LEGENDS OF HERALDALE IV

OUR FINAL ACT

Table of Contents

LEGENDS OF HERALDALE IV

OUR FINAL ACT

By Brian McNatt

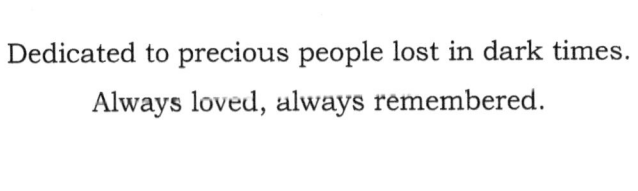

Dedicated to precious people lost in dark times.
Always loved, always remembered.

PROLOGUE

The refugee village balanced on the knife's edge between the crashing waves of the Northern Sea and the vast snow fields. Glaciers groaned out on the waters, loosed sharp cracks as pieces broke and fell or ground together in their jumble; at night, many a sleeper's dreams were troubled by the tumult. The black rock shore weathered the rush and beat of the waves. The air stung of frost and sharp salt. The early evening sun lay obscured past pallid grey clouds. Rain was promised for the night.

From the shrouded west came a lightning bolt high in the sky, skimming the dark roots of the clouds and trailing behind it a rolling roar of thunderclaps to draw the eye of every gryphon, minotaur, and Wolf-Lord calling the village their home. The hearts of the former quailed at the sight of the deadly, blistering light. Many had fled from it or the rumor of it, fled home and land, fled war and loss for a precious, precarious peace there on the edge of the world, past notice or care. Or so they had thought. Before their eyes, the lightning bolt fell like a star. The good earth shuddered as it struck. Some gryphons reached for their loved ones. Others reached for a weapon. Laura the minotaur, town alchemist, ran to the eastern forest for help.

The steam of melted ice and snow rose to meet the hanging clouds, so that to onlookers it seemed for a moment as if a volcano had cracked open on the edge of town and begun spewing its heat into the gathering storms. Lord Mordred rose as a shadow in the midst of the obscuring steam, unbothered by the crackling heat encompassing him. His unicorn guise was shed, the Wolf-Lord standing proud and free in his birth form for the first time in too long. He stepped from the impact of his Elemental landing, and there stood for a moment, eyes closed and muzzle turned into the breeze coming in from across the ocean. The bracing cold and tang of salt, across his armor and through his fur, black cape billowing like wings behind him. He felt no war on the wind. Empress Nova's tyranny lay far behind him, almost forgotten past the personal errand which took him so far from home and duty. It felt to him as if shackles, worn for so long their terrible weight was barely noticed anymore, had been sundered from his wrists and neck, leaving behind . . . possibility.

"The reach of the Empire is vast, my lord, but I have found its border. A daughter of Morgana le Fay lives to the east."

The loud rush of wings and landing bodies spurred Mordred to open his eyes. Ahead, between him and the main bulk of the refugee town, a small flock of gryphons had gathered. Young gryphons of various kinds, stout of body, eyes wide with their terror at the wolf's coming. They wore no armor but carried long spears of dull metal.

Mordred eyed the quality of the metal for a moment, deemed it mere iron, and grinned. He advanced with a lazy stride. The gryphons retreated at equal pace like a wave parting before a ship's prow, most of them, a few managing to stand their ground. Mordred grinned wider and kept on toward these trembling fools, with a sudden jerk of his head impaling his throat on one of the sharpened blades. A cry rose from all around, the starling-gryphon holding the spear screaming loudest of all. And Mordred continued to grin and continued to walk, fangs gleaming red with the gushing blood rising up his throat, streaming from his torn-through throat to stain fur and cloak. His voice as he spoke was thick and wet, every word a torture.

"Next time, bring only your finest Lunar Steel if you wish to kill me!" He held his right hand out to the side.

For a moment a lightning bolt was grasped in those greedy claws, and then the bolt was a spear of white metal, bright as if it gleamed in the sun. At the sight of the weapon, many of the surrounding gryphons dropped their own spears and fled, or else looked with hope to a gathering fury to the east. Mordred paid it no heed and kept his gaze locked on the starling-gryphon's. "Oh, but I misspeak. There will be no next time!"

Mordred swung his spear for a decapitating strike. The gryphon, too late, let go of his weapon and raised arms and wings as if to ward off the blow. But before it could reach him, the long and sturdy blade of a black sword blocked it, barely wavering for all the strength Mordred had put into the attack.

A hush descended on the scene for a moment, and then cheers rose from the assembled gryphons. Mordred growled and followed the blade until he saw it was another Wolf-Lord who held the sword. She stood as tall as he did, as heavily muscled as he was, her fur as perfectly white as his was perfectly black. Hair red as blood on the snow fell in long waterfalls down her broad shoulders and back, a few tresses caught in the breeze. Her black-feathered cloak billowed in the same breeze, the more fearsome mirror to Mordred's own cape.

Before he could speak the cutting remark he had prepared for this meeting, the other Wolf-Lord drew a fist back, and then SLAMMED it into the center of Mordred's cuirass. Metal screeched as the armor crumpled beneath the blow, the remark—and all of Mordred's breath—knocked from his rattling chest as he was sent tumbling five feet back and onto his ass.

The cheers of the gryphons grew louder yet.

For a long second, Mordred remained where he lay and wondered how he got there. Then he tore his ruined cuirass off so it would stop pushing into his tenderized flesh and levied himself back to his feet with his spear, swaying there a moment as he regained his bearings. He looked up at the feel of a cold blade against the side of his neck, into the perilous face of the other Wolf-Lord. "Before you ask," she spoke, voice deep and almost musical, "know that this is Lunar Steel. The very finest."

Mordred bared his teeth but made no further attack. "I come here at the report of a . . . mutual acquaintance."

"Morgana le Fay?" asked the other Wolf-Lord.

"Commander Bevin," corrected Mordred. To be the bigger wolf between them, he buried his spear blade-down into the snow, and then waited until his counterpart had lowered her sword back to her side before continuing. "I was curious why my most faithful servant failed to complete the retrieval mission set for her. The report she gave me only fanned those flames. I had to come and see for myself. You are Princess Candida, I presume?"

"I go by Holly, now," corrected the other wolf. "Holly le Fay. And you are Lord Mordred."

"The very same." Mordred regained his grin. He could not help himself. Everything so far was as Commander Bevin had promised him, flooding him with a joy wholly distinct from what he felt in times of violence, something sweeter and yet closer to grief as well. He felt tears gather in his eyes and for once made no effort to wipe them away. "You are the daughter of Morgana le Fay."

Holly spared a glance to the audience gathered for their confrontation before she answered, mostly a sea of gryphons, among them a few minotaurs and other Wolf-Lords. At the front of crowds stood a three-tailed kitsune of orange fur, and at her side stood the lone unicorn, a young filly with a pinto coat and the same blue eyes of her mother. "I am one of them, yes. And you are the lone child of Queen Morgause, better known among unicorns and gryphons as General Nero."

"I am!" Mordred didn't know what to do with his hands. He couldn't get his muzzle into anything but a smile, and he had the horrible sensation his tail was actually wagging. "And so, we are cousins of shared blood and flesh. And I am . . . so pleased to finally meet you. Commander Bevin told me all she could about you."

Holly said nothing for a moment and her features gave away nothing aside from a reluctance to meet his eyes with her own. But soon she gestured past him with the blade of her sword, over the snowy fields south of the town and along the forest of aspen, holly, and pine. "Go. This needs more privacy."

"Holly, be careful," spoke the kitsune onlooker. She'd placed a hand on the back of the filly unicorn's neck, as if to keep her from charging forward. "You know the stories told of this monster. If even half a true, he puts all the rest of your family to shame."

Holly looked briefly to the kitsune and put on a smile like a mask. "I have taken his measure. This will not be long. Keep the others safe. Go along, cousin."

Mordred made no objection. He even left his spear behind as he turned and started in the direction indicated, the snow cold and crunching beneath his footpaws and the breeze taking the murmurs of the crowd behind them. Holly le Fay hurried up to stride beside him and the pair walked in their own silence, and Mordred could not take his eyes off of her. In the many hundreds of years since the fall of Gateway and his abandonment as the rest of the Wolf-Lords fled Heraldale, she was only the third other wolf he'd ever laid eyes on. He drank in the sight of her like one starving, stumbling upon an oasis in the middle of a vast desert. The solid curves of her warrior's form. The bright brilliance of her yellow eyes. Even the scars Mordred could glimpse where her clothes did not cover, a rarity for Wolf-Lords with their healing powers. Holly seemed—

"If you keep staring at me like that, my wife will have questions when I get back."

Mordred snapped his head away, teeth bared. He glanced around them and stopped walking, forcing Holly to do the same. "This is far enough," he snapped. "We have our privacy."

"Aye," agreed the other Wolf-Lord. She stabbed her sword into the stony ground and looked at him anywhere except his eyes. "Why did you come here?"

"It is as I said. Commander Bevin told me all and I simply had to see, to meet you. Heraldale, as you can imagine, doesn't have the Wolf-Lord population it once did. I . . . cherish, any brush with my kind I might have. It has been a pleasure to meet you, violence and all."

"I wish I could say the same to you." And to her credit, the white-furred Wolf-Lord did look regretful, roving gaze taking Mordred in as he had taken her in. "Meeting family . . . it should be a chance for joy. But these refugees are under my watch, my protection, and I have heard too much of you and your evil acts."

"It is war," said Mordred. He smiled and held his arms wide to his sides as if to encompass all around them. "It is war and I am winning. Evil acts? Only evil paid back onto evil. They may cower now beneath your guardian's blade, but those gryphons of yours are the enemy. They will always be the enemy. They burned our homes and drove us from our lands. They killed us and our children where we stood, and took everything that remained for themselves. I only return the favor."

Holly stood unperturbed. "You do it in service to a unicorn, a mad empress with delusions of godhood. In the Old War, the unicorns did all you say the gryphons did, and worse, but still, you serve one for your own ends."

"And you've taken one as a daughter," snarled Mordred. He glanced back the way they came, back to the kitsune and filly at the front of the distant crowd. He put every ounce of possible disdain into his voice. "Doomed yourself to be the loyal nursemaid, no pride or honor, to be left behind with the spring days of childhood."

"Perhaps." And here, Holly gave a theatrical shrug. "But better still, I deem, to be a nursemaid than an attack dog. Someday, in the natural course of things, we will both be discarded. Only one of us, though, will be remembered with love."

Mordred grit his teeth. "If I had known you were such a sentimental soul, I would have brought my spear along with me. It is hard to be sentimental with a spear buried in your chest."

Fresh silence fell over the pair. Mordred took the time to examine the land his estranged relation had chosen to call home. It was a cold land, not quite desolate, the fields of snow and broken stone hemmed in by forests vast and dark to the east and west, and to the north by the glacial sea. Farther still, past the forests, rose the dim, pale ghosts of mountains. In the air hung the cry of gulls, and the scent of salt, and the hushed weight of the snow. In Heraldale, there were few places which grew so cold, and fewer still which were inhabited.

Yet, in its remoteness, its inhospitable nature, there was a great safety. The wars for which Mordred was both herald and captain would not come there, not until all else lay conquered or ruined. And then, Mordred thought, he might come back only to find—

"Stay here, then."

Mordred's train of thought crashed and burned. He blinked and looked back at Holly, found her head held high and her shoulders squared, the same grim authority overtaking her as he had first seen when her sword blocked his spear. "What madness do you speak?"

"A last chance," answered Holly. "I do not know why you were left behind when our kin at last fled Heraldale those many, many hundreds of years ago, but those days are gone. You can simply . . . leave. Leave Heraldale, leave your master's wars, rejoin your kind here or to the east and find peace. Maybe even happiness. Nothing is stopping you except your own need to keep hurting others, but it does not need to be that way."

The speech ended and silence once more descended. Mordred stared, stunned to the heart. For the first time in the long years since the deaths of Lancelot, Grimhilt, and all others whom Mordred had loved, he wavered. For the length of a breath, the strength of Lord Mordred fell to a weariness which years later would've made even Princess Galaxy or Sir Brynjar pause in pity. He became an old wolf, whose life had been drawn out far longer than it ever should have been by his use of a unicorn form, full of war and loss, the spring days of his childhood faded away to nearly nothing. Who could not remember the beauty of his mother's face, nor the song of her voice, nor the touch of a friendly hand.

Holly stood before him and held her hand out for him to take. For a moment, Mordred stared at this final lifeline and the scales of destiny teetered, ready to shift. For a moment, he raised his own hand with a hope to take hers. For a moment . . .

The spear flew from its resting place to smack solidly into his raised hand. Mordred swung with the force, forcing Holly le Fay to jump backward and away to keep her head on its neck. Mordred glowered at her retreat, fangs bared and Lightning Elemental crackling. Steam rose as the nearest snow melted from the heat. "I won't let go of my hate," he snarled. "I won't forget what's been lost. I will make the hurt and tremble in fear to my last breath."

"To your last breath, then," said Holly, and then lunged, sword thrusting for Mordred's heart. But he fled before her, roaring away into the sky and far away on a bolt of lightning in the same manner as he had arrived. Back to Heraldale and the unknown doom of his death at the talons of Princess Galaxy and Sir Bifrost in the years to come.

CHAPTER ONE

The lonesome Imperial troop carrier flew over the cursed and conquered lands of Schwarz Angebot, high in the cold northern climes of Heraldale. Harsh, ever-storming winds rocked the blocky craft, keeping the refugee gryphons hidden within huddled close together against the storm. At the head of the craft stood a golden eagle-gryphon, tall and strong. Beside him sat a slim palomino unicorn minding the magic-threaded crystals of the craft's control console. The gryphon, Brynjar, stared out the windows dominating the head of the troop carrier, despairing as he watched the wretched land pass beneath them.

"My mother told me this was a good land . . ."

Beyond the troop carrier's windows lay a blasted waste. Overhead, dark clouds filled the sky from horizon to horizon, spitting at times a heavy, hissing rain, at other times great fields of lightning to set the ground below ablaze. They passed factories in their flight, towering, city-like factories spewing thick clouds of noxious smoke. Mines carved through the mountains and the forests were all but gone, the Avalon Empire eating away at the land and its people for every last good.

"It can be beautiful again," said Owain, trying to force some cheer into his voice. "After the war. We can set things to right here."

Brynjar didn't know if he believed the unicorn. He didn't have time to think about it. One of the troop carrier's many enchanted instruments let out a warning ping. The air trembled as a pair of somethings as large and heavy as their carrier closed in behind them, the gryphon refugees whispering their fear. One, a hawk-gryphon bereft one of her wings, broke from the group and joined Brynjar and Owain at the head of the craft, followed by a quiet Elk warrior. "What's going on?" asked Captain Junko.

"A good question," said Brynjar, looking to Owain. Much of the color had drained from the unicorn stallion's features. "Trouble?"

"Big trouble," said Owain, setting the guidance spires to stay their course as he focused his attention on the pinging enchantments. "We have at least two Imperial air-yachts following behind us. At least, I assume they're air-yachts. They're the right size, but without seeing them . . . crap!"

Brynjar didn't need to ask why the sudden swearing. The pinging had grown louder, and from the left slowly glided into view the metal prow of a scouting air-yacht. "Verdammt."

"They're trying to get ahead of us," said Junko. "If they get ahead of us, will they be able to see inside here? Has anyone noticed if the windows are clear from the outside?"

Brynjar and Owain shared a look, the realization hitting both at once. They had never noticed.

"Great," continued the hawk-gryphon. "Just great."

"I can cast an illusion to make us all look like unicorns," said Captain Hywel. "But it won't be able to last for very long with a group this size."

"It's still our best bet," said Brynjar. "Owain, get ready to share some magic with Hywel to help—"

A new sound filled the air, replacing the pinging. A sharp snap and crackle, and below it a hissing. All eyes went at once to the red glow of the troop carrier's built-in communication crystals mounted overhead. Brynjar shared another look with Owain, who after a moment nodded and stood to his full height. The tip of his curved horn touched the crystal and sent a small bolt of his minty green magic into it. "Hello?"

"Unidentified troop carrier," spoke a harsh, impatient voice, echoing distantly from the overhead crystals. "This is Lieutenant Hatch, of the Northern Heraldale Scout Corps. Identify yourselves at once or you will be brought down. You are in restricted airspace."

Owain swallowed. To Brynjar's admiration, when he spoke his voice carried none of the nervousness of his body. "Lieutenant, this is . . . Captain Urien of . . . prisoner transport. We are on our way south to secure fresh captives for Lord Beauty."

"Is that so?" responded the unicorn on the other end of the communication crystals. Several seconds of silence passed, Brynjar certain he could hear any number of warning sounds within the silence. Then, "We find your story unsatisfactory, seeing as Lord Beauty is at this moment away to the east securing captives for herself. Would you care to try again?"

Brynjar almost loosed the bitter curse in his heart. Almost. Keeping silent, he grabbed a long sword from the wall-mounted weapon racks and strode to the forward right corner of the craft. Taking one deep breath, he stabbed with his full body weight, burying the blade into the rune-covered wall down to the hilt.

The hissing, sparking sound of spells and machinery failing in concert.

The troop carrier slowly pitched forward and to the right, a surprised cry rising among the gryphons behind them as the carrier listed inexorably toward the rocky mountain cliffs below them.

"Unidentified troop carrier!" demanded the soldier through the communication crystals. "Explain yourselves at once!"

"I'm sorry, sir!" shouted Owain, shooting Brynjar a death glare as his magic returned to working the carrier's control rods. "Missed damage from a storm we passed through, sudden failure in . . . in a magic channeling to the forward-most guidance spire! Please assist! We are going down, we—OH GOD!"

There was little need to fake the panic. The troop carrier struck the ground hard, carried on across the craggy, snow-laden rock for several yards through sheer momentum, barely stopped with its front fourth hanging over a sheer cliff edge.

Without prompting, everyone within the carrier scurried to the rear of the craft, Brynjar the last to come, bringing the heavy sword with him. Owain looked like he wanted to ram the sword into Brynjar's unmentionables. "That was your best idea of how to get out of that situation!? REALLY!?"

Brynjar shrugged. "Well, we're out of it."

"We are out of nothing!" hissed Junko, seeming too nervous to raise her voice for fear the communication crystals were still working. "We're in here, and they're out there, and now they're going to try coming in here, and you're standing there, and—"

Two heavy thuds rang out from somewhere outside. Silence fell in the carrier. Brynjar, despite his confidence of moments before, swallowed and looked to Owain, the unicorn swiftly joining him at the far rear of the troop carrier, where the wall would, at the pull of a lever, slide down into a boarding ramp.

The seconds passed. They heard muffled voices from outside, distant at first, and then drawing closer. Brynjar counted three distant voices he was certain of, and maybe a fourth. His grip tightened on the hilt of the sword he had procured for himself, his broken and healed-wrong talon protesting the strength put into the grip as he tried to remember the distant lessons his mother Ida imparted on him regarding fighting with a sword. He could only half-remember one lesson, something to do with the pointy end. He glanced at the weapon he held and guessed it to be less the stabbing kind and more the swinging kind, but with lives on the line . . .

The hiss of releasing steam filled the air, making Brynjar flinch. He saw the rear of the carrier tremble, felt the gears grinding as damaged mechanisms were forced into motion. He readied himself, felt more than saw Owain beside him doing the same. The seconds passed . . .

The rear of the carrier did not lower into a ramp so much as it crashed down into one. The unicorn soldiers on the other side had a moment to dance away from the falling slab of metal, then Brynjar flew forward with a leap, sword swinging with all his might.

Swish.

One unicorn fell, his head flung far by the force of Brynjar's blow. Another unicorn, swiftly recovering, tried to charge forward to stab her horn into Brynjar's side, but Owain charged and buried his horn where her neck met her shoulder. A horrid, gurgling scream rent the high cliffs and gullies, and then she fell, her blood gushing.

Hywel took the next unicorn soldier, battering him down with a barrage of magic bolts.

The last soldier turned tail and began to run for the nearest of the landed air-yachts. Brynjar dropped his sword and flew after the unicorn, tackling him to the sharp, biting rocks. They rolled for a moment, the unicorn kicking, head jerking around in blind, whinnying attempts to catch Brynjar's face on his horn. Brynjar clung close and tight, wings beating for leverage. Talons found the unicorn's throat through the joints in his armor, dug in, tore. The unicorn began to drown in the flood of red, struggles hitting a fevered pitch before slowly weakening They turned to shudders in Brynjar's grip as his whole front ran warm and red.

Then, silence but for Brynjar's labored breathing. He let the body go and slowly stood, wincing as he placed his weight wrong on his broken talon. He tried to ignore the hot wetness of the unicorn's blood all across his front as he looked around, making sure there were no more enemies to be seen. "Is that all of them?"

"I think so, I—" began Owain, before stopping, his gaze gone past Brynjar, eyes wide and full of swears he could not find the breath to utter.

Brynjar followed his gaze, felt his own breath catch. A final Imperial soldier, a mare, stood on the deck of one of the pursuing air-yachts, her horn glowing with her purple magic as she trained a railing-mounted automatic crossbow at the small group. Close enough, merely a few yards, it seemed unlikely they could dodge away if she began firing. Close enough, too, for Brynjar to see the fear in the unicorn's brown eyes.

"You're Sir Brynjar and Sir Owain," she said, startling Brynjar with how young she sounded. "You're real. The Rescuer and the First Deserter."

"If that's what they're calling us these days," said Owain, daring a step to draw even with Brynjar. "I guess that's us. You?"

"Delma. I . . . I . . ." The unicorn's magical grip on the weapon disappeared. She stepped aside and away from it, visibly trembling as her magic removed first her helmet—

(Oh God, thought Brynjar, *she's so young.)*

—and then, with growing haste, the rest of her white barding. Beneath it, her coat was a deep brown, her mane and tail tawny yellow and cropped short. Her eyes shone wet with tears. Armor gone, she turned and marched stiff-legged down the air-yacht's boarding ramp, looking like she was doing her best not to start hyper-ventilating. "I want to go home," she said, barely over a whisper.

"What are we doing about this?" asked Hywel, joining Brynjar and Owain at the front of the group.

"Nothing," said Brynjar, draping a wing each on Owain and Hywel's backs. "If you've seen a more obvious surrender, tell me about it later."

"I want to go home," the mare, Delma, repeated as she reached the snowy stone ground at ramp's end. Her gaze had gone glazed and distant as she turned away from the scene, stiff steps taking her away back toward the northwest. "I want—"

A crack of bone and a puff of blood as an arrow suddenly buried itself in the back of the unicorn mare's head, causing Owain to startle beneath Brynjar's right wing, a horrified groan escaping him. The mare managed another two steps, then fell with the clatter of a puppet bereft its strings.

For a moment, the air swelled with a silent horror, Brynjar staring breathless at the corpse, heart stopped. Then he spun to see who had loosed the killing blow. Captain Junko stood upright a yard from the troop carrier's lowered ramp, a crossbow in her talons. Her eyes met Brynjar's and showed no remorse. "There," she said. "That's all of them."

Brynjar growled and stomped forward, stopped from doing worse by Hywel hurriedly pressing against him. "She was surrendered," Brynjar snapped. "She was no threat!"

"She could have warned others about us," Junko snapped back, passing the crossbow off to another gryphon at her side. "She WOULD have warned others about us."

"You saw her, she was practically a child! She just wanted to go home!"

At this, Junko scoffed, dropping down to all fours and flaring her one remaining wing. "So did I!"

Brynjar continued to glare, but said no more to his fellow gryphon. After a moment he backed away a pace, allowing Hywel to relax beside him. Brynjar looked down at himself, grimaced at the mess all over him. Wiping at where the blood had splattered across the front of his neck, he found it was already beginning to dry in the strange, arid air of Schwarz Angebot. "Verdammt. Hywel, take a gryphon and see what can be scavenged from the air-yachts. There's sure to be food. Wait. Before that, do you think you can cast anything to hide us?"

The Elk looked around for a moment, frowned. "There's too much here to make invisible, but . . . I think I could manage an illusion of heavy fog or something to obscure us from a distance."

"Do it. Owain," started Brynjar, stopping as he noticed his unicorn was no longer at his side. He looked behind, his heart flagging as he saw Owain knelt beside his murdered countrymare, head lowered and eyes closed. Brynjar watched the vigil for a moment, then turned away to reconfigure his duties. "Junko, make sure the others are all calm and alright, let them know the situation is under control."

"I'll take your word for it the situation is under control," the hawk-gryphon remarked, before turning and returning to the rest of the gryphons beginning to poke their heads out of the troop carrier.

Brynjar watched her go for a moment, then turned and set off away from the scene. He did not go far, only a few yards. Even so, the air-yachts and troop carriers became no more than vague impressions in Hywel's false fog as Brynjar sat down and began to slowly and thoroughly clean away the unicorn soldier's blood with talonfuls of the mountain snow. He tried not to think as he worked. He did not want to think about the warmth he was cleaning away with cold, nor the sounds of the soldier's desperate gasping for breath through a throat rent asunder, struggles weakening, the last, half-whispered cries for help . . .

Brynjar slapped his face with a heavy ball of snow, growled, and resumed cleaning himself, slowly and thoroughly to make the most of the limited means at his disposal. He focused on the physical act, let himself fall into the old habits of his days at the forge long ago in Featheren Valley, when there had been nothing to fill the hours of the day but work and resentment. It was easier than he expected.

Eventually, a long time later, Brynjar heard the sound of approaching hooves and turned to find Owain approaching. Brynjar's heart fell at once as he saw the blood caked and dried all across Owain's head and neck, his horn stained red. Brynjar cursed himself for his idiocy. "Oh, hun . . ."

Owain laid down beside Brynjar, legs tucked primly beneath him. No more words passed between the pair as Brynjar began to clean the unicorn with snow, careful with his sharp talons as he scrubbed his lover down.

Combed through his mane and over his eyes, down his snout and neck and chest. Owain shivered beneath the touch of the snow. His eyes kept locked with Brynjar's as the gryphon worked, the unicorn tense. Brynjar went slowly and carefully, meeting Owain's gaze, close enough in his dutiful work for their breaths to mingle. His talons stroked the curved horn until at last it sparkled its usual pristine white, and all sign on the unicorn of their vicious work was gone.

By the time he was done, the figures of the many gryphons traveling with them could be seen moving through Hywel's illusion fog, no more than shadows as they stretched their limbs and relieved themselves. Brynjar looked from them in the distance to Owain before him, cupping the unicorn's head in his talons and carefully touching his beak against Owain's cheek in a gryphon kiss. "There. All done."

Owain at once sagged, the tension bled from his body in the safety of their intimacy. He leaned in to nuzzle against Brynjar neck to neck, a sign of affection Brynjar eagerly returned. The unicorn's voice when he spoke was weak and full of regret. "That could have been me. Three, four months ago, that would have been me with tears in my eyes, not wanting to fight, just wanting to go back home."

"I'm sorry."

"It would have been me with a bolt in the back of my head. If not for you and Galaxy. I had a chance to change . . . and I took it."

"I'm sorry."

"Me too," said Owain. "But you couldn't have saved her any more than I could've. And you can't punish Junko any more than I can. She's too much the leader of the gryphons we saved. They'd never stand for it."

"Even so. If I ever found myself the chance to get my talons 'round her throat for this . . ."

"It'll be after a long line of comeuppance," spoke a new voice.

Brynjar and Owain parted and stood, Brynjar looking to Hywel trotting their way and feeling a smile tug at the pliable corners of his beak. He went to greet the Elk, nuzzling him neck against neck as he had with Owain. "Glad to be on the same page. You find something in all this mess?"

"Unfortunately," said Hywel, who right then seemed to be doing his best not to look Owain's way. "Certain unicorns were supposed to bring you the good news, but he took his time and now there's bad news to go with it."

Owain shuffled on his hooves beside Brynjar. In response, Brynjar spread and rested a wing on his unicorn's back. "There was a good reason. Anyway. Best get the good news out of the way first. Don't want to risk a good mood."

Owain laughed, and Brynjar knew from the laugh things could not be so bad yet, however they looked. "Alright," said the unicorn. "Despite the severity of your mid-air swordplay, I think I can repair the troop carrier with parts salvaged from the air-yachts. An hour or two of work, but we'll be flying out of here easier than we flew in."

"Okay. What's the bad news, then?"

"It's best to see it yourself," said Hywel, the Elk turning and trotting back to the collection of Imperial vessels. Frowning, Brynjar followed, Owain keeping beside him. They went to the far air-yacht from the carrier, to an array of documents scattered across a wood crate. Beneath the documents lay a map of the region marked here and there with red ink, with more of the ink the farther north and west the map went.

"What's all this?" asked Brynjar.

"The leader here said this was a no-fly," said Hywel, who nodded toward the papers. "There's why."

Brynjar glanced at the papers, then to Owain. "I can't read unicorn."

Owain picked up the papers in his green magic, eyes narrowed at first as he read through them, then growing wide. "Oh my God. They're orders for termination from Lord Thoth. Lord Mordred was killed in battle with Galaxy and a King Vigdis of Gateway. Empress Nova is retaliating with . . . with the culling of gryphons in Avalon-controlled territories, and the total razing of gryphon towns. Thoth is overseeing the operation personally."

Brynjar's rear legs gave out beneath him. He sat, staring first at Owain, then around at the gryphons he, Owain, and Hywel had rescued from the Avalon Islands. He watched them wander the scene and remembered the farmhouse shed the way he did in his nightmares, the metal shack shaking with the bodies dead and dying crammed inside, talons grasping out at Brynjar, begging for help.

"How many?" he asked. His voice sounded thick to him, heavy with the tears he felt threatening his eyes.

"You don't want to—"

"How many?" Brynjar asked again, turning to look at the unicorn. "Please."

Still, Owain hesitated before answering, his own tears falling freely. "All of them."

For a long and terrifying moment, Brynjar could find neither his words or his breath. His mind quailed at the enormity of the horror before him, the madness which had fallen over the land. He dropped his gaze back to the map and its scrawled words as if looking at them again might change them, make them not only legible, but sane.

They didn't, but as he stared, Brynjar's eyes saw suddenly past the orders, saw the map itself. He traced the markings of forests and rivers, of mountains rising tall and narrowing to crowded valleys. His horror crystallized into a sharp gut-stab of grief as he realized he knew the land around them, hidden though it had been before by smog and snow.

Some cry must have left him, for Owain sidled closer, horn alight with the green magic of a healing spell. "Brynjar? Are you alright?"

"No," whispered Brynjar. The pain was a physical thing, a scaled and muscled thing. It wrapped around Brynjar and squeezed from all sides, crushing lungs and heart and hope. He staggered back to all fours, turned and made a stumbling run back to the troop carrier and then past it. He stopped at the cliff edge its first few inches teetered over so precariously and stood to catch a breath which wouldn't come, which couldn't. The air seemed too thick. The sky was too dark, a late dusk before its time, but peering down below, he began to discern in the gloom the shapes and contours of a mountain valley almost familiar . . .

"Brynjar, don't," spoke Owain, voice draped in a forced calm. "Don't. You've seen enough. You don't want to see what's down there, not now. Please . . . please, stay here."

Brynjar heard, but could not yield. He had to see, no matter the pain. And there was pain, as he took wing and dove over the cliff edge into the shattered mountain valley, the pain his heart had always feared the most. He passed the shattered ruins of the governor's fortress in a blink and a glance, past where a ribbon of waterfall had once graced the sky from a cleft in the mountainside, landed beside the turgid, ash- and wood-choked remnants of a once-proud river. Brynjar might never have recognized it alone, but he could never mistake the high and sheer mountains rising to the east and west of the narrow valley for anywhere else. The pain returned full-force as he stood there.

Featheren Valley. Home.

Brynjar came to stand by her side, a golden wing draping across her back. A quarter-mile behind them the underside of the Titan lit up, hundreds of scarlet beams flashing down. For a moment evening turned to noon as the village, its buildings, its people, burned in a flash of magical heat. Then they saw only fire and smoke. No sound carried across that distance, not the rumble of explosions, not the cracking of centuries-old homes, not the hissing of the river boiling away to nothing, not the roaring of the flames, not the screams of the dying.

"Our home..." Galaxy struggled to find the words. "Our home's gone!"

The fires were long gone out, gone cold. Most was grey ash, lingering in the air and across the months like a curse upon the land. Few buildings remained standing. Those few were hollowed-out husks of blackened and crumbling stone. Even the scavengers had already come and gone, eating long and well on the carrion the Empire had left them.

Somewhere in the unseen distance, wolves howled. Brynjar flew high so as not to disturb the fields of ash. Against his will, he saw the ghost of what had once been overlaid what now was. He saw the tavern he had worked, serving liquor to the increasingly broken gryphons who came in from the mines every night. He saw the smith's home, where he had worked the forges in secret to make rebellious arms for the gryphons of the valley. The fair field. The outdoor market where any gryphon willing to fly deliveries could earn a decent coin. Home, his and Galaxy's, his and Ida's, his and Sascha and Siegfried's. His tears stung in his eyes.

He flew until he couldn't, until the pain and the poisoned air grew too much for him. He half-landed, half-fell into the dunes of ash which carpeted the cold valley, and there beneath the char boughs of a barren tree he lay, half-propped on his talons, shaking as he hung his head and wept. He remembered the tree before him. It had been a peach tree, one of many in the valley, though this one had been his mother's favorite. Squirrels had lived in its trunk, and whenever he had gone to the tree to grab a few peaches with the twins, he brought them back to Ida with nonsense stories of all the squirrels' lives.

Now there would be no more silly stories, because the squirrels were all dead. No more peaches; the tree was dead. There were no more late nights of ale and song, or early mornings at the forge. No more desperate haggling with gryphons in as dire need as him and his family. No more winter festivals or summer candies. The old was gone. It could never come back. The history, the culture, the home, all wiped away.

"But where the old world dies," whispered Brynjar, the words seeming to come from somewhere far outside himself, "there is room for the new. The old . . ."

So there, he wept. For his home, for the people he had known, for the war. He wept for the long journey and those lost along the way. He wept for Owain's late father, Governor Urien. He wept for Ida, his own mother, who Brynjar's deep heart told him had died while they were apart.

Brynjar wept, and then he stood. He looked around a final time and saw a pack of yellow-eyed wolves many yards away, a dozen of them with furs ranging through black and brown and grey. They stopped in their prowls through the ruins at the attention and looked his way. Dread struck Brynjar afresh, the wolves seeming both ghosts of the past and a doom of the future. He thought of Lord Mordred, who Owain said was dead, and of whatever other Wolf-Lords remained out there in the world.

Yielding the staring contest to the wolves, Brynjar took wing once more and flew as fast as he could go back the way he had come. Behind him the wolves he had seen raised their heads and howled high and loud. From the haze of the ruined valley, countless unseen more raised their howls in answer.

CHAPTER TWO

Bevin's first operation as a military commander had been to Baumbrücke, a mountainside village along the southern edges of the border between Gryphonbough and the lands formerly known as the sovereign nation of Schwarz Angebot. Bevin had been young. Growing up the ward and protégé of Lord Mordred had allowed for ego and indulgences which in hindsight had begged for disaster, if Bevin was honest with herself. But she had been talented and ambitious, and Lord Mordred had been cruel, and some tragedies had to be lived with.

It had been the early days of the war with Gryphonbough, but the war was not the reason Bevin went to Baumbrücke. She and her soldiers in pursuit of a fugitive, a traitor and deserter from the Imperial Navy. Bevin couldn't even remember the fugitive's name now, or what he looked like, but she remembered well the quiet of the village as she and her soldiers swept the streets, knowing Baumbrücke the last chance to catch him before he slipped beyond reach into Gryphonbough.

It had been raining for three days, a cold autumn rain. Bevin remembered the weight of her soaked-through barding. The muddy streets sucking at her hooves with each step. The shadows of the thatched roofs all around, full of watching gryphon eyes. Bevin did not even notice the flight of crossbow bolts until her second soldier fell to them, but from there, it was nothing but a mad struggle for survival.

Even after so many years, Bevin could not bring herself to remember the soldiers she had buried, the gryphons she had murdered for a cause she now realized to be monstrous. But she could remember the temple, all black stone and high towers, perched at the top of the village and too large for it, too old for it, too . . .

All those years later and the temple still stood. Bevin saw it through the sheets of late winter rain as she landed her air-yacht in the village square, a towering black monument, vague and ominous. After years of heightening war, the temple was all there remained to see of Baumbrücke. The town was abandoned. Some buildings had been destroyed, the arcing bridge the town had been named for chief among them, but mostly the buildings had been left to ruin beneath rain and muddy landslides. Bevin knew of ghost towns, of whole populations fleeing in the wake of war and its accompanying horrors, but she had never bothered to go to one before. They unnerved her.

As the air-yacht settled onto its landing struts, the half-dozen Elk soldiers accompanying Bevin stumbling from the sudden and unfamiliar motion, Bifrost landed beside her and looked around at the otherwise-empty village square. She looked nervous, thought Bevin, who couldn't blame her after the brush with disaster at Markhaven. Yet still, the way the raven-gryphon stood on her rear legs in the Gateway custom, Mordred's old Lunar Steel spear clutched tightly in her talons and blue scarf looking so weighed down by rain it threatened to choke her, the sight was also amusing. "Boo."

Bifrost flinched, though did not squawk as Bevin had hoped, and looked at the unicorn reproachfully. "That was as lame as it was mean."

"I couldn't resist," said Bevin, looking away with a toss of her mane and a smirk. Her gaze swept the dark, abandoned buildings surrounding the square, trying not to look inexorably up the long path toward the higher cliffs and the black temple overlooking them. Lord Beauty, after all, could have been lurking in wait anywhere. She wasn't, Bevin knew damn well where the

Lord of the Empire was waiting, but she could have been, all the same. "I'm a mean mare."

"Tell me about her," said Bifrost, voice carrying a forced lightness to Bevin's trained ears. Around them the Elk had fanned out, casting detection spells for illusions and other trickery, while gryphon soldiers deployed larger, mounted versions of their artificial spell-casters in defensive positions around the air-yacht. "Lord Beauty. Please. You must know her somewhat from your time . . . well, your time abroad."

Bevin chose to ignore the absurdly idiotic attempt at tact. "Lord Beauty is evil."

"Uh-huh." Bifrost's voice dripped with derision. "My friend, I spent days at the torturous mercies of Lord Mordred and Lord Thoth. THEY are evil. The whole Avalon Empire is evil, or at least enough of the people and institutions are evil for the whole to count."

"A lot of words to try not saying I was evil too, but okay." Bevin tore her gaze up, up to the storm drenching their small company. Through her new Lightning Elemental, courtesy of the late Lord Mordred, she felt the power of the storm, the charge before each lightning bolt, the raw, hot energy spike and boom like a living thing. She felt this, but . . . not as she would've expected. With the power of her new Elemental, she could reach out and touch those natural bursts of power, feel them, call them . . . yet her own lightning, her inner spark, kept quiet within her. Present but inattentive, as if, for all her joy in having it, the Elemental could not care less to have her. Bevin tried not to worry that the Elemental still yearned for its old master, the late Mordred, and resented being shuffled off to a unicorn such as her, but . . .

Bifrost still stood beside her, waiting for more. Bevin sighed. "It's like . . ." she began again, trying to find the right words. She had never been much of a philosopher. "It's like how . . . okay, you are a good person. King Vigdis, he is a good person. Brynjar and Owain, they are good people. But Galaxy is GOOD. You understand me?"

"I think so," said Bifrost. "So, Lord Beauty—"

"As fake a name as Captain Blackbird," Bevin heard herself snarl, quickly reining herself in as one of the surrounding soldiers looked her way. "Blackbird's real name is Kanti, 'to her friends.' But what I mean is, Lord Mordred was an evil person. Lord Thoth is an evil person. Empress Nova, for sure, is an evil mare. They're evil in wrath, in greed, in ego. But Lord Beauty is evil to a higher purpose. Evil with thoughts of nobility. There's a difference. You know it when you feel it."

"It looks like I might be learning it rather soon," said Bifrost.

Bevin followed the raven-gryphon's gaze to the old, dark temple. She made out the dark shape of an Imperial troop carrier coming down for a landing in whatever counted for the ancient temple's courtyard, flanked by a number of—

"Wyverns?" asked Bifrost.

"Who do you think Mordred learned her necromancy from?" answered Bevin. She turned and cast her attention upon the heavy casket of darkest wood and strongest steel, and the hateful Wolf-Lord corpse kept guarded beneath triple layers of defensive spells within. "Stay and guard the ship. I shall go on from here."

Bifrost snapped her head toward Bevin so fast her neck popped. "What!? But Gal said to keep together! And you just told me Lord Beauty is—"

The casket, alongside its defensive enchantments, carried a lightening spell. Bevin hefted it up from the air-yacht's deck with a levitation spell as easily as if it were a mere sack of flour and started down the landing ramp. "Galaxy's not here, she doesn't get a vote. And anyway, I told you Lord Beauty was evil. I didn't say she was powerful, not as she is."

The sky flashed with lightning, throwing the buildings, the forests farther down, the mountainside farther up, in jagged-sharp relief. Thunder rumbled. Bifrost hurried halfway down the ramp after Bevin. "But you don't have a powerful Elemental anymore, it's not working for you like it should! Please, a soldier or two, anyone! Don't go alone!"

Bevin did not slow her stride as she started through the village, though Bifrost's remarks—as pure in care and concern as they were—annoyed her. Her Lightning Elemental kept quiet, but a blinding bolt from the storms above answered her call without hesitation, scattering from her horn and dancing fleetingly around her. "You forget, Sir Bifrost. I'm never alone."

It was a long walk through the village and up the winding, ill-tended path to the ancient temple, made longer by the rain and mud. Bevin, lost to thought and the heat of lightning coursing through the storm, hardly noticed. She marched on, thinking, pondering, looking for the angle to reveal the true meaning of this entire meeting. She had learned well from Mordred. She knew how close Mordred and Lord Beauty had once been, though she had never asked them why. For a while, years ago, she had wondered if Beauty was another Wolf-Lord secretly operating in Heraldale, the same as Mordred and Captain Blackbird, but no mere Wolf-Lord could command such magics. She had wondered if the pair were lovers, or former lovers, broken apart by Mordred's secrets. In the end, Bevin had been forced to settle for their shared history with the Knights le Fay as the source of their close relationship, as anticlimactic as it seemed.

Somewhere in the near but unseen wilderness, wolves howled to the storm. Ascending the last rise before the temple, Bevin thought she knew better now, or was at least beginning to.

Before her, the path broadened into a rock-strewn lawn, and then the black temple proper. To the right, an Imperial troop carrier sat steaming in the rain, a quartet of soldiers in white barding loitering near the lowered ramp and glowering at Bevin. She ignored them, focus straight ahead. The temple was a forbidding sight, a rectangular block carved out of the mountainside, cornered with tall obelisks. There were no windows, and no doors except the main entrance, a massive, gaping entryway revealing its cold, dark innards.

"Go on, then," shouted one of the nearby soldiers, voice a harsh bark. "Get going, you traitor!"

The other soldiers echoed with shouts of "Traitor!" and "Murderer!" Bevin ignored them and continued on into the temple, mindful to carry Mordred's casket behind her to ward off attacks of opportunity.

The innards of the temple were dark, lit fleetingly by lightning glimpsed through an open-air roof. The barren foyer emptied the temple into a grand cathedral interior. The stone floor was cracked through and littered with bones. Towering statues of robed Wolf-Lords guarded the four corners of the temple, cold, dead braziers collapsed at their pawed feet. The air of death and broken holiness hung over the whole of the temple, cold enough to draw visible breath, heavy and still. Those who came there remembered it in their darkest dreams long after.

Bevin paused beneath the broad arch separating the foyer from the central chamber and waited.

"At last," spoke a voice from the far end of the room. Bevin looked, and saw staring out at her from the deep shadows a pair of glowing star sapphires, like eyes. Another moment and the unicorn mare they belonged to stepped forth, her snow-white coat blinding against the surrounding gloom, her storm-grey mane and tail lashing about as if untouched by the rain of the storm above.

Bevin dropped the casket in front of her, the BOOM of its crash to the stone floor as deafening as any blast of thunder as she drew her longsword in her magic and leveled it at the other mare. "Lord Beauty."

"Commander Bevin," spoke Beauty, inclining her head once, seemingly unconcerned with the sword aimed her way. "I knew you would come. How are you adjusting to the late Mordred's Lightning Elemental?

How does it compare to your old Stone Elemental? From stone to lightning. Such a wild shift."

"I handle it fine." Keeping her grip on the sword, Bevin shoved Mordred's casket across the floor with a burst of magic, halfway to the Lord of the Empire. "The prisoners of war. Release them. No tricks."

"No tricks," agreed Lord Beauty. "I signaled for them to be sent down to your waiting air-yacht the moment you entered my temple. They should be getting there any moment now. And you know, it's strange. I have to wonder why you insisted on coming alone . . ."

Bevin ignored the unasked question, instead shifting a sliver of her magical focus to activating the personal communication crystal secured to the front of her barding. "Sir Bifrost, do you read me? Have the POWs made it to you?"

"Yes!" echoed the crystal. "We're almost through loading them up. All 14, as promised. Which means you're going to be coming back down here ASAP so we can leave, right? Mission accomplished? Bevin?"

"In a moment," said Bevin, never taking her eyes off Beauty. "Keep on your guard. I want to talk some first."

"Bevinnnn," whined the crystal, "for God's sake, stop pulling a Gal—"

Bevin deactivated the communication crystal, dropped it to the floor, crushed it beneath a hoof. She never lowered her sword or dropped her gaze from Lord Beauty. The crystal-eyed unicorn watched her in turn, calm and knowing. At a flash of lightning, she smiled. "Talk. You want to talk to me. Well, I can hardly imagine what you might want to talk about all alone here, cut off and beyond communication with any stupid gryphons. It might give certain fools the wrong idea regarding your loyalties."

Thunder rumbled overhead. Bevin marched out from under the arch, felt again the charge in the air, the raw power waiting, merely waiting, to be called down. If only her own Elemental power would rise to match it, she would have no fear.

"Ridiculous, of course. Your loyalty to family, your sense of duty in the name of morality, is unimpeachable. You would die before you knowingly betrayed Princess Galaxy. No. You didn't come here alone to talk and you didn't come to change sides. I know why you accepted my offer of an exchange. It's because you're a true-hearted soldier."

Bevin stopped walking, struck nervous by the observation. She feigned disinterest, looked around, noted the wyverns lurking half-hidden in the shadowed corners. She realized with a sudden drop of her stomach these were not undead wyverns as she had first assumed, but living, breathing wyverns, armored in black steel and leather. And riding atop the wyverns . . . the grey-furred, armored forms of Wolf-Lords, eyeing her as a curiosity and little more, hate tempered with disdain.

"A soldier," Lord Beauty continued, voice rising as she stalked toward Bevin, slowly closing the two yards left between them. "A brute. You've been so all your life. Driven by Mordred's command. Driven by vengeance. Driven by a desperation to live. Only now, Mordred's dead, you're alive and free, and you have absolutely no idea what to do with yourself. And like all weaklings, that terrifies you more than anything else, so you fall back on your oldest and truest crutch. Being a soldier. A brute. A killer—ah, that's it. Of course. A soldier, alone with a priority enemy target, surrounded by all the power you could ever want. You've come here to kill me."

Bevin charged. One of the Wolf-Lords leapt off their wyvern mount to intercept her. Bevin tried to strike them down with a bolt of lightning from her horn, but the energy only crackled fitfully along the shaft for a moment before dispersing. Hurriedly she switched tracks and conjured a spell chain from her horn, snagging it around the Wolf-Lord's throat and yanking them in faster than they'd timed for, impaling their heavy form onto her enchanted silver sword. There was time enough for a solitary scream, and then the wolf burst apart into a quick-lived inferno of cinders, swiftly snuffed out by the rain.

Cries of horror, dismay, rage rose from the remaining Wolf-Lord onlookers. Bevin ignored them and kept up her charge, swinging her sword for Lord Beauty's throat—

Bevin froze in place, her blade the barest inch from the other mare's neck. Snarling, Bevin struggled against the paralysis, though her blood ran cold in understanding.

Lord Thoth stepped out from the shadows behind Lord Beauty, each step of the sphinx strengthening his psychic hold on Bevin. Fear. Now she felt fear, the fear made bitter by Lord Thoth's obvious smug satisfaction.

"I only told you to come alone," said Lord Beauty, pushing Bevin's sword away with her silvery magic and stepping closer, until they were nearly muzzle to muzzle. "It was entirely your idiocy, or perhaps arrogance, that made you think the same of me."

Bevin gave up her struggles, knowing well the futility. She focused instead on the power of lightning high above. She could not let her guard down, not even for a moment, or else the sphinx might read whatever he wanted from her mind. But Lord Beauty kept talking in front of her, and her words came like a slow and vicious venom.

"Your arrogance . . . such arrogance. And such rage. Such hurt for all you've lost and desperation to cling to whatever you can keep. Now that I think about it, you seem so familiar. Lord Thoth, what's your professional opinion on the matter?"

The sphinx nearly—but not quite—giggled at the invitation to an emotional attack, ragged mane growing yet more matted as he stepped out into the rain to stare at Bevin more closely. "Oh, I know exactly what you mean. It's pathetic, really. All her hate, and she's still Lord Mordred's daughter."

Bevin's breath stilled at this claim. Her rear legs kicked with no real aim, her mane in her eyes as she looked between the two Lords of the Empire. "No. I am the daughter of Sir Lancelot. I am the half-sister of Princess Galaxy. I—"

"Are Lord Mordred's daughter in every way that matters," insisted Lord Thoth. He drew close enough to reach out and drag his bared claws down Bevin's throat, enough pressure only to draw the smallest pinpricks of red through her white coat. She could do no more than squirm in his psychic grasp. Squirm and listen. "Your home destroyed in childhood. Your family murdered by or fled in despair from enemies they once thought were friends. Taken in by those enemies, raised by them to be a perfect little soldier."

"Shut up," snarled Bevin. She struggled still harder, managing to move a front leg enough to bat away his claws. But she could not bat away his words as they dug through her flesh and to her heart.

"You betrayed those who raised you for a new master, a chance at revenge," Thoth continued, smile swelling in what seemed his victory. "You found Princess Galaxy, and Mordred found Empress Nova. Blessed royals you'd do anything to keep the good graces of. Forget being Commander Bevin. Forget even being Sir Bevin! You are clearly LORD Bevin, made everything you are by the dearly departed wolf whether you like it or not!"

"For God's sake," spat Bevin, looking desperately from Thoth to Lord Beauty. The words had struck closer to home than Bevin could stomach, and it took all her willpower to keep from screaming. "Kill me, damn you! Or take me back to Avalon so Empress Nova can have her way with me. But have a little heart and shut the sphinx up!"

"Hey!" But Lord Thoth chuckled, voice verging strangely hysterical. It gave Bevin, rattled to her core, something to focus on. He looked a mess she realized, fur unwashed and mane tattered. Perhaps . . . the escape of Brynjar and Owain . . .

"NO!" Thoth's shout was more startling than any crack of thunder. Bevin grunted as the telekinetic hold on her body tightened, Thoth stomping close enough to smack her across the snout with his claws out. "Don't think their damned names! I won't hear of it! I will kill that gryphon RAT! Slowly! Snap every bone in his body and drag his throat out through his beak! And then I'll take his wings and—"

"Thoth," said Lord Beauty, and with the word an overpowering magic draped over the scene, cracking the stone floor and buckling Thoth's legs. "STOP."

Thoth loosened his telekinetic grip on Bevin, enough at least for her to breathe again. The moment he did, the weight of Lord Beauty's magic vanished. Thoth scrambled away from the pair of unicorns, staring at Lord Beauty with wide, terrified eyes. Bevin did the same. She had felt such staggering magical power only thrice before. From Empress Nova. From Galaxy. And years before, journeying to the east . . . the cult, their leader . . .

"That's right, Thoth," continued Lord Beauty, sounding pleased now. "Just like that. Just enough for her to squirm, if she wants. Listen to me, Bevin. The Avalon Empire is failing. Anyone not lost in a sycophantic haze can see it. Empress Nova is losing her grip. Soldiers, inspired by you and that other . . . unicorn . . ."

"Owain," gasped Bevin.

"Yes, him. Soldiers are deserting where they're not being mass Harmonized. The citizenry is in despair, miserable in their lives but unable to imagine any other way of life. All it would take is one more catastrophic blow to send everything tumbling down."

The attack, thought Bevin, hurriedly turning away from the thought, focusing on Lord Beauty and her words. But a glance aside at Thoth and the sphinx's eyes were alight with delight, grin curled and knowing. And Bevin knew he had heard her glancing thought.

"I had hoped Lord Mordred would live and see the culmination of all my fun," Lord Beauty continued, snapping Bevin's attention back to her. "I had hoped to have them at my side. But your family ruined that. Not the first of my hopes and plans to be ruined because of your rotten family. So, now that I have you here all alone, I am going to indulge myself a little. I will kill you. But slowly. Slow enough you will get to watch as I kill all your family—

At this threat, without a thought to slow her, Bevin at last loosed a blistering burst of lightning from her Elemental, the lightning in the storms answering in kind. The power fell and foes were scattered, thunder rending stone asunder. Thoth shrieked and tumbled, burning, psychic power fled. Gem-eyed Beauty stood unbowed, untouched beneath a conjured shield. Bevin charged her, lightning-driven, thrusting horn for the other mare's heart—

The wave of magic sent Bevin flying back to the broad archway separating cathedral from foyer. She landed hard, a leg-kicking tumble she barely turned into a role to stagger back upright, lightning abandoned for a shield spell against any possible follow-up attack.

Lord Beauty seethed before Bevin. The air around the storm-maned unicorn wavered with heat. The falling rain evaporated before it could reach the floor, the surrounding puddles blasted away. The walls were breaking, the statues crumbling from the heat and pressure. Only Mordred's casket remained untouched.

"REVENGE, BEVIN! REVENGE FOR MORDRED, PAID IN FULL BY EVERY MEMBER OF YOUR HOUSE! MY SISTER'S WORDS SHALL RING TRUE YET!"

And for the briefest moment, there appeared to Bevin's dazzled eyes no unicorn, but a tall and slim Wolf-Lord woman in black robes and silver armor, a broad antlered helm upon her head.

Then the vision was gone, and so was Lord Beauty, and so was Lord Thoth, and so were Mordred's casket and the Wolf-Lords and wyverns who had remained lingering on the sidelines. The darkness of the temple returned, a blasted, melted ruin now. The rain fell. Lightning lit the sky and the thunder sounded. Bevin did not move from her spot, did not move a muscle until the sound of gryphon wings and Bifrost frantically calling her name reached her dazed ears. She looked to the raven-gryphon at her approach but only half-saw her, mind instead a whirl as it repeated Lord Beauty's parting threat over and again. "My sister's words shall yet ring true . . ."

"What was that?" Bifrost sat beside Bevin, cast her gaze over the unicorn in naked worry. "Are you alright? Are you hurt? Let me see."

"Nero, on revenge her soul did cling," muttered Bevin, thinking. She knew the words, had memorized them and many more after her farthest travels afield. But she had not thought of them in . . . "Lost herself to the evil of the Burning King . . . Thou shall know revenge by more dread. Revenge on . . . every member of your house . . ."

Bifrost's talons touched her and Bevin jerked, backing away with a whinny and toss of her mane. The beat of her heart drowned out the rain. She could barely focus on the gryphon before her beneath the nauseating wave of horror crashing over her, threatening to sweep her off her hooves. All her family, the faux-unicorn had promised. ALL her family. "Oh God, oh God! We need to get back to Gateway! NOW!"

CHAPTER THREE

The dream felt old, ancient, almost forgotten in the tribulations and haunting visions to come since. Lush green forests stretched below Galaxy. The sky swelled with blue immensity, puffs of clouds like breaking waves. The sun kneaded its gentle warmth upon her back and wings. Her heart light, Galaxy sang into the bracing wind. She saw unicorns among the shadows of the trees, unicorns and Elk, laughing and whole and free.

A break in the forest revealed a majestic river. Unicorns and gryphons lounged together along the banks. Owain and Brynjar caught Galaxy's eye, sitting together atop an outthrust rock, her dearest friend and eldest brother resting with necks entwined. Near the rock stood a unicorn mare, her coat white and her mane and tail gold. Bevin, proud Bevin, entertaining children with a mad dance, sparks of lightning spitting from her hooves and horn. On the opposite riverbank, Bifrost the raven-gryphon sat knitting a blue scarf of prodigious length at prodigious speed. Her sister, the blind seer Carina, fed it with equal swiftness into the white flames of a lit brazier.

Carina did not watch her work. Her fire eyes, hidden beneath her dark blindfold, gazed skyward at Galaxy. Meeting the gaze without pause, Galaxy left the river behind and flew on over the forest. She remembered what came next.

"Galaxy."

Galaxy looked left. A yard away flew a dead gryphon. Ida, Galaxy's adoptive mother. Dead five days without a final goodbye. Dead without forgiveness spoken.

"Mother."

"I'm dead, Gal. And I'm the lucky one."

Laughing suddenly, the dead gryphon crumbled into flame and ash. The pain grown old, Galaxy went wearily through the motions of reaching for her mother. She barely winced as the flames leapt over and consumed her left arm from talons to shoulder, a battering gust of wind scattering the limb and Ida to the void.

Chains shot from the forest, wrapped around Galaxy to squeeze the breath from her. Wanting to see the dream through to the end, no matter the hurt, she gave no struggle as they dragged her down, past the treetops, into a shallow, black-rocked gully dotted with muddy pools. The chains drew tight to the ground, holding

Galaxy flat. Sharp rocks drew pinpricks of blood from her belly.

Hooves clacked on stone. Before Galaxy stood the Dream Unicorn, towering above her, his snowy coat blinding in the gully's gloom, his storm-grey mane and tail lashing with lightning. His silver horn shone with might. His star gaze struck Galaxy with utter contempt. She weathered the loathing with a glare of her own, talons clenching as she tested her magic against the chain.

"Blind." The unicorn's muzzle split open into an impossible smile. The skin pulled back, back, back, tearing down the length of neck, chest, torso, sloughing off, revealing blood-smeared black. Before Galaxy's eyes now stood the Wolf-Lord, Mordred of Avalon, also dead five days yet still haunting her dreams.

"Blind!"

Cracks appeared in the black-furred Wolf-Lord's body, glowing white, spreading. Flames licked the edges of the cracks, skin and flesh crumbling away, leaving behind a scorched stench and blackened bones wreathed in white fire.

Screams echoed from all around Galaxy. She saw the forest aflame, fire lashing like angry serpents. The sound of crackling wood and bursting trees rang thick, but never louder than the screams. Burning unicorns and gryphons stumbled out of the forest. They fell headfirst into the gully, smoke-wrapped falling stars shattering upon the sharp rock. Galaxy breathed deep, increasingly untouched by the hazards of the dream vision. A quick pulse of the magic of the Waters of Life dispelled the chains from her, ridding her of every wound as she rose.

Fire consumed all else. Before Galaxy stood the Burning King, 40, 50, 60 feet tall, black bones and white fire scorching Galaxy where she lay. The skull's eye sockets stared down at her, full of the fire of dying stars.

"BLIND!"

"Not anymore!" Galaxy screamed back.

***

Galaxy tore herself from the old dream-vision, back into waking reality. For a blink, her quarters in the Gateway palace trembled around her. A cold wind fluttered against her scarred back from the open balcony. In front of her the hearth burned with merry brightness, set so by some unthinking or unaware member of the lean palace staff.

Galaxy remained on her personal nest of blankets and pillows and stared at the fire in the hearth. Pondered. Long ago, seeming a whole lifetime ago, she had been burdened with a terrible, inexplicable terror of fire. It had been with her all her life, since her first waking memory. A deep gut fear, an unthinking fear, a sickening fear. It kept her cold on winter nights and unable to do her share of the cooking. Now, after the many months of her journey from Featheren Valley, having faced unicorn armies and Wolf-Lord monsters, wyvern swarms and the horrors of the undead, and worst of all, the treacheries of those she'd trusted, Galaxy knew better, felt better. The fear remained, would probably remain all her life, but now she understood it perfectly. She was afraid of fire because something LURKED there.

"You took longer this time than last. What happened?"

Galaxy stretched her wings and stood to all threes. She no longer stumbled or swayed from her lost left arm, not as badly as she once did. She turned at her leisure to her sole audience. Carina, sister of Bifrost. A gryphon, for reasons Galaxy could not yet articulate, who Galaxy did not wholly trust. "I wanted to see it to the end this time. I wanted to see how the vision changed."

"That's a dangerous want, your majesty." Carina stood from Bifrost's nest against the wall and strode over to the hearth. Talons reached. The flames arced out to wrap around the talons, the leg, disappearing with a sizzle and flash into the dark gryphon's chest where the heart might have been. Carina kept talking. "Dangerous, even if you ignore how visions can be a way for others to look into you just as readily as you look into them. Even ignoring that. History is full of people, even the naturally psychic sphinxes, losing themselves in their visions, no longer able to tell the Dream from waking reality. It would be a shame to lose Heraldale's last hope to a random flight of fancy, I think."

"I could almost see it this time," Galaxy persisted. "Something beyond the Burning King. Bright and shining, like a jewel, but cold. Colder than his fires, but similar. Someone else out there. She felt familiar to me . . ."

"As I said, your majesty," said Carina, turning from the now-barren hearth to tilt her beak down in a smile at Galaxy. "Flights of fancy. It would do better to focus on the Empire. On Empress Nova. The Burning King has hunted and haunted the dreams of Heraldale for centuries. Leave him to it a few centuries more."

Galaxy nodded in acknowledgment of the point, then turned and marched out onto the balcony, bracing into the stiff late-winter breeze. She stood solitary, talons on the balustrade as she watched Gateway. The view still awed her with the sheer scale of the city and its populace, though recent days had drained it of any power to calm or reassure. The noon clouds hung heavy and low, dripping down into the city in an eye-stinging fog. The old, hazy sun cast the scene in eerie yellows, and the winds from the south brought the faint but foul stench of smoke and sulfur. The Dragonback Mountains were awake, and it seemed the heat of their anger grew day by day.

Yet even so, spirits remained high wherever Galaxy looked. The city-state had been invigorated by General Madara's attempted coup, by the arrival of the Elk, by the laying of plans for a final strike against the Empire to capitalize on Lord Mordred's recent death at Galaxy's talons. For the first time since Galaxy had arrived, she even heard singing on the wind, songs a far cry from the mournful melodies which had once haunted the palace's endless halls.

A far, far cry from distant Featheren Valley to the north. She could not wait for Brynjar and Owain to be there with her, to know the tide was truly turning this time.

With this thought, Galaxy closed her eyes and with the swiftness of old practice opened herself to magic within and without. The darkness blossomed into light. All of Gateway shone. She felt the unyielding metal and stone of the city. The deep, growing greens of the farmland. The cold immensity of the inland seas. Most of all she felt the people of Gateway, gem stars in a night sky, each individual gifted with their own personal magic, each magic unique. And Galaxy, who knew she herself shone blinding to any able to perceive magic, giggled with exhilaration at the beauty, her closed eyes wet. The world burned with magic.

"Do you see our sisters?" asked Carina from somewhere behind Galaxy. "Do you see them still?"

"No," said Galaxy, not needing more than a cursory search to be sure her unicorn half-sister, Bevin, and Carina's sister, Bifrost, were nowhere in Gateway or the surrounding seas. "I watched them leave my current range last night, as expected. Northward, as expected. If all went as hoped, they should be on their way back already."

"As expected," said Carina, and nothing more. Galaxy understood the blind gryphon's worry. The central difficulty with secret plans, Galaxy had quickly realized, was the need to keep them secret. The plan to teleport a small infiltration team into the late Lord Mordred's fortress to destroy the Grand Harmonium from the inside, only six days away, required the utmost secrecy. This meant acting as if the only major developments in the war were Mordred's death and the new alliance with the Elk. This meant, when Lord Beauty sent her offer to exchange a dozen prisoners of war for the Wolf-Lord's body, they needed to accept it or else risk the Empire asking WHY gryphon lives suddenly weren't a priority. And Galaxy knew it made sense to send Bevin on the mission, the former Imperial among them the one most certain to recognize a potential trap.

But Galaxy disliked not having her sister at her side. She disliked the mystery of why the Empire would even want Mordred's body back. She wanted the war over. She wanted her family back, all of it, together.

This train of thought broke as Galaxy noticed a ripple spreading through her vision, the sudden but expected arrival of new magic. They came from the northwest, fast and unwavering. If they had not sent a notice of their intent late the night before, Galaxy imagined they would have been swarmed by gryphon soldiers by now.

New to Gateway, not to Galaxy. To her, two of the approaching magical signatures were breathtakingly, heartbreakingly familiar. "They're here."

"Go to them," said Carina. "Don't keep them waiting."

Needing no further push, Galaxy spread her wings and leapt from the balcony. She soared with the speed of magic to the flat top of the ziggurat palace. Already, hundreds of gryphon and Elk soldiers stood in formation, spears raised and banners flying. Many cheered as Galaxy flew over the twin armies of red and grey, the Elk firing off sparklers of magic from their antler-like horns, the gryphons raising a wordless song of heraldry and valor. Galaxy flew faster for it, beak up in a gryphon smile, her heart racing.

Despite all her speed, King Vigdis and Queen Gwendolyn already waited near the black obelisk at the center of the palace roof with their personal guard, their gazes trained on the skies to the north in watch for the awaited arrivals.

Vigdis the condor-gryphon, strong and regal in his armor, looked over at Galaxy's landing and greeted her with a nod. "Gal. Border scouts alerted us the moment they started over the waters. I made sure they have a full honor guard on this last leg of their journey."

"Thanks, Vig." Galaxy fought the urge to pace, remaining talons combing at every errant feather itching at her nerves, to the obvious and quiet amusement of Gwen at her other side. "Sascha and Siegfried should know—"

"Leading the honor guard, of course. The first to say hello."

Galaxy relaxed and wiped at the tears threatening to blind her.

A gryphon's call echoed from the clouds above. A great shuffling rang as the whole of the assembled host stood at full military attention, Galaxy looked up at the call, giving up the tears as they came. A dozen gryphons in the grey armor of Gateway descended into view, wing blades glinting in the shallow sunlight. Galaxy saw Sascha and Siegfried, the lone swan-gryphons in the group, their joy a radiant song on the wind. One waved the weathered flag of Gateway. The other wielded a flag Galaxy did not immediately recognize, full of the colors of spring. The old, forgotten flag of fallen Schwarz Angebot.

An Imperial troop carrier followed the gryphon honor guard out of the clouds and down toward those waiting on the flat palace top. It was a clunky, boxy airship, larger and less elegant than the air-yachts Galaxy knew from her travels, smoking and battle-worn. More gryphon soldiers followed after the troop carrier, but the craft was all Galaxy had eyes for. She watched it descend, slow, turn to face boarding ramp-toward the trio of assembled royalty, settle onto the palace roof with a sudden drop and clang of over-stressed machinery finally giving up the ghost.

For a long heartbeat, all was silent but for the hiss of steam from the carrier. Metal whined as the rear of the ship slowly lowered into a ramp. The first one down the ramp was an Elk Galaxy recognized after a moment as Captain Hywel, lending his side to a one-winged hawk-gryphon. Vigdis fluttered his own wings in unease. On Galaxy's other side, Gwen stamped a hoof and whispered in a voice choked with relief "My Hywel . . ."

The pair barely made it off the ramp before the Elk stopped and looked about them warily. His eyes went first to his queen in equal relief. He started walking again, saw Galaxy and slowed, eyes widening. His voice cracked as he spoke, not to Galaxy, but to those behind him. "She's here! The hippogryph!"

More gryphons came down the ramp, young and old, soldiers and civilians, some limping and some managing to walk strong, all together the most hurt and frightened group of gryphons Galaxy had ever seen. Some stood clustered together, uncertain and disbelieving of their successful journey to safety. Some staggered a few steps toward Galaxy before stopping, muttering exclamations in the vein of "Hippogryph!" or "Her leg!" or "Grimhilt!" Hywel and the first gryphon down separated, the Elk galloping the short distance to Gwen to twine necks with her, the gryphon limping over to stand at attention before Vigdis, her remaining wing arcing around in a wavering salute toward him. "Your Majesty . . . Captain Junko, reporting again for—"

Vigdis reached out with wings and front legs, the smaller gryphon entirely disappearing into the hug from her king.

There was laughter then, and twin cries of "Brynjar!" from the Twins. Galaxy looked, and there at last she saw them, Brynjar and Owain descended last from the craft, one of Brynjar's wings draped over Owain's back.

Flags thrown aside and forgotten, Sascha and Siegfried flew around their lost sibling and laughed, laughed and cried, swooping in for a moment's hug, pulling away to hug Owain, flying, repeating the process all over. Brynjar and Owain joined in on the fun, dancing and prancing about with the pair, adding their laughter to the song. The laughter rang out, loud and bright, bright as spring and the war's end, and the ripples of it danced across the deep well of Galaxy's sorrow. She dared a single step forward, dared a single word, barely whispered. "Brynjar."

The golden eagle-gryphon slowed in his celebrations, stopped, smile calming but remaining strong as he and Owain turned at last to Galaxy. The world quieted. Galaxy didn't know how long it lasted, the long-sought meeting of gazes, relishing the sight of each other like the first gasp of air after a deep and frigid dive. Brynjar looked older than Galaxy remembered. She had never seen her brother so worn, or weary, or sad, the grief well-hidden but lingering behind the joy in his eyes. Yet he did not seem broken by any of this, only greater and wiser.

"Gal. You've gotten old," observed the golden eagle-gryphon, and it felt too much like the truth to dispute.

Galaxy moved first and Brynjar met her, wings and front legs encircling her, beak brushing the back of her neck as he held her close. Owain appeared, pressing close, eyes wet as he nuzzled her cheek, Brynjar taking them both beneath his wings. Galaxy returned the affection and cried, unable to talk, unable to breathe, wishing only for the moment to last forever. They were together again.

CHAPTER FOUR

Hours passed as Galaxy and her family attended to their duties. Galaxy went among the gryphons her brother and Owain had rescued from slavery in Avalon, using the Waters of Life within her to heal and mend what she could. Limbs could not be regrown, she knew this herself, but scars could be faded down into nothing and the vigor of a hale heart could be restored. Brynjar and Owain, meanwhile, alongside Captains Hywel and Junko, debriefed to their respective royals all they had experienced during their grim journeys through Avalon, from the cruelty of their captors to the misery of the common folk.

Duties done and travelers fed, Galaxy at last took Brynjar to see Ida. The statue of her in the old le Fay temple, at least. And it was here, as she, Brynjar, Owain, Sascha, and Siegfried, stood gathered together among the stone memorials to loved ones long gone, when Galaxy realized how much they had changed, all of them, in their time apart. In the days before, Brynjar would have spoken long and bitterly on the particulars of his mother's death. Would have raged and thundered. Would have found ways, valid or not, to lay the blame at least somewhat at Bevin's hooves.

Now, though, Brynjar stood quiet. He listened as Galaxy recounted the flight of the dragons, the cause of her journey to Gateway, all the troubles they found there, General Madara's brief coup. He asked once about the fate of Madara and Noble Master, heard they were both waiting chained in the dark of the palace dungeons for the war's end, nodded, and fell silent, staring at the statue of their mother with tears running down his cheeks. The twins, Sascha and Siegfried, sat at his sides in shared mourning, their wings overlapping. Galaxy stood a few statues away, giving the blood family their proper space. Owain had disappeared somewhere among the levels and rows, whispering something about trying to find his own family there.

"I want to go back to Featheren Valley," said Brynjar. "Once this is all over. I want to rebuild. It won't be the same; it can't be the same, too much was lost, but . . . it would be good to rebuild something. And Mother's family was from Featheren Valley. It was home."

"We'll close the mines," said Sascha. "Lots of explosives. Make sure no gryphon will ever have to work them again. And we'll rebuild up into the mountains, past that dumb governor's castle, make the valley better than it ever was."

"I want to build a school," added Siegfried. "Teach gryphons all the subjects the Empire forbade, just like Mom taught us in secret. And there'll be singing, too. All sorts of singing, every day and all day, and double at breakfast. They'll have to rename it Featheren Valley of the Gryphons That Wouldn't Shut Up."

Brynjar laughed. A bright, honest laugh, the sort Galaxy had almost never heard from her eldest brother. He looked over at Galaxy and nodded her over. "What do you want, Gal? When this is all over?"

Invitation given, Galaxy joined her family and thought the question over. "I think . . . I like Sascha and Siegfried's ideas. There should be a school. A big one. Not just for gryphons, though. People should be able to come to it from all around, if they want. Brynjar, you and I . . . and Owain, and even Bevin, I guess, we've grown from being around others. We've learned from them and they've learned from us. I want a school, after the war is over, where gryphons and unicorns, and Elk, and sphinxes, and . . . Sheol, anyone, can come and learn and see other ways of life. This all started because for one reason or another, unicorns of Avalon began thinking their way of life was better than everyone else's, right? But if they can see how others live, see the commonalities as well as the differences . . . maybe we can stop that from happening again."

After a moment, Galaxy noticed the stares from her siblings and realized how much she had been rambling. "I'm sorry, it's just . . . ideas I've been having—"

"Good ideas," said Siegfried, trilling as the swan-gryphon leaned over to adjust Galaxy's black scarf. "I like the ideas. Trying to teach unicorns to sing like gryphons sounds fun."

"Or at least funny," added Sascha, throwing in her own bad attempt at a whinny that had the rest of them chuckling.

"I like the idea."

Galaxy ducked her head around the front of her siblings, corners of her beak turning up in a grin at the sight of Owain trotting back up to them. "Owain! Get in on this! What do you want after the war is over?"

Sascha, ever courteous beneath her teasing, pulled away from Brynjar enough for the unicorn to wriggle in against the golden eagle-gryphon if he wanted. He did, getting further chuckles from Galaxy and Siegfried and bringing a bright blush to Brynjar's cheeks. Owain paid neither any heed as he leaned against Brynjar and sighed. "After the war . . . I guess everything's going to be different. Someone will have to figure out new leadership for Avalon. There'll be no need or want for a unicorn governor over Featheren Valley, but I'd like to stay with you all anyway and help rebuild."

"Not that I'd ever let you out of my grasp," growled Brynjar, wrapping his left wing close around Owain, to an appreciative whinny. The unicorn sighed again. "And then, I suppose, Galaxy will find herself queen of all the newly-liberated Schwarz Angebot, to rule over it from her family's old ancestral castle."

All humor fled from Galaxy's heart upon this news. "Oh Sheol," she muttered, sharing looks with Brynjar and the twins. They looked as thrown off by the realization as she felt. "I never even considered . . . Sheol. I don't even know the NAME of my family's old ancestral castle. I've never been there, or thought about it, or . . . I have no idea . . ."

"Calm," said Brynjar, reaching out to stroke his talons through the feathers of Galaxy's neck, a fair mimic of her usual stress coping mechanism. "Calm. One worry at a time. That's all for after the war. Let's just worry about the war for now. And besides, you'll do fine. You'll be a great queen, Gal."

Slowly, Galaxy relaxed. They all trusted her, she realized with wonder. Brynjar, Owain, Sascha, Siegfried. They trusted her like nobody else, even though in Galaxy's estimation, if anyone in their small family was fit to be a ruler, had the head and the heart for it, it was Brynjar. "God. Your blind faith is humbling. I—"

Galaxy's personal communication crystal tucked away in her scarf chimed with an incoming signal, high-pitched for urgency. Sharing a new look with her family, Galaxy drew the crystal out with her magic and twisted the small spar at the top to activate it. "This is Princess Galaxy."

"Gal." It was Vigdis, his voice graver than Galaxy had heard since the Battle of Markhaven. "Sir Bevin and Sir Bifrost are back with the prisoners of war. There's been a . . . development."

Galaxy stood from the group cuddle, Brynjar and Owain standing with her without question. "Is everyone okay?"

"As far as we can tell," spoke up another voice. Queen Gwendolyn's. "But Bevin's in something of a panic. Get here as quick as you can."

Brynjar rested a wing on Galaxy's back. Owain touched a hoof to her side. Galaxy glanced at them, nodded. "We'll teleport there right away. Clear space around Bevin, there'll be a number coming with me."

Sascha and Siegfried elected to stay there a little while longer and find their own way back. Galaxy nodded, then closed her eyes and reached out with her blazing red magic. Reached across the many miles of

Gateway separating the abandoned temple and the ziggurat castle, past hundreds of thousands of lives. She felt, distantly, the familiar touch of Bevin's magic, alike hers in the way of blood family. Using this as her anchor, she teleported herself, Brynjar, and Owain—

—Into Vigdis's throne room. Galaxy opened her eyes and looked about, her heart already dropping. There was Bevin, of course, and Bifrost, the raven-gryphon hurrying forward the moment the errant magic had dissipated to twine necks with Galaxy. Vigdis and Gwen near the map table, as well as High General Shan and High General Odin, and a small number of the lower generals from both Vigdis and Gwendolyn. Captain Hywel, as he had since returning with Brynjar and Owain, stood watchful at Gwen's side, head high and eyes alert.

"Oh dear," said Galaxy, pulling reluctantly away from Bifrost. "You were downplaying—"

"Princess Galaxy," echoed a voice, low and trembling.

Galaxy startled at the sound of her name, and then startled again at she who spoke it so. Bevin stared at her wide-eyed and wild, pacing like an animal kept long in a too-small cage. Galaxy had never seen the unicorn so distraught; even in the days when the loss of her magic and death seemed certain, she had held steady and reserved. Now, she looked like she might break to pieces beneath an errant breeze. A glance around told Galaxy everyone else found it as disturbing as she did. "Bev?"

The unicorn stopped her pacing—barely—and looked to Galaxy. Words left her as if they came up jagged in her throat, a painful struggle. "Do you trust me, your majesty?"

Galaxy blinked. She had expected much, teleporting to the throne room, but not this. "Yes, of course. I trust you with my life."

"Do you trust me with the fate of the world?" asked Bevin next.

Galaxy's answer came no slower. "Yes. I do."

One small weight at least seemed to lift from Bevin's burden. In its place came guilt. "I failed you and many others today, more than you know. There is so much still that needs to be said . . . explained . . . and I don't know where to start. But I need to leave Heraldale."

For a moment, Galaxy didn't think she had heard her sister rightly. There was simply no way . . . "What?"

"We can deal with that nonsense in due time," snapped Vigdis, slapping talons upon the map table for emphasis. "We have far more pressing matters right now. Lord Thoth was also at the prisoner exchange."

Beside her, Galaxy felt Brynjar, Owain, and Bifrost shudder at the name. She couldn't blame them. They had each spent days, weeks at the cruel mercies of the . . . "Sphinx. Oh verdammt."

Bevin nodded. "He didn't get much. I made sure he didn't read much from my mind. That was one benefit, at least, of being raised by Lord Mordred. Her dislike of Thoth was infamous throughout the Empire. But he did get some, before I realized he was there. That there's going to be an attack against the Empire. The date and time of the attack, perhaps, I'm less sure on that."

"Enough to ruin everything, either way," growled Vigdis. He looked at Bevin in disgust for a moment more before looking to Galaxy again. "Bevin thinks she might have killed Thoth in retaliation before making her . . . apparent escape, but we can't take that chance. We need options. Today."

"Before that," said Owain, "could we have a quick recap, you know, for anyone who might have been held captive in Avalon and missed out on a few things?"

"It's one week until the spring equinox," said Galaxy. "Our plan, such as it is, is to use Mordred's frozen teleport spell in three days to teleport a small assault team into Hiraeth Arian, the central stronghold of Imperial power on the mainland. With Bevin's knowledge of the fortress's layout and Elk invisibility illusions, we will destroy the Grand Harmonium from within with a series of strategically placed explosive spells. From there, a flock of Gateway troops will swoop in during the confusion and secure the fortress before the Imperial soldiers can respond. Hopefully, with their Lord of War dead and their superweapon lost, the Avalon Empire would be forced into peace talks. Hopefully."

"Only now," spat General Odin, sounding every year of his considerable age, "they will be expecting something to happen that day, and we can't risk assuming that our knowledge of the Grand Harmonium is secret."

"It's not," said Brynjar, drawing many eyes to him. Galaxy realized, dismayed, how long he and Owain had been exposed to Lord Thoth's mind-reading powers. "Although," Brynjar quickly added, "Owain and I didn't know about the frozen spell during captivity. They don't know about that. Won't be expecting attack from within."

"Can we move the time of attack forward?" asked Owain.

General Shan shook her head. "They'll have had the hours it took Sir Bevin and Sir Bifrost to return here to ready their defenses. Less time to do that then it will for us to ready our attack."

"Send more infiltration teams to attack from the inside, then," suggested Galaxy. "We use the frozen teleport spell for our initial infiltration, and then we can use my magical signature for Bevin to teleport more soldiers in with herself."

This time, it was Gwendolyn who shook her head. "My people have had much time to study the frozen spell while it was in our possession. There are several triggers designed into the spellcraft that, after discussion with Vigdis's people, are keys to defensive enchantments around Hiraeth Arian. Tied specifically to Lord Mordred's magical signature. Our best guess is that only one of Mordred's teleports could get through without triggering an alarm. At best."

"At worst," provided Vigdis, "a quarantine spell, like the kind you dealt with in Port Oil. Worse, perhaps, disintegrating people going in as well as out."

"Then we attack later," continued Brynjar. "Lull them into the idea that discovery has made us too wary to continue with the attack."

"I like that least of all," said Gwen. "We're already cutting closer than I like to the planned activation of the Grand Harmonium. We still don't know exactly how it will work, but our guess that it will draw from the energy of the Dragonback volcanoes seems ever more likely as they grow more active day by day. I'm sure you noticed that on your way in here."

"We need a distraction," declared Vigdis. All other chatter ceased. All attention turned to the condor-gryphon. "We need a feint. Another attack, elsewhere, large enough and at critical enough of a target that the Empire will believe it's the attack they were warned of."

Mutters around the table. Galaxy shared a look with Bifrost as the raven-gryphon laid a wing across her back, Galaxy's worries clear in the other's rainbow eyes. "It could hurt us terribly," Galaxy said aloud. "A target like that could fend off an attack. We could lose if we bit off more than we could chew."

There was an unspoken fear all around the table in sync with Galaxy's words. It was impossible not to think about the last major attack Gateway launched, flying to join the Elk in battle against Lord Mordred in the failed defense of Markhaven. They had been victorious, but only thanks to Galaxy.

"It's a risk we must be willing to take," spoke Gwendolyn at last. It was her right to do so. Her troops would most likely be those in greatest danger. "We are too close to ending this war to back away now. We Elk are prepared to do what we must to reach the war's end."

"As are the gryphons," agreed Vigdis. He looked then to Galaxy, nodding. "What say you, princess?"

Galaxy swallowed, hating as ever the sudden attention. This time, she did not seek the eyes of her companions. "It mostly seems to me that all we have to decide is where to strike and with who. The Imperial forces to the north?"

General Odin shook his head. "They are a danger to us, but not an immediate one with the natural defenses of our inland seas. More, they will not be a great enough priority for the Empire to focus its attention on in the event of an attack. A diversion like this calls for a target absolutely instrumental to the Imperial strategy, a target that they absolutely must not lose or falter in."

"One problem with that," said Brynjar. "You're already hitting the biggest target the Empire has for your main attack, other than the Avalon Islands themselves. What could compare?"

Shared looks crossed the table, desperate scanning of the map before them for somewhere, anywhere, they could strike at. Galaxy thought she saw it first and hated herself for it. Hated herself more than words could measure. "Gryphonbough."

The throne room fell deathly quiet. Not a feather ruffled or breath sighed free. An excruciating pain flickered across Vigdis's features, gone as quickly as it came, but terrible all the same. "Explain, Gal."

Galaxy wasn't sure she could, not well enough to excuse reminding Vigdis of the battle he'd lost his mother in. But if she had to try, and she did . . .

"Ignoring Mordred's murderous tantrum across the Heraldale Midlands, conquering Gryphonbough was the Empire's last great military victory, and their first major progress in the war since the fall of Schwarz Angebot. It gave their common soldiers confidence again. It gave the Empire land access to the United Zakarian Confederacy. It gave them vast woodlands and farmlands to support the desiccated husk of a country Brynjar, Owain, and Hywel tell us Avalon has become. If I were in charge of the Empire, it would not be a conquest I'd want to lose."

A war of emotions played out across Vigdis's face. His expression hardened as the inevitable end was reached. "I shall lead the attack myself."

The throne room burst into predictable protest. Generals begged Vigdis's safety. Court officials pleaded how much Gateway needed him. Galaxy wondered at how the condor-gryphon weathered the storm, silencing it after a moment with one raised wing. He stared the throne room down, head high and eyes alight. "The attack must look convincing. It must look predictable.

It must look, above all else, TEMPTING. Whatever the risk, we must do what we must do."

"Whatever the risk," Gwendolyn agreed.

"Whatever the risk," Galaxy echoed. She looked to Brynjar and Owain close at talon, thought of the hardships and risks which had brought them back to her, took solace again in having them there. Her family, together again, could accomplish any—

"Wait," said Galaxy, startled as she hurriedly scanned the gathered crowd. Her heart sank as she realized the obvious, realized the one voice they had not heard in too long. "Where's Bevin?"

Vigdis glanced around, frowned. "Gal?"

"Already on it," said Galaxy, charging a teleport spell as she reached out to her sister's magic. Distracted, she did not remember Bifrost's physical connection until the spell had been cast and the pair teleported to the corridor outside the royal library, coming within a hair's breadth of slamming Bifrost's beak into the wall.

"Whoa!"

"Shoot!" hissed Galaxy, looking to Bifrost, then the wall, and then back to Bifrost. "That was close. Sorry. I should have said—"

"It's alright," said Bifrost, the raven-gryphon smiling, though Galaxy saw how her heart still beat staccato from the sudden teleport. Bifrost looked away first, dropping her wing from Galaxy's back as she frowned. "The royal library? Is Bevin much of a reader?"

"If she is," said Galaxy as she led the way inside, "that's at least one thing she and I have in common, though this hardly seems like the right time for a good book."

"Didn't you go spend several hours in Port Oil's bookstore in response to finding a magic-draining monster running loose there?"

Galaxy was feeling too relieved to give much thought to the kindly tease. In the moments before teleporting, there had been the fear of Bevin following through on her claim of needing to leave Heraldale, and Galaxy would teleport and find herself aboard an air-yacht or troop carrier heading for who-knew-where. Her arrival at the royal library, though confusing, was nonetheless reassuring. Bevin had not gotten far yet.

They found the unicorn in question bunkered down at a far table, a multitude of tomes concerning Elementals and how to commune with them laid out before her and a look of ferocious concentration upon her muzzle. Galaxy approached slowly, letting her wings rustle loudly enough for her sister to hear her approach, not speaking until she had joined her at the table. "Something I should worry about?"

Despite the care Galaxy put into her approach, Bevin startled up from the main book of her focus, a quick whinny escaping her before she saw Galaxy and settled down. "Oh, you."

"Yeah, me," said Galaxy. She tried to keep her tone light even as her worry grew. She could not remember a time when the soldier had been so startled, not even in the depths of her sickness. "Now come on, talk. The rest of us came up with a . . . I won't say it's a good plan, but it's one we can at least all be unhappy with together. What's going on? You were rattled when you got back. Even more rattled than an enemy sphinx reading one stray thought should have left you."

"Yes, I was rattled," said Bevin, gold magic glowing from her horn as she closed the books around her. "For more than one reason. I'm still rattled. But now I can't remember one of those reasons."

"You can't . . ." Galaxy frowned, shared a look with Bifrost, looked back with a forced smile and laugh. "It can't have been too serious then, if you've forgotten already. Right?"

"No," said Bevin. The unicorn turned and slid between Galaxy and Bifrost, marching for the exit. She motioned for them to follow with a toss of her head. "No, it's deathly important. Why was I gone? Where was I to get my thoughts read by Lord Thoth?"

"A prisoner exchange," said Bifrost, hurrying after Bevin alongside Galaxy. "I was there too. We went to trade Lord Mordred's body for some gryphon prisoners of war."

"From who?"

"From," began Galaxy, stumbling in her walk as her thoughts stumbled. "From . . . Lord Thoth? He's the only Lord of the Empire remaining, right?"

"Right," said Bifrost. But then the raven-gryphon jolted to a stop between the library aisles and the doorway out to the rest of the palace, confusion writ large across her face. "But wait, no, how could he have surprised you with being there to read your mind if he was who we were going to meet in the first place?"

Bevin stopped her march and turned to Bifrost. "Exactly! Something doesn't add up. Our memories don't add up. I came here from the meeting for a reason, I know I did, but now I can't . . . it's like something has been cut out from the fabric of my mind. It's not there, but I can almost . . . almost make it out by feeling around the edges of the hole . . ."

"And now we can't remember either," said Galaxy. Her heart thundered in her chest and she felt nauseous down deep in her belly, a horrid mixture of confusion, fear, and awe driving her to pace as she thought. This could only have been the work of a spell, but she could not imagine any spell powerful or complex enough to affect their memories both so thoroughly and so precisely. And then there was the question of how it had been cast upon them in the first place . . .

A thought. Galaxy stopped her pacing and went to the broad doorway into the palace library, eyes scanning the soft rose marble, the delicate traceries of—

"Runes," she said. "Here, on the inside of the doorway. Wolf-Lord runes. I've seen their like before, away north in the underground ruin Brynjar, Owain, and I fled through at journey's start."

Bevin and Bifrost joined her at the doorway, the latter tracing the ancient symbols in an arc all along the inner sides of the doorway. "These are a variant I'm not familiar with. They're old, but not as old as the surrounding stone. They were added later. Maybe when . . ."

"You can feel the magic in them," said Bevin. "Where are they drawing the magic to power the spell from?"

"There you all are!"

Galaxy jumped at the sudden shout and spun around. Brynjar was hurrying up the corridor toward them, Owain hot on his heels. An idea came to Galaxy. "Brynjar! Who did Bevin and Bifrost get back from meeting to trade for prisoners with!?"

Brynjar skid to a halt, frowning at what to him must have seemed the strangest of questions. "Lord Beauty, wasn't it?"

Galaxy sagged with relief. She had a moment to smile as her memory snapped back to fullness, Bifrost sighing in relief beside her.

And then the doorway into the royal library exploded.

CHAPTER FIVE

Galaxy waited until the dust had settled before dropping the shield spell around herself, Bevin, and Bifrost. "Well, that was dramatic. Alright, sound off. Who's not dead?"

"Not dead yet," reported Bevin, the unicorn backing away nonetheless and eyeing the smoking remnants of the now-jagged and crumbling library entrance as if they might blow again.

"Would you believe me if I told you that wasn't the first time a library has tried to kill me?" asked Bifrost, before turning away to intercept the palace guard rushing in response to the sudden explosion.

"I probably would," Galaxy said to her retreating back.

Brynjar and Owain hurried over, looks of panic upon their faces. "What in blazes," began Brynjar—

"An enchantment," answered Galaxy, looking again at the burnt and broken marble scattered around them. "A spell trap, just in case. There was some kind of memory removal spell over the library. It made any of us who entered completely forget about Lord Beauty. I guess the reintroduction of the removed knowledge from outside its sphere of influence pushed the spell matrix into a fail state."

"I'll pretend I understood that," said Brynjar. "How did the spell get here? And why?"

"I . . . don't know." Galaxy turned away to her sister. "Bevin?"

The unicorn did not look to the sound of her name. Bevin faced away from them, toward the north wall of the palace library, eyes narrowed. Galaxy followed her gaze and blinked, frowned as well after a moment as she found herself staring at a tall and sharply arched doorway of black stone and shining silver, the corridor beyond wrapped in shadows which wholly defied the bright sunshine filling the main of the library, deep shadows no gryphon sight could pierce.

"How long has that been there?" Galaxy asked, though she could guess the answer.

"Since we broke the memory spell," said Bevin. The unicorn walked forward until she stood before the tall doorway and then stopped, looked back at them all. "It could be dangerous. Someone should stay to deal with things here."

"I will," said Bifrost, rejoining the group. "Talk with the palace guard, fill King Vigdis in when he shows up over all this ruckus. And I'm sure my sister's on her way as we speak, just itching to do her whole, you know . . ."

"Wise, blind seer thing," said Galaxy, grinning. She stepped forward past Brynjar and Owain and pecked a gryphon kiss against the side of Bifrost's beak. "Thank you. I'll fill you in on everything we figure out when I get back, I promise."

Bifrost smiled and leaned down to return the kiss. "I'll hold you to that. Stay safe."

"Always do."

"Heh. Liar."

Somewhere behind them, Owain groaned and looked to Brynjar. "Oh God, is that what we've looked like to everyone else this whole time?"

Galaxy ignored the remark, kissed Bifrost's beak a final time, and then joined Brynjar, Owain, and Bevin at the shadowed corridor. She noticed Brynjar giving her a Big Brother Look and turned to him with a smile. "Owain makes you very happy, no?"

Brynjar's cheeks flushed red through his feathers and he looked back to the dark corridor, a wing lifting to rest across Owain's back as he cleared his throat. "So . . . what is this, exactly?"

"If we're lucky," answered Bevin, "answers to questions I've been asking for many years."

"And if we're not lucky?" asked Owain.

"Answers to questions I've been asking for many years . . . followed by swift yet agonizing death."

"The usual deal, then," said Galaxy. Nobody laughed. The four of them were already walking. Galaxy could not remember starting to walk. She glanced back and saw the light and life of the palace library already an impossible distance behind them, each step they took sending the doorway farther and farther away. "Oh. Spooky."

They walked on with no telling for how long. Around them reigned the darkness of the corridor, no light to guide their way. To Galaxy, the others were dim shadows within the greater darkness, ideas and echoes of form and movement rather than whole, physical beings beside her. They walked until Galaxy thought it impossible for them to still be within Vigdis's palace, until she knew this corridor was more magic than stone and they had gone far, far afield. Yet it seemed impossible to stop now, the mere idea of turning and going back a total impossibility.

"When I was young," spoke Bevin, shattering the silence of the corridor, "I had . . . dreams. Perhaps visions. A white unicorn with a storm mane and a storm tail, hooves of—"

"Silver," Galaxy finished, stomach dropping. "Tinged perhaps with the vague feeling of fire. I've . . . seen them too, in my dreams. At first, at journey's start, I thought they were my father, of whom I knew nothing about. Then, I began to realize . . . to fear . . . that it was the Burning King inside my head somehow. Reaching out to me through the Dreaming. It's what Bifrost's sister, Carina, thinks."

From the darkness, Galaxy felt Brynjar's other wing settle across her back. The silence stretched on. She hastily added "But it's not so remarkable as all that. I've been told the Burning King has haunted the dreams of Heraldale for centuries."

"I heard those words myself, once upon a time," muttered Bevin. More silence. When next Bevin spoke, it was on a tangent Galaxy almost couldn't follow. "I've never told you how I came to realize Lord Mordred was a Wolf-Lord, have I? Or about Captain Blackbird, for that matter?"

"Captain Blackbird's a Wolf-Lord!?" said Owain, voice startled in the dark. "God, Brynjar and I did miss a lot."

"No, you haven't told us," said Galaxy, frowning. "There's a lot you've never told us, I reckon."

"A lot," Bevin agreed. "A lot which I regret, which I feel shame over, which I would rather never think about again, if I could help it. And some things for which I can feel a . . . ghost of pride at. Only one thing, really. It takes some explanation. We might have talked about this before, but unicorns don't replenish ourselves as quickly as other species. Every child, every filly and colt, counts. In the military, there is even a protocol that at regular periods, mare soldiers must take a leave of absence to do their duty for empress and empire. They return to actual active duty as swiftly as possible, all foals born to military mares fostered by unicorns who for one reason or another were found unfit for combat."

"I remember there being a few such colts around when I was growing up," Owain added in, hoofsteps gaining a bit of a trot. "They were good playmates, until we moved to Featheren Valley."

Galaxy had a thought. A wild, head-spinning thought, but before she could put it to question, Bevin spoke again. "I'll try to keep the story brief. The better part of three years ago, a caregiver fled Avalon, fled Heraldale, with two such children. I led the unit sent after him. The mission took us to the Wolf-Lord nations half the world away. The caretaker had been slain and the children stolen from him in turn by an infamous cult among the Wolf-Lords, the Cult of the Burning King.

With . . . local help, we found they had been stealing children from all across the lands for the sake of some kind of eldritch ritual. Blood magic of the darkest order. Captain Blackbird was among the local help. I eventually returned to Avalon, thinking the cult had been destroyed and the nightmare finished . . ."

"But, considering you're still talking about it now," said Galaxy, setting aside her impossible thought for later, "and in some kind of connection to Lord Beauty and the Burning King . . ."

"A threat was made," said Bevin, gaze staying forward. "In the prisoner exchange, after I had blasted Thoth away with lightning. A threat made by Lord Beauty against our family for the death of Lord Mordred and for my part in stopping that cult. A threat against all our family."

"All our family is here in Gateway," said Galaxy, able to hear the tinge of desperation coloring her voice. "As safe as any of us can be in this war. Bevin—"

Before she could finish, the corridor ended. It seemed the darkness fled away into nothing around them, leaving them standing in a new room, dazzling after the preceding dark. Galaxy blinked and turned a slow circle, slipping out from beneath Brynjar's wing as she took in the sights around them. It was a large room, at least as large as Vigdis's throne room. Carved from black volcanic stone, a high ceiling twinkling with glowing crystal spell batteries arranged like winter constellations. Lining much of the walls stood statues of Wolf-Lords in white stone, arms raised and palms up to the ceiling, titans holding the heavens aloft. Across the floor were tables of more white stone, turning grey with the dust of time, many laden with weathered scrolls and leather-bound books, others burdened with strange items of gold and crystal. A few of these unfamiliar instruments still whirred and puffed languid breaths of steam, but most lay dead and broken.

"What is this place?" asked Galaxy, walking over to the nearest of the tables. On it stood a broad ring of purple crystal atop a silver pedestal. Staring through the ring, Galaxy saw the wall beyond magnified tenfold, but within the ring itself there hovered the ghostly, barely-glimpsed impression of distant Rotwald. "A prototype viewing portal, maybe . . ."

"This dust," said Brynjar, joining Galaxy's side. "Nobody's been here in years. But . . . it's nowhere like the state the Wolf-Lord city of Hollereich had been. It hasn't been THAT long since someone else was here . . ."

"Galaxy!" shouted Owain. "Come here!"

Galaxy, Brynjar trailing behind her, joined Owain and Bevin on the far side of the room, where the floor rose several steps from the rest and began to twine with strange symbols in silver and gold. The wall there featured no statues. Instead, upon it was painted a dominating mural of a Wolf-Lord. Galaxy's heart skipped a beat at the sight of her. The Wolf-Lord was tall, but willow-thin where Lord Mordred had been a towering brute of muscle. White fur, the cleanest white, with stormy grey hair reaching far down her back. The Wolf-Lord wore simple robes of black and armor of silver. Her yellow eyes stared out at the world with startling hatred, seeming to Galaxy almost alive.

Above the mural were three words scrawled massive.

MORGANA LE FAY

"The founder of the Knights le Fay?" Galaxy asked, turning briefly to give the secret room another glance. "The creator of the Elk?"

"The Two-Hearted," said Bevin. Her voice rose with shocking venom, a hatred which startled Galaxy, as used as she was to hearing it reserved solely for Mordred. "The Sorceress. Queen of Dark Realm and leader of the Cult of the Burning King. She was the dark monster of their history, the evil sister of General Nero, banished transformed into a hated form long before our betrayal of and assault on the Wolf-Lords."

"Banished for what?" asked Brynjar.

Galaxy could not answer. She stared transfixed at the mural, eyes roving it, seeing details with startling, horrifying familiarity.

Galaxy heard hooves clacking on stone. Before her stood the Dream Unicorn, towering above her, his snowy coat blinding in the gully's gloom, his storm-grey mane and tail lashing with lightning.

"A threat has been made against all our family," said Bevin in repetition, looking from the mural down to Galaxy. "With the threat came a vision of Lord Beauty transformed into Morgana le Fay. I need to answer this threat. To the east outside of Heraldale are . . . friends, of mine. They've fought Morgana before. They've beaten her."

"The Wolf-Lords," said Galaxy. It was not a question. She looked to her sister and held herself as tall as she could to hide her heart as it broke. "You are going to the Wolf-Lords. Morgana is one, Mordred was one, so you hope . . ."

"This is something I need to do," insisted Bevin, not fleeing from Galaxy's gaze. "I had a chance to kill Lord Beauty before, stop this madness before it could start, but I just . . . my Elemental wouldn't . . . I failed. This is the next best choice I can make now. I'd rather go with your blessing, as my princess if not my sister, but—"

"You'll go either way," finished Galaxy. Her voice was low and steady, but only barely. On the inside she wanted to scream, to rage, to throw things at anyone standing too close. She had only hours before gotten what remained of her family back together again, a miracle in the face of the war. The unicorn before her now threatened to break the family up even worse, traveling farther and to even more uncertain ends. Galaxy wanted to scream . . .

Instead, she looked her sister in the eyes and said "Not alone. The attack on the Grand Harmonium can't spare both of us, but you aren't doing this alone again." It took all of Galaxy's willpower not to insist on going along herself. It had been to the lands of the Wolf-Lords that the dragons had fled, in the hour of her greatest failure. More than anything other than ending the war, Galaxy wanted to see the dragons again and make amends. Make sure, at least, they were settling into their new lands as easily as Mordred had promised.

"I understand," said Bevin, stance relaxing; not wholly, Bevin wouldn't wholly relax until the war was over or she lay dead, but enough to be noticeable. She looked away from Galaxy at last, to the quiet watchers of the debate. "Brynjar?"

"If it needs doing," said the golden eagle-gryphon, "I'll do it. To war's end."

"To war's end," Bevin and Owain both echoed.

"To war's end," said Galaxy, voice muted as a sudden, unnamable, unreachable fear swelled in her heart.

CHAPTER SIX

Even with all need for haste, they could not depart immediately as Bevin wished. Considerations needed to be made to account for Bevin and Brynjar's absence in the attack plan, supplies secured, Vigdis and the rest informed with as much as Bevin felt safe sharing. Her deepest worries, of Bifrost and the blind seer Carina, and the statue of the Burning King in the palace gardens, Bevin kept to herself, Galaxy, and Brynjar.

"I promise you, Bev. Vigdis would stop in a heartbeat if we gave him reason not to pray to that statue. He's certainly not involved in any of this like . . . well, like Carina probably is. It's just something to do to keep the spirits up with him."

"Maybe. If there's anything I learned being raised . . . being KEPT by Lord Mordred, like a pet and nothing more, it's that people can be in on things without knowing until it's too late. Be careful."

Galaxy's downturned beak spoke volumes across their quarters. "Bev, about Mordred—"

"No. Focus, back to the task on hoof."

They spent most of those many hours reviewing Bevin's memories of the insides of Hiraeth Arian, the rooms and corridors, the troop complement, the security enchantments and pathways to best circumvent them, everything Bevin thought Galaxy would need in her absence and could be covered in the relatively brief time allotted them. It was slow going, and with the unspoken discomforts sprung between them, neither got through it too happy.

***

Brynjar waited until dark to go down to the palace dungeons. He kept his anger down to a simmer as he waited through the hours of discussion and debate among Galaxy and Bevin and Queen Gwendolyn, among King Vigdis and his generals and his counselors, among Sir Bifrost and the raven-gryphon's strange, too-knowing sister.

Brynjar waited, and when it was time and he guessed he would not be overly missed, he slipped away from the rest and ventured through the palace. The soldiers there, all but worshipping him for his rescue of the prisoners and escape from Avalon, were too eager to point him in the direction of the dungeons, down stairwells and ramps, past locked gates and heavy steel doors all swung eagerly open at his asking. One sparrow-gryphon soldier, perhaps guessing his thoughts, even offered Brynjar her spear and a promise to heed no shouts or screams she might hear for the rest of her guard shift.

Brynjar took the spear and the promise.

Far below the earth, below the clean, orderly, sun-kissed face of the palace, the royal dungeons lurked cold and wet. Brynjar delved down the broad, echoing corridors, his way lit by a lone torch held tight in his talons. Cells passed to his left and right, thick iron bars rusting, the insides choked with shadows banished only briefly by his flame before he moved on. The air lay cold and heavy, silent but for the thud of Brynjar's steps, the ruffle of his feathers as he explored the dark, and the subtle yet harsh rasp for breath he followed farther and farther down and in.

In the farthest cell along, Brynjar found High General Madara. The hawk-gryphon lay on the stone floor of the cell, wings bound at his sides and primary feathers plucked, his gaze on the wall as he lay with his back to the bars and the corridor beyond. Here the air stank with old blood and fresh waste, Brynjar grimacing despite his anger at the thought of how rarely gryphons must come down to tend to prisoners.

"I've been waiting for you, princess," said the limp and lifeless form on the cell floor. "I knew eventually you would come to gloat at your stranglehold on Gateway, on my king. Your cursed unicorn blood would drive you to it. I can see it now. It all makes sense. The scars and hurts are a ruse. You came to Gateway to twist and subvert. Only sense to make of it. Nothing else works . . . best interests at heart . . . WELL!? GET ON WITH IT! MOCK ME, FILTHY HALF-BLOOD FREAK!"

"I am not Princess Galaxy," said Brynjar. "And my sister is no freak."

General Madara lay still and silent for a moment, before slowly sitting up and turning to face Brynjar. Eyes shuttered by deep purple bruises grew wide at the sight of the golden eagle-gryphon, the traitor hurriedly scuttling back and away from the bars. "Sir Ida!? N-no . . ."

"Sir Brynjar. Son of Sir Ida. Adoptive brother of Princess Galaxy." The rage struck as he spoke. The hate, the all-consuming loathing, until there was nothing Brynjar wanted to do more than throw the spear through the bars of the cell and put the traitorous hawk-gryphon out of everybody's misery.

"Impossible," said Madara. He stared at Brynjar as if looking at a ghost. "You were taken prisoner by the Empire. We all know it. We all know it's impossible to escape Avalon. You can't be here . . ."

"You have a pathetic idea of what's impossible," said Brynjar. He set the torch into a sconce in the wall, the better to let him grip his borrowed spear in his talons. "And here I am. Escaped. Reunited with my family. Well, the family that's still around."

Madara swallowed. His gaze turned from Brynjar to the head of his spear, wicked and sharp in the wavering light of the torch. "And so . . . and so you have come to kill me. Avenge your mother. Do what my weak king and your weak princess couldn't. Good. Good to know there's one true gryphon left in Gateway, one true gryphon of resolve."

Brynjar's beak ached from how tightly he pressed it closed. "Princess Galaxy is a lot of things, but my sister is not weak. I could only dream of having her resolve. If I did, maybe I wouldn't be standing here, staring at the most pathetic gryphon I've ever seen, holding a weapon of murder. If I had her resolve, maybe I'd be up in the palace, enjoying what time I could with the loved ones I still have."

"But you are here," hissed Madara. The hawk-gryphon stood and lunged for the bars, grabbed them in his talons and hauled himself up, belly exposed to Brynjar. "You're here and you want to kill me, so do it! Go on! It's what you want to do, it's what you deserve! A true gryphon of action! Do it! DO IT!"

Brynjar stared. The spear lowered, the point forged to pierce the strongest of armor aimed for thin skin and guts.

"You know how my soldiers found your mother dead?" asked Madara, voice a hissing venom in Brynjar's head. "Lying between that unicorn, Bevin, and the remnants of a grenade. Her whole front half perforated with shrapnel, her insides turned to burnt mulch. I can just imagine it, the unicorn using a burst of magic to throw your mother in the way of the bomb! Can you imagine it!? Can you hear in your head the cry of anguish, the sizzle of flesh, smell the rush of blood, hear her last dying gasps!? Betrayed, used as a shield by the unicorn filth! You know that's how it happened because you know unicorns just like I do! You know it, you know, you know, you—"

***

Gwendolyn entered the secret chamber within the old le Fay temple and looked around, a frown growing in her heart but her expression kept carefully neutral for the sake of her pair of guards accompanying her. The room was all as Galaxy and the others had described it. Dusty and harshly lit, cluttered with the outdated and eccentric magical and scientific instruments of ages past. It felt like a tomb, and merely stepping in,

Gwendolyn felt she wouldn't have been surprised to find a few mummies left scattered about.

Her hooves carried her farther on of their own volition. She kept her pace slow and her head on a swivel, examining carefully the work Galaxy and friends had been putting into cleaning the place up, books dusted and restacked, tables mended, tools returned to their proper places. The work of hours, surely, but against the vastness of the room and all it contained, the efforts so far looked like little more than the idle attentions of the bored.

"I shall set my own servants to the task," she said to herself, the first words spoken aloud by any in her small group in a long while. Gwendolyn saw her guards had begun to scatter through the room, their attentions caught by this trinket or that, and she had to smile. It was understandable. They stood in the workshop of their creator. It was the closest Elk kind had ever come to having a place of holiness.

"In distant ages and ancient woods there dwelt an elk named Erentil.

His many-pronged antlers arcing high proved him true the battle-king.

Grey was his coat, as the oaks of his realm, where oft he roamed in grim mood.

Of many he sired, all sons silver-coated, their prongs the ire of hunting men.

And daughters too he duly delivered, gold as the sun and glad of their goodness.

Unicorns too lived in that wood, who stood and delivered onto Erentil scorn.

'Horns over antlers,' they'd answer his call, and for a horn he would trade all.

Pure does not promise good, the wise ones wrote, of which the elk could

Truly attest. East and west Erentil trod, to find and ease to his troubled thoughts.

The unicorn beauty he loved, though in truth a lowly elk was he. But lo,

At western edge of the wood one morn, he met a woman by travel worn.

For food she begged, and drink, and freedom from an unnamed fear.

Daring Erentil could not answer no, and so led her to secluded dale.

A feast on gathered fruit he fed her, and water too from snow-fed river,

'til at last the lady bowed down low and thanked him for his grace.

Then like a veil lifted from his eyes, the elk beheld no beggar-woman, but

Fearsome and fiery Morgan the Fae, wielder of magic both wicked and fair.

Before her he bowed, knees buckling, his better by far.

'Good elk,' she spoke, words like the wind, 'What is your wish?'

Then Erentil told her of his travels and troubles, his hope for a horn.

'For kindness a reward, oh lord of my realm.' Morgan reached out

Her hand to the hart, resting upon the brow of the old battle-king.

And Erentil felt a light flood into him, magic and might to master the True.

Taller Erentil stood, his antlers felt strange, more solid now yet light.

Thus born were the Elkish, beloved of Morgan, her bairns thereafter."

Gwendolyn came to a stop before the towering mural. Morgana le Fay. Morgan the Fae. The entity to whom all Elk owed the gift of magic and greater civilization. She stared at the image and tried not to think about all she had heard Galaxy, Bevin, and the others discussing. Their theories, their fears. Morgana le Fay, walking the realm free and empowered again. Working with the Avalon Empire. Spreading chaos, worshipping the Burning King. But like always happened, once she tried not thinking about it, she could think of nothing else.

"She is our creator," she said aloud, ears twitching to hear her own voice. The scuff of Elk hooves meandering behind her told her how her people continued to wander. A part of her supposed it made a certain terrible sense. Toqeph, the Prime Unicorn, had created the Wolf-Lords and then turned to evil, to be cursed and banished away as the Burning King. Morgana, his prize creation, had made the Elk who and what they were and then turned to evil, to be cursed and banished away.

Were creation and evil linked? Were they hereditary? Was it a doom, continuing down the line step by step? Gwendolyn's father, the King Erentil of the old poem, had turned to cowardice and evil in later days, had come to serve Avalon and betray his vows. One more link in the chain.

Now Gwendolyn stood before the mural, wondering to herself, only herself, if she might be the next link.

"My queen," called out the voice of Captain Hywel from somewhere distant in the secret chamber, startling Gwendolyn, forcing her to look away from the mural and to him as he trotted her way. She smiled at his approach. After a moment, he returned the smile. "My queen. We should get some rest, shouldn't we? Tomorrow . . ."

"Yes," said Gwendolyn, fully turning away from the mural and briefly surveying the room. Her guards continued their idle explorations, and suddenly fear struck her, a near certainty at any moment one of them would trigger an old and forgotten trap and be utterly destroyed.

As if somehow seeing this errant fear in her remaining eye, Hywel stopped before Gwendolyn and turned, voice raised and bursting with full military authority. "Guards! Attend to your queen!"

At once, each Elk soldier stopped whatever they were doing, be it rifling through the pages of a weathered book or picking through a vase full of gold rings, and moved to assemble themselves before Gwendolyn and Hywel. As soon as they had done so, the latter turned again and smiled up at the former. "Is that better, your grace?"

Gwendolyn stared, barely having the presence of mind to nod yes, it was better. She looked her old friend, her oldest friend, up and down from hooves to antler-like horns and back, and felt an old, familiar stirring. For the first time in her life, she chose to act on it.

"Soldiers," she said, addressing her guards. "You are relieved for the night. Return to your barracks and get some rest, for tomorrow we go to war. Hywel, come with me."

The assembled guards, after a moment of confusion, all bowed and popped away with the staccato flash of teleport spells. Hywel looked strangely up at her, confusion in his eyes. "My queen? Where—"

"Tomorrow I go to war, old friend." Gwendolyn strode past the shorter Elk, head high and focus on the doorway from there back to the royal palace. "Tomorrow, I might die. Or the day after, or the day after that. But tonight, I go to my bedchamber. My lonely, lonely bedchamber . . ."

A moment's pregnant silence passed, and then the scuffing of hooves on stone as Hywel hurried to follow after her.

***

The night was dark. A full, heavy, pregnant dark, no stars or moons to hold it back, to light the hearts of those for whom no sleep would come.

As he had done more and more in the weeks and months of his rule, Vigdis sat before the statue of the Burning King in his royal garden, eyes closed and talons clasped tightly together, and he prayed. He had always been a gryphon of deep prayer, even in the long-distant days when his mother and all his bothers were still alive. It had always seemed a good way to pass the time and give himself a quirk. Andor, grey-feathered in the face before his time, had been the political brother, the destined king. Guntram after him had been the military brother among them, the general, the soldier, returned home by Lord Mordred in more pieces than Vigdis had the stomach to count. And so, Vigdis had made himself the religious brother, the praying brother.

Nobody ever answered his prayers. Not in any way he could remember. Nobody ever spoke back during his long vigils through the night, eyes closed and talons clasped, warmed only by the eternally-burning fires beside the statue. Most nights he did not mind the Terrible Silence, or told himself he did not mind. Someone was listening out there. Someone had to be listening.

But then there were the nights, and days, where Vigdis' faith threatened to fail him. Where the dread thought entered his head about how all this was pointless, wasted time, how there was nobody and nothing out there listening, and if there was, they thought Vigdis and all like him a deluded fool. The nights after his mother, Vigdis the Elder, died, were the worst. He remembered coming close, so close, to taking the statue and hurling it from the garden to the palace courtyards far, far below, let it shatter to countless unrecognizable pieces. He came so close . . . but then came . . .

He felt them, there in the present moment. Talons, wicked and sharp, caressing his right hip and side, sending shudders up his spine and down his wings. Beside him the soft, husky voice of Carina crooned, its owner pressing insistently—no, needfully—against him. "Your grace, ohhh, your grace . . ."

Vigdis opened his eyes. He saw first the statue of the Burning King, seeming to grin madly down at him from the dark. Then he looked down and saw Carina as he had expected, the raven-gryphon caressing his side and looking up at him, grinning, her blindfold gone, her eyes nothing but white fire burning in the depths of their sockets. The sight, as it always did, sent a new shiver of revulsion through Vigdis. But even so, his right wing spread, draped over Carina, dragged her in to press warm against him. He could not stop himself. God above, he could not stop himself.

"What do you pray for?" asked Carina, once the seer had settled herself in comfortably against Vigdis.

"Victory in battle tomorrow," he answered, forcing his gaze to return to the statue in front of them. "For us to win through the day and the days to follow, and for Galaxy's plan to work, and for the end of the war."

"All the old songs," Carina remarked. "And does the Burning King answer?"

"No," snapped Vigdis, not caring how harsh his voice turned. "He doesn't answer. He never answers. Every day and every night I speak into the Void. Every day and every night, NOTHING speaks back. It's enough to drive a rational gryphon to . . . to . . ."

"Think not of the rational, your grace," said Carina, voice turned softer yet, soothing as her talons resumed their grooming along Vigdis' side. "You think too literally, my friend. Your prayers have been answered in so many unspoken ways. In Princess Galaxy. In the Elk. In our learning of the Grand Harmonium before it was too late. In—"

"You?" Vigdis asked, the condor-gryphon feeling ashamed now of how he had snapped at her earlier. He had always snapped at her in their private moments, and she never made a fuss, which only served to sharpen the shame to a knife's edge.

"You flatter me," whispered Carina. She had begun to nibble at him, her beak slowly nipping and caressing its way up his neck toward his own beak. "What prayer could I possibly be the Burning King's answer to?"

Vigdis shuddered, keeping his gaze on the statue a greater and greater struggle. His talons dug into the soft dirt of the garden. He almost screamed in terror and countless other emotions as Carina's beak found his and began tracing along it with quick gryphon kisses. Terror, yes. He had come to pray before the statue terrified of tomorrow. Tomorrow, when he would fly once more to battle. Battle in the same land his mother died in. A hopeless battle, dependent wholly on others, Princess Galaxy and her companions, to see the day through to victory. And in his terror, Vigdis prayed to not be . . . to not be alone, that final night before the end. He had prayed for anything other than the lonely dark of that cursed night.

"Nobody has to be alone tonight," Carina promised, and at her words and the warmth of her breath against his beak, Vigdis yielded.

***

Brynjar rejoined his family in the quarters Galaxy had been sharing with Bevin and Bifrost in time to listen to the twins tell another fanciful tale of childhood in Featheren Valley. He laughed along at the appropriate moments, clapped alongside all the rest when the story was done, and did his best to ignore the way Galaxy watched him, an all-too-knowing look upon her face.

CHAPTER SEVEN

Bevin woke in the dark minutes before the sun, haunted both by fears of what she would find in the days ahead and by the words of Lord Thoth.

"You betrayed those who raised you for a new master, a chance at revenge. You found Princess Galaxy, and Mordred found Empress Nova. Blessed royals you'd do anything to keep the good graces of. Forget being Commander Bevin. Forget even being Sir Bevin! You are clearly LORD Bevin, made everything you are by the dearly departed wolf whether you like it or not!"

As the sun rose, bleeding the deep haze consuming the sky from horizon to horizon to a bright, bloody red, Bevin donned her barding. It was a gift to her from Queen Gwendolyn and the Elk, made by her own armorers and fit for a royal, thick leather dyed white and the finest steel enameled in red, with gold clasps and gold filigree as bright as Bevin's mane and tail. Emblazoned upon left and right flank was the sigil of old Schwarz Angebot in the brightest blue to match her eyes, declaring to all who saw her and knew their lore who she served.

The air blowing in from the balcony was dry and sour, itching the eyes like the grit of a sandstorm. Bevin sheathed her sword at her side and turned to find Galaxy awake and watching her. Further on behind her, Owain and Brynjar secured the last of their well-worn travel bags, the golden eagle-gryphon's own armor far plainer, though not lesser in quality.

"No last breakfast or final bit of joking around before you go?" asked Galaxy, voice low, full of a solemnity wholly new to her. "No farewells?"

Bevin hesitated in the midst of all her worries, and then went to her sister, kneeling down on one front hoof so they could better see eye to eye. "I think I can manage a farewell, this one time."

She had barely finished speaking before Galaxy was there with her remaining arm wrapped around her thick neck, the hippogryph's face pressed into a shoulder. The pain of it swept through Bevin's heart like a tide, and she whinnied and hurriedly draped her head over Galaxy's neck to return the hug. Both knew it might easily be the last they ever saw each other.

"Come back when you are done, safe and victorious as you always are. That's a command from your princess, lord knight."

Bevin shuddered as the command fell over her like a heavier set of armor and closed her eyes for a breath. "As you command, my queen. And queen you are, crowned or not."

The hug broke as Owain and Brynjar came over, the gryphon going to Bevin's side and the unicorn staying at Galaxy's. At a look, Galaxy hurried forward to give her brother a hug as well, before backing away as swiftly as she'd come. There seemed then too much left unsaid for any of it to be said, but somehow Galaxy managed "Keep our family safe, Bevin. All of it."

Bevin slowly nodded, then looked to Brynjar beside her. "Ready?"

"As ready as any gryphon ever could be. But, sudden thought, how are we getting there? Is this some kind of new, secret Imperial teleport spell or something? Something you found in that secret chamber?"

As amusing as the gryphon's guesses were, Bevin shook her head before closing her eyes to concentrate. "No. I just already have an anchor over there."

Whatever the reactions of the others were to this, Bevin neither saw them nor cared. She focused, called forth her personal magic, allowed her thoughts to sink into the warm, steady flow of certainty and strength. It carried a feeling of summer, her magic, heavy and gold, hot and relentless and, if she wasn't careful, joyous.

Bevin's thoughts reached, searching. Through Gateway, beyond Gateway and its surrounding seas, farther and farther east and north. She felt her magical anchor out there, waiting, magic reaching out for like magic. Farther than she had ever teleported before in her life. She only had to concentrate . . . and reach . . . and cast—

Bevin knew the teleport was a success when there came a BOOM of displaced air and sudden engulfing of ferocious cold. She staggered from this and the sudden exhaustion, slipping and almost falling as she found the ground beneath her hooves now uneven and slick with ice. A bracing wing from Brynjar kept her standing, though, the golden eagle-gryphon gasping at their new surroundings. "Bevin . . . wow."

Bevin opened her eyes at Bifrost's words and felt the last of her quiet worry slip away. The teleport spell had worked. The old, almost-familiar sight of Eishaven spread out before her. The two of them stood beneath a broad archway of stone atop a short hill, the ground beneath them and the individual stones of the archway inscribed with Wolf-Lord, unicorn, and even sphinx runes, the runes slowly losing a blue glow Bevin knew, if she had been looking, had burned blindingly at the moment of her teleport.

"A spell catcher," she remarked, focusing her attention for a moment away from the town and to their arrival point. By the lack of wear, she guessed it a new addition. "Keeps people from just popping into place anywhere in town, or . . . accidently teleporting into other people or buildings . . ."

Brynjar gave no response, his attention still turned away, focused on their wider destination. Bevin chuckled and shook her head, following his gaze. Eishaven was bigger than she remembered from the last time she'd been there, less a refugee town and more a city. More buildings now, and larger ones, and from what she could tell from their short hill in the far west of the town, the harbor had been especially expanded, the waters before the town full of many masts and many ships. The populace, too, seemed expanded. Before, Bevin remembered mostly gryphons, a dire scattering of minotaurs and Wolf-Lords. Watching, gryphons still dominated the town, but now there were sphinxes too, zakarians, kitsune and Jackals, and far, far more Wolf-Lords than she would have expected.

And there were unicorns, she noticed, trying not to, trying not to wonder if they were Imperial unicorns deserting a sinking ship or non-Imperials driven there by war and conquest. Either way, the sight of the town, unblemished and thriving, came as a grand relief to

Bevin, who had feared quietly to herself the whole while they were tarrying too long and would come too late at a time when too late was worse than not at all, come only to a smoking, blasted ruin. But no, the Foe had not been there yet. They had time.

"What is this place?" asked Brynjar. "I thought we were going to the Wolf-Lord nations?"

"We are," said Bevin, starting down the hill. The pair of them got looks from passerby as they walked, gryphon eyes spotting the sigil of Schwarz Angebot and growing wide in awe. None seemed to recognize the mare who wore the sigil. "This is a small northern corner of those lands, nearest to Heraldale. This is Eishaven, a refugee town and the point of this journey, as Galaxy has already guessed. Safe in the keeping of local help. The place has grown since last I traveled here. It was mostly gryphons then."

Beside her, Brynjar's head turned on a swivel, trying to look everywhere and at everything. A flock of gryphons in blue scarves like Bifrost's flew overhead, singing songs of promising hunting grounds. On one street corner, a grey-furred Wolf-Lord helped a pair of minotaur children fashion some kind of snow monster, too many carrots forming too many horns and pieces of coal working for too many eyes. In the doorway of a tavern, a two-tailed kitsune, her fur white as the falling snow, was helping a nightingale-gryphon carry a load of fresh produce in from a delivery cart, chatting with each other as if the oldest of friends.

Walking through it all, Bevin realized with a dim sort of self-loathing how, two or three months ago, she would have found the entire scene abhorrent. Now, she found it . . . charming. Happy. She imagined Galaxy would be over the moon to see such a diverse town working and living together so perfectly. Maybe, once the war was over, they could find an excuse to come back . . .

"Where are we going?" asked Brynjar, taking wing to better navigate the crowds. "Going to meet that local help you mentioned?"

"Yep."

"Who are they?"

Bevin kept her brisk pace through the snow-strewn streets even as her thoughts turned reminiscent. She remembered, with the regret of wishing to have known her better, a white-furred Wolf-Lord and a four-tailed kitsune. "Old lovers of Captain Blackbird's. One was a princess, Blackbird told me once, disgraced and cast out. The other was once a monk of the Nameless Order, who are supposed to stand guard against the return of the Burning King. Refugees who made a home here and opened it to whoever needed them. Blackbird loved them both dearly."

"Loved?" asked Brynjar. "Past tense?"

Bevin began to answer when a sudden roar from high above had the both of them and at least a few of the others on the street ducking their heads or raising wings as shields. Bevin looked up, her breath stolen as a pair of dragons, one green and the other gold, flew over the town toward the harbor, pursued by a laughing Wolf-Lord riding a wyvern. "Dragons are here . . ."

"Aye, they're here alright," grunted a white-furred minotaur minding a road-side scroll stall, ears flopping as he shook his head dismissively. "Hear there're even more over in Romulus, and even the kitsune islands. Some kind of great migration going on. Suppose it was only a matter of time, the way the war was going. Fishing and hunting are going to become nightmares if any more move here."

"Are there many?" asked Brynjar, circling around Bevin to meet the minotaur eye to eye.

"As big as dragons get, there don't really need to be many, do there?" The minotaur shook his head again and sighed, looking wistfully away to the south of town. "Still, the young ones at least have livened up the park, though every comment I hear about having to make sure our children don't get snatched up as snacks is more tasteless than the last. Some gryphons, I swear."

"Children? The park?" asked Bevin, a thought stirring, unwanted but undeniable. "Can you tell us where that is?"

It was not as long a walk as Bevin had feared, only a quarter-mile down south until they reached the Old Lumaine Inn, a left from there, past two houses, and there they were. Close enough, Bevin didn't start to rethink her actions until the two of them stood at the park gates, and by then, Brynjar's curiosity needed sating.

It was a good park, Bevin thought as she stopped a pace past the entrance. Wide, separated from the rest of the refugee town by a rough wall of loose stones reaching half up Bevin's neck, the gates wrought-iron and well-tended. Within, Bevin saw a frozen-over-pond, a pair of Jackals skating intimately across it. There were many trees, alone and in clusters, and even more children of all kinds running, flying, playing.

It was easy to pick out the lone unicorn filly among the hordes of gryphons and wolves and, yes, even a few dragon young. A lone unicorn filly, still blessed with the handsome pinto coat of her father, a rare coloring among unicorns, but her eyes . . . the same bright sky blue as Bevin's own, and the same as Galaxy's.

"Bevin . . ." Snow crunched as Brynjar landed beside Bevin, the golden eagle-gryphon watching the filly play a game of tag with a starling-gryphon child. The astonishment of recognition colored his voice. "The filly. Who is she?"

"Nessa." Bevin swallowed. It hurt to say the name. The very sight of the young filly was a stab of pain through Bevin's heart, the extremity of the grief at seeing again paths not taken surprising her. "My anchor here. My daughter."

". . . pull the other wing."

"It's not a joke," said Bevin. Her eyes remained trained on her filly. There was a brief whinny of alarm as one of the dragons joined the game of tag, but then she took off, and Bevin got to marvel at how much the filly had grown and what a little athlete she had become. "It's just a long story."

In the course of the game playing out in the park, the young unicorn turned in the direction of Bevin and Brynjar. Another moment and she stopped her galloping around and turned to them again, staring now. Her eyes grew wide and filled with emotions it hurt Bevin to see. She saw fear at the forefront, confusion, curiosity. The filly backed away a step as the seconds dragged by, but to Bevin's relief, she did not run.

"Hey, kid," said Bevin, after the silence had gone on for too long. She dared a step forward, heart lurching as the filly backed away to keep the distance between them. "Nessa, I didn't come to cause trouble. I came to see . . . your parents, and Kanti if she's here. Please take me to them."

Nessa stood and watched the pair for a moment longer, long enough for Brynjar to shift and flutter his wings uncomfortably beside Bevin. But at last, the younger unicorn turned and began a swift, stiff trot eastward, out of the park. Without a word, Bevin followed, ignoring Brynjar's efforts to catch her attention as he in turn followed after her.

***

The sun at their backs was swiftly disappearing behind the dark swell of a storm rapidly approaching from the west when the three of them came to the statue. It stood in the middle of a broad field of snow and ice, halfway between the great bulk of Eishaven-proper and a smaller scattering of buildings running the edge of a vast pine forest. The statue stood as tall as the Wolf-Lord it portrayed, a marble-like stone as white as the wintery surroundings gleaming in the soon-to-die sunlight. Holly wreathes lay with care around the feet of the statue, more of the distinctive red and green draped over the statue's broad shoulders and wound around its neck. The statue wore a smile, as well, a sad smile which reminded Brynjar frightfully of Galaxy in ways he couldn't say. Perhaps he could have, if he was not still trying to wrap his mind around the sudden revelation BEVIN, Commander Bevin, Sir Bevin, was somehow a mother. Had been the whole time and there'd never been a word about it.

And if she's a mother, Brynjar's thoughts continued, *Gal's an aunt! God!*

A creature Brynjar guessed to be a kitsune stood between the statue and the forest, staring up at its face. She—Brynjar guessed the creature was a female—stood a head shorter than the statue and far slimmer of build, the deep blue cloak she wore all but hanging off her. Her orange fur was messy and ill-tended, her four tails hanging limp behind her. Her ears perked at the crunch of their many footsteps in the snow, but otherwise she made no move, no recognition of their presence, not even the filly's.

At once, even though he had never met the kitsune before, had never even spoken a word to her, Brynjar felt he had found a sister of sorts there in Eishaven. He recognized the grief so deep it bordered on despair, sadness which threatened to swallow the world and everything good in it. His own was still so fresh, a part of himself still in Gateway, looking at the statue of Ida.

"Mom!" called Nessa, quickening her pace the last few yards to reach the kitsune's side. "Mom, visitors. She came back like she was not supposed to."

Brynjar watched the kitsune's brow crease at these words, her gaze slowly dragging down from the statue to take in their approach. The grief was dampened— though not wholly snuffed out—and anger appeared. Her voice when she spoke was low and raspy, with an accent Brynjar didn't recognize. "You beast. How dare you show your face here again. Not one step—"

"Is that her?" asked Bevin, her head turned to keep her gaze on the statue even as she circled it to where Nessa and the kitsune stood. The question was abrupt, but Bevin's voice, Brynjar heard, rang full with a soft respect he had never heard from the unicorn before, respect and an unaccountable awe. It, almost as much as the reveal of Nessa, hammered in to Brynjar how little he knew of the situation.

The kitsune blinked, seeming as caught off-guard as Brynjar was. Slowly, the set of her shoulders relaxed, the hand holding Nessa back behind her as Bevin approached falling again to her side. She nodded stiffly, looked again to the statue. "Yes, it is. Is this all you came here for? Finally found the free time in your busy tyranny schedule to pay your respects to the wolf who saved Nessa's life?"

"It is not the least of reasons I am here." Bevin at last looked from the statue to the kitsune, gold mane and tail whipped aside by the strengthening winds.

From where he stood a ways back, not wanting to intrude on the strange reunion, Brynjar couldn't see Bevin's expression, but he knew the unicorn well enough now to recognize the pain in her voice. "There's a lot we all need to catch up on, Shun. A whole lot. We might want to take this inside."

The kitsune, Shun, scoffed. "I doubt it's that much."

Bevin glanced aside to share a look with Brynjar. He raised an eyebrow and nodded for her to go. She nodded back, turned again to Shun, and took a deep breath. "I defected. A new hippogryph was discovered, named Galaxy, the lost daughter of the late Queen Grimhilt. This is one of her adoptive siblings, Brynjar. Say hello, Brynjar. We fought. There was a magic monster. Lord Mordred tried to kill me. I joined up with the hippogryph for revenge. We found out the Empire's building a doomsday weapon. We found out the hippogryph and I are half-sisters. The dragons ran away. There was almost a coup in Gateway. My sister killed Mordred. The Elk allied with Gateway. I got a new Lightning Elemental. Lord Beauty of the Empire, I think, is secretly Morgana le Fay, and she has sworn vengeance on my family for Lord Mordred's death. ALL of my family. I came to make sure Nessa is safe, whether I'm welcome or not."

"Alright," said Shun. "Let's take this inside."

***

The cabin was large, thought Brynjar, sprawled on a gryphon-style bed of pillows and blankets in the hearth-lit den, listening to Bevin recount their various journeys to the kitsune in greater detail. Too large for only Shun and the child, Nessa, to be calling it home. In the orange firelight, Brynjar saw strange weapons in cases mounted on a wall, between portraits of Shun and Nessa, Shun and a white-furred Wolf-Lord identical to the statue outside, a portrait of the three of them, plus another Wolf-Lord, black-furred and garbed in unfamiliar yellow robes, smile far kinder than any Brynjar had seen Mordred wear. There were shelves of books all gathering dust, and in one corner, shoved behind several plush, high-backed chairs, a small table covered in old alchemist tools, these too gathering dust. It spoke to Brynjar of a home once full to the brim, now falling apart.

Distantly, Brynjar heard Bevin's voice cease and returned his attention to the proceedings. Nessa had been banished upstairs to read quietly in her room. It was only the three of them down there in the den, Bevin pacing near the doorway to the front hall, Shun standing at the hearth, her back to them and her arms crossed over her belly.

"That's the last of it," Bevin added after a moment of silence. "You know everything I know. No, more, actually. That day, confronting the cult. I was busy with the fortress defenses. I only ever caught a glimpse of the leader from a distance. A white Wolf-Lord, emaciated, a big, antlered helm. Was that really Morgana le Fay? Or a pretender?"

Shun's shoulders hunched at the question. Her head hung for a moment and she rubbed her eyes. The room warmed as the fire in the hearth grew. Without saying a word, the kitsune cracked her four tails through the air like whips. Brynjar startled and sat up at the burst of magic he felt from this, eyes widening as, sweeping outward from the hearth, the room changed around them. It became a black, fiery mountaintop—no, a volcano. Twelve sacrificial altars lined the edge of the volcano's mouth, and upon each altar was bound a child of a different species, Nessa among them. Among the altars, motionless as a diorama, stood three figures. There were Shun and the black-furred Wolf-Lord from the paintings around the house, strange swords drawn as they charged the third figure. Morgana le Fay, Brynjar guessed. She was tall like Mordred, made taller by the antlered helm she wore, though rakishly thin and elderly compared to the brute the late Lord of War had been. Though like Mordred, this Wolf-Lord wielded a spear.

"Years ago," spoke the real Shun, turning at last to observe this scene, "the Cult of the Burning King, led by the legendary Wolf-Lord Morgana le Fay, twin sister of Queen Morgause—"

"Who?" asked Brynjar.

"The first Wolf-Lord," answered Shun, seeming unbothered by the interruption. "She was known to gryphons and unicorns in the Golden Age as General Nero. Anyway. Morgana stole children from across the world. Her plan was to sacrifice them to free Toqeph, the Burning King, from his eternal torment enshrouded by the Eternal Flames, so that he could lead the Wolf-Lords in a return to Heraldale. But Morgana was stopped by her own daughter and heir, my wife, Holly."

As Shun spoke, the scene around the three of them shifted. Morgana knelt defeated at the lip of the volcano. Beside her stood the white-furred Wolf-Lord Brynjar had seen in drawings around the house, a long and wild mane of red hair caught frozen in the cindery winds, a black sword in her right hand as she stared down at her fallen mother.

"Before the final blow could be struck," said Shun, "Morgana fled. The children were returned to their homes, all but Nessa, who stayed with me and Holly as our daughter. With her blood mother's hard-fought blessing, of course."

"She would have been Harmonized if I brought her back to Avalon," said Bevin, voice soft, tone flat and restrained. "It was . . . the best thing for her, staying here."

Once more, Brynjar startled. His gaze turned to the unicorn, true wonder striking him as he realized. Before, he had thought the thing Bevin felt a "ghost of pride" at was helping to stop a mad cult. Now, he thought it was at being able to let go of her own flesh and blood for the other's own good, despite such an act surely going against every spark of what she knew as a soldier and citizen of the Avalon Empire. There were worse things, Brynjar decided after another moment, to be proud of.

"So, it was the real Morgana le Fay that day," said Bevin, unknowing of Brynjar's thoughts. She stared hard at the scene revealed to them, eyes raking over the image of Morgana for more than he could guess at. Then they turned to the other Wolf-Lord. "What happened to Holly le Fay? Captain Blackbird only ever told me, drunk and sad, that she is gone now."

"Gone. Yes. That's the word for it. Gone." Shun stared at the Wolf-Lord with the crimson hair for a long moment, cyan eyes growing visibly wet with tears and all the strength looking to leave her. Even after the illusion disappeared with another whip-crack of her tails, returning them to the warm and empty den, the kitsune stared where Holly had stood, seeing through it to somewhere else. "Two years ago, Spell Rot swept through Eishaven like a wildfire. Many fell ill. Many died. Both Nessa and I were among the former, and were very, very much in danger of joining the latter. To save us, Holly went on a quest for the Waters of Life. Certain parties . . . took offense at this. She succeeded, but didn't survive in doing so. Things . . . kind of fell apart for all of us after that."

"I'm sorry," said Bevin.

Shun laughed weakly at this, rubbed her eyes again, at last turned a withering glare at the unicorn. "What did you come here for, commander? Why are you bothering us, what do you want? From what you say, it sounds like your savior of a sister has things well in hand, I don't know why you felt the need to come marching back here, opening old wounds and filling our heads with enough bad news to fuel plentiful nightmares."

"I'm here for Nessa," answered Bevin. "Lord Beauty, or Morgana, whatever you want to call her, she threatened my family. Princess Galaxy can take care of herself. Sir Brynjar here as well, to a lesser extent."

"Gosh," said Brynjar, "thanks for the vote of confidence."

Bevin continued. "They can protect themselves, but there are those who can't. Most of Eishaven, for example. Come back with us to Gateway, where you can be behind every possible safety measure until the threat is dealt with and the war is war. Or . . . and this is my preference . . . come with me to deal with Morgana permanently. You've fought her before. Together, we could—"

"No."

Bevin stumbled over her words and stopped. Brynjar frowned. Shun looked back and forth between the both of them, shook her head, turned to stare down at the fires in the hearth with fallen shoulders. "Just . . . ignoring the insanity of you thinking that taking Nessa into the middle of an active war is the SAFE option, everyone in Eishaven is here to keep out of the war your people started. Begging us to get involved now is only going to get people killed. I don't have the heart for that. You're wasting your time."

"But Morgana—"

"Has left us alone so far," said Shun, keeping her back to the others. Her ears lay flat against her head and her tails hung limp behind her. "Has done so for years. A vestige of regard for her daughter's wife and child, perhaps. I don't know. But I do know I have Nessa's safety to think of, and you're asking me to forget about all that for some impossible quest to kill Morgana le Fay. Why should I put that all at risk?"

"Then who can help us?" asked Brynjar, stepping forward.

Shun's ears perked and she turned to regard him with a raised eyebrow. It was the first serious consideration she had given him the whole time, her attention before then only for Bevin. "What was that?"

"For your wife," Brynjar repeated, standing firm at the heat in the kitsune's voice. He knew Galaxy would have been better at this impossible negotiation task, but she wasn't there and Bevin was hopeless. It had to be him. "So her sacrifice to save this little town isn't in vain. Whatever holds Morgana at bay, it won't stop Empress Nova. If the Avalon Empire wins in Heraldale, sooner or later they will turn their gaze here and to the rest of the Wolf-Lords. It will be all your worst fears and more. The skies stained with smoke and poison. Villages burned down to skeletons and ash. Your Nessa will be lucky to die."

Shun tensed and looked over her shoulder to the doorway from the den to the cabin's central hall. From there rose the stairs to the second floor where the filly in question waited, perhaps listening. The kitsune's tails waved fretting behind her, a hitched breath in her chest, fists clenched and trembling. After a lingering second, she spoke. "The lands to the east of here used to be called Romulus. The royal family there, all evil brutes, were killed or . . . otherwise indisposed after it was found they used slave labor, the greatest crime among Wolf-Lords. That and other indiscretions committed by its last queen, Celeste. The other Wolf-Lord and kitsune nations were content to let the land and its weary people wallow in its fallen misery, aside from a few key, affluent cities on the coast. Then, the dragons came and began settling the mountains, making folks . . . nervous."

Brynjar held his breath and watched, trying not to show his trembling fear, trying to ignore the way Bevin looked at him as he watched the kitsune. This was it. He felt it.

After a moment, Shun gathered herself and continued. "There is a gathering there, representatives from the Wolf-Lord and kitsune nations, and from the dragons, to hash out how they all might live in peace. It is a . . . fraught, topic." You might . . . MIGHT . . . find your succor there."

Brynjar nodded and looked to Bevin. "That sounds like our best bet."

"It probably is," said Shun. She looked to the window as the light faded in the den, raised the fire in the hearth with a wave of her hand. "The hour is late in this part of the world. You can both stay the night. Tomorrow . . . tomorrow you shall have transport to the summit. It's the most help I can provide. I have to think of my daughter."

"Thank you," said Brynjar, Bevin echoing him the next second. He looked past Shun then, to the window in the western wall behind her. He saw the day was all but gone and realized how far north and east they must have traveled for night to come so early.

An early night, he thought to himself. *And a long wait yet until morning.*

CHAPTER EIGHT

The red sky over Gateway lingered into night. Few flew the corrupted skies for fear of choking ash and poisonous volcanic gasses. The bleak and bleeding sky tempered the joys of recent victories, leaving the city and its surrounding lands sullen and waiting, watching for the balance to tip more certainly toward glory or doom.

Galaxy tried to keep her mind off such matters the best she could. As Vigdis and Gwen further refined the battle plans for the coming days, Galaxy busied herself by further exploring and sorting through Morgana's secret chamber. It was the work of hours and days, full of the strangest tomes and magical instruments she had ever seen or heard of.

Galaxy's magic sight let them find the exact location of Morgana le Fay's secret chamber easily enough. As Galaxy had guessed from the journey, the chamber wasn't within Vigdis's palace, a secret teleport of some kind hidden in the darkness of the corridor. The chamber lay in secret beneath the statue room of the old le Fay temple, accessed from a hidden set of stairs built beneath the statue of Morgana le Fay. Upon discovery, Vigdis had wanted to post a guard there immediately in fear of it being used to infiltrate the palace in a moment of crisis, but Galaxy managed to dissuade him.

"Nobody knows about it. Posting guards there, even without a big announcement or anything, will draw people's attention. Posting a watch in the palace library makes more sense, I would think."

"Gal, look at this!"

Galaxy blinked as the sudden voice snapped her from her wandering thoughts and back to the present. She looked up from the ancient array of black crystals she had been examining for magic traces as Bifrost flew over to her, a large book of black leather held with the greatest care in the raven-gryphon's talons. "What have you got there?"

Bifrost carefully set the book down on Galaxy's table. The front cover of the book looked blank at first, but at a tap of Bifrost's talon, words appeared across it in a flowing silver script.

THE ANNALS OF THE KNIGHTS LE FAY: A HISTORY.

Galaxy stared, awe-struck. Bifrost giggled beside her. "This should make some lovely bedtime reading, I should think. So much lost history, right here at our talontips! And before you ask, I checked before coming over. It reaches all the way to right before the war against the Avalon Empire started, so it's going to have at least a little something about your father!"

"Sir Lancelot . . ." Galaxy swallowed, the unknown figure exactly where her mind had first gone upon seeing the book. Talons trembling, she opened the book to the first page, watched with professional interest as the silver words appeared on the well-preserved paper before her very eyes. "How would they do that, I wonder? It's not pure ink. Some kind of ink and metal mixture. Ink doesn't hold magic, nor does paper."

"Has to be silver in there," said Bifrost, sitting at Galaxy's side. "That holds magic fine for long periods of time, though, not very much at once, and it must be further diluted by the ink. But what activates the spell to make the words appear? Touching the book?"

"No," said Galaxy, slowly flipping through the pages and watching the words appear as she came to each one. "Unicorns would hold a book and move its pages with their magic, not by touching it. Unless . . . perhaps by the slightest touch of our breath? The sensitivity enchantments must be off the charts. How does it not trigger for every page at once?"

Bifrost sidled closer, a wing draping absently across Galaxy's back. "There must be breaker enchantments in the binding you trip with each turn of the page. Go back a bit, I'm curious how long the words linger once you've moved on."

"Great ancestors before us," cried Siegfried from far off in the chamber, the swan-gryphon sorting through his own stack of books at Galaxy's behest, "Get a room, you two!"

From nearer the Morgana le Fay mural, Sascha broke out into laughter, nearly dropping the brass scales she had been cleaning of cobwebs. Galaxy's cheeks flushed with embarrassment. She glanced over to find herself nearly beak to beak with Bifrost, a matching blush barely to be glimpsed through the raven-gryphon's dark feathers. At once she looked away, swiftly closing the book as the incorrigible twins kept up their laughter. "Er, thank you for this. It's . . . fascinating."

Before either could say more, Carina slid in between the pair, setting a pair of tightly bound scrolls beside the history book. "The idiots are correct. This is hardly the time or place for . . . flirtations. We stand in a room of solemn history. We must treat it with the utmost respect and digni—"

"Hey Sascha!" shouted Siegfried, taking to the air with a dirty yellow globe. "Catch!"

"Sheol yeah!" answered his twin, joining him in the air with talons open. "Pass it to me! Hit the Wall Wolf's nose for 20 points!"

Carina squawked in alarm, wings smacking Galaxy and Bifrost in their faces as she spread them and took to the air. "No! That's an antique!"

"Cool," crowed Siegfried, throwing the globe past Carina to be caught by Sascha. "Check out my antique technique!"

Galaxy watched, amused as her siblings relentlessly teased and tormented Bifrost's sibling, passing the globe back and forth in midair to the blindfolded seer's mounting frustration. A glance at Bifrost showed her to be as entertained as Galaxy was, watching the ongoing show with wide smile and bright eyes.

Rainbow eyes, Galaxy thought to herself. Beautiful eyes.

"We should probably put a stop to that before somebody loses her temper," said Galaxy, after a minute had gone on and the game showed no signs of stopping."

"Nah," said Bifrost. "My sister's enjoying that, even if she'd never admit it out loud. I haven't seen her play like that since before . . ."

Bifrost trailed off, but Galaxy could guess well enough what went unsaid. She looked again at Carina chasing after the Twins and their stolen globe, the seer struggling more and more to keep the laughter from her voice. "What happened to give her those fire eyes? To give her such a sense of . . . of . . . destiny?"

Bifrost's smile weakened. She looked down from the scene, talons moving absently to take one of Carina's scrolls and start undoing its bindings. "That's a long story that can be quickly summarized as I was a coward and Carina paid for it. She has never told me of her resentment and I have never asked about it. Another bit of cowardice, I suppose."

"You've gone to battle beside me," said Galaxy, touching Bifrost's talons with her own to still them. "You faced Mordred beside me. You are no coward."

"Different kinds of bravery," remarked Bifrost, shrugging. A ways off, Carina had finally gotten hold of the globe. Turning it in her talons, she oversaw as Sascha and Siegfried began to carefully dust an extensive alchemy set.

Unbound, the scroll rolled open. Eye drawn by the movement, Galaxy glanced down, gasped in delight and gave the scroll her full attention. Before them lay a complete map of the night sky as seen from Gateway, dark and deep blue background, the moons, stars, and planets crystalline motes of glimmering light, each marked with their name beside them in the languages of the unicorns, the gryphons, the dragons, and the Wolf-Lords. It was the most extensive star map Galaxy had ever seen, but what had spurred her to gasp was the sensation of magic and how the motes of light on the scroll ever so subtly moved.

"Enchantments," she said, picking the star map up in her magic and turning in a slow circle, watching with glee as the perceived angle of the stars subtly shifted in response. It was so slight she didn't think she would even be able to notice without her gryphon eyes. "It doesn't merely show the night sky here, it tracks the night sky! Do you think this is in real time? Or is this only how the night was when this was made?"

"Only one way to find out," said Bifrost, grin returning as she looked to the dark corridor back to the palace.

But there was no finding out. Leaving their siblings to continue their work, Galaxy raced through the corridor, flying out of the library and through the halls to her quarters. She barely kept the door from slamming as she flew in, mindful of tired and lonely Owain sleeping in the far corner. She flew on past him, to the balcony, thoughts already calling to mind what she could remember of where the stars should be—

But there were no stars. Galaxy landed, the old star map dropping forgotten from her talons, nearly rolling off the balcony and down to be lost in the city below as she stared about, heart sinking. No stars, only cloudy darkness painted in overbearing red, as if the whole world burn inside a kiln. The same bleak sky loomed across the whole of Gateway, from the peaks of the palaces to the harbor slums, and all who looked up to the fiery darkness driven by foul winds from the south felt a despair, as if winter would never end and the warm of green growing things was only a distant dream.

Watching from her balcony, Owain's soft snores behind her and the sour wind curdling through her feathers, Galaxy felt this same great despair. She missed Bevin, having grown so used to the unicorn's presence in the past few months. She missed Brynjar, having only gotten him back the day before after so long apart. She missed her mother, Ida, now dead and burned, never to be seen again but in Galaxy's nightmares. She missed them all and hated how they threw themselves into dangers unknown while she sat waiting for her turn. It burned at her. It wasn't fair.

"I'm not sure there is any such thing as fairness," Owain had said, after Galaxy confided her mood to him. *"But there is hope. We have seen worse days than these,*

and we survived. We can all stay strong a little while longer."

Galaxy had appreciated the wise words at the time, but hours later, it was difficult to appreciate wisdom in the lonely dark, the future unseen but full of threats, the past a litany of sorrows, and the present one sleepless hour after another. Oh, how the Foe must have slept so well in the deep heart of night, with fear and confusion ever their ally, twin iron hooves ever advancing the bloody cause of empire.

There came the temptation to join Vigdis in his garden for prayers, the thought banished as swiftly as it came. Vigdis, as good and worthy a king and a friend as he was in all other respects, prayed to the Burning King, and it was the Burning King who left Galaxy unable to sleep in the first place. She did not think she could take another night of the Sheol vision, chasing the fiery unicorn across the broken plains and poisoned waters toward a Gateway fallen to ruin. Or worse, the flying dream, peace and joy burning to ash and cinders before Galaxy's helpless eyes. Or the most dangerous of all to her heart, the dream of the white Wolf-Lord, full of icy sorrow and grim resolve . . .

The sound of wings in the night startled Galaxy from the downward spiral of her thoughts. She looked up, a welcome warmth coming to her heart at the sight of

Bifrost coasting in for a landing. The raven-gryphon met her lightly, sharing a smile with Galaxy before joining in on the city-watching.

The night passed in companionable silence. At some point, Bifrost's right wing reached out and draped over Galaxy, so large compared to her. Galaxy accepted it, leaned against the raven-gryphon and sighed. It was a comfortable moment . . . and yet, the air felt thick with expectation. A peculiar nervousness stole over Galaxy as the minutes passed on. She felt as if something which had been building for a long while, something bright and unspoken, something made perilous by the perilous world around them, was come to a head, to be grasped or left to fall, to be spoken or . . .

An insight Galaxy had never considered before struck her, a saving touch to her nerves. It felt as true as the beat of her own heart.

"Love is the bravery to ask."

Bifrost shifted, looked down at Galaxy and the soft words whispered. Galaxy looked up to meet her gaze, saw herself reflected in those startling rainbow eyes, knew at once the question's answer.

I love you.

I love you too.

"But why?" asked Galaxy, voice a weak croak. "Or how? How can you love me, when your passing glance always holds such pity?"

"Not pity," said Bifrost, "though pity on its own is not a true evil. Sorrow, my princess. Sorrow at the sorrow I see always in your passing glance, in your unspoken word, in your cold body as you lay dreaming your dark dreams. When we met, beside that mirror pool, your heart was in the bright throes of autumn, but ever since, winter has fallen over you. And I would have so beautiful and wise a soul as you know spring again."

Galaxy looked into the other's eyes and this was the truth, every word of it. And again, those all-consuming words passed between them, unspoken but understood.

I love you.

I love you too.

Wings spread and flapped, and both lovers rose together in a narrow gyre. Wingtips touched and talons caressed, and gazes found each other again and again. And high above as they rose, the wind for a moment shifted, a keen, unlooked-for gale from the east sending the bitter southern winds into disarray. There came, for a moment, a break in the cloud cover, and down through the tatters fell the quiet beauty of the stars. And those who looked up and saw this brief gift felt the doom lift from their hearts, if only for that night.

Galaxy and Bifrost rose up through this break, up through the fiery haze to where the stars hung free in their cold, crystal clarity. The air chilled and breath came in misty bursts. There they hovered with beating wings and locked eyes, and the magic of gryphon song came over them.

> *"You are enough.*
> *You are enough.*
> *Courageous and kind*
> *And one of a kind.*
> *My dear, you are enough."*

The tears scattered from Galaxy's eyes, lost in flight as she answered the raven-gryphon's verse.

> *"You are enough.*
> *You are enough.*
> *Whatever the world brings*
> *With you I can sing.*
> *My dear, you are enough."*

Together, their voices rose in a song which carried far on the winds.

> *"You are enough.*
> *You are enough.*
> *To see beyond the war*
> *And whatever more*
> *We must face*
> *Whatever we must fight*
> *To the end of the world*
> *To the end of all strife*
> *My dear, you are enough."*

They stayed high over the world a long while. There, where the clouds spread below them like fields of snow. Where every breath came cool and precious. Where moons shone bright as the sun and the stars seemed close enough to reach out and touch. They held each other, Galaxy resting her head against Bifrost's chest, content in the raven-gryphon's hold, their bodies together warm and warming.

"You're crying," said Bifrost.

Galaxy knew and could not stop. The tears streamed cold from her eyes, freezing upon her cheeks, scattering into oblivion with the beat of their wings. She cried because she knew this moment was perfect, the lone perfect moment in all her life, and struggle as she did, she could not imagine another moment like it in her future.

Her future. Dark, smoke-choked down in the muck of war, consumed in fire and beating hooves, misery piled upon misery. There was no promise their plan to attack and destroy the Grand Harmonium would work. There was no promise Vigdis' and Gwen's military campaign would win through. There was no promise Bevin would find the truth of Lord Beauty out east and return home with Brynjar. There was no promise of a future at all with the Dragonbacks awake and Avalon on the march.

"Gal?" asked Bifrost, barely pulling away, enough to look Galaxy in the eyes.

Galaxy swallowed and met Bifrost's gaze, lost as ever in her rainbow eyes. "Promise me. Promise you will stay at my side. Whatever happens. Whatever we face, in Hiraeth Arian and beyond . . ."

Bifrost stared, her scarf tossed by the wind. The talons of her right arm came up to caress Galaxy's cheek, brushing away the tears as they froze. "Galaxy. You are my queen, now and always."

Their beaks touched in a gryphon kiss, longer than they had ever shared before. Their wings stilled, pulled tight around them, and together they fell. Down from the moons and stars, down through the clouds to the dark and burning world below, turning, falling, breathless as they held each other. When the time came, they would pull away, wings spreading, catch themselves and fly again safely, but as they fell, they were one in body and soul.

CHAPTER NINE

Brynjar woke early, before the sun had even begun to rise. For several minutes he remained on the floor of the small guest shed he and Bevin shared and listened to the howling northern winds subtly rocking the wooden walls. The wind brought him an ancient memory, childhood even before going to live in Featheren Valley with his mother and siblings. He remembered nights where the gales howled through the northern ranges of Schwarz Angebot, nearly tearing young Brynjar from his cliffside perch, where he watched the Northern Lights as if they were the only sight in the cold, dark world to behold.

Featheren Valley lay too far south for the Lights to reach them. Memory had faded. But now, there . . .

Brynjar rose and left the shed, careful to keep his steps light for Bevin still sleeping on the far side of the single room. The cold outside struck hard but welcome. A harsh wind nearly slammed the door out from Brynjar's grip. On the edge of the woods along the east of Eishaven, the bare branches overhead ran like cracks through the early, early morning sky.

Many stars, but no Northern Lights.

Brynjar sighed, spread his wings, flew to and then through the refugee town. The sun was still only an impression of light along the southeastern horizon, but already much of the town was awake and busy, focused mostly along the docks. Late-night fishermen were coming in and early-morning fishermen were loading their boats to head out. The lights of the taverns and inns were all on, the smoke of cooking breakfasts rising from their chimneys. From one especially large building, a smithy, rang already the roar of fires, the musical clang of hammers.

Brynjar landed on the snow-packed road in front of the smithy, listening and yearning. He felt again the grief of his unexpected return to Featheren Valley, lesser since the reunion with his remaining family but still potent. He thought of his days at the forge, the work he had left behind. Hardly much at all, he saw now, not enough to accomplish anything with, but even so . . .

"New arrival, eh?"

Brynjar blinked, found in his drifting thoughts he had begun to cry, the tears scattering frozen in the cold wind. He turned and found an elderly magpie-gryphon had joined him before the smithy, her beak turned up in a knowing but kind smile. "It can be overwhelming," she continued, looking to the building, "to see something familiar done in peace, free of the fear of soldiers coming in to take what they like. Where are you from, young man?"

"Schwarz Angebot, at first," Brynjar answered, shaking his wings. "Then Featheren Valley, then just . . . hopping around, I guess."

"Featheren Valley," the magpie-gryphon murmured, looking away and frowning. "I'm sorry, young man I don't believe we have anyone else here from there. I could ask around to be sure, but I'm usually among those who greet newcomers . . ."

"It's alright," said Brynjar. Past the other gryphon he could see the sun begin to truly rise. "I know where my family is. I'm only passing through here to help a friend. She needed to find something out."

"I see. Well, I hope your friend finds what she's looking for."

"Yeah," said Brynjar. "Me too."

***

The Sun crouched low to the east as Bevin walked the beach, the unicorn idling the hours away as they waited for Shun to ready for the trip. Soon after dawn broke, the frigid winds brought bleak grey clouds across the vast sky, though to the palpable relief of many in

Eishaven—Bevin and Brynjar included—little fell but a few unsteady, scattered snowflakes.

Still. The north seas rolled beneath the winds, frothy green and dark. The black stones of the beach, rolled smooth by the relentless workings of the sea, clacked like Go stones beneath Bevin's wandering hooves. The smell of cold and salt dominated all else, forcing Bevin to keep up a low-yield respiration spell over her face to keep her eyes from stinging.

Some yards ahead, a lighthouse of the old unicorn style stood tall and forlorn at the end of a long, upthrust spur of black stone, a startling tower of untouched white among the various shades of black and grey. Bevin made for it, an idle curiosity roused by the thought of a unicorn aside from her daughter living there at the cold edge of the world.

Before much longer, Bevin saw the other unicorn in question, a mare, on a slow march toward the lighthouse from the other direction. It was an older unicorn, veritably elderly, her coat grey and thinning, her wispy mane and tail at the mercy of the winds. Old, yet carrying the heavy packs upon her back with an admirable steadiness of step.

Even so, Bevin lit up her horn with her golden magic and lifted the largest of the packs from her fellow unicorn's back. The other mare glanced up at Bevin at the sudden lightening of her load, said nothing as they reached the main door into the lighthouse together. The yellow glow of the stranger's magic as she worked the door locks was weaker than Bevin's, more alike to daisies than the brilliant Sun they grew under.

Then, they were inside with the warmth. Bevin closed the door behind them and glanced around. It was a warm home, large with the liberal use of space enlargement spells, but not empty. Cluttered, in fact. A ramp led up to the upper floors where the actual lighthouse work went on. There on the ground floor stood wooden mannequins adorned in old armor and barding, a large nest of blankets, bookshelves stuffed to bursting, a blazing hearth, a cramped—for a unicorn—kitchen area, and along the walls, both weapons and paintings of unicorn knights and castles mounted blindly, without thought of rhyme or aesthetic.

"By the hearth will be fine," said the other unicorn, dropping her own packs near the door. They were the first words to pass between the pair. "I shall make us steaming tea."

"I don't mean to intrude," said Bevin, moving to obey the command as she did. Her interest had been piqued. The tone of an old and veteran soldier rang clear in the other's voice, impossible to fully lose no matter the years or distance. "I'm only passing through."

"Nevertheless, steaming tea to hearten the soldier far from home."

Bevin allowed herself a fleeting smile as she set the packs near the hearth as requested. Fleeting, for the stranger's words recalled to her mind Lord Beauty's words from the day before.

"A soldier. A brute. You've been so all your life. Driven by Mordred's command. Driven by vengeance. Driven by a desperation to live. Only now, Mordred's dead, you're alive and free, and you have absolutely no idea what to do with yourself."

"I won't be a soldier forever," said Bevin, as much to herself as to her host. Her idle eyes roamed from her finished task, taking in the old treasures of war gathering dust on the walls and on their mounts. "Not forever."

"Oh, is that so?" The hiss of a tea kettle accompanied the amused, musing words. "Running from the war, are you? I ran from a war once, long ago. Only, it didn't feel like a war, not by the end of it. It felt like the end of the world. Everything I knew, gone. So much lost, even for the winners. Do you take brandy with your tea, Sir Bevin?"

"It's not something I'd say no to," said Bevin, voice trailing away as she stepped closer to a short sword mounted in a place of special importance over the hearth. Her eyes narrowed. The blade was strange, looking made more of dense purple crystal than of steel. A flick of her golden magic to wipe away the gathered dust, and Bevin saw a white rose engraved into the center of the crossguard. She swallowed and turned to the other mare, saw her setting a pair of wide wood bowls onto a low table. "You were a Knight Le Fay."

"Yes, I was," said the other unicorn, pouring generous portions of brandy into each bowl of tea without pause. "The priestess branch. Sir Nimue. One of the last Le Fay knights, alongside that rotten Mordred stirring up trouble."

"Mordred is dead," said Bevin. "Killed by Princess Galaxy of Schwarz Angebot several days ago."

Nimue added another dollop of brandy to her bowl, then gestured for Bevin to join her as she knelt down at the table. She looked stricken. "Mordred dead. Then I am the last knight. The very last."

Bevin knelt and drank brashly from her bowl, thinking desperately how she wanted to talk about anything else than Mordred. The tea burned down her throat, gave her voice a rasp as next she spoke. "I am . . . Sir Bevin. My father was Sir Lancelot of the Knights Le Fay. Did you know him?"

"As a friend of a friend. We unicorns are of course long-lived, and the Knights were never really that large of an institution. Everyone eventually knew everyone by one degree or another. What do you want to know?"

Bevin took a moment to think the question over, tilting her bowl with a hoof as she did. It was not a question she had ever given any thought to answering, because she never thought it would be asked. "All that you can tell me, I guess. I lost him when I was young. I didn't have time to really get to know him at all."

"All that I can tell you." The elder unicorn sipped at her own tea, seeming unbothered as she nodded. "Aye. I can do that. Sir Lancelot. Skilled and fearsome and powerful. He was a right brash and arrogant fool of a knight. Jumping horn-first into the most appalling danger left, right and center, all but throwing himself into flights of arrows, into bursts of dragon-fire, into the dens of robbers and killers to flush them out. Sometimes you'd swear he had a death wish, the trouble he got himself into."

Bevin stared. She had expected much, but not this. "Ah. So that's where Galaxy gets it." If nothing else, Brynjar would appreciate knowing who in the family tree to blame for his prematurely-greying feathers.

Nimue didn't look like she heard Bevin. The elder unicorn's brown gaze turned distant and sentimental as she continued. "He was the best to have at your side in any fight. And in the holiday contests he always won—

except against Mordred, on the rare occasion—but he never made you feel lesser for losing. His every passion burned, as quick to love as to anger, though never bitter. He found that in others, I think. In your late mother, Lady Elaine, and in the late Queen Grimhilt. No accounting for taste, I suppose, even when you are as old as I am."

Bevin nodded. This, too, reminded her all too well of Galaxy.

"He enjoyed a fight, but he didn't enjoy war. He didn't enjoy THE war. If it hadn't been for the war, I think he would have left the knights for Grimhilt. Left the knights, his duties, all of it for her, and you, and the sibling he wanted to give you. He was quite known to be as proud of you as any unicorn could be."

"I can't imagine doing that," admitted Bevin. It was the first time she had ever admitted this to anyone. Yet Morgana and Lord Thoth had known her all the same. "Empress Nova. Revenge. Princess Galaxy, I am a soldier. I have my . . ." But Bevin didn't know how to finish the declaration. She had meant to say duties when she'd started, but her heart told her chains.

"You feel bound in your life," observed the elder unicorn, watching Bevin closely. "I've seen it before. Long ago, I knew a knight much like you. Raised by those they should've hated, possessed of a fierce, vigorous heart. But the years and the clash of what they felt they owed and what they could give weighed them down and chipped away at them. They became, after a while, a hateful, wretched thing, so consumed by ideas of what they MUST be, they no longer saw what they COULD be."

Bevin's throat had gone dry as the other unicorn talked. There was no more tea to wet it. Around them, the lighthouse groaned beneath the force of winter gales, a lonely and haunting sound. "I think . . . I am already such a thing," she admitted, unable to look up at her host. "I remember my years with Lancelot, and I try so hard to, to slot them back in as really my own, but . . ."

"But Mordred saw you through your most formative years," continued Nimue, voice worn but not unkind. "Made you the mare you are today."

"Forget being Commander Bevin. Forget even being Sir Bevin! You are clearly LORD Bevin, made everything you are by the dearly departed wolf whether you like it or not!"

"Maybe I don't want to be!" hissed Bevin, snapping her gaze back up to her host, putting all the hate Mordred had taught her into her glare. "Maybe it's an awful thing, to be the daughter of Mordred! Maybe I'd rather they had . . . had . . .

A piece of flaming ceiling dislodged and came crashing down toward the unaware Bevin. Right before it could crush her, however, tendrils shot forth from the open front entrance, grabbing the piece of ceiling and throwing it to the side. Grimhilt froze where she flew, no, actually hovered away a pace as a towering black unicorn strode into the flaming cabin, eyes dark with some unfamiliar emotion as he took in Lancelot's corpse.

"Nevertheless," said Nimue, "these are all things you cannot change. And until you resolve this conflict within yourself, you will never be able to use Mordred's Lightning Elemental to its full potential."

***

Bevin found Shun standing once more at the statue of Holly le Fay, dressed warmly in heavy garb for travel. The four-tailed kitsune looked over at the crunch of hooves through the snow and frowned. "There you are. Your gryphon friend's been back ages. We thought we might have to go looking for you."

Bevin had nothing to say to this and no time to think of anything. The whir and crackle of an Imperial troop carrier descended upon the snowy field. Bevin tensed for a fight, but the troop carrier which appeared over the eastern forest and flew in their direction was not adorned in the colors of Avalon, but in heroic shades of red and white.

The troop carrier swung around the pair on the ground and landed with its rear facing their way. The boarding ramp lowered and a black-furred Wolf-Lord dressed in heavy brown jacket and pants marched out, her curly black hair and long red scarf at once catching in the cold northern winds.

Lady Kanti le Blackbird, known better throughout Heraldale as the gryphon smuggler Captain Blackbird.

Kanti gave the barest glance of acknowledgment toward Bevin as she crossed the remaining yards of snow, before her gaze drew like a magnet to the statue of Holly le Fay. There, a rush of love, sorrow, and misery filled her every expression. Without a word, Bevin backed away, allowing the newcomer the space to stand beside Shun in front of the statue. For several minutes the pair stood in a silence rife with what went unsaid, the love and the hurts, the grief and regrets, until at last—

"I missed you."

Shun's ears twitched at the choked-out words. Her tails stilled behind her. Her back grew stiff, a flood of shifting wants and moods storming across her muzzled face. She stared almost desperately toward the statue so near at hand, hands clenching as the storm was wrestled down with a supreme act of will. "I know."

The black Wolf-Lord looked to the kitsune and waited a moment, visibly desperate for more to be said. When nothing came, she plunged on regardless. "I haven't forgotten what you asked of me. I promise. Return with a way to save her, return with a way to avenge her, or don't return at all. I haven't forgotten, and . . . and I almost have a way. For vengeance. And then . . ."

"I remember what I asked of you, Kanti," said Shun, still not looking over. The kitsune's shoulders were hunched and she had drawn subtly away from the wolf. Bevin, watching carefully and quietly from the sidelines, thought it the most hurtful thing she had ever seen. "I remember what I demanded of you that day, with the wound still so fresh."

Another, deeper silence fell over the scene. Kanti reached a hand out, but it wavered before it could reach Shun's shoulder, fell meekly back to her side. Instead, the Wolf-Lord looked over to Bevin and put on a brave smile. "Sir Bevin, my favorite unicorn. It seems you accepted my invitation to leave Heraldale after all."

"So it seems," agreed Bevin.

Kanti's smiling mask remained firmly in place. "Well, if there's luggage to load, load it now. I thought there was a gryphon as well?"

"Present!" called out Brynjar, flying over from Shun's cabin. He landed, allowing—to Bevin's quiet horror—the Nessa to slide giggling off his back. The giggling stopped as the filly caught sight of Bevin staring at her. Several silent seconds passed where all Bevin could turn her attention to was the nervous child in front of her, a silence broken only by the swish of Shun's tails across the snow, by the twitch of Brynjar's feathery wings, by the crunch of Nessa's uncertain hooves. Bevin, a yearning in her chest, knowing exactly what Galaxy would want her to do . . .

. . . turned and stalked toward the troop carrier, head high and voice rigid as she called back "Brynjar, Kanti, come on. Time is of the essence."

"Good grief," Bevin vaguely heard Brynjar mutter, following after.

"Safe travels!" Shun shouted, the words stuffed to bursting with forced cheer of the same breed as Bevin had heard on more than one occasion from Galaxy. And the child said nothing at all.

CHAPTER TEN

It was only a few short hours to their destination, Blackbird—*No, her real name's Kanti*, Brynjar reminded himself—promised them. Four hours at the reconfigured troop carrier's most comfortable cruising speed.

"Enough time for us all to start getting tired of each other in such close quarters," the black-furred Wolf-Lord, flashing a toothy smile too full of forced cheer from the pilot's station. "And yes, there are snacks in the left-hand storage lockers. That long one at the bottom's enchanted for frigid cold, if you prefer a chilly lager."

Several seconds passed. When Brynjar realized Bevin wasn't going to ask the pertinent questions—or speak up much at all, judging by her glower—he asked instead "Where is our destination?"

"The old castle of Cairn Romulus, which crowns the Grand Black Mountains," answered Kanti, gaze returning forward. "Of the fallen nation of Romulus. Once upon a time, it was the royal stronghold of Celeste, the last queen of Romulus. They were a cruel and wicked queen, and eventually they and most of their children killed each other, and the last two fled to parts unknown to survive, and the castle was left to whoever would bother to tend to it."

"And now?"

"Now," continued the Wolf-Lord, "it will be serving as neutral ground as representatives from the other Wolf-Lord—and kitsune—nations meet with representatives from the dragons to hammer out just how they're going to coexist." She glanced Brynjar's way again. "You'll want to be on your toes, I wager. The most dire victims of unicorns and gryphons getting together to commiserate our sufferings, and a unicorn and gryphon want to walk right in and ask for help. I hope you understand you'll be lucky if all they do is laugh their heads off before throwing you out."

"Even so," said Bevin, "we must try. Even if only to warn them."

Brynjar glanced back at the unicorn where she sat subdued near the rear of the airship, an eyebrow raised at the relative softness of her voice, her words. Then he returned his gaze out the craft's forward window to watch the lands shift beneath them as they flew. At the start, the view was all snow and barren rock, a sea of white and grey pockmarked by herds of black-furred snow-bison raising their shaggy heads to watch the craft rush over them. Once, Brynjar spied a bronze-scaled dragon flying higher and straight east to their southeast path, swiftly disappearing into the distance.

Before much time passed, the barren cold transitioned to more of the northern pine forests such as Brynjar had seen bordering Eishaven. The hills rolled in dark shades of green and grey for as far as even the gryphon eye could see, broken by thick rivers and steep gullies. At perhaps an hour into their flight, they passed low over a large lake, large enough to have a large island of its own at its center. A town ringed the lake, buildings of wood and stone, with ships and tall bridges connecting to the central island like wheel spokes.

"It is Villa Rocheuse," said Kanti, unprompted. "Began as a pearl farm, became an iron mine. I imagine, if they are smart, many dragons will find a place of employment there." She did not specify if she meant the dragons would be smart or the mines.

Eventually, Brynjar had his fill of sightseeing and joined Bevin in the rear of the craft. Minutes passed in silence for the pair. Brynjar preened his wings. Bevin nibbled distractedly at a dried hay cake, her gaze boring through the metal wall opposite her. In such a manner, half an hour passed in peace and quiet, mellow as a yellow spring butterfly.

"So," said Brynjar, switching from his left wing to his right. "You're a mom."

"in ainm Dhia!" growled Bevin, a nearby storage locker blowing open from the unicorn's burst of magic. "You had to say it, you just had to say it!"

"Which means Gal's an aunt," Brynjar continued, feeling calm as a rock before a raging storm.

"Brynjar, you insipid gryphon, if you say one more word—"

"Which means I'm an uncle," Brynjar finished. He raised a wing, blocking the thrown hay cake from hitting an eye. The wing protected less effectively from Bevin's scream, echoing through the enclosed troop carrier as fiercely as a clap of thunder. It set Brynjar's head ringing. "Ow. Perhaps I pushed that too far."

"YOU THINK!?" Kanti shouted from the front of the craft. "If I didn't have the guidance spells enabled, I could've crashed us there!"

"No," said Bevin weakly, only the dregs of her earlier anger remaining. She stared at the fallen hay cake, unreadable to Brynjar but for her weariness. "No. That anger was uncalled for. I might have struck with lightning rather than food. This whole . . . journey, has me unbalanced."

Brynjar was touched by the concern for him. He stood and walked closer to where Bevin sat, felt amused at how her whole body stiffened up at him sitting close enough to hug her with a wing if he wanted to. He didn't want to, not really, the entire thought sounding weird in his head, but he liked the idea of holding it over the unicorn's head like a threat.

"So," he said again, more carefully this time. "You're a mom."

"You're a dummy," Bevin answered back, but there was no true venom in her voice.

"You must have been young when you had her," he continued.

"I was of age," she bit out. She refused to look his way. "I wanted . . . I wanted it over with so that I could focus on my military career, for Lord Mordred's sake. Just another duty for me. I never even saw her again after the birth until I was recruited among many others to go after the rogue caretaker. Her father."

Brynjar tried his very hardest not to laugh at the phrase "rogue caretaker", coughing to cover up whatever sounds might have slipped out. "There's a story there, but I won't press you for it. I am curious, though. Until Port Oil, you were a true believer in the Empire. How did you stop the cult and rescue the kids but not bring your own daughter back home?"

It took Bevin long enough to answer, Brynjar had begun to think she wouldn't answer at all. Her voice sank low and full of remembrance. "She didn't want to come back home."

Brynjar waited. Eventually, Bevin continued. "Technically, it had been Shun and Candi . . . and Holly le Fay who'd rescued Nessa from the cult, a little while before I teamed up with them and Lady Kanti here to destroy the cult. Afterward, I was . . . overly aggressive in demanding the filly back."

"By that," added Kanti from the front, "she held a couple boulders the size of a house over our heads and threatened to drop them."

Brynjar remembered the early encounters with the unicorn on their journey and nodded. "That does sound like you, Bevin."

"I almost killed them," said Bevin, as if Brynjar had not spoken at all. "But then, Nessa, this dumb little filly who was barely old enough to talk in complete sentences, got between us. She was scared. Scared of ME. But she still tried to stand and protect the people who'd saved her."

Bevin's voice hitched on the last word. Brynjar looked over and saw how wet the unicorn's eyes had grown. But there was pride in her voice, too, pride beneath the pain. "Yeah," he said, "that sounds like you, Bevin."

"Does it?" Bevin looked at him then, the most vulnerable he had ever seen her. "Does it really? I never stopped to ask where she had gotten the nerve. I just turned and walked away. And that was the last time I saw my daughter until yesterday."

Bevin's gaze returned to boring a hole through the airship's side, but only for a moment. Then she frowned, shook her head, and growled "Why are we even talking about this in the first place? We're flying into unknown waters, a continent away from our best backup, on the precipice of utter catastrophe, and you want to talk family!"

Brynjar didn't want to, but he had to admit Bevin spoke true. He looked to Kanti at the pilot's station. "She's right. What are the politics, where we're going? What are the Wolf-Lord nations and who might listen to us?"

"Easy questions to ask, not to answer." The Wolf-Lord tapped a trio of oval crystals in a panel in front of her, then stood from her chair and joined Brynjar and Bevin at the rear of the airship with a swish of her red scarf. Brynjar's alarm must have been more obvious than he'd wanted, for she grinned and jerked a thumb over her shoulder. "I put in the route and activated the automatic pilot system. That is, a complex array of interlocking spells which operate . . . no, never mind, such technical details are wasted on gryphons like you. Don't worry. I can tell they go over Bevin's ponderous horn as well."

"Information," growled Bevin, stomping her hoof on the grated metal floor for good measure. "We need it. Now."

"Right, right." Kanti sat cross-legged before them, fingers interlocking in her lap in a clear gesture of thinking. "The basics, at least. With the fall of Romulus, there are five Wolf-Lord—and kitsune—nations we can look forward to having to convince about Morgana le Fay. These are Fenris, Akela, Tabaqui, Okami, and Inari, named for the founding families who overthrew and imprisoned Queen Morgause—sorry, that's General Nero to you unicorns and gryphons—once it became clear she was more obsessed with exacting revenge on Heraldale than establishing a new home for our people."

"Imprisoned?" asked Brynjar.

"For trying to harness the power of the Burning King," answered Kanti. "Guarded by the Nameless Order, kitsune monks who will no doubt be representing Okami and Inari in the coming discussions. Shun used to be one of them, but don't think that means you can trust them. They're all bastards of the highest order, and I'd love to see them all killed in the most gruesome—
"

Kanti caught herself, cleared her throat, continued. "Akela. Home of grand temples and renowned universities of learning. They of all the nations fell the most harshly upon Romulus for the use of slave labor. No kings or queens, but ruled instead by several affluent houses. Despite this, their main delegate will be Guru Veda, a great alchemist . . . and a good friend. She played a pivotal role in saving Eishaven from its Spell Rot epidemic several years ago. We will find our best support with her, I am sure.

"Fenris is the easternmost Wolf-Lord nation. Technologically advanced. Usually the most reclusive, but recently—relatively speaking—had a marriage alliance with Romulus. They will most likely be represented by Duke Managarm, the Star-Clad."

Bevin laughed. Brynjar almost laughed, kept it in at the last moment, said instead "That's . . . quite the title."

Kanti shrugged. "It partly began as a joke at their expense. The day they were named a lord of Romulus, they set out to build a fortress on the southern coast all their own. The night it was finished, a meteor fell demolished the whole thing, bankrupting Managarm utterly. In their devastation, they took the metal of the meteorite and forged a helm and cuirass with it, then spent two decades as a mercenary, earning greater riches than all they had lost. There is rumor that they are quite mad, and that the helm of meteor metal gives them visions when they were it outside of battle."

Strange choice of delegate, thought Brynjar, though he did not say it aloud.

"And as for the last, Tabaqui . . ." Kanti shrugged. "I cannot tell you much. It is a land of many rich families and many powerful mercenary groups. The delegate does not seem to be anyone of note, almost disposable. I don't think they're taking the situation with the dragons all that seriously."

"Which means they're not likely to take us seriously," said Bevin.

"Not . . . well, not necessarily," said Kanti, a strange note of fiercely subdued anger in the Wolf-Lord's tone. "Morgana le Fay is a very . . . touchy, subject for us Wolf-Lords. The greatest, most reviled traitor in our history. When Shun's wife, Holly, revealed to the world that Romulus was using slave labor, she was widely hailed as a hero of the highest order. But when the rumors spread she was an illegitimate daughter of Morgana le Fay herself . . ."

Here, the anger breached the surface, hands clenched and fangs bared. Deciding the topic had gone on long enough, Brynjar looked aside to the front of the troop carrier. "You think we're getting close, now? Anything we need to start preparing?"

Kanti blinked and followed Brynjar's gaze over her shoulder, before standing and striding back to the pilot's station. "You're right. Not much longer now. Just keep an open mind and be honest and I think . . . I think this will go well."

Brynjar and Bevin shared a look, then joined the Wolf-Lord at the front. Brynjar's gaze swept through the viewport. They had left the forest behind for the most part and now rushed over gold-grassed meadows crisscrossed with rivers. Ahead, far ahead, he saw high black mountains. "Gal would have loved this trip."

"Aye," said Bevin.

Ahead, the black mountains rose higher, and Brynjar could begin to see the grand castle built onto and at least partly into the whole of the central peak's north and eastern mountainsides. Black stone, a vast keep and high towers gleaming but bannerless, wide outer walls encompassing courtyards and gardens. Near the keep and between several of the towers spread a smaller, glass-ceilinged hall. In the air above and around the castle, Brynjar saw Wolf-Lords in widely varied armors riding wyverns which seemed a far cry from the feral, savage beasts he and Galaxy and Owain had encountered on the way to Port Oil, these wyverns strong and groomed and regal. He saw as well strange airships unfamiliar to him, circular rather than the boxy or triangular craft the Avalon Empire favored. Wolf-Lord airships, he guessed.

Dragons, too. A dozen of them of various shapes, sizes, and scale colors, flying the air or crouched along the defensive walls of the castle. Most of these were watching the approach of Kanti's troop carrier and looked ready for a fight, Brynjar realized with a start. More began to gather as Kanti drew the airship down for a landing in one of the emptier courtyards, Wolf-Lords in armor joining them.

"The Imperial Palace is bigger," remarked Bevin.

"So's the Gateway palace," said Brynjar. "But I suppose size isn't everything."

"Easy to say when you're a golden eagle-gryphon."

"You nervous?"

"Trying not to be," answered Bevin. "You?"

"I wasn't," said Brynjar, "but then we started landing and now I'm having the most terrible flashbacks to when Galaxy, Owain, and I went to the Elderpine Forest and met the Elk. Everything straightforward at first. They're friendly. There's a problem they need solving. We solve it. They're not friendly. Sudden dagger in the back."

Kanti glanced their way. "God, cheer up a little."

They landed with the hiss of steam and groan of settling metal. Systems powered down and Kanti led the way down the lowered ramp, a hand raised and a jovial shout to the nearest of the Wolf-Lord soldiers approaching them. Brynjar brought up the rear, head craning around to take in their surroundings more closely. The Imperial Palace of Avalon was bigger, but it was stark and inelegant, in aesthetics more a tomb than a home for royalty. Cairn Romulus, despite the name, was the opposite. White, verdant courtyards. Fountains of elegant stone- and metalwork. Walks lined with fragrant rows of apple trees. Flags flying from every tower, shining with silken gold. Everywhere Brynjar looked, he saw wealth and beauty in abundance.

And yet . . . the air was cold and carried the stench of the dead. The soldiers, marching in the distance or standing close at attention, stank with fear beneath all their arms and armor, flinching for every errant sound. And it was only soldiers he saw. Even Empress Nova had need of her servants and court officials.

It was a show, Brynjar thought to himself. A performance put on for the dragons perhaps, to make the Wolf-Lords seem in a stronger position.

Then Brynjar took a deep breath and forced himself to set aside the thinking which before had made him consider returning the young dragon, Ashe, to the Dragonbacks as only a potential political maneuver. He looked around at the living Wolf-Lords in their armor and uniforms, looked at the resplendent architecture all around, the money and care which had gone into the castle over who-knew how many generations. He remembered the ruins he and his family had fled through, beneath the mountains to Port Oil, the grandeur of old tarnished and lost by war.

A hall larger than any seen in the unicorn fortress opened before them, the walls lined by towering statues, twenty feet tall each. They stood on two legs, arms stretched upward to hold the ceiling up, their heads and legs like those of wolves . . .

The three stood on a stone pathway a dozen yards wide. It wound through a vast emptiness, as if the mountain itself had been hollowed out, ceiling above and floor below lost in shadow. All around them towers of stone rose into and fell out of sight, hundreds of doorways or windows dotting the mammoth structures. They resembled giant stalagmites and stalactites, yet were surely the work of the Wolf-Lords, the last monuments of their greatness. Their stone sparkled weakly, embedded with or naturally possessing light-emitting crystals that twinkled like stars in the mountain darkness, just enough to see them by.

"They don't owe us, or the dragons, anything," said Brynjar. The words escaped him as Kanti finished speaking with the guards. "Anything at all."

Bevin nodded. Her gaze was to the mountain's peak high overhead, to a glint of bright pink flying over the white of the snow. She said nothing.

CHAPTER ELEVEN

They would be seen only one at a time. As a guard led Brynjar to whatever quarters allowed them for their stay, Bevin and Kanti were led through the broken ruins of the castle to a wide, sunlit hall of marble and glass. Much of both were broken. Ivy and moss grew in, gathered around shallow pools fed by thin trickles of water falling from a ceiling mostly caved-in. Flowers grew among the moss and fallen stones, splashes of pink and yellow and blue. Bevin breathed deep as she entered the room, refreshed despite her misgivings. The air was cool, fragrant, and calm.

Two-thirds of the way down the beautiful ruin stood four high-backed thrones made of a cloudy black crystal. In the thrones sat a diverse range of beings. On the far left sat a grim Wolf-Lord of grey fur, cloak, and raiment, masculine in form, and on their head rested an unadorned black helmet, hinged to cover the upper half of their muzzle. Duke Managarm, surely.

Beside them sat a red-furred kitsune dressed in dark blue robes of an unfamiliar style, eight black-tipped tails curled around to drape over his lap. Beside him in turn lounged a startlingly white-furred Wolf-Lord of feminine form, head tilted to the side in curiosity as they stared at Bevin with bright red-pink eyes. Aside from their thick fur and the long white hair falling in rivers down over their shoulders and front, they wore no coverings. The monk of the Nameless Order and the Lady Gauri. And on the far right of the assembled—

Bevin startled and stepped back, mane tossed in agitation before she could stop herself. Lady Gauri laughed and clapped, their voice like over-sweet syrup as they turned to the black-furred Wolf-Lord in maroon dress to their left. "Guru Veda, you startled the poor thing! Shame on you! Oh, doesn't anybody have a carrot to help calm the beast down?"

Chuckles echoed from the surrounding shadows. Managarm sighed, already sounding tired. "Gauri, shut up."

Bevin only half-heeded their words, the bulk of her attention remaining on the final wolf in their number. Guru Veda sat calm in her throne, hands folded in her lap, a gentle smile on her muzzle, her eyes hidden beneath a black length of bandage wrapping which reminded Bevin at once of the blind seer Carina.

From nearby, Kanti cleared her throat. Bevin took a deep breath. "I . . . beg your pardon for my reaction. I simply did not know there would be a fire priestess among you. I have cause against the Cult of the Burning King."

"As do I," said Veda, leaning forward in her throne and gesturing to herself. Her smile was bright and eager. "Former fire priestess, I promise. Though, I must admit to my own surprise. I did not know that wretched little cult had any presence in Avalon."

"Not in Avalon," said Bevin, beginning to feel marginally less on-edge as she found at least one of the four willing to talk with her rather than at her. "But in Gateway, a very large presence. Including the gryphon king, Vigdis. There is a blind seer, Carina—"

"We're not here to discuss the politics of gryphons," growled Managarm, managing to sound frustrated and bored all at once. "We weren't here to discuss unicorns or gryphons at all, until Lady Kanti here came begging for an audience, and that, only for a dear favor I owed her. Speak your piece so we may return to the matter of the dragons invading our lands."

Gauri loosed a theatrical groan. "They're not 'invading our lands', you old mongrel. They're refugees, come flying with their tails between their legs. I say again, let's show them mercy."

"And I say again," said the duke, "there is very little practical difference between a horde of invaders and a horde of—"

"I believe that somehow, Morgana le Fay returned," said Bevin.

The guards stalking the dark corners of the hall ceased their pacing and muttering. Gauri stopped tapping their claws against the sides of their throne. Managarm spluttered and half-rose from their throne. Veda gave no reaction.

The Nameless Monk stiffened in his throne, a frown twisting his muzzle. "That is a serious claim to make, unicorn. Explain yourself, thoroughly. Leave no detail unspoken."

Bevin, accustomed to such commands as a soldier, obeyed thoroughly and without question. She told her of first visit to the Wolf-Lord nations and brief conflict with the Cult of the Burning King, fighting alongside Kanti, Shun, and Holly le Fay to rescue kidnapped children planned for some eldritch ritual. She told of the visions of the Burning King which frequented Gateway, and which Galaxy had admitted to experiencing as well. She told of the prisoner exchange with Lord Beauty, of the Wolf-Lord soldiers who had been there and of the brief, terrifying vision of Lord Beauty revealed as Morgana le Fay herself. She told of the strange enchantment over the palace library to rid memory of Morgana, placed long after Wolf-Lords were driven from the city.

Once finished, she waited, quiet and anxious.

"What is your proof?" asked Gauri, voice quiet and restrained.

"I am experienced with the memory sharing spell," answered Bevin. "I can take each of you through the memories of these occurrences and let you see for yourself, if you are comfortable with a unicorn casting spells around you."

Even as she spoke, Bevin saw none but Veda were comfortable with the notion. The other three looked to the black-furred guru, who turned her own blindfolded gaze upward to the broken roof and clean sky in apparent thought. "Well?" asked Gauri after a long moment of nothing. "You know the most about magic and junk. Is it safe? Can this sort of spell be, I mean, can memories . . ."

"You're asking," spoke Veda, "if we can trust whatever memories the spell shows us. I would answer that it depends very much on the unicorn in question. Certainly, memories can be altered with the right spell, even destroyed entirely. And then of course, we all know how unreliable memory can be even without getting magic involved. Show 10 wolves the same scene and you'll come away with 20 unique retellings, each given with utter certainty of authenticity, is my personal experience."

Bevin's confidence began to wilt. This was already turning out no better than going to Lady Quetzal about the Grand Harmonium had.

"No unicorn is putting their horn near my head," huffed Managarm, beating a fist down against an armrest for emphasis. "Forget memory nonsense, one quick jab and she'll have your eye on her horn. Can't trust unicorns for a moment, have only to look to the dragons to know that."

"My fair duke, please!" spoke Kanti, stepping forward to stand beside Bevin. "Your own heir was one of the children taken by the Cult of the Burning King! You've met Holly! You can confirm certain facts here yourself!"

At this, the Nameless Monk shot a sharp glare in the duke's direction. Managarm spluttered for a moment, then rallied. "I met the so-called Holly 'le Fay' once, at the return of my heir, and I know you, Lady Kanti, but what do I know about this Sir Bevin? She admits to until very recently serving the Avalon Empire. She admits to being the blood daughter of Sir Lancelot of the Knights Le Fay, which on its own is nearly enough to get her thrown from the walls of this castle, let alone thrown from these chambers!"

Bevin frowned. "I'm sorry. I fail to see what my parentage has to do with anything."

"A great deal," said the Nameless Monk. "Sir Lancelot, of the Knights Le Fay, the order which spearheaded the genocide of the Wolf-Lords and kitsune of Heraldale. Founded, obviously, in distant times by Morgana le Fay. And we have been informed by trusted sources that he fell in love with Queen Grimhilt of Schwarz Angebot. Strong enough love to have a hippogryph child with her. Tell us, soldier. What did Queen Grimhilt allow to happen to the northern dragons of Heraldale?"

Bevin's stomach fell, and with it, much of her hope. She shared a look with Kanti, but the smuggler seemed as much at a loss for how to avoid answering as Bevin felt. She looked back to the four on their thrones, each watching and waiting for the answer everyone already knew. Bevin swallowed. "Queen Grimhilt allowed for the wholesale genocide of northern dragons at the horns of the Avalon Empire. At the horns of my people. But this doesn't matter to—"

A deep, bone-rumbling growl sounded through the old hall, followed by the snarl "IT DOESN'T MATTER?"

An old and total terror seized Bevin as the heavy gale of broad, beating wings assaulted the hall from high above. Through the broken roof, a blue-scaled dragon descended into view, horned and winged, long-necked and thick-tailed, feathered wings tucking against his back like a cape as he landed. The floor cracked and the pools scattered through the hall rippled from his weight.

"THOSE DEATHS . . . MEAN EVERYTHING . . ."

"I present," said Veda, with a gesture to the newcomer, "Mammon, one of the two dragon representatives for these negotiations."

The dragon curled behind the four, draped himself over a moss- and grass-strewn mound of rubble. Thick black claws reached out and carved down the length of the nearest wall. His burning green eyes remained on Bevin, who took a moment to find her words after the impressive introduction. "One of . . . where is the other?"

CHAPTER TWELVE

Ashe was gone by the time Bevin and Kanti returned with their guard escort. Brynjar asked for a moment to talk with them before going to meet the representatives and the guard allowed it. He asked to do so in private and the guard turned around to face a wall, but otherwise remained. Brynjar grimaced, but hadn't really expected to be allowed privacy anyway.

"What's wrong?" asked Bevin.

"Ashe visited," said Brynjar, watching one of the guard's ears twitch. He focused on the relevant bits of the conversation. "She says one of the representatives is really Lord Beauty, or at least associates with her closely."

The guard turned, a quick turn, a quick glance at them before turning back to the wall. Kanti growled, baring her teeth and clenching her fists. Bevin's expression remained tightly controlled. "She couldn't tell you which one?"

Brynjar shook his head. "Never been around them one at a time to tell apart."

Bevin nodded. "Then we'll need to be on our guard. It could be any of them."

"Not Guru Veda," said Kanti. The Wolf-Lord stood with all the agitation of pacing the room, her tail lashing against her legs. "She is a friend. She was a friend of Holly's and wept at the news of her death. Morgana once shoved Holly into an active volcano."

Brynjar blinked. "Her own daughter?"

Kanti nodded.

"And your Holly survived?"

"It's a long story, but—"

"Time's up," growled the guard. "You coming, or are you canceling?"

"Coming," said Brynjar. He gave a last look to Bevin, a strange, new concern filling him. It took him a moment to recognize it as the same sort of concern he always felt for Gaaxy, Sasha, or Siegfried. Familial. They were, after all, brother and sister, of a sort. "I know I don't need to ask, but you will be careful?"

"I should be asking you that," said Bevin. Then she surprised him by stepping closer and curling her neck against his in a unicorn hug. It lasted only for a moment, but long enough for Brynjar to feel the armor around the soldier's heart abandoned, if only for the length of the embrace. "But I will be. Thank you."

It was enough to help Brynjar follow after Kanti and their guard escort with head high.

***

Standing before the four representatives—five if counting the blue dragon—Brynjar was reminded more than he liked of being brought prisoner before Empress Nova and her court. There was more curiosity than contempt from the Wolf-Lords and kitsune present, but the acidic hostility remained in the air, setting Brynjar on edge even before the first word could be spoken.

"You surely know how strange this is for all of us," said the blindfolded Wolf-Lord, Veda. "By all accounts, gryphons and unicorns get along as well as . . . fire and water. Yet here you come together, bringing the strangest, most foreboding stories. If you would introduce yourself to us . . ."

"I am Sir Brynjar of Featheren Valley," he began, gaze moving from one throne to the next, taking each of them in. "Son of the late Sir Ida and Sir Kurt, of the late Queen Grimhilt of Schwarz Angebot. Adoptive brother of Princess Galaxy, the hippogryph."

"That would make you siblings of a sort with Sir Bevin," said the helmed Wolf-Lord, Managarm.

"I suppose," said Brynjar.

"God, you're handsome," said the albino Wolf-Lord, Gauri.

Brynjar blinked. "I . . . am taken."

Gauri grinned, teeth gleaming as they leaned forward in their throne. "Wolf-Lords of Tabaqui and Akela don't tend to practice monogamy."

Brynjar stared. Managarm sighed. "Gauri, shut up."

The Nameless Monk grit his teeth and leaned forward in his throne to put the quarrel behind him. "Sir Bevin came asking for our help. She came with claims of our most infamous villain, Morgana le Fay, working in a place of power within the Avalon Empire under the name of Lord Beauty, likely for purposes of revenge. Do you have anything to add? Other than your family tree?"

Gauri laughed. Brynjar ignored them and thought back to the weeks spent in Avalon. Weeks he'd rather forget if he could, but he knew he never would. Weeks still lingering with him in the scars and burns, the broken talons which had never set quite right again.

"It is a natural response among living creatures to avoid pain when they can. But this can be a delicious trap in itself. A familiar pain can lose its edge. The victim, knowing only the pain for too long, will retreat into their own mind, as immune to it as the stars. Being so prepared for pain, they don't how to handle . . . pleasure."

"I was recently a captive of Avalon," began Brynjar. The words came halting to him, each word bringing with it memories, each memory refreshing the phantom pain. "Myself and my partner, Sir Owain. Lord Beauty was one of those who oversaw our torture. Won't harm you with reports of what they did to us. During escape, overheard a soldier planning to defect. Heard rumors of Lord Beauty as a fire priestess, as practicing ritual sacrifice."

Guru Veda clicked her tongue. "Horrible. Did you believe such rumors? Did they seem . . . believable, based on your interactions with Lord Beauty until then?"

"Very well, then, stupid gryphon. Pain will break the bond of your hearts."

Brynjar didn't need to think about it for even a moment. "Absolutely. Lord Beauty . . . she spoke to Empress Nova as an equal, and Nova spoke to her the same. Nobody else with such privilege, not even other Lords of the Empire. Beauty is a monster. Can't think of anything more monstrous than ritual sacrifice."

"I can," growled Mammon, the dragon dragging claws up his ruined throne. "A great many things, gryphon. Slavery. Hunting for sport."

Brynjar hung his head. He could not argue against the dragon.

"That's assuming if it happened at all," said Managarm. "You are a biased source, gryphon. And soldiers wanting to justify defecting will believe or make up any outrageous rumor they can to make their treason seem the reasonable action. You come asking for us to interfere with your war, but no reasonable leader of wolves could ever justify doing so on no more than rumor and hearsay."

"Now hold on a moment, there!" To Brynjar's surprise, Kanti stepped forward, a hand gesturing wildly around them at the old throne room. "If I might have the floor a moment—"

"Granted," said Veda, grinning toothily at the other representatives as they shot her annoyed looks.

"More of history than any of us would like is nothing more than hearsay and guesswork," continued Kanti after a moment's nod to Veda. "Sheol, this very moment we all stand—or sit—in an example of this. Two years ago, while on a quest to find a cure for Spell Rot, Holly le Fay was captured by her family and a Nameless Monk and brought here to face punishment for her supposed crimes against Romulus. Somehow, she escaped, Queen Celeste and the heir to the throne died, and half a dozen more Nameless Monks were all killed in some kind of vicious battle. The whole nation of Romulus fell to ruin until the dragons came, and nobody knows how! We're all making guesses to this day what happened in this room, but nobody knows except the last two members of the Romulan royal family, Maurus and Caelestis, and nobody knows where in the world those two are!"

The Nameless Monk shifted in his seat, frown deepening on their muzzle. Brynjar watched as Kanti carefully made no show of having noticed this, wondered what had happened he lacked the context to understand, remained quiet as Kanti gestured toward him. "You all asked me here as a character witness of sorts for the whole of Heraldale, a more objective viewpoint as you deliberated how deeply you should welcome the dragons to your lands. If their flight from the unicorns and the gryphons was as warranted as our peoples' flight so many centuries ago. I'm afraid in this one instance I cannot be entirely objective. In my guise as the smuggler Blackbird, I have fought and triumphed alongside this gryphon and Bevin. I believe what they have to say. I believe we Wolf-Lords need to do something about it."

At these words, Managarm stiffened in their throne, muzzle drawing back in a snarl as they banged a fist down. "Do not presume to tell us what we need to do! They killed us on the field and in the streets! They butchered our children and drove us from our homes! If you ask me, it is already an act of incomparable mercy that we haven't gone to Heraldale ourselves to wipe both sides OFF THE MAP!"

"Like your Morgana?" asked Brynjar.

This cut Managarm off even as they drew breath for the start of another tirade. They paused and slowly unclenched their fist as they suddenly found themselves the focus of several new, speculative looks from the other representatives. Behind them, even Mammon seemed to eye them in a new, unpleasant light.

"I think," said Guru Veda, smiling softly, "we all have much to debate. Lady Kanti, Sir Brynjar, if we could have privacy for now . . ."

CHAPTER THIRTEEN

The white-furred Wolf-Lord stood on the black-rock shore, the sky a sullen grey. Her crow-feather cloak pulled tight around her as she watched the tumultuous northern sea, the wind billowing her long red hair out behind her. Waves tossed and churned white by storm winds crashed against the black shore, filled the air with frost and the tang of salt. The Wolf-Lord beheld it all, barely felt the cold, lost in her thoughts and—

Galaxy jerked awake, found herself staring out from the thrown-open balcony doors to a pre-dawn sky, Bifrost curled all around her and still blessedly asleep. Galaxy gripped as tightly as she dared at the wing draped over her and stared ahead, willing the dream— and the overpowering sensation of grief it had brought— NOT to be an ill omen.

***

The sun rose for Gateway, glimpsed too briefly at the horizon before disappearing as the sky turned its full bleeding red. An apocalyptic red. With the day came the dread and anticipation. It reigned in the gryphon soldiers assembling upon the ziggurat palace in full arms and armor, helms enchanted against the thick, ashen air. It reigned in the air-yachts crewed by Elk soldiers rising even with the top of the palace, antler-like horns alight and magic batteries charged and protective enchantments reinforced and expanded. It reigned in the kings and queens of this proud force, gathered together near the towering black obelisk at palace roof's center.

"The day has come," said Vigdis, head high as he surveyed all arrayed before him. Galaxy, kitted in her black armor despite not being a part of the attacking force, followed the condor-gryphon's gaze, the horrid knowledge passing through her head how this would be her last living look at many of them. Gwendolyn stood near in full queenly armor, Captain Hywel at her side. High Generals Odin and Shan. Bifrost, her blue scarf joined now by blue and gold armor bearing the sigils of the Floating Mountain. Carina, unarmored and unarmed, the seer draped in the air of grim foretellings. Owain, fitted in red armor much the same as the barding gifted to Bevin. Galaxy wished then for Bevin and Brynjar to be there with her, there at the end of all things.

"War comes for us," Vigdis continued, drawing Galaxy's wandering thoughts back to him. "But we are ready for it. Today, Queen Gwendolyn and I fly north with the brunt of my forces and staves of teleportation. When we reach the outer reaches of Gryphonbough, we shall bring forth the full might of Elk-kind and engage the Imperial forces holding the southern fortresses by evening. The defining battle of our age, one to draw every eye in Avalon our way. No matter the cost."

"No matter the cost," Gwen echoed. Looking to the Elk queen, to her friend, Galaxy had never hated a phrase more deeply.

"We shall strive for personal victories with all our hearts," Gwen continued, taking over for Vigdis. "God willing, we will win. But win or lose, the Grand Harmonium must fall. Galaxy."

At her name, Galaxy closed her eyes and took a deep breath, holding it for several seconds before slowly releasing it. She opened her eyes and rose into a hover to better see all those assembled. "Tomorrow, I lead the assault on Hiraeth Arian and the Grand Harmonium. We will destroy it from within and seize the fortress for ourselves. And, if there is even a shred of decency left in Empress Nova or any of the sycophants she surrounds herself with, that will be the end of it. The war will be won."

She allowed a moment for those words, for the unfamiliar dream of victory, to seep in before speaking again. "None of us are who we were when this war began. Many of us weren't even born yet when it began. But it will be us who end it. All of us together. The roads of all our varying lives have brought us together for this. Gryphons. Unicorns. Elk. People of Gateway, of the Elderpine, of Vogelstadt, of Avalon. You are all so brave. Let's see this through together, once and for all."

"Once and for all," they each echoed.

Galaxy landed and watched as Gwen and Captain Hywel shared a final word before the Elk queen turned and marched away to board an air-yacht. Vigdis nodded to Galaxy once before taking wing, High General Odin at his side. A call went out as he rose, repeated from all around, and suddenly the assembled gryphon soldiers rose to follow their king, hundreds from the palace roof, thousands more from the surrounding city. More and more gryphons and air-yachts, enough to hide the sun if the Dragonbacks had not already done so, and following after them came a song of steadfastness and farewell. It was sung by soldier and civilian, by those flying away and those staying behind, by Galaxy with a breaking heart, by Owain beside her, tears gleaming in his eyes and streaking down his cheeks.

"Hold the paths that bring us near
Hold all those we hold most dear.

"Hold the peaks, lofty and grand
Hold the beaches of snowy sand.
Hold the forests, trees all in bloom
Hold the roads, quiet as the tomb.

"Hold those reaching their last rest
Hold those who pass the last test.
Hold the night, so silver and black
Hold all those not coming back."

It took a long while before the great host slipped at last from sight. Many had stayed upon the palace roof to watch the departure. Elk soldiers remaining behind to be teleported for battle. Gryphon soldiers staying as part of a home guard in case all went wrong. Family members and friends watching loved ones off, each hoping the departing army was not the last time they would ever see them. Galaxy, standing between Owain and Bifrost, a wing draped over each of their backs, found herself fitting uncomfortably into "Most of the above."

It was the sound of distant thunder which finally drew their gazes from the north. Galaxy drew her wings in and turned to the south with a frown, listening close. The thunder rumbled again, south and high above. As it went on, Galaxy beheld flashes of forked light dancing within the folds of the overhanging clouds, one bolt bright enough to make her blink and shake her head even from such a distance.

"Volcanic lightning is a fascinating phenomenon," began Bifrost, voice full of forced cheer. "There are many factors that can go into it, but the most integral from current understandings is the collision and fragmentation of volcanic ash particles near the—"

"Bifrost," said Owain, and the raven-gryphon quieted.

"So far away," said Galaxy, watching the lightning blaze through the clouds. "Volcanic lightning from so far away. Too far away. If there had been an eruption to cause THIS, we would have felt it from here. But there's the lightning, all the same."

"I feel something," said Owain. The palomino unicorn took a step forward and raised his head, a dazed look in his features Galaxy didn't like. There was a shimmer around his horn, his magic half-summoned forth. "It's like this pressure, all around and over us. It's all of a sudden, like a spell, or a thought."

Galaxy felt it too. She stepped even with Owain and closed her eyes. She slowed her breathing and, with more difficulty than it usually took her, quieted her thoughts until it was only her, her own magic, and the magic of the world all around her. She saw something wrong at once.

"It's like . . . the world's been stained," she tried. "The stains left from a horrid, choking smoke. And to the far south . . . there's . . ."

A wildfire of magic churned far away before Galaxy. The Dragonbacks burned with magic, a rising, rising inferno, tendrils breaking forth like long, grasping talons to rake the sky with lightning.

Something changed. Something within the firestorm of magic looked back at Galaxy. She opened her beak to scream—

—and found herself slapped back to the waking world. The scream cut off into a startled yelp before it could even start, Galaxy sitting down and bringing her talons up to her stinging face. In front of her stood Carina, body language torn between terror and fury. "Do not look!" the seer hissed, her wings spreading as if to block Galaxy's mortal sight of the south. "Do not look with your magic eyes! Would you blind yourself, the way a fool blinds himself by looking into the sun? Do you think whatever you see would be worth that loss?! Fool!"

The words sparked Galaxy's ire far more than the physical blow. She shrugged off Bifrost's attempts at a helping talon and stood again, hobbling forward to glare straight on at the bandages hiding Carina's fire eyes. "I don't trust you, Carina. I never have. I get the feeling you've never trusted me either. And I'm getting tired of you playing up this all-knowing seer act, like you're always knowing more than you're letting on. I don't have time or the patience for it anymore. Just tell me one thing, fire priestess. Do you stand with me or against me?"

"Gal, stop, my sister—"

Carina held her talons out and Bifrost went quiet. Whatever hid behind her bandaged gaze did not waver from Galaxy. "I've told you once before, in the Dream. The destiny my Burning King chose for me. A raven-gryphon helping a hippogryph to her full potential. A fire priestess helping a hippogryph bring peace to the world. You have nothing to fear, my princess. I am here for you."

Galaxy nodded, not out of satisfaction but out of hearing all she had expected. "That's what you think, but I see you missing two vital details. It's BIFROST, your SISTER, who helped me reach that potential, and you are NOT the only fire priestess in Heraldale!"

***

Lord Thoth limped into Empress Nova's throne room, feeling sad and pitiable, shying away from the looks of barely-restrained contempt sent his way by the soldiers guarding the door. They did nothing to hide their snide thoughts from the sphinx, the open gloating at the black scars of lightning covering so much of his body now, his ruined rear left leg, the lingering blind spots in his eyes. Lord Thoth felt only relief when the doors slammed shut behind him and the special metals built into the throne room cut off his natural sphinx telepathy.

Across the throne room from Lord Thoth, Empress Nova and Lord Beauty sat laughing. Paranoia born of decades in service to the pair of unicorns, or whatever in Sheol Beauty truly was, bellowed to Lord Thoth how he was the subject of their laughter, a final joke gone the way of Lord Mordred, who despite all other faults, at least had possessed the decency not to laugh at him.

"Lord Thoth!" shouted Empress Nova, sitting suddenly straighter atop her dais of a throne and looking at him, her shattered body crackling like tumbling stone from the movement. "There you are! Come here, sphinx! Lord Beauty has just been telling me the most wonderful of news!"

"Yes, indeed," said Lord Beauty, looking Thoth's way as well. Her star sapphire eyes were blank as usual, but Thoth's paranoia told him she was grinning at him, laughing at him on the inside, eager to see the lame sphinx walk the distance. "Walk ALL the way over here. This news needs to be shared CLOSE."

Thoth swallowed and took a step at the command veiled in the sweeter words of invitation, took another step, loosed an unwanted gasp as his bad leg gave out and nearly dropped him to the floor. He looked down at himself in the gleaming floor's reflection, a burned and horrid beast. Sir Bevin had wounded him with her lightning, had ruined him in ways he realized with dawning horror Lord Mordred had always been able to, if she'd really wanted. Fur had been burnt away where there had been fur, the bared skin of his face and throat and chest cracked and blackened by the heat, the flesh ashen and raw. Droplets of blood oozed forth with each harsh and fought-for breath. The burns dominated the right side of him. He was lucky to still have his eye . . .

"Lord Thoth," said Empress Nova, voice no longer so jovial as it dragged the sphinx's attention back up from his reflections. "I said . . . come here."

Lord Thoth stood as straight and strong as he could manage and began walking toward his empress and fellow Lord of the Empire. Halfway there, his strength faltered as all had known it would and he gasped his pain. Every step forward his limp grew more pronounced, the pain immense, as if the bone was ready to snap in half.

Then he was there before the dais throne, shaking, his maimed front right leg seizing up from over-exertion and clutched uselessly against his chest. He took a long, shuddering breath to steady himself, then looked up at the pair and tried to smile his usual smug smile. "Empress Nova. Lord Beauty. The good news?"

"The most wonderful of news," Empress Nova corrected, her air of cruel glee returning, though this time, to Lord Thoth's relief, not entirely directed at him. "You'll truly get a smile out of this."

"My hopes for Lord Mordred's body were well-founded," said Lord Beauty, drawing Thoth's attention to her. "Organic material gathered from it was the last piece the Architect Spider needed. Together with the material the late Lord Mordred collected from the Dragonbacks—"

"And the world will be yours to lose," Thoth finished, looking again to Empress Nova before him with fresh wonder and fresh fear. He sunk into the deepest bow he could manage in his current state. "My most incredible, most awe-inspiring, most all-powerful Empress, once more your wisdom and might have reshaped the course of Heraldale's destiny beyond anything even I, with the fullest faith in you, could have imagined."

"I know, I know," said the unicorn, giving her mane a toss. "All true. You were always such a flatterer."

"Only for you, my empress," Lord Thoth continued, limping closer still and biting his bottom lip in pain at the movement. "For only you in all Heraldale and beyond could ever inspire such flattery, or be deserving of it. It, it pains me to be in such a foul, pitiable state in your presence. And with your total victory close enough to TASTE, we might . . . turn certain considerations toward a post-war world. If you would command Lord Beauty here to rid me of my wounds so that I could more efficiently bring the Sphinx Hierarchy into the fold . . ."

Empress Nova made a great and needless show of thinking the request over, leaning back as she sat and raising a leg to scratch a hoof against her chin the way a gryphon might have used a talon. Then her cracking muzzle twisted into a grin. "Hmm . . . no."

Lord Beauty barked with laughter. Lord Thoth sagged. "My . . . my empress?"

"You have been a disappointment to me lately," continued Empress Nova, lifting her head and looking away. "An utter disappointment. You shall stay like this until I grow bored of your suffering. I like you more like this. So sad and pathetic now. We can hardly bare to look at you."

At first, Lord Thoth's jaw worked but no sound came out, the impossibility of the situation driving all sense out of him. "But, but my empress, I have ever been a loyal servant of yours. Surely as your power expands to all horizons, you would see a known and loyal face on the sphinx throne?"

More laughter from the unicorn pair, more laughter from all around as the soldiers guarding the throne room joined in. Lord Beauty strode forward, a front leg lifting, a hoof pressing against the flesh of his burned and ruined shoulder until he cried out and stumbled back. "King Thoth, he begs!" she cried out, each word pierced with laughter. "All these years, the kitty's dreamed and schemed for King Thoth! King of the sphinxes! King of the fools! KING OF THE DEAD!"

Thoth backed away, at last speechless in his misery. Everything grew blurry, and every breath was harder than the last as damaged throat and damaged lungs struggled against the panic and pain.

"He's crying!" someone called out, the following laughter ringing louder than any which had come before. "Big kitty kitty is CRYING!"

"It makes me yearn for the dignified fury of Lord Mordred!"

"Someone! Cream and a saucer at once!"

"ENOUGH!" shouted Empress Nova. The throne room fell silent, all eyes turning to her as she stood and limped her own way down from her dais. Lord Thoth shook beneath the burning weight of her red eyes. "The Empire, of course, recognizes the breadth of work you have done for us. We would not have an end to that. Stay there a moment and listen close."

The white glow of Empress Nova's personal magic covered her horn. Terror stabbed through Lord Thoth's heart as he thought, for one moment, he was about to be subjected to some new form of the Harmonization spell.

But then the magic slipped up from Empress Nova's horn into an orb of shining light, dim enough to look at, and as Thoth looked at it the magic slowly solidified into an orb of milk-white crystal shot-through with veins of black.

"My generals bring me word," said Empress Nova, levitating the crystal orb over to Thoth, "that their scouts report a massive army of gryphons and air-yachts departing Gateway and heading north. They scattered the small garrisons stationed at their northern borders, and now seem to fly to Gryphonbough with reckless haste."

Thoth blinked, looking from the frozen spell to his empress and back again, thoughts slow to collect as the moment of trauma passed. "The . . . the attack I gleaned from the traitor Bevin's thoughts . . ."

"So it would seem," said Lord Beauty.

"I have a command for you, my sphinx," said Empress Nova. "Take my crystal of magic and go to the former Gryphonbough capitol. Stay there and await further orders."

Thoth did not trust the moment of relative peace to last and grabbed the orb with his telekinesis as quickly as he could. He tucked it close to his good side, then looked up at his empress, still fearful. "Greatest and most glorious Empress Nova, I, I am not a general."

"No, you are not," the unicorn agreed.

"I-I am not a soldier."

"No, you are not."

"Then why would you—"

"Because," and Empress Nova almost purred the words, "one thing you are is mine."

CHAPTER FOURTEEN

They were allowed to wander the castle grounds, as long as a small guard of soldiers kept with them. Brynjar thought this patronizing, but also not worth the trouble of complaining over.

The abandoned open-air gardens Brynjar eventually found his way to still carried the faintest trace of the care and attention they had once enjoyed. Brynjar, never one for plants, took his time taking it all in as he ambled aimlessly about. Thick creepers ran unheeded along floors and up breaking stone walls. Flowers, once in orderly rows, burst like shrapnel across the scene, riots of intermingling reds, blues, pinks, yellows, purples; most of them, Brynjar couldn't name, their size and petals as varied as their colors, their clashing scents an assault upon the senses. Grey plants sprouted tall as the golden eagle-gryphon's shoulder, spreading thick leaves a dark, oily green.

"It's not going well in there," he eventually said.

"No," agreed Bevin, joining him among the flowers. Kanti trailed close behind, right hand resting on the handle of heavy-headed mace hanging from the Wolf-Lord's belt. "It really isn't."

"And you," said Brynjar, looking to Kanti next. "You and the fox have some kind of history, don't you? Bad blood? I get the feeling that's hurting us."

The black Wolf-Lord gripped at her mace tighter and failed to meet Brynjar's gaze. He sighed and looked away, beginning to pace. The garden, at first peaceful and calming, began to feel like an enclosing trap around him. The sense of time being wasted, of chances slipping away, took hold of him and would not let go. It took all he had not to scream up to the sky. "This very moment, Galaxy and Owain must be risking their lives in battles to decide the fate of the world, and here I am . . . playing ambassador to people who'd rather wear my feathers in a cape . . ."

"In fairness to you, I've seen far worse ambassadors in my day."

Brynjar stopped his nervous-winged pacing and turned as Guru Veda joined them in the garden. The blindfolded Wolf-Lord cleared the mold from a stone bench with a dismissive wave of her hand and accompanying burst of silver magic. The act, and the magic, both seemed strangely familiar to Brynjar, though he couldn't place either.

"What's your news?" asked Bevin.

"That's some unwarranted brusqueness toward the only representative in your corner out there," answered Veda as she sat down. She turned to Kanti, smiled with well-disguised contempt down at the shorter Wolf-Lord. "I hope you don't let them talk to you that way. You deserve better, little wolf. Losing all your loves as you did . . ."

If this struck a nerve in Kanti, the pirate did not show it, only sheathing her sword and asking "Your news?"

"What are our chances?" asked Bevin a moment later than the Wolf-Lord.

Veda turned to the unicorn first. Her smile dimmed. "Your chances are . . . not to be mentioned in polite company. You have me, of course. I am well aware of the threat of cults getting involved in wars. A number of the dragons believe in the threat of Avalon to these lands, but they have no power to lend you. Lord Managarm would rather eat silver than trust in the word of a unicorn on anything. Lady Gauri is sympathetic to the dragon cause and potentially to yours, but they are young and came here prepared to treat everything as a joke, and they will follow the lead of the Nameless Monk on any important matters. Speaking of . . ."

Veda looked back to Kanti, smile brightening again. "Bold move there, bringing up the old royal family. I thought that crusty old Nameless Monk was going to stand and bolt right for the door."

Fangs were bared and ears folded back, but otherwise Kanti remained unmoved. "It's been years. I'm tired. However else this journey fares, I will have revenge. I promised her so."

"I remember what I asked of you, Kanti. Return with a way to save her, return with a way to avenge her, or don't return at all."

Brynjar grimaced and closed his eyes.

"But you are here," hissed Madara. The hawk-gryphon stood and lunged for the bars, grabbed them in his talons and hauled himself up, belly exposed to Brynjar. "You're here and you want to kill me, so do it! Go on! It's what you want to do, it's what you deserve! A true gryphon of action! Do it! DO IT!"

Brynjar stared. The spear lowered, the point forged to pierce the strongest of armor aimed for thin skin and guts.

Brynjar opened his eyes again and watched Kanti with a new keenness of understanding. He knew, without needing the full history, the pain the Wolf-Lord felt, knew the words she spoke, knew he might have spoken them himself on another day. The fresh burst of knowledge only served to make him feel more tired and defeated by the journey.

"I wish this could all be over with," he said, drawing all eyes to him. "We should be back out west, fighting with the rest of our loved ones. Fighting's all I've ever been good for, anyway. Leave the wolves and the dragons to find their peace together, if they can."

The sound of leathery wings passed overhead, accompanied by a heavy shadow gliding over the grass and stone. Veda's head jerked upward for the briefest moment, almost faster than Brynjar could've noticed the movement, and then a grin spread along her muzzle. "You may be pleasantly surprised to learn those negotiations were going fairly well before your arrival. One of the great tragedies of the driving of the Wolf-Lords from Heraldale, besides the . . . the obvious, is how close our peoples once were in culture and craft. Prized miners, builders, crafters. Each peculiar among the nations of Heraldale as the only practitioners of trial by combat to settle disputes. I can't say for the dragons, but those practices still linger among the Wolf-Lords at least. It is my hope they can be the start of a renewed bridge between our divided people someday."

Again, there came the sound of leathery dragon wings from somewhere overhead. Brynjar looked up as quick as he could, but only caught the last flash of pink scales disappearing beyond the edge of the nearby walls. He frowned and wondered what Ashe could be playing at, listening in on conversations without announcing herself or joining them.

Before Brynjar could say any of this aloud, a brown-furred kitsune cleared his throat from the doorway into the main hold of the castle. His two tails hung low and stiff behind him as he addressed the group at large, though the main bulk of the young fox's attention was on Kanti. "My master, the Ambassador Monk, requests a private audience with you and your companions. . Immediately."

***

The Nameless Monk had taken what looked to have once been the castle's main throne room for his own use, warning Brynjar of an ego not to be trifled with. A dark hall draped in gold pillars and red banners, lit only by sparse brass braziers. The stone floor was pitted, cracked, and scarred with old burns, calling to Brynjar's mind a vicious battle fought there once upon a time. It seemed to him in every way the inverse of Empress Nova's throne room, yet still a place of evil.

The Nameless Monk, sitting with legs crossed in a meditative pose at the foot of the steps up to the broken throne, opened his eyes as the small group of Brynjar, Bevin, and Kanti approached. "Punctual. That is a good habit."

"What do you want, fox?" snapped Kanti, the black Wolf-Lord's voice a growl as she took the lead among them.

"Peace and quiet," answered the Nameless Monk, gaze focusing on Kanti. From where he stood a little behind, Brynjar barely repressed a shudder of revulsion. He knew well the thick contempt oozing through the kitsune's words. It hadn't been so long at all since he'd heard the like of it directed at himself, from both Empress Nova and Lord Thoth.

"You ask for quite the rare commodity, where I come from," remarked Bevin, the unicorn's hooves clacking loud through the dark room as she moved to stand even with Kanti.

"But not so rare where I come from," said the monk. His smile was full of teeth. "At least, not until recently. The arrival of the dragons seeking a new home has disturbed the waters. I don't like that. None of us in the Nameless Order like it. Life was good and settled and orderly. We kept our affairs in order and nobody wanted to make trouble."

Brynjar saw Kanti's eyes narrow. "We literally stand in the ruins of Romulus, the royal family dead or . . . missing."

The monk made a dismissive gesture with one of his four tails. "The fall of Romulus came from within. The royal family brought it on themselves with their dalliances with Morgana le Fay. What troubles us now comes from without. From Heraldale. We do not want trouble from Heraldale. A dozen kitsune, at most, still live to even remember it firsthand. There are warmongers among the ruling classes of our nations, you've met one in Duke Managarm, but the common people do not care. The dragons are enough to tolerate. We want no more."

A snort, a stomp of hoof, a toss of mane from Bevin. "That's too damn bad, then. Lord Beauty is your foe, Morgana. That makes her YOUR responsibility."

The monk's back stiffened. His eyes narrowed. Around them, the fires in the braziers grew until they towered nearly to the ceiling, banishing the shadows and nearly scorching Brynjar with the sudden rush of heat and choking air. "Do not presume to tell me of my duty, unicorn! I am a member of the Nameless Order! It is our solemn vow to guard against the return of the Burning King and the freeing of Queen Morgause from her eternal prison! Duties beyond the mortal ken of witless fools stumbling—"

But then, he stopped even as Kanti looked primed to explode back at him. With a clear show of titanic effort, the kitsune breathed out and shook his head, the fires dying back down to their original states. His slighted pride stalked unspoken behind the iron bars of his eyes as his gaze roamed to Brynjar once more. "We get . . . off-topic. We waste our own time. I did not summon you here for argument. I have summoned you here . . . for a compromise."

Kanti snorted, clearly unbelieving. Brynjar shared a look with Bevin, eyebrow raised. The unicorn subtly shook her head. Brynjar nodded in agreement, then looked back to the monk and asked "What sort of compromise?"

The monk's smile returned. "Officially, the Nameless Order stands beside the other representatives. There is not enough proof in your mere words to take action regarding the situation in Heraldale. Unofficially, the Nameless Order is prepared to send 500 of our most powerful kitsune sorcerers to Heraldale to deal with your so-called Lord Beauty. They await only my word . . . and your payment."

The pliable corners of Brynjar's beak turned down in a frown, the frown growing as he saw Kanti grow dangerously still at this offer. He thought he had a good idea what the "payment" would be, with the little context he had gleaned over the course of the trip, but he wanted to hear it said aloud. "And that payment is?"

The monk visibly relaxed. His tails even began to wave and curl behind him. "Somewhere in the north, between these lands and your own, there is a village of refugees. Among them is a former monk of the Nameless Order. A traitor, to be more precise. She fled our lands, took a name for herself, and murdered a fellow monk in so-called self-defense. Worst of all, she associated with the wretched spawn of Morgana le Fay, the late Princess Candida—"

"Her name was Holly! Holly le Fay!" growled Kanti, stomping closer toward the monk before Brynjar hurriedly placed a wing on her shoulder to stop her.

"I don't care," remarked the monk. His gaze never left Brynjar. "What matters is that the Nameless Order will provide support to win your war. All you need to do is surrender to us the traitor, 'Shun'. That's all."

"Never!" screamed Kanti, tearing herself from Brynjar's touch and storming forward until she stood the barest breath from the monk. "Never! You'll have her over my dead body, and I will have my own justice long before that! A justice wreathed in the blood of the Nameless Order."

Now at last, the Nameless Monk stood, tails flicking in agitation as he glared up at Kanti. "You sling death threats at a monk of the Nameless Order. In all the lands of the Wolf-Lords, the lesser people would suffer death for such an affront."

Kanti's hand dropped to the mace hanging from her belt. "Luckily for me, I am no lesser folk."

Brynjar watched the growing confrontation, torn. His every idealistic, moralistic impulse rebelled, repulsed by the offer and the thought of giving up someone who had only shown him and Bevin kindness to what was surely a gruesome death. But he couldn't deny the cold side, the pragmatic side, the voice which long before had told him to regard Ashe in only practical terms on the way to the Dragonbacks. It was, in truth, an appallingly appealing offer. The price for winning the war—one life, one kitsune, one nobody—a mere pittance, the slightest trifle compared to the hundreds, the THOUSANDS more to be lost if the war dragged on much longer. Surely, it was monstrous to deem all those lives as meaning less than the one life asked for.

But then, a feeling of déjà vu struck Brynjar. He remembered standing in another hall, months and lifetimes ago, standing together with Galaxy in Governor Urien's castle as Lord Mordred gave the hippogryph an offer. Serve Mordred, serve the Empire, or see all they loved be destroyed.

"Ignore him!" Brynjar struggled with his restraints. "They killed my father, widowed our mother, orphaned you, conquered us, enslaved us! I'd die rather than know you do anything for unicorn filth in my name!"

"No," said Brynjar, perking as he heard Bevin speak the same. They shared another look, but it was Brynjar who continued. "No offense, but betraying that trust . . . just isn't a price I can pay again."

The Nameless Monk remained silent and staring. Iron shutters had fallen over their expression, and not or word and not a thought of what they felt could be read. Not until he spoke. "You may leave now. I hope you understand what you have done. The dragons have their demands concerning the gryphons of Schwarz Angebot and the unicorns of Avalon. You may find, in the hours ahead, certain ears are far more willing to entertain them."

"A risk I'm willing to take," said Brynjar, and then no more. He turned away and started for the doors out of the ruined throne room, Bevin following close behind. He heard Kanti come at last after a long pause, tread heavy and slow.

"What now?" she asked, once the doors were behind them.

"What else can we do," said Bevin. "See what the other ambassadors have to say to us and hope Galaxy and the others can manage without us a little longer."

CHAPTER FIFTEEN

After some difficulty with the stairs made for two-legged beings, Bevin found Lady Gauri atop the ramparts surrounding the mountainside castle, knuckles against the stone as they looked over the parapets at the bleak late-winter lands beyond.

For a brief while, Bevin contented herself with watching, giving the Wolf-Lord the choice to break the silence when ready. A frosty wind blew from the west, teasing through Gauri's white fur and setting their white hair drifting behind them. Bright pink eyes scanned the horizon, full of wants Bevin only dimly remembered from her own lonely childhood.

"I am the last scion of a noble house," spoke Gauri at last, breaking the silence. "In the old days, when the wolf nations were new, pirates from the Remnants of Metavore plagued us. A great ancestor of mine raised the banner to fight against them, and many rallied to their cause. It became a noble protective order, bearing perhaps only a shred of the renown and respect of the

Nameless Order, but something you could see with your own eyes the good you did with your own hands. But it has been decades since those marauders plagued us. I am the first in my family not to have had the chance for bloody glory by my age. Instead, I am accustomed to leisure and frivolity, and the scorn of those older than me."

"Soldiers fight to safeguard the frivolity of others," said Bevin, though as she spoke, she thought of Vogelstadt, of Lady Quetzal's pigheaded resistance to getting involved and ending her realm's summer days, and thought of how such things could only be allowed to go so far.

"A great-grandparent of mine, rest their bones, went to Heraldale for a while in their youth," continued Gauri after a moment. "They went in the guise of a dragon, with thoughts of exploring our underground cities we left behind. I never really asked them why, but I think they had dreams of recovering lost treasures and old arts. Pieces of our history and culture we couldn't take with us when first we fled our lands, if anything remained to be found."

Bevin closed her eyes and sighed, guessing the end to the story. She remembered the abandoned city she and Lord Mordred had chased Galaxy and the rest through near journey's start. She remembered the wolf bones half-crumbled to dust in their age and the wyverns gone feral and mad in their isolation.

"It was a bad time to be a dragon in northern Heraldale," continued Gauri. "The first attempt by unicorns and gryphons to do to the dragons what they'd done to the Wolf-Lords, the subsequent counterattack, and Quetzal's 'taming' of the dragons with the Oath Spear, all still within living memory. The unicorns hadn't even recovered to form their empire yet. Tensions were high all around."

"I can imagine," said Bevin.

"Maybe you can," admitted the Wolf-Lord. They shifted their stance, fluffy tail tucking against a leg as they looked to Bevin. "After they came back, they never stopped talking about what a sad, miserable place Heraldale turned out to be, how the people there squatted in ruins without a thought. No others in my family repeated their journey. We've been content to take their word for it. The arrival of the dragons here, now, lend credence to their word. It . . . stirs pity in the heart, things I am not used to feeling. I'd rather it all quiet down again and let me return to the golden days of frivolity I have always known."

Bevin watched the Wolf-Lord carefully. "But."

Gauri bared their teeth. "But that's the thing about KNOWING things. It's so damn hard to STOP knowing.

There gets to be a point where you need to know MORE, no matter how terrible. And when nobody else is willing . . . you do what you gotta do."

Slowly, Bevin nodded. "How may I be of service?"

Gauri turned to fully face Bevin at last, chin up and shoulders squared. For the first time, they looked as if their thick fur might not be enough against the frigid mountain climes. "The memory spell. Show me everything."

Bevin frowned and looked around. Aside from some Wolf-Lord soldiers minding the main courtyard and a scattering of dragons up high in the skies overhead, they seemed to have the whole world to themselves. "Are you certain? The others didn't seem to trust the method."

"Screw what the others think," snapped Gauri. If anything, she held her head higher. "Duke Managarm is a rotten old wolf who'd go to war with the world if it cared to look in our general direction. The Nameless Monk . . . they take children from their homes and names from their children to fill their ranks. They took a cousin of mine and made them into . . . into nothing. And as for Guru Veda . . . I don't know. It doesn't really feel like she's TRYING, if that makes any sense. She's saying all the right words, but it feels like she's only going through the motions. And I don't buy that story of only formerly being a member of the Cult of the Burning King. She's the only former member I've ever heard of. No, screw them all. I'll make up my own mind."

Bevin repressed a smirk, but only barely. Sparing another glance around to be sure nobody was paying them undue attention, she stepped closer to the young Wolf-Lord, close enough to lower her head and touch horn to their forehead, if she wanted. "Very well, if I have your express permission. I shall show you . . . what shall I show you?"

"The war," said Gauri. "The war and the hippogryph, everything you can show me about both. Up until you left with that dashing gryphon friend of yours."

This smirk, Bevin failed to keep to herself. "He's already taken."

"Hm, a crying shame. Are you?"

Commander Bevin stood beside the stone slab, the mask of her expression all cold stone as she dragged the cloth aside with her magic. She took in the slender pinto unicorn splayed out on the table with a careful soldier's regard, taking in the bruises of a neck which had been broken and then later reset for presentability, the deep stab in the side, the burns for which there could only be so much done to hide them. The unicorn stallion had gone down fighting.

"Kelan . . ."

With the lone whispered word, the stone of Bevin felt the mask crumble from her. Blue eyes welled with the tears she could not stop, trailing down her cheeks to patter the mortuary floor.

Bevin took a deep, steadying breath. "Once."

Gauri, to their credit, did not press. After a moment, Bevin continued. Stand level with me, my lady. Keep eye contact. If you have any understanding or grasp of magic—"

"Gather it to my forehead," said Gauri, smiling on as they looked into Bevin's eyes. "I have no real talent for magic, but on a dare, I once spent two years shapeshifted into a unicorn. I think I can manage what you need."

Bevin nodded in approval, then dipped her head further down to touch the tip of her horn to the young wolf's forehead. She took a moment to familiarize herself with the feel of the other's magic, soft and bubbly and vanilla-sweet. "Good. Now, focus. Ignore all else. Everything else slows down and falls away. You see . . ." As Bevin spoke, she drew up and pushed out her magic in a steady flow, remembering as she did so, remembering . . .

A cabin as it burned down. Sir Lancelot—father— gutted and dead on the floor among the traitorous gryphons who'd brought him down, the unicorn child sobbing as Lord Mordred loomed into the doorway to claim her.

A small, cozy gryphon home. A flurry of spell bolts. A golden eagle-gryphon, Ida, collapsing to the floor with a gasp, the memory of a tall, uncaring unicorn in the doorway. "Miss hippogryph. I am Commander Bevin. My Lord Mordred would much appreciate an audience with you."

A shabby hall far from the splendor of Avalon. Galaxy and Brynjar standing before Mordred, rejecting the disguised Wolf-Lord's offer to serve Avalon, the offer turning to blistering lightning, to commands for them to be taken away.

A dark ruin, the shadowed halls of the abandoned Wolf-Lord city drawing a pained gasp from the observing Gauri. In the memory, Bevin and Mordred watched apart as their soldiers cleared the scene.

"I feel that you have a question on your mind."

Memory Bevin closed her eyes, took a steadying breath, and opened them again to meet her Lord Mordred's gaze. "I wonder what makes the wyverns a higher priority than the hippogryph, sir. These creatures are dangerous, but they have been limited to underground. The hippogryph spreads dissent and rebellion wherever she goes. The Empire's enemies will rally around her."

"*The hippogryph orphan is only a child. Our enemies may flock to her, but more likely than not they will crush her in doing so. Hmmph. Almost a shame.*"

From within the memory but not a part of it, Bevin watched her old self and frowned. It did little for her ego to see what a blowhard and a tool she had been.

An alleyway shrouded in morning mist fresh off the ocean. An equine figure encased horn to hoof and snout to tail in stone. The confident gaze of Commander Bevin, her horn glowing a stark gold against the white of her coat. "I am Commander Bevin. You are under arrest. Come peacefully and you will not be harmed. There is no need for this to come to violence."

The fight. The spell chain. The fall. The rescue. Bevin awoken by an unwanted touch.

"*She caught me as I fell.*"

"*Indeed she did.*" *Beak turned up in a smile, Blackbird turned to look eastward, to the area of Port Oil cast in shadow by the surrounding cliffs.* "*Such a merciful, heroic hippogryph. Unicorns and gryphons could learn from her, I think.*"

Bevin huffed. "*What would YOUR people know of heroism?*"

Blackbird shrugged, that smile never leaving. "*Oh, wouldn't you like to know?*"

"YOUR ORDERS DESTROYED MY HOME! MY LIFE! MY FAMILY IS BROKEN BECAUSE OF YOUR ORDERS!"

"I was only a child when the gryphons came, came and... slaughtered my family before my eyes, set... fire to our home with me locked inside. I should have died then. I would have... if not... for Lord Mordred. He saved me, raised me. He is... the closest thing I have to family left."

The battle against Spell Virus, Mordred's betrayal of all Bevin's trust as he came on his ship to destroy Port Oil, her grief-fueled act of cowardice in wanting to abandon the city and flee, all whirling past the observers in a barely-discerned rush. Owain's shining achievement.

"Bevin, don't you understand? Everything we were taught is wrong. Wrong! Unicorns aren't any better and gryphons aren't any worse just because they're unicorns and gryphons! Don't you realize that? Don't you even realize you're standing there, talking about sentencing tens of thousands of innocent people to their deaths as if it's a little bit of bad weather!?"

Victory. Weeks of wandering Heraldale without purpose passed unseen. Then, the bridge, Mordred's true wolf nature shining through. Bevin and Princess Galaxy standing together at last.

Not to, heh, monologue, but you can't possibly think this absolves you of . . . ANYTHING you did at my command? The blood . . . staining your hooves. The stench of terror . . . BAKED into you. The sobs of the innocent ECHOING through your head at night. Khehehheh. Stupid, stupid Bevin, crying out for some greater purpose—"

No bridge, then, but a campfire. Hesitant allies and burgeoning friends gathered around. Sir Bevin. Sir Brynjar. Sir Owain. A quest to return Ashe the dragon home. The joy of training Galaxy in magic. A quest to rescue Sir Bifrost. Close calls and terrible truths—

"SISTER!"

The Grand Harmonium. The flight of the dragons from Heraldale. The long, stumbling journey south, the weight of the world on Bevin's back.

"It's all so much," whispered Gauri. The young wolf's heart sounded close to breaking. Bevin couldn't deny it.

Quetzal slammed a fist down, cracking the stone of her dais. "It was war, child! Choices needed making! Heraldale had been devastated by the dragons, they NEEDED taming! A strong fist to show them their place! Call it monstrous if you wish, but I did what I had to do for my people, just as your mother did all those years ago. And what have you done in comparison, if you think you can judge me? Allowed your home valley to be destroyed? Lost the support of the Elk? Lost your FAMILY? Rid Vogelstadt of all that stands between it and the horrors and devastation of WAR!?"

"At least she was out there fighting!"

King Vigdis. The failure of Bevin's Stone Elemental and news of her eventual doom. The flight to Gateway. They passed like gale winds, leaving her and Gauri on the balcony of the Gateway palace.

A ways away, Galaxy and Memory Bevin stood together, panting from the exertion and staring down at their assailant. Then Galaxy turned and kicked the gryphon with a hoof.

"You're a child," remarked Bevin.

Gal turned to her. "We need to stop getting into arguments like that when there are way more important things to worry about for the next . . . forever."

"I should have killed her the moment I had the chance." Memory Bevin sat in front of the hearth, shivering despite the fire blazing. She favored her front right leg, the limb decorated with bruises from a bad trip across a rug. "Back on that bridge, back in the Elderpine Forest. After I'd saved you. I should have galloped straight at her and sliced her head right off her shoulders. But instead . . . instead I had to ask why. I had to rage at her. I could have kept all of this from happening, all of it, if I had just . . . KILLED her . . ."

Bowls and decanters smashed to the floor. Memory Bevin stood among the splintered stone and shattered glass, sobbing. "I SHOULD HAVE LEFT HER THERE! I SHOULD HAVE LEFT THE MISERABLE, STUPID HIPPOGRYPH THERE WHERE I FOUND HER! I'D HAVE LIVED! RECOVERED! KILLED MORDRED! I HAD SO MUCH MORE TO DO! IT'S NOT FAIR!

"BUT I COULDN'T—" *As suddenly as it had come, the rage broke, crumbling beneath the very words it had dragged out of her. The Bevin in the memory nearly crumbled as well, a slight and pitiable creature.* "But I couldn't leave her there."

A firebomb filled the whole world, then disappeared behind a rush of brown and gold. Once more, Ida lay sprawled before Bevin, body perforated and smoking. Another life taken, more blood on her hooves.

The attempted coup. The repercussions. The plan for the assault on the Grand Harmonium. The late Lord Mordred's Lightning Elemental—

"I can," *laughed Bevin.* "I can!"

"REVENGE, BEVIN! REVENGE FOR MORDRED, PAID IN FULL BY EVERY MEMBER OF YOUR HOUSE! MY SISTER'S WORDS SHALL RING TRUE YET!"

The memory spell's connection broke. Immediately, exhaustion from its prolonged use struck Bevin. She whinnied and stumbled nearly to the stairs, unsure of when or where she was. Gauri hurried forward and braced against her shoulder, steadying her until Bevin could steady herself.

A look passed between the pair. The Wolf-Lord's eyes glimmered with tears streaking freely down their cheeks. They backed away and roughly scrubbed at their face with the heel of a hand, huffing in embarrassment as they did. "I . . . God, that was . . . something else. That was a lot. More than I could've expected, or . . . or . . ."

Bevin gave no apology. The young wolf had, after all, asked for everything. Instead, she questioned her own daring, or perhaps audacity, to invite someone else so deep into her mind and heart. If it had all failed . . . "Do you believe any of it?"

Gauri dropped their hand and snapped their still-wet gaze to Bevin. Seconds passed as they visibly struggled with their answer, ears flattened against their head and tail batting the air viciously behind them. Then, "I do. All of it."

At once, the weight of the last few days lifted from Bevin's back, the grief and dread she had refused to speak turning to a relief sharp enough to blur the corners of her vision with tears of her own. Someone believed them. Someone who could actually provide aid believed them. The journey had not been in vain, not wholly. "Thank you," she managed.

"Morgana . . ." whispered Gauri in mingled horror and wonderment. And then again, louder, the horror becoming the greater portion as their eyes widened and their hand grabbed at Bevin's side. "Morgana! Your empress, the harm-harmony—the mouthful spell Your empress is a unicorn and can only use it on unicorns, right!?"

"And Elk," answered Bevin, startled by this sudden change in the other's demeanor. "Why—"

"If your empress is allied with the nightmare of my people," said Gauri, "then Morgana has access to that dread spell! She could Harmonize Wolf-Lords and kitsune as Nova Harmonizes unicorns and Elk!"

And suddenly, Bevin could see it, a vision in her mind as startling for its clarity as for the horrors unveiled. The fleets of Avalon appearing on the horizon. Eishaven burned to the ground, the refugees there rendered into eternally-smiling slaves. The castle of Cairn Romulus thrown down, the dragons dying or fleeing once more before the marching hooves and gleaming horns. The cries and terror of the wolves in the face of a second, more complete genocide, the sins of Heraldale brought to fruition. All the world condemned to be the vassal of Nova.

"People need to be told," said Gauri. "At once."

Bevin, shaken to her hooves, nodded. "Tell your people, ready them. Tell the dragons. I—" She paused and mentally ran through her options. Brynjar and Kanti were trying to persuade Lord Managarm. They had already been to see the Nameless Monk so recently, going back so soon might do more harm than good. "I'll go to tell Guru Veda. She might know how best to proceed."

CHAPTER SIXTEEN

They found Duke Managarm in one of the larger courtyards, among a small gathering of dragons. The courtyard had been cleared of debris and the encroaching nature, new training dummies set up down its length, stacks of crated weapons and archery targets. Managarm stood before a gryphon-shaped dummy, stripped down to pants and fur—aside from their ever-present helm—and flanged mace in hand, beating the dummy down as the hissing conversation of the dragons washed over them. A dozen or so Wolf-Lords watched the small meeting from pillared balconies overlooking the courtyard, their own forced conversations doing little to hide their nervous watching of the hissing dragons.

Those hisses became snarls at Brynjar's approach, but Kanti swiftly took the lead, making a point of adjusting the sizable barrel of beer she carried on one shoulder. "Managarm! Quit with the bicep-aching and join me for a drink! It has been too long!"

"It can't have been too long, milady." THWACK. "We have never joined for a drink before at all." THWACK. "The feat to celebrate the return of my heir does not count." THWACK.

"All the more reason to finally have one now," answered Kanti. She set her barrel on its side atop a pair of crates, Brynjar following suit with the pair he carried tucked under his wings. As he worked, he tried to catch Ashe's eye from the crowd, succeeding only for a moment before she hurriedly looked from him back to Mammon, the only dragon who seemed at ease as he lounged curled in the sun.

A final swing took the gryphon dummy's head off. Managarm let their mace fall from their grip to hit the ground with a heavy thud, then looked at last to the newcomers. Their yellow eyes locked on Brynjar. They smiled, all fangs. "Hail, villain."

Brynjar refused to answer to the call. Kanti sidled in between them, an earthen mug held out to her fellow Wolf-Lord. "A drink, to the miseries of politics?"

Managarm huffed. "A toast I would make gladly, but I doubt the dragons would much appreciate me making merry with . . ." They gestured toward Brynjar. "I believe the appropriate slur is . . . featherbrain?"

Chuckles ran among the dragons, a streamer of black smoke billowing from between Mammon's lips.

Brynjar kept his features carefully neutral as he wondered how Kanti had ever talked him into this, while the smuggler in question raised an inquisitive eyebrow. "If I'm being honest, I got the impression you hate the dragons almost as much as you hate gryphons and unicorns."

"I do!" said Managarm, arms held out as if to encompass the whole courtyard. "And they know it! But at my age, that key word, 'almost', really makes all the difference. And I find there is a sort of honesty in hatred, in enemies, especially when there is another enemy to hate together.

Brynjar closed his eyes and took a deep breath. He thought of Gateway for a moment and all his loved ones left there, the dangers they faced to give him and Bevin this slim chance. This sort of talk was nothing. He had heard worse.

"I shall go ahead and ignore how much sense that makes," said Kanti sitting herself down on a nearby hay bale. The mug was still held out in offering. "I still propose a drink. To honest hatred. It may please you to know our dear gryphon friend here worked at a tavern for many years. He shall serve us as he's accustomed to."

"Not entirely as I'm accustomed to," added Brynjar, unable to help himself. "I was accustomed to spit in the drinks bound for unicorn soldiers before serving them."

The sound of dragon laughter was far less unnerving when it came at Brynjar's remark and not his expense, he decided. Even Managarm looked a smidge disarmed, smile less cruel and more speculative as they at last sauntered over and took a seat opposite Kanti. "Oh, well . . . what sort of ale is it you've brought me anyway, Lady Kanti?"

"An old lager from the north of Heraldale, hardly brewed anymore, for how thoroughly Avalon has destroyed the crops for it," answered Kanti, offhandedly motioning for Brynjar to set to work. He did so with half a bit-back remark. The short-hafted mallet and stave felt precious and familiar, and the smells which struck as he vented the cask resurrected memories of late nights in taverns lit amber and gold by roaring hearths, the roused cheer in crowds come in from days of brutal labor, every respite a miracle in itself. Brynjar felt the softest of tears well in his eyes, but his talons remained steady as he poured the first mugs and passed them around. If any saw his weakness, even the dragons kept quiet about it.

Managarm half-drained their mug in three hearty gulps, then loosed a sigh and settled more comfortably on their makeshift seat. "That is a worthy brew. This is the sort of diplomacy I am better suited for, if I must do it at all. It has been such a chore to sit in chairs among ruins and listen, my only entertainment whatever nonsense that Gauri can come up with. I wasn't made for it. I can handle the terror of the battlefield far better than the dullness of the—" But then, to Brynjar's amusement, they seemed to notice the dark smoke rising from the nostrils of the dragons present and hastily took another swig.

"Well," said Kanti, "if that's your attitude about this, I hope the dragons are getting everything they can out of you outstanding representatives of our people."

"I . . . can't say that they AREN'T doing that."

The time passed in this relatively peaceful manner, Kanti and Managarm drinking and regaling with tales of old battle, Brynjar serving drinks as he was needed, the lounging dragons watching and listening with a reluctant but growing interest. At some point, nobody noticed when, Ashe moved over to lay nearer to the lone gryphon among them, striking Brynjar with an aching jolt of nostalgia for those distant days of him and his family and friends traveling on the air-yacht, when the whole war had seemed so much simpler. Impossibly simpler.

It was as Brynjar was tapping the second cask when Managarm addressed him again, voice surprisingly steady and clear for how much they had drunk. "You, gryphon. Your finger there was broken and healed poorly. Do you call those fingers? I don't know."

Brynjar paused and glanced at the digit in question, thoughts returning to the night of his escape from the imperial warship. A bright spot for him among many bad days. "Oh, this. It happened weeks ago, when my partner and I were prisoners of the Empire."

Ashe stirred at this remark and looked to him. She was not alone. Managarm nodded gravely. "Torture."

Brynjar shook his head. "No, Lord Beauty—or so I knew her at the time—preferred burning and cutting to breaking. This came from the escape."

The grey Wolf-Lord leaned forward. Kanti sat aside, trying not to smirk too obviously. Brynjar caught her eye and frowned, but after a moment shrugged. "It was good luck. A unicorn soldier I had caused ill fortune to in a previous battle visited me in my cell, bribing her way in for some personal revenge. Stomped on my talons 'til they broke. Started monologuing, which was almost worse. Gave me a chance to get out of there, though, so . . . can't complain. Escaping the ship was only the start of escaping Avalon, though, and as we were hunted there just . . . never seemed time to set the break properly to heal it, not before it healed wrong."

Managarm raised their mug. "A toast, then, to broken bones and fools making bad decisions for revenge."

"I'll drink to that," said Kanti, and then proved her words by emptying her mug. As she passed it over to Brynjar for a refill, she continued "It reminds me of the one time my dear late Holly accompanied me on one of my Heraldale trips to pick up fresh refugees from a small village of no name, gryphons who already had family over here. It all was going well—ignoring the weather, storming like the end of the world—until a passing patrol of unicorn soldiers spotted the gryphons waiting near the docks and tried to arrest them. Holly jumped in, as she always did, and her thanks for it was a right into her gut. I should mention at this point that Holly was physically disabled and didn't possess a Wolf-Lord's natural invulnerabilities, so you didn't need silver or Lunar Steel to kill her."

The Wolf-Lord tapped high on herself, nearly where belly met chest. Brynjar and Managarm both winced in sympathy. Kanti nodded. "Nearly took her lung out, but you'd never know it from looking at her. She just wrapped her freakishly strong arms around that unicorn's neck and held him there while she glared the other soldiers down. Held them off until the rest of my crew could intervene. Never let her on my Heraldale-bound ships again."

"She sounds like she was wonderful," said Ashe, nearly startling Brynjar enough for him to knock the beer casks over. It was the first time she or any of the dragons had spoken since his and Kanti's arrival. "You must have been scared. And angry."

"Absolutely furious," agreed Kanti, downing the last of her beer. "Only two people in the whole world were angrier at her over the stunt."

"Who?" asked Brynjar.

"Her wife," answered Kanti, "and her doctor."

It should have led to an explosion of laughter all around. Brynjar could see it building in the final moments, ready to burst. There should have been laughter, and a great swell of comradery between them and the dragons and the Wolf-Lords. Managarm had thrown their head back, mug on the precipice of spilling in their lap—

KRAKA-BOOM!!!

At the deafening roar of thunder rolling across the courtyard, Brynjar did knock the beer casks over. Managarm toppled from their seat. Kanti shot to her feet. The dragons hissed and snarled, rising up with half-furled wings and looking about for the attack which seemed upon them.

More cracks of thunder rang. Brynjar looked to the noise and saw bolts of lightning shooting skyward from the glass and stone grand hall where the main meetings with the diplomats took place. Already, Wolf-Lords and dragons were hurrying to the scene from all across the fortress, and with barely a glance spared between them, Kanti hopped onto Brynjar's back and he took wing.

The flurry of lightning had long ceased by the time anyone arrived to the meeting hall. Brynjar descended through the shattered and smoking roof, landing with a splash in one of the mossy pools. He stared around, confused and aghast. The thrones had all been blasted away, banners burned and stone cracked. At the center of the hall, before the thrones, lay two bodies, motionless. One seemed only sleeping. The other lay wheezing at the center of a growing pool of blood, a long sword stabbed through her chest and pinning her to the floor.

"GURU VEDA!" The Nameless Monk stormed through the gathering crowd, heedless of the blood as he knelt before the grievously harmed Wolf-Lord. In smooth motions he drew the sword out of her and tossed it aside, a hand wreathed in flames pressing first over her stomach and then against her back to cauterize and end the bleeding. The Wolf-Lord, blindfold torn free, groaned and squirmed in pain from this, but did not awake.

"Great Toqeph," whispered Gauri, padding over to stand beside the monk. And as the words echoed across the scene of battle, eyes turned from the dying guru to the unicorn sprawled only a yard away. Brynjar stared at Bevin with the rest and felt his hope die.

CHAPTER SEVENTEEN

Bevin found Guru Veda in the main meeting hall, standing alone amidst the shafts of cold light falling through the broken roof. Despite all her sense of urgency, Bevin skid to a halt across the mossy floor and eyed the scene. The air, already thick with the wild scents of the flowers and moss and clear pooling waters, felt charged with an arcane energy. It reminded her, more than anything, of the temple where she and Morgana had exchanged Lord Mordred's body, but bereft the ancient sense of watchful death.

At a hoofstep forward, one of the guru's ears twitched. Veda turned slowly to look at Bevin, an overly familiar grin spreading on the dark Wolf-Lord's muzzle. "Lord Bevin, a pleasure—and a surprise—to see you here. Is your Elemental still giving you trouble?"

"I'm dealing with it," answered Bevin. "And it's Sir Bevin, please." She continued approaching the other, sparing a glance around at the otherwise empty hall. "I didn't know where your quarters are or who to ask, so this was a wild guess. Didn't expect to find you here either."

"Ah, so you've been looking for me." Veda turned to fully face her. "Has there been a development?"

"Lady Gauri has joined our side," said Bevin, allowing herself a moment to relish in this small piece of good fortune before going to the far larger, more terrible realization. "They let me show them my memories and realized the real danger of Morgana le Fay working with Avalon. The Harmonization spell."

Veda's smile had been dimming the entire time Bevin spoke, but at this last reveal it died entirely. "The Harmonization spell. Yes, I am aware of this piece of magic—"

"Nova is restricted to Harmonizing other unicorns and Elk," Bevin pressed on, pacing from one end of the thrones to the other, barely even looking at the dark Wolf-Lord, the anxious energy from before returning to her tenfold as she laid it out once more. "But Morgana could Harmonize the Wolf-Lords! It perfectly explains why they're allied in the first place! Even that Nameless Monk must put whatever his problems are aside in the face of a threat like this."

Veda took a moment to answer, a familiar but strange tone entering her voice. "Yes, I believe you are correct. The threat of the Harmonization spell being used on them, or even the rumor of such a threat, would be enough to rally the wolf and kitsune nations together. I'm surprised such a danger occurred to Gauri."

"As am I, but I talked with them, they're not as they first appear to—"

"I'll have to remember to kill them the first chance I get."

Bevin stopped her pacing at the far end of the lined thrones from the Wolf-Lord, unsure she had heard correctly, a dread deep in her gut that she had. She looked, and the Wolf-Lord smiled back at her, muzzle cast in new and frightening shadows by a cold purple glow from beneath her blindfold. "No . . ."

"No, what?" asked the Wolf-Lord, sauntering closer. In the space of those two words, her whole demeanor shifted, head high and shoulders squared, every idle thought of humility and honor slipping away for royal arrogance. "No, you couldn't possibly have been raised to be this stupid by Lord Mordred—"

Instinct and training triumphed thought and Bevin whipped her head about, conjured spell chain spanning across the distance to slash across the Wolf-Lord's face. She stumbled aside, nearly falling before regaining her balance. A quiet moment as the torn blindfold fluttered to the cracked floor, then the Wolf-Lord stood back to her full height and looked back at Bevin.

The star sapphire eyes of Morgana le Fay shone bright in the dim hall. Amusement had returned to her. "No lightning? Still floundering beneath the embarrassment of daddy issues life decided to throw your way?"

"Morgana!" Bevin didn't know how and she didn't care. She snarled and whipped the chain at her foe again, this time aiming to noose her neck and drag her in for a quick stab of her sword through the heart—

But the chain froze mid-swing at a gesture from Morgana, a second gesture causing it to rust away to nothing. "Bah. Child's play."

Bevin cast a spell at the Wolf-Lord's feet and the stone softened to a consistency nearly of thin cake batter. But Morgana barely began to sink before a snap of her clawed fingers brought her back to the surface, the stone returned to normal. "Guh. I'm bored. You're boring me."

Bevin readied a cutting spell, then paused. She reviewed all that had happened so far, considered her options, and looked to the nearest door. "Guards! Guar—"

Morgana stood beside Bevin in a blink, face a mask of fury. With a snap of her fingers, she drew Bevin's sword from its scabbard, the unicorn rearing back and away in full expectation of the sword being turned on her. As such, all words were startled from her as the Wolf-Lord instead stabbed the blade through her own gut.

"Guh! Auck, that hurt a little! Hah, now let me show you some real power!"

Morgana thrust a hand out, fingers clutching. Bevin whinnied as she felt an invisible magic seize her and lift her off her hooves, squeezing her with bruising force. Her legs kicked in panic, mind shooting back against her will to an abandoned tavern in Port Oil, to the wrath of a hippogryph squeezing until bones broke and blood seeped—

The lightning came of its own accord, bursting from Bevin without thought or aim. It crashed across the thrones and against the walls, up through the roof to the open sky beyond. The thunder deafened, echoing and rolling from all sides, buffeting the pair like gale winds. But the pressure across Bevin's body was unrelenting, cutting off air. She kicked harder, gasping for breath, watching with rolling eyes as Morgana hovered toward her like a puppet dragged along by its strings, whispering in a harsh, unknown tongue. Arm still outstretched, those crooked claws grasping Bevin by the base of the horn—

Then, darkness and unknowing for a long time.

CHAPTER EIGHTEEN

The first battle of King Vigdis's Gryphonbough campaign took place over the Fortress Upon the River. This was the keystone of Gryphonbough's southern border, built straddling the Greenleaf River and home to one of the kingdom's most important trading posts, for it served as a connective hub between Gryphonbough, Gateway, and the United Zakarian Confederacy. General Lugus of the East Army had captured it late in the war, a hideously brutal and stupid general. In an infamous act of devotion to Lord Mordred, he rounded up every gryphon from the fortress and surrounding city, every man, woman, and child who had failed to escape, and slaughtered them. The 3,100 lives taken by this act of barbarity, each of the dead bolstering the Lord of War's necromantic ranks, earned Lugus the moniker of Butcher. He wore it with pride.

Vigdis's wrath upon the Butcher and his forces was less a battle and more an Act of God. At the command of their king, flocks of geese-gryphon dropped two dozen spell-guided pillars of iron from 20,000 feet up. 19 hit their target, obliterating the main span of the fortress across the river. Then, in the early twilight, Vigdis led the next bombing run across the town and remaining Imperial defenders, firebombs and smaller flechette-spitters raining down like locusts upon the helpless grain. In half an hour, the entire site and its conquerors had been wiped from the map.

Vigdis flew on.

Twilight fell toward true night across sleeping Hummingburgh, now named New Little Avalon by newly-installed Governor Kay. Once it had overseen the vast reaches of woodland composing the majority of Gryphonbough's lumber industry, its oaks contributing to ships and cities as far away as Aliton and the lands of the sphinxes far to the southwest. Now those goods went only to Avalon, taken there by the blood, sweat, and tears of gryphon slave labor.

Queen Gwendolyn led her host through the camps of the gryphons and their masters, her illusion spells leaving them unseen and unheard. Chains were shattered, wounds healed, and weapons passed out. Then the fires were set. By the time Governor Kay knew anything was amiss, his soldiers were being driven burnt and bloodied through the trees and his own gates torn asunder.

Gwendolyn galloped on.

Near midnight's first stroke, with two more Imperial-held towns broken behind them, the forces of Vigdis and Gwendolyn came at last to the Plains of Donar. Here they slowed, Vigdis and his guard flying down to stand alongside Gwendolyn and her knights. Many miles ahead opened the heavily forested Valley of Woden, where waited the capital of Gryphonbough. The capital, distantly seen, blazed in the night with many lights, the skies above whirring with air-yachts and crystal drones. On the plains, Vigdis beheld many dozens of Imperial fortifications, unicorn soldiers scurrying among them in the many hundreds. He and Gwendolyn had come wanting to provoke a fight, and it seemed at last they had succeeded.

For a moment, Vigdis faltered. The remnants of his mother's last, failed battle upon the plains could still be glimpsed all around them, and the air lay heavy with the smoke of death and the cold hunger of Sheol. So many of the brave souls around him now would never see home again, perhaps himself among them . . .

"An avenging wind comes from the south, heralding great doom," said Gwendolyn, drawing Vigdis's eye to her. The Elk Queen stood tall and ready, her antler-like horns bright with magic and her eyes all the brighter.

"Shall we sweep the old orders aside to make room for the new?"

"Make room for the new . . ." And as suddenly as the anguish and dread had struck, they fled. Vigdis held his head high again, remembering why they fought against such odds. Not for personal glory or victory or survival, but for the hope of those coming after. "Yes . . . Gwendolyn, once the front line has been broken, scatter your people to the sides and harry all who flee. I will strike through for the valley."

"Fly fast," said the Elk Queen, and nothing more.

Vigdis spread his wings and returned to the air, to the fore of his host, sword swinging free and sheath falling away. He held the sword Cortana, a great cry arising from his gryphons as the blade shone with the starlight.

"FLY NOW FOR HERALDALE!" Vigdis shouted, voice ringing with all the strength and clarity of song. "FLY FOR THE HIPPOGRYPH! FLY FOR HOPE! FLY FOR THE WAR'S ENDING! FLYYY!"

The gryphons, and the Elk upon their airships, flew, a shadow over the earth thousands strong, the beating of their wings a storm and the glow of their spell staves a starfield.

Below, the Elk charged at speed, their horns alight with the magic of shield spells and their hooves a deafening thunder.

Against the two armies, the Imperial defenders loosed a withering storm of magic bolts and blasting spells. The Elk shields lit up and held strong. The gryphons returned fire with their staves, magic bolts and lightning bolts and blue-hot streaks of fire. The air crackled with the raw magic unleashed by the clashing foes, and for five glorious seconds the night itself was banished by harsh spell-light.

Then the gryphons, Vigdis at the head of them, crashed into and through the returning charge of Imperial air-yachts and crystal drones, and the Elk stormed over the unicorn defenses, and battle was truly joined.

CHAPTER NINETEEN

Dawn rose, the sky aflame with the volcanic haze. Galaxy woke slowly, felt cool, dewy grass beneath her, felt a wing blanketing her, felt a warm body soft and gently breathing beside her.

Bifrost made an excellent pillow.

Slowly, not wanting to wake the other, Galaxy wriggled herself free of the wing, turning over, a hoof kicking up a small spray of dirt and a wing pinned awkwardly at her side. Her horn dug into the dirt. Her cheeks flushed at the sound of low chuckling from the raven-gryphon. "You're adorable when you're trying to be subtle."

Galaxy stood, frowned at Bifrost as the raven-gryphon stretched. "You were awake before me."

"Yes, your highness."

"And you just . . . let me make a public fool of myself."

"I mean, there's nobody here but us trees, but . . . yes, your highness."

"And you . . . realize I just really want to kick you right now, right?"

Bifrost grinned and stood, shook her wings before fixing an askew feather from Galaxy's crest. "Yes, your highness."

Galaxy opened and clacked her beak closed twice, strangling her brain for any more questions to ask. None came and she sighed, pressed her head to Bifrost's chest, defeated. The raven-gryphon really was an excellent pillow.

Bifrost's wings came around to hold Galaxy close, and for a moment the pair stood there in the heart of the palace garden, alone as they had been beside the Elderpine moon pond at their first meeting, a lifetime ago.

"It's time," spoke Owain from the edge of the clearing.

Galaxy had heard his coming hooves in the underbrush and did not startle, only sighed again and pulled away to look toward him. "Yeah, it is."

***

None of them had an appetite, Galaxy least of all, but still they ate what breakfast they could. In the armory, Galaxy watched via mirror as sparrow-gryphon attendants helped her into her black armor, the weight of each plate of hardened, enchanted steel familiar and welcome. Some advisor or other of Gwendolyn's insisted Galaxy try for an enchanted prosthetic to replace her lost limb, but Galaxy carefully shut him down. She felt more used to the disability now, and trying to fix it then, so suddenly and so close to the most important hour of her life, of all their lives, seemed like it was daring for something to go wrong.

"Today," she said, more to herself than to anyone else, "is not the day to tempt fate."

They assembled, to Galaxy's quiet amusement, in the palace garden, in the clearing before the statue of the Burning King. Herself; Owain; Bifrost; Captain Hywel; Bevin's owl-gryphon compatriot in the Gateway conspiracy investigation, Souma; and some distance away, watching from the statue's side, Carina.

"We all know the plan," said Galaxy, as beside her Bifrost ran through a final check on her satchels and the frozen blasting spells stuffed within. "We're only going to have one shot at this. Captain Hywel, do you have Mordred's frozen teleport spell?"

The Elk captain magically levitated the crystal out of one of his satchels in answer, wincing as he did. Everyone there winced along with him. The spell, a blood-red crystal shimmering with a harsh inner light, looked angry. If Galaxy did not see it before her with her own eyes, she wouldn't think spells even could express emotions. More worrisome was the way the grass smoked and hissed when Hywel set the frozen spell on the ground.

"Right," Galaxy continued, returning her gaze to the others in her rough circle. "We use that to teleport past all of Hiraeth Arian's outer defenses and into the fortress itself. From there, under cover of Elk invisibility illusions and with the guidance of memories from Sir Bevin, we make our way to the Grand Harmonium. We set the blasting spells at key structural stress points within the weapon. After they are all set, I send a magic charge to detonate them all at once. With the Imperial defenders in disarray, Gateway soldiers will fly in to seize the fortress."

"After which," added Hywel, "we can contact Queen Gwendolyn and King Vigdis and tell them to end their battles in Gryphonbough. Empress Nova would have to be mad not to listen to our demands for a surrender after all this."

"You'd be surprised how mad she truly is," said Owain. The lone unicorn's gaze was away to the east, his ears twitching his nervousness. "Our one shot is still terrible . . ."

Galaxy watched her old friend for a moment, recognizing the look of longing and worry in his eyes. She felt it herself. She sighed and reached a wing out to his shoulder, slowly drawing his attention to her. "I know," she said. "I wish Brynjar and Bevin had gotten back in time for this too. But they didn't, and we can only hope that whatever's keeping them is important. I'm sure it is."

"We still should have heard something from them by now though, right?" asked Owain, his voice all doubt. "Personal communication crystals can't reach across such vast distances, but we surely should've heard something, found some way . . ."

"And now you know how I felt the last month and change while you were enjoying your Avalon vacation," joked Galaxy, trying to lighten the mood. And though Owain did snort in amusement and toss his mane, his gaze remained dark as he returned his attention to their planning.

"Alright, okay," he said, "I suppose if worst comes to worst, Brynjar and Bevin are at least as far from the Empire as you can physically get."

A quick laugh was shared around the group at this observation—

"There is nothing to be afraid of, my friends."

Against her better nature, a shiver ran down Galaxy's spine and killed her tense laughter. She looked over with distaste as Carina sauntered over to their small group. Galaxy didn't want to dislike the raven-gryphon, despite their previous acidic encounters and Bevin's suspicions. Galaxy had hoped the seer was there to see her sister off and wish them good luck. It seemed not.

"It is the will of the Burning King that this war be ended," continued Carina, stopping before them. Her attention through the blindfold was reserved solely for Galaxy. "You have surpassed horrors and wonders to stand here now, with the tools that you have. Today is your day. So I have been shown. Have faith."

The seconds passed before anyone spoke. "I feel more confident already," joked Bifrost, voice sounding tight to Galaxy. "Wish us luck, sis. See you soon."

Carina glanced at Bifrost, her easy smile turning strained. "Yes, of course. I'll see you soon, victorious and safe."

From there came the plunge. Galaxy stretched her wings across Owain's and Captain Hywel's backs. Across from her, Bifrost did the same across Souma and Owain from the other side so her wingtips brushed Galaxy's. Mordred's frozen teleport spell shone in her talons, old and fragile. Galaxy barely tightened her talons and the crystal cracked. Magic flooded out, washing over them in a furious scream. Galaxy closed her eyes to the blinding flash of light—

The wind and the cool grass disappeared, the distant song of the city silenced. In their place, Galaxy felt stone beneath her, heard the building-lightning hum of machinery and the deeper, bone-quivering crackle of layered enchantments. She opened her eyes to darkness, panicked for a heartbeat before thinking to light her horn with magic. Owain and Hywel followed her lead. They found themselves in a large room, large enough the far corners remained in shadow despite the magic light of their horns. Wood boxes were stacked high and far along one wall Galaxy could see, with all the rest a dull, smooth grey stone. It reminded her, horribly, of the ancient and abandoned Wolf-Lord bunker she and her companions found Ashe the dragon hiding away in.

"This is hardly what I was expecting," said Owain.

"You said the teleport spell was meant to bring the dragon here," said Hywel, turning and daring a few paces from the group to look around. "The dragon never came, so they left the room alone. I feel a lot of magic in these walls, though. Enchantments to reinforce them. Perhaps the whole fortress is like this."

"Either way, there's got to be a door," said Galaxy, joining the search. Before too long, the red light of her horn illuminated a long stretch of clear glass in place of wall. At the far end of this, she found a solid steel door inscribed with runes of enchantment.

"Here, everyone form up. Hywel, keep the illusion spells ready."

As they regrouped, Galaxy mulled over the source of her disquiet. She glanced over as Owain sidled up beside her, Owain meeting her gaze and nodding. "I was expecting some resistance from the start."

"Me too."

"The halls beyond are abandoned as well," said Souma.

The group stood in silence for several long seconds, uncertain. Then Galaxy growled and shook her head, igniting her horn with fiercer magic. "We're wasting time."

Enchantments collapsed and the door yielded to her magic. As she entered the corridor beyond at the head of her group, she felt a flicker of magic overhead. Enchanted lighting crystals lining the upper walls flickered to life up and down the corridor and each connecting room Galaxy could see. Hywel startled at the sudden flood of light from all around, but Galaxy quickly raised a wing to signal for them to still. More seconds passed and the long, white-walled hallway did not flood with Imperial soldiers, nor did any alarm start blaring.

There was only the harsh white spell-light and the increasingly-noticeable stench of decay and the dead.

"Motion-activated lighting spells," said Galaxy, breathing a sigh of relief. "I remember these from Bevin's memories now. It's to conserve power during stretches of inactivity. Nothing to worry about. Come on, this way."

They moved quickly from there on, barely pausing long enough at each room they passed to check for unicorns, traps, or worse. Down long corridors and branching paths they hurried, a feeling in the back of Galaxy's thoughts, small but growing, that they were running out of time.

After a minute, they reached one of a number of magic-drawn lifts in the fortress, Galaxy following Bevin's memories to call the lift to them. The seconds passed as they waited, Galaxy glancing around to keep the rest of her party in sight. Owain, Bifrost, and Hywel clung close, almost comically so, their heads on swivels as they kept a similar lookout. Souma was some ways farther off, curiosity drawn to a nearby glass wall. Galaxy could vaguely understand his curiosity. It was the first such observation window since their arrival—

"Oh God," said Souma, every head in the group snapping toward him at the muttering. "Everyone, come see this."

Galaxy hurried over, stumbled to a shocked stop as she caught sight through the glass of what had her ally so rattled. Dead bodies hung by heavy hooks. More corpses than she cared to count, perhaps hundreds by the look of things. Some were unicorns. Some were gryphons. Some, rarer, were sphinxes or minotaurs. Some were ancient, withered and dry. Others were fresh, the blood still gleaming from wounds which looked like they could have been inflicted that very morning.

"Storage," said Galaxy, drawing all attention to her. "Lord Mordred's storage for her necromancy. She could have fielded an army from here."

"I guess she had to store them somewhere," said Bifrost, gaze returning to the view through the glass. "I guess the Empire was happy to forget this floor even existed. But God above save us, you'd think they'd want to get rid of the bodies . . ."

". . . no," Galaxy answered, forcing herself to look away from the horror, back to the lift. It had arrived while they were gawking and now waited for them. "You forget. Lord Beauty, too, is a necromancer. Now SHE could field herself armies."

Bevin's memories took them up a dozen floors from the warehouse of the dead. Two unicorns stood waiting for the lift as it came to the floor Galaxy's group needed.

Galaxy flinched back, almost casting a spell to blast the pair away before feeling Hywel's invisibility spell cast over the group.

"Huh," said one of the unicorn soldiers, looking the seemingly-empty lift up and down before turning to his companion. "That sure took its time getting here."

"And so, we see the need for proper and steady maintenance," said the other soldier, boarding the lift. Galaxy carefully squeezed by him as he passed, turning to make sure they were all off as the first soldier joined him. "Everything's been falling to pieces since Mordred died and those foreign wolves began poking their noses around the place. Give me the creeps, no knowing what they're whispering to each other in their weird, foreign tongues."

"Whatever." The first unicorn soldier's horn glowed as he activated the rune combination for the floor they wanted. As the lift rose out of sight, Galaxy barely caught him start to ask "Hey, you ever wonder why—"

"Close call," Bifrost barely breathed out beside Galaxy. She nodded, turned, and continued on. The memories Bevin had shared gave her a basic idea of Hiraeth Arian's layout, from the outer wall defenses and air-yacht landing platforms to the inner core of the fortress, down where it delved into the mountain itself, an eternal mine and underground gardens utilizing old

Wolf-Lord techniques to render the late Mordred's seat of power wholly self-sufficient in case of siege. Galaxy could lead them to the fortress's command center, the hub from which all enchantments and wards were controlled and maintained. She could lead them to the mess hall, or the multitude of armories, or to the late Lord Mordred's personal quarters.

With some difficulty. It had been impossible to plot the most direct route to the Grand Harmonium before the mission began, for they had no way of knowing where exactly in the fortress Lord Mordred's teleport spell would send them. Filling Galaxy's brain too deeply, too thoroughly, with picture-perfect Bevin memories of Hiraeth Arian could have caused brain damage, or worse, an altering of Galaxy's personality.

"And believe it or not," said the gold-maned unicorn, loosing a whinny of amusement, "the world doesn't need two Bevins."

They passed five patrols of varying sizes as they made their wandering approach to the connection point. Each time, their group pressed against the walls to let the Imperial soldiers pass, knowing well how the illusion spells they were under did not hide sound. They fought only once, when a trio of soldiers stepped out of a room right as Galaxy's group passed by the door, knocking into Souma before anyone could react. Swords, talons, and horns did the bloody work quietly, without an alarm raised. A spell to banish away the bodies, another to hide the blood, and they continued on.

Not much later, they came to a corridor shorter than those before, culminating in another heavy steel door emblazoned with two crossed unicorn horns. Galaxy quickened her pace, wings flapping at her sides. "This way!" she dared to call out. "We can cut through the northern hydroponics garden and be there in just two more hall—"

Then Galaxy stopped. She barely noticed as the others behind her staggered to not run into her, barely noticed anything beyond the strange looping sensation inside her head. Her eyes turned, her head following, drawn like a magnet to another heavily secured door at the end of a clean, brightly lit branch in the corridor.

"Gal?" asked Bifrost from beside her. "Something wrong?"

Galaxy didn't know. The door held no markings, no runes, no signs or warnings. Even so, Galaxy drew near and knew a dread unmatched by any other in her life. It felt like her shadows lay beyond the door.

"Gal?" tried Owain next, somewhere close and yet far away. "Gal, you still with us? Are Bevin's memories failing?"

"No," said Galaxy. She couldn't say more. Her throat had closed and refused to open for more than mere breath. As she went, unseen tendrils of magic hanging from the ceiling caught on her like spider webs, each one burning for the briefest moment, each one—GO AWAY, GO, BE GONE—yelling in her head for her to turn and resume the gallop for the Grand Harmonium, all in an unfamiliar voice.

The door was not locked. It slid into the wall and out of the way with the barest pressing of Galaxy's magic. She entered the unknown room beyond, made it only a few feet before stopping, the breath driven from her. Behind, she felt Owain and Bifrost start to come in after her and then stop, crying out in horror of the scene.

It was a large room, lit in harsh whites from all sides so no shadows could be found. In widely-spaced rows from one end of the laboratory to the other stood tubes of crystal and glass. Inside of each tube, floating in liquids Galaxy could not begin to guess at, were dozens of . . . creatures.

Hobbling forward on numb legs, wings dragging at her sides and jaw slack, Galaxy passed from one row to another, taking in the horror of the creatures around her. She could not bring herself to call any of them hippogryphs, each uniquely malformed and mercifully dead. In one tube, a creature floated with the body and head of a unicorn, but each limb was an oversized, featherless wing. In another tube, a creature torn between gryphon and unicorn, no limbs at all but the wings on its back, its beak curving horridly to the side like a spiraling horn of alicorn. And in another tube, a shapeless creature with two heads, one gryphon and one unicorn, both limp in their preservative fluids and both with mouths open as if screaming.

Galaxy heard the sound of Souma retching behind her. Bifrost swiftly joined in. Owain came up beside her, pausing as she stopped in front of a tube, no more or less horrific than any of the others. The creature inside ALMOST looked like an older Galaxy, ALMOST, but it lacked hindlegs and its talons were alicorn horns sprouting from stunted forelegs.

"Gal . . ."

"What is all this?" asked Galaxy, looking from the horror to her friend. She thought her voice was calm and controlled, but at the sight of the unicorn flinching away she laughed, barked out "What is this!? WHAT IS ALL THIS!?"

The nearest tube cracked. Owain backed away to the rest of the group. Galaxy watched him go, felt an anguish like she had never imagined burn her from the inside out, wanted to scream.

But their eyes were not on her anymore. They stared past her. Galaxy turned, her heart stopping at the sight of the unicorn standing at the far end of Galaxy's row and watching her. Galaxy knew this unicorn . . .

Before her stood the Dream Unicorn, towering above her, his snowy coat blinding in the gully's gloom, his storm-grey mane and tail lashing with lightning. His silver horn shone with might. His star gaze struck Galaxy with the most horrible contempt.

The unicorn before Galaxy now was a mare, and her eyes were carefully carved star sapphires, but in all other respects it was the unicorn from her visions and nightmares, before her at last and in the flesh.

"Lord Beauty," said Owain.

Galaxy readied a shield spell, certain in the next moment a shout for the guards, or a blast of powerful magic, or even a crude charge at them with lowered horn. But Lord Beauty only looked away, to the cracked tube and the fluids slowly beading along the crack. "A shame about this one," she said, her tone wistful as if discussing a soup gone wrong instead of an abomination against nature. "She was almost viable. Close enough, at least, to be worth harvesting for the next try."

Galaxy groaned in a mute, stomach-churning horror. She couldn't stop herself. Looking into the clear glass of the tube, she couldn't see anything close to 'viable' in the loose collection of . . . parts, on display. "Was she conscious?" she asked, looking back at Lord Beauty. "Were any of them?"

Lord Beauty looked at Galaxy, tossing her mane in a unicorn shrug. "They were meat, Gal. But even meat will scream if it can breathe."

The horror was too much. Galaxy wanted to banish the moment away to the deepest recesses of her nightmares. Unable to, she began to pace along the rows, circling Lord Beauty, barely holding herself back for the right opening to attack. "Don't you dare talk to me with such familiarity. You're a monster."

"But we are so familiar, aren't we, Gal?" The gem-eyed unicorn remained in place, turning her head to keep Galaxy within sight. "Certainly I have become plenty familiar with you over the course of my experiments. I know you better than you know yourself, body and mind. Your contributions to the peace efforts are greatly appreciated."

Galaxy stopped. A new anger was born by the unicorn's cryptic remarks, bursting through the wariness and fear which had been at the forefront of her thoughts so far. "What contributions? What are you talking about? What IS all this!?"

"Gal, stop!" cried Bifrost. The raven-gryphon started toward Galaxy, stopped as Lord Beauty looked her way. "Just take her down! She's only trying to distract us from the Grand Harmonium!"

"Oh? Am I?" Lord Beauty glanced aside, toward the door they first came through. "I thought we were having a lovely discussion on the latest advances in genetic engineering, but if you're all really in that much of a rush, who am I to stop you? I'm sure none of you mind all these . . . unanswered questions."

Galaxy warred with herself. She wanted to stay. She wanted to fight Lord Beauty, demand answers for who she was, for why she'd wanted the late Lord Mordred's body, for all the horrors in the lab around them.

"Gal," Owain started, getting no further. The room began to shake, a low but rising rumble in the air. Barely on the edge of hearing at first, but then it rose, building and building until it was a thunderous, rolling BOOM crashing over them from all directions. More of the surrounding preservation tubes cracked. The lighting crystals overhead flickered, hissed and spat their wavering power supply. The walls began to warp, the metal twisting as if rent apart by massive forces on the other side.

"Gal!" Owain cried, struggling to keep steady on his hooves. "What is this?"

Galaxy didn't know. Overhead, a light crystal burst, showering the small group with shards of smoking, blackened crystal. A titanic crush of noise shattered the scene, Galaxy reminded horribly of the collapse of Grimhilt's Folly in the Elderpine Forest, as loud as a hundred dragons roaring, a screech of metal tearing and stone shattering. The floor heaved beneath them, rising for a slow second in the direction of the Grand Harmonium, then falling into crumbling ruin, as if something had briefly pulled on the fortress itself before letting go. The shaking ended and only the head-crushing rumbling remained, even this gradually growing more bearable.

"That was dramatic," said Lord Beauty, sounding close to laughter. "Maybe someone got to Nova's pet project before you?"

The remark sent a bolt of fresh fear through Galaxy. Fear as nonsensical as it was all-consuming. Galaxy took wing and sped back to the corridor, ignoring Owain and Bifrost's shouts for her to wait and think. She blasted the door aside with a spell, found the corridors darkened and twisted at a strange angle. The doors at the far end hung askew, the next corridor awash with sparks raining from shattered lighting crystals, the walls half-collapsed, splintering fissures running through the floor. Galaxy ducked beneath a mass of twisted grating and spitting wires from the ceiling—

—and then stopped against a cold, snow-flecked breeze. She stared ahead, stunned. The whole of the far wall was gone, taking the last few yards of the corridor and much of the connecting rooms along with it. Beyond, Galaxy saw a dark, cloud-shrouded sky, snowfall tossed about by harsh mountain winds.

Even as Owain and the rest of her group neared from behind, calling for her, Galaxy flew ahead again, out through the fortress's outer wall and into open sky. The mountaintop was littered with stone and metal debris. For one desperate, dizzying second, Galaxy thought Lord Beauty told true and some unknown third party had destroyed the Grand Harmonium for them.

Then she registered the debris still falling and slowly looked up. She saw at last in person the dark tower of the Grand Harmonium, hovering high in the sky like an Imperial warship angled to face downward. It was a tall craft, taller than Galaxy had expected or imagined, rough black armor plating all across the outside like the shell of some long and horrid flying insect. From its bottom hung four angled spires, magic arcing between them, and distantly, Galaxy could see matching spires at the top of the weapon.

Owain's hooves clattered to a stop at the corridor's edge behind Galaxy. "Merciful Toqeph, it flies. Of course it flies. What good is a stationary super weapon?"

A second sound caught Galaxy's attention, higher-pitched than the deep roar of the Grand Harmonium's flight spells. As the second hum rose higher and higher in intensity, it became accompanied by the creaks and groans of metal under terrible stress. Then came the stench of cooking air like before a lightning strike, and the ferocity of the wind grew, grew. Galaxy realized what was happening a moment too late, getting out a fractured "No!" before the whole of the floating weapon disappeared in the crash and flash of a mass teleport spell.

Above them, the unobstructed stormy sky and falling snow once more.

"Where did it go?" asked Owain, his voice a mere trembling whisper after all they had witnessed.

Bifrost's voice mirrored Owain's. "The sheer magical power needed to move and teleport something that big . . ."

Galaxy swallowed and turned. She flew back into Hiraeth Arian, ignoring her companions. She flew back to the laboratory, found Souma the owl-gryphon and the Elk captains Hywel and Ithel still there, as well as, more importantly, Lord Beauty. "You. You monster. Where did it go?"

"She's been talking, your highness," said Souma, trembling where he leaned against a wall. "She's been telling us horrible things. Things we never needed to know, never wanted to know."

"Well now she can talk to me," said Galaxy. Her horn shone, a shield spell springing to life with sharp edge against Lord Beauty's throat. "Where did the Grand Harmonium go!? I will ask only one more time, and you best start answering because fighting Lord Mordred has given a GREAT imagination for inflicting pain!"

"Good Lord," said Lord Beauty, looking down at Galaxy with an expression of honest admiration. "A lesser mare would be trembling in fright right now. Lord Thoth would be screaming. You truly are at wit's end, aren't you? You had this whole thing planned out, victory was so close you could practically taste it, and now it's all slipping away like the last seconds before Armageddon."

Galaxy tightened her beak until it hurt, pressed the shield edge harder against the unicorn's throat, watched the skin press in, split, droplets of blood beading beneath the fur. "Where did it go?"

"If you want to know," said Lord Beauty, lifting a foreleg up, "I can take you right now."

Galaxy looked down at the offered leg and the possibilities promised. She looked aside to Owain and Bifrost at the laboratory door, neither looking quite sure what was going on anymore. She thought of how much she loved them both, and Brynjar, and Bevin, weighed all the danger she had ever dragged them into against all the danger she had ever saved them from. The danger she could save them from.

"Owain," said Galaxy, reaching her decision. "Get them back safe to Gateway. Get Gateway prepared for whatever's coming. I love you all."

She saw it, the realization sweeping the room. Owain began to shout for her. Bifrost spread her wings to fly to her. Galaxy did not give them the chance, dropping the shield spell and grabbing Lord Beauty's leg in her talons.

Crack-BOOM.

CHAPTER TWENTY

Before anything else, Galaxy felt the weight of an incredible magic pressing upon her, a magic with an almost physical, tangible presence to it. She let go of Lord Beauty and hobbled back a pace, keeping herself standing with a rush of her own magic as a counterforce.

The room around Galaxy now was a near-perfect copy of the Imperial throne room Brynjar and Owain had shared in their memories of their encounter with Empress Nova, though the steel-webbed window ran all along the outer wall rather than loom only behind the throne. The sky revealed outside was dark and stormy, wracked by lightning. At the throne room's center stood a pedestal roughly throat-level to Galaxy. Atop the pedestal sat a black orb shot through with veins of white lightning.

Near to the pedestal stood a large metal tube, large enough to hold Brynjar and smooth all around but for a small, blacked-out glass window on the surface facing Galaxy.

"The hippogryph. At last, we meet."

Though wary of putting her back to Lord Beauty, Galaxy turned to face the voice. There she saw the dais throne, and upon the throne, a white unicorn mare all covered in cracks, as if her body were as hard and brittle as alicorn and breaking apart with age. Yet no age shone from the mare's glowing red eyes, only glee and a loathsome admiration of power.

"Empress Nova," said Galaxy, backing away and to the side to keep both of the mares in sight. "This is a meeting I've been wanting for a long while. Not how I expected it to happen."

"That is a shame," spoke the Empress, standing from her dais and carefully stepping off. She stumbled as the leg splintered beneath her, the limb reassembling to Galaxy's horror as she continued walking. "For this is exactly as I have hoped for. Have longed for. You bowing before me, a trusted Lord of the Empire at my side, and all the world within my grasp. Yes, today is beautiful."

Galaxy narrowed her eyes and puffed out her chest. "You're delusional, 'your majesty'. I will never bow to you. I'm too powerful for you to make me bow. Even better is how, for all your power, you are literally falling to pieces in front of me."

Empress Nova paused in her slow trudge toward the pedestal as if to ponder Galaxy's point, nodding and continuing on after a brief moment. "True. Surviving the wrath of the dragons after the foolish assault on their hoards centuries ago, and the resulting delvings into the deepest magics to make sure this never happened again, has left me scarred and broken in body, and the longer this physical form is away from the rejuvenating lands of Avalon, the worse it will become. Soon, if I do nothing, I will die my last death."

Empress Nova reached the pedestal and looked from Galaxy to Lord Beauty, broken snout forming into something like a smile. "Thankfully, we can do something, can't we, oldest and most treasured friend?"

Lord Beauty answered with a flicker of magic from her horn. Galaxy startled back as the orb atop the pedestal lit up, a bolt of energy stabbing forth from it and into Empress Nova's throat. A scream echoed through the throne room. Galaxy watched, confused, horrified, mesmerized, as the albino mare's body turned to stone before her eyes, the stone spreading through the Empress with a horrid slowness as every ounce of her titanic personal magic was drained away. Her neck cracked afresh as she turned her head to look at Galaxy, red eyes burning in the last few moments before unseeing stone overtook them.

Then it was done. A tall statue of a unicorn mare stood where Empress Nova had once been, menacing in its own way but unbalanced and fragile. Even as Galaxy watched, the statue tilted over from its uneven pose, fell, its head and front legs shattering as it hit the floor.

Even before the final echoes of this crash had died away, Galaxy noticed the swirling, near-blinding white light of Empress Nova's stolen magic already fading from the central orb. It was draining away, dancing across the floor in thin bolts toward and into the metal container. In a sudden crash of perception, she understood, every piece of the puzzle slotting into place. "No!"

Rising into a hover, Galaxy loosed a blasting spell at the container. A shield spell from Lord Beauty blocked it. The unicorn danced forward and under Galaxy's next attack, a cutting spell sent in the storm-maned mare's direction, Beauty's next shield spell knocking Galaxy back and into the nearest wall.

Distantly, Galaxy noticed the faint sounds of battle outside. She shook her head and gathered her wits, firing off a pair of rusting spells, one at the container and one at the pedestal holding the control orb. Yet her follow-up charge was halted as she beheld Lord Beauty block one of the attacks with a shield spell and the other with her own body. "No. That shouldn't—"

"Be possible?" offered Lord Beauty, muzzle pulling up in a grin as she stalked forward. Aside from the thick, discolored blood now dribbling from between her teeth, the mare seemed unharmed. "Fool. Utter fool. A spell like that could never harm me. I MADE that spell. I made ALL spells. All your pitiful grasps for power spring forth from ME!"

At the heart of the throne room, shield spell clashed against shield spell, Galaxy's red versus Lord Beauty's glittering silver. Sparks of magic cascaded all around them, the floor scorching, the glass of the windows cracking.

The unicorn buckled beneath the struggle. Galaxy pressed her advantage, trading the shield spell out for a blasting spell which sent Lord Beauty tumbling backward. The mare struggled on her back a moment, legs kicking frantically before she managed to squirm around into righting herself. Right as she stood again, Galaxy flew in, turned in mid-air, kicked her muzzle with both rear hooves.

"Gah!"

Lord Beauty staggered. Galaxy grabbed her in her magic, spun, threw her into the far window. Metal bent and glass cracked from the impact.

"GAHH!"

As the unicorn fell, Galaxy turned back to the container, heart dropping as she saw the orb was almost empty of the stolen magic. She ignited her horn for the strongest shield spell she could muster, intent on utterly destroying the container and whatever waited within.

Conjured chains snagged around her neck and yanked her back. She gagged at the tight hold on her throat. The shield spell fired astray, sped past the container, blew out a hole in the far wall large enough to fit an air-yacht through.

The orb grew completely dark. Galaxy paused mid-turn to launch a freezing spell at Lord Beauty, looked instead to the container as once more Empress Nova's heavy magic swamped the room. Still held tight by Lord Beauty's conjured chains, she watched with bated breath as a seam appeared in the surface of the container, slowly opening and spilling out a billowing rush of oily white fog. "What have you done?"

"I have birthed the war's end," said Lord Beauty, voice betraying none of the battle they had fought mere seconds before. "It was your lost limb which made this all possible. The Waters of Life infuse EVERY piece of you. The balance between unicorn and gryphon took some trial and error, as you saw. Genetic material from

Mordred's body, the mutability of Wolf-Lord matter, served as a stabilizer. The final results . . ."

A shadow appeared within the swirling mists, hovering, slowly lowering. Hooves clicked on the metal floor. Talons clacked. Out of the mists, dispelling them with a flap of her wings, strode a hippogryph. She looked in nearly all respects identical to Galaxy, but freshly made, all her limbs in place, free of the scars and tattered feathers from Galaxy's lifetime of struggles. She was completely white, from the tips of the wings she now sat admiring to the bottoms of her rear hooves. All white but for her eyes, Empress Nova's eyes, red and glowing.

"Look what we have done," said Empress Nova, switching from admiring her wings to watching how the light caught in her talons, the curve of them, the deadly sharpness. "I'm young again. I'm beautiful again. I'm STRONG again!"

All sound fell away. The burst of magic came and knocked Galaxy back, shattering the throne room's windows. Another burst, the air itself crackling with the raw power, tore through the throne room, tearing away the roof and walls with storm-like ferocity. Galaxy felt Lord Beauty's conjured chain drawn away and rooted herself in place with shield spells all around her.

The assault ceased. Galaxy dropped her shields and staggered forward, panting from the exertion. Ahead of her she heard the new Empress Nova walking, saw her approaching the central pedestal and its orb as she talked.

"At last, I am perfected. At last, the glory that has forever been my rightful due is before me. At last, all unicorns and all gryphons, all the world over, shall bow only to ME!"

"No," said Galaxy. She pushed aside her fear and marched forward, horn ignited for her next spell as she eyed the former unicorn. "Not yet. I'm not letting this go any further. I will destroy the Grand Harmonium with my magic alone if I have to, but I'm not letting you near a single gryphon to Harmonize."

"Not letting me near . . ." The white hippogryph repeated herself a moment, then chuckled, the chuckles growing into full-bellied laughter, setting Galaxy's nerves on edge. "Not letting me near . . . young fool, have you been so distracted as to not look around you even once? Do you not see where we are and realize the true depths of your failure?"

Galaxy stared, not comprehending for a moment. Then she looked away from Empress Nova to the world now revealed beyond the ruined Harmonium throne room. A battle raged all around. Gryphons, thousands of them, flew through the dark and storm-ridden skies in desperate struggle against four Imperial warships and their accompanying swarms of air-yachts and crystal drones, magic bolts and firebombs filling the air with blistering light and heat.

"No." Galaxy tried to run, tripped, took air, flew to the edge of the throne room to look down. Her heart stopped, no breath coming as she beheld the distant forms of Elk on the ground many hundreds of feet below, fighting their own pitched fight against unicorn ground forces. "No!"

Vigdis and Gwendolyn's attack to liberate Gryphonbough.

"Young fool," spoke Empress Nova from behind Galaxy, voice full of utter contempt. "At last, you understand. There was no hope for you and your people's pitiful resistance. Every attack has been foreseen, every struggle planned for. The Avalon Empire, MY Empire, will take EVERYTHING YOU LOVE AND RULE OVER IT FOREVER!"

"NEVER!" Galaxy screamed as she turned, no thought for spell or craft as she loosed a blast of raw magic from her horn straight for the other hippogryph. Empress Nova stood her ground and countered with her own blast of magic. The blasts met, pushed against the other, magic scattering in the blowback. For a moment each attack held in perfect balance—

A sudden, wet SHLUNK resounded through the throne room and Galaxy shuddered. Her magic cut off, Empress Nova's following suit soon after, Galaxy only dimly noticing as a deep, wet pain blossomed inside her. She coughed and tasted blood thick in her beak, thick in her throat. She looked over as Lord Beauty pulled free of Galaxy's left side, the unicorn's horn gleaming red from tip to root.

Galaxy coughed again, the blood thicker in her throat now, choking. She struggled to get a breath in as she staggered, fell, left wing pressing futilely against her stab wound as white coat stained red. She tried to concentrate, to summon her magic to heal herself—

A conjured chain from Empress Nova lashed out, striking Galaxy's head. The bare magic she had gathered for a healing spell scattered from the strike.

Nova struck again. Again. Reared back with wings spread, chain lifting high, Galaxy barely able to see her through blurry and dimming vision. "And now, the end! The last gasp of gryphon song! And as you die, so ends the final act in your pitiful story of rebellion!"

The chain swung down. Galaxy, dazed and bleeding, watched it come, managing a last thought for Brynjar and Owain, for Sascha and Siegfried, for Bevin . . .

Bevin . . .

Yet at the last second, Empress Nova stopped her attack short and leapt back, a massive sword swinging through where her head had been moments before. And suddenly Vigdis was there, wings flared, dauntless Cortana shining true with each swing as the towering condor-gryphon forced Empress Nova and Lord Beauty back. "Gal! Get out of here! Now!"

"Nu . . . no, I can . . . can heal . . ." The Waters of Life. Galaxy blinked, head heavy and body cold as she tried to concentrate. All she needed to do was call on the Waters of Life—

Ahead, Beauty stabbed Vidgis the same as she had Galaxy. Vigdis grunted but kept his footing, switching to hold his sword with one set of talons while the other reached down to grip Beauty's neck and squeeze. His head craned back, eyes catching Galaxy's with their desperation. "Gal, go! Now!"

Galaxy's magic wavered, her sight of the pitched battle growing black around the edges. Her body was freezing. Distantly, she felt a magic, half-familiar. Unthinking, she reached out to it with her own magic, her last sensation a feeling of vertigo as the last darkness closed in all around.

"Bevin."

CHAPTER TWENTY-ONE

The battle was lost. Lost the moment the Grand Harmonium appeared over the battlefield, hardening the Imperial resolve, heightening their ferocity.

On the ground, new foes had joined in the battle, fresh and relentless. Wolf-Lords in the hundreds, returned to Heraldale from distant lands of exile in bright and terrible armor, stormed across the battlefield, scattering their foes upon black spears from which blistering spell bolts flew. Upon their banners and cuirasses, they bore the white rose, the sigil of Morgana le Fay, and with their aid, the unicorns pushed forward and the Elk fell back. It was a hard, slow, bloody retreat. Gwendolyn, keeping to the thickest of the fighting, made the unicorns and wolves bleed for every inch, every foot, every yard of ground they forced the Elk host back. The air boiled with screams and smoke, the ground churned to mud and littered with bodies.

Gwendolyn screamed as she fought. There was no time for deliberate thought, no space. Unicorn soldiers came at her and she blocked with shield spells, stabbed and slashed with her spear, battered with her hooves, parried and gouged with her horns. Blood and the smoke of ozone hung heavy on her tongue. A hundred gashes and dents ranged across her tattered armor, the attrition of hours upon hours of fighting. Crystal drones dove at her from overhead as she struck them down with blasting spells, their sharp shards scattering against her, some cutting, some burying in splinter-deep. One lucky stallion caught her face with his horn, tore her eyepatch away. The blood poured freely.

From behind, calls for a full retreat, for the Elk to turn and flee, to teleport back to Gateway. Gwendolyn bellowed for her people to hold. They needed only to hold for Galaxy and the rest . . .

Then a lull came over Gwen's surroundings. The battle parted around her, an eye in the storm. At a sudden urge, Gwen looked up. Her breath stole from her.

Before and above her floated Morgana le Fay. In dark robes and silver armor, and a heavy antlered helm, she looked as if the hidden mural in Gateway had suddenly sprung to life.

"Queen Gwendolyn," spoke the subtly glowing figure, silver fires trailing from her clawed hands as she gestured to the carnage all around. "Take your people and flee. Abandon this war. Join me far away in safety. Why fight? The unicorns and the Wolf-Lords are your brethren. Stand with them. Find peace."

Gwen nearly fell prostrate. Her legs trembled with the urge, her vision blurring as her eyes filled with tears.

"Come to me, my eternal bairns," said Morgana le Fay, smiling, star sapphire eyes shining bright as she gestured Gwen forward. "Come to me. Remember how I made your kind in ancient times. Gifted you magic, gifted you civilization. Come to me. Leave all else behind and serve me as you were meant to. Forever and ever and ever."

Gwen wept, the tears heavy and hot down her cheeks. She looked around at her people fighting and dying alongside the gryphons, the last companions against Avalon's tyranny. Here was their maker, their god, offering an end to it all, if only Gwen would bow . . .

"It's a risk we must be willing to take," spoke Gwendolyn at last. It was her right to do so. Her troops would most likely be those in greatest danger. "We are too close to ending this war to back away now. We Elk are prepared to do what we must in the name of peace."

Gwen wept and her legs trembled, but she remained standing. "No. You are the old order. We fight for the new. We will not yield."

Morgana's offered hand dropped back to her side. The lips of her muzzle pulled back in a snarl as she began to drift upward and away, her voice a rising crash of thunder. "No. The old order . . . STANDS!"

Like a puppet yanked by its unseen strings, the figure of Morgana le Fay flew away, back toward the Grand Harmonium hovering far away and high overhead. Halfway there the illusion failed, revealing to a startled Gwen the beaten and bloodied form of King Vigdis.

The strings were cut. The puppet fell.

"NO!"

Gwen charged at full gallop, through the nearest unicorn line, bursting past them to nearly fly across the broken fields of Gryphonbough to where she thought the falling gryphon would land. Magic bolts from unicorns ahead and behind grazed unfelt past her. Exhaustion and fear fell behind, horns igniting with all the magic she had left. Once, twice, three times she tried to catch Vigdis, each time managing only to slow the plummeting condor-gryphon.

A final try, a shield spell buckling almost immediately beneath his weight, mere yards above the ground and enough at last to turn the fall non-fatal. Even still he hit the muddy earth with a bone-jarring thud and roll, wings flopping broken and useless beside him.

The next instant, Gwendolyn tripped over him and fell, rolling twice in the muck. A stab of pain, a scream as one front leg twisted wrong.

Gwendolyn lay panting on the ground, head twisted painfully by her horns. She had landed where she could meet Vigdis' eyes where he lay, the condor-gryphon panting for breath, eyes swimming with tears of pain and fear. She saw despair in those eyes.

From somewhere distant, she heard the cry of "CHARGE!"

Gwendolyn could not pull her eyes away from Vigdis'. They each knew and understood, the tears coming fresh again to her eyes. They had hoped in the war's end. They had believed in it, fought for it. But now . . .

Slowly, Gwendolyn stood, nearly falling twice from her broken leg. She hobbled over to the fallen Vigdis, her magic flickering as she tried to help him get back to all fours. But he could not.

From behind, the drumming of many hundreds of hooves. Gwendolyn swallowed and turned, nearly falling again as her broken leg gave out. She saw them, the hordes of fresh Imperial troops thundering across the battlefield toward her and the fallen Vigdis. She looked away briefly, back toward her own people to see the line breaking beneath the wolf-led assault, to see them turning and fleeing along with the scattered gryphons overhead. She nodded, accepting this. A last steadying breath through the pain as she turned to face again the oncoming host. Beside her, Vigdis at last regained his footing, breath weak but gaze unwavering.

Queen Gwendolyn of the Elderpine Forest and King Vigdis of Gateway stood tall together at the end, their heads unbowed, their gazes unfaltering.

And then the swiftest of the unicorns, their horns piercing, their heavy hooves beating, swept over them.

***

Doom stormed through Hiraeth Arian on iron-clad hooves. The straight-edged corridors echoed with bellows and screams, with the clanging drum of hooves, the snap and hiss and crack of spell bolts burning through the air, striking walls, striking shield spells, striking flesh.

Owain jolted as a bolt grazed a front leg. He snarled, dropped his faltering cover for a moment to fire off his own bolt, raised the shield spell again as he watched the unicorn soldier fall away with a burning cough from his smoking throat, the injured knocked aside by the others still in pursuit.

Owain continued backing down the corridor, covering the rear as Hywel led their desperate try for the outer landing pads of the Imperial fortress, their best hope for a weakness in the anti-teleportation wards, for an escape. Between the two spell slingers, Bifrost huffed and grunted, dragging a half-conscious Souma with her, the owl-gryphon still sizzling across his gut and wings from where the spell bolts struck him. Still sizzling, still breathing, but from what Owain could hear over the clamor of battle, not for much longer.

Another spell bolt slipped past Owain's shield. He glimpsed it strike Bifrost in the shoulder, the raven-gryphon squawking in pain, nearly losing her grip on Souma. Pained rainbow eyes rolled, found Owain's gaze, were full of pain and mounting panic. "Faster!" she panted. "Hywel, God, faster!"

"I'm trying!" the Elk shouted back. He spun to fire off three bolts past Owain's shield to down another soldier, before turning and half-galloping for a turn in the corridor. "I'm only half-guessing which way to go, I don't—oh crap, stop—"

Owain turned to see, nearly tripped over Souma. He saw past Bifrost as the Elk skid to a halt and raised a shield spell, barely in time to stop a volley of bolts from perforating his whole front. One slipped through and took off the top half-inch of his right ear. Hywel screamed, stumbling legs sending him reeling against the wall behind him. The bolts continued to come, pummeling his shield spell.

More shouts back the way they came, more soldiers. Owain focused on them, his backwards retreat down the corridor ceasing as a grim certainty filled him. He heard Souma grunt, then felt Bifrost stood beside him, the raven-gryphon unslinging a crossbow from her back and immediately putting down one of the soldiers advancing on them. As she did, she loosed a swear Owain knew Galaxy must have taught, by its inventiveness alone.

God, he was going to miss Gal. He was going to miss Brynjar. He was even going to miss Bevin. "It's been an honor, Sir Bifrost."

"Likewise, Sir Owain." Bifrost loosed another bolt, but rather than reload, she paused, then dropped her crossbow. Owain looked over, watched her dig around in the pack at her side a moment before bringing out the frozen blasting spells originally planned for the Grand Harmonium.

Owain looked from the blasting spells to Bifrost, the raven-gryphon meeting his gaze without flinching. She nodded, slowly. After a moment, Owain swallowed and nodded back, looked again to their foes. Their ranks had been reinforced while Owain looked away, half a dozen back the way they had come, another nine or ten driving Hywel to the floor with their barrage of spells. It was clear to Owain there could be no teleporting their way out and no fighting their way out, which left them only . . .

"To decide the quality of our deaths," Owain whispered. He breathed deeply in and out, did not close his eyes as he reached out and gripped the explosive spells in his magic. The seconds passed and all he could feel was the heat of the spells, waiting for the right pressure from him to set them off and swallow both the small scene of battle and the surrounding hundred feet in a blue-hot inferno. All he could see were Bifrost's eyes watching him, scared but unyielding. All he could hear were the shouts and taunts of the Imperial soldiers, the snap of their spell bolts, his own beating heart, his own rushing blood.

"After the war . . . I guess everything's going to be different. Someone will have to figure out new leadership for Avalon. There'll be no need or want for a unicorn governor over Featheren Valley, but I'd like to stay with you all anyway and help rebuild."

Owain's horn brightened to trigger the spells, but then he paused, ears perking. Confusion ran through the Imperial ranks, then alarm. Owain watched, confused and amazed as the rain of spell bolts at them slowed, then ceased as the soldiers firing them were all cut down from behind.

"Bevin and Brynjar returned?" guessed Bifrost.

For a moment, Owain could see nothing but moving shadows in the smoke of the fallen-silent battle. He dropped his shield spell to keep from wasting any more magic he might need, felt Hywel reluctantly do the same, the Elk muttering strangely breathlessly "What is this? Backup?"

"Maybe," said Bifrost. I don't—"

An Imperial soldier stepped into view. Owain stiffened and nearly fired off a spell bolt at the bay-coated mare, stopped himself at a talon gesture from Bifrost. The moment allowed the mare to step closer, looking as wary as Owain felt. She wore no helm with her barding, her black mane shorn short and stiff. She eyed Owain up and down with an unmistakable awe in her gaze. "Are you, are you . . . Sir Owain? The First Deserter? Please say yes."

Owain shared a quick look with Bifrost. "Ye . . . yes, I am."

At this, the soldier heaved a deep breath and her eyes welled with unshed tears. Owain, startled, thought back to another time not so long ago, to another soldier and another escape.

"I want to go home," the mare, Delma, repeated as she reached the snowy stone ground at ramp's end. Her gaze had gone glazed and distant as she turned away from the scene, stiff steps taking her away back toward the northwest. "I want—"

"Hywel, don't!" snapped Owain, glancing the Elk's way. He found he needn't have bothered, the Elk at the moment fallen on his side, eyes half-glazed as he focused his struggling magic on healing a long and terrible tear across the side of his neck.

"No!" Owain took a step toward the fallen Elk, hesitating to add his own magic into the mix and risk interfering with Hywel's own efforts. At the sound of more hooves in the distance, the soldiers who had come to their aid turning to guard the corridors, Owain looked again to the first mare. "We need to get out of here. We need to get him to the other Elk."

"You can," said the mare. She blinked away her tears, stood tall even as, too close for comfort, sounds of fighting began again through the fortress corridors. "There are more of us. Not many. Others went to disable the wards. Not fully, not for long, but a small group like yours can slip through without harm Go! Hurry!"

Immediately, Bifrost draped one wing over Owain's back, the other falling across Souma and Hywel to bridge them together for the teleport spell. Owain readied his magic to make the jump back to Gateway, then hesitated, looked down the corridor one way and then the other. The sounds of fighting grew, the deserters beginning to fall back already. He looked to the mare. "You're all going to die."

"We're all going to fight," she corrected. "It's the best we can do."

CHAPTER TWENTY-TWO

Bifrost collapsed the moment the Gateway palace roof was beneath her again. She barely perceived her surroundings through the haze of grief and pain, the hurried rush of guards and other onlookers, Owain's shouts for Elk healers to aid in the struggle to save Hywel and Souma, the bitter, ash-smelling rainfall. Again and again, her mind replayed the scene in Lord Beauty's laboratory, the sight of the Grand Harmonium in the air, the sudden and grim resolve of Galaxy. Beneath the repetition was the hurt, the sense of betrayal that Galaxy, though probably with the best of intentions, had not trusted the rest of them, had not trusted HER, Bifrost, to go with her to whatever end awaited.

Beneath the rain, Bifrost let her tears fall.

"What is the meaning of all this!?" demanded High General Shan, the elderly gryphon stumbling in for a landing beside them. "What happened? Where is

Princess Galaxy? Has the Grand Harmonium fallen? Someone, speak!"

"We failed," said Owain, voice distracted and trembling. Hearing it, Bifrost remembered that she was not the only one hurting. "Gal, Gal is gone. Teleported away with uh, with Lord Beauty. Going after . . . Grand Harmonium. I've almost got this bleeding stopped, Hywel, almost there, just hold on. Almost . . ."

"I don't understand," begged Shan. "The Harmonium was gone? Did the frozen teleport spell not take you to it after all? Why would the princess go with Lord—"

"It doesn't matter," said Bifrost, fighting not to break. She forced herself to all fours, one rear leg somewhat dragging as she did, though she held forth a wing to ward off an Elk starting over to help her, nodding him instead to where Owain had moved on from Hywel to the owl-gryphon, Souma. "It doesn't matter how or why," she said again, looking to Shan. "The attack failed and the Grand Harmonium, flying like any Imperial warship and capable of mass teleport spells, could be anywhere in Heraldale. Could even be on its way here, right now. Contact Vigdis and Gwendolyn. They need to call off their attack and get back here at once. The diversion failed."

Shan nodded and turned at once to the nearest soldier at her side. The hawk-gryphon at once took wing, flying for the black obelisk at the center of the palace roof. Clustered there at the base of the black obelisk were six thick rods of iron and crystal, each two yards tall and floating a beak-length off the palace roof. They were the work of tireless enchanters from Gateway, Vogelstadt, and Wedjet, magical explorers who had worked through blood and sweat to recreate even poor facsimiles of the grand teleportation towers the Wolf-Lords of old had once taken for granted.

Yet even as the hawk-gryphon flew, Bifrost saw the teleport spires light up at their peaks. In a moment, the air was filled with the bright flash and deafening crack of teleports, dozens of them, then hundreds. Those already gathered on the roof fell silent as they were joined by more Elk and gryphons, mud-spattered and battle-worn, smelling of smoke and bloodshed, each one wide-eyed and delirious.

Three minutes passed and the retreat to Gateway was finished. Bifrost, having taken to the air to better see the returned host, counted no more than 200 gryphons, perhaps two-thirds that many Elk. The last through turned at once and destroyed the teleport spires, grabbing them in their magics and smashing them to pieces against the palace roof.

"No, no, stop!' cried Bifrost, rushing over, but the deed was already done. She stared down at the ruined spell machines for a long moment, thoughts clicking and clacking like the misaligned gears of a shoddy clock. Then she looked up and around, surveying the gryphons and Elk, her search desperately driven by her mounting fear. "Where is King Vigdis? Where's Queen Gwendolyn?"

The nearest of the gryphons and Elk, those who could hear Bifrost, began to fall beneath the weight of the ashen rain, sobs wracking their bodies. Bifrost continued to turn in her slow circle, heart hammering away in her chest and tremors beginning to strike her as well. "Please," she begged. "Where are Vigdis and Gwen? Someone? Anyone?"

"They're gone."

Bifrost froze, then looked to the voice. High General Odin stood near to the black obelisk, armor scorched and broken, gaze going past Bifrost to nothing. "They're gone."

"No," said Bifrost.

"The Grand Harmonium came upon the battlefield," said Odin. "More terrible than any warship I saw. Lord Beauty was there, and . . . and a white hippogryph. I think it was Empress Nova. Then the battle was lost. My king was . . . lost . . ."

The last of Odin's faltering words were barely to be heard, for a great and terrible wailing of grief began to rise from the hideously reduced host of gryphons and Elk. Some fell to the palace roof to beat their heads against the stone. Some sat shrieking, tearing feathers from their bodies. Some looked with frightening want to the edge of the roof and the long, long drop beyond it.

Bifrost sat. For a moment she tottered on the brink of utter insanity, the immensity of the pain, the grief, the despair all around her and deep within her more than any frayed mind should withstand.

But then, from somewhere near, Owain asked aloud in a shaking voice "But where's Galaxy?"

Suddenly, Bifrost had a patch of mental footing, a thought, a tether to grasp with all her talons, wherever it might lead. She stood again after several tries, turned, and looked to Owain. "I know who to ask."

***

They found Carina in the palace garden, crouched before the statue of the Burning King and with her talons clasped together in prayer. Approaching, Owain snorted as if he had never seen anything so worthy of contempt and disgust. Bifrost, flying to reach her sister first, could not put to word or thought how she felt beyond a growing dismay, a despair at the failure of all hopes and trusts.

Carina looked up at their approach, corners of her beak turned up in a smile at first, the smile faltering almost immediately. "Bifrost? Owain? You are back already? That's not right."

And suddenly, Bifrost could put her feelings into thought, into words, into action. She landed, reared back, and punched her sister across the beak. Carina staggered back, a shocked cry escaping her, and Bifrost advanced, punching her again, then spinning with wings outstretched to knock Carina's legs out from under her. The other raven-gryphon fell onto her back, wings sprawled out, and before she could move, Owain came and stood on Carina's right wing with both front hooves, pinning her to the garden floor.

"That's not right," said Bifrost, echoing her sister's words as she paced in front of the purported seer and prophetess, the Priestess of Fire and all that such titles entailed no matter how Bifrost had tried to ignore or excuse. "That's not right, you said. Why would you say that? What were you expecting to happen? Where were Owain and I SUPPOSED to be?"

"With Princess Galaxy," said Carina, voice for once fearful rather than full of knowing smugness. "In Hiraeth Arian, the smoking ruins of the Grand Harmonium before you. What—"

Owain brought his head down into Carina's face, perilously within reach of her beak if she decided to peck at him in self-defense. "Did you see this? I mean actually, honestly SEE this with whatever you're using for eyes under that blindfold? Did you see it!?"

"I've told you what I've seen!" Carina's head snapped back and forth between Owain and Bifrost, her chest heaving with the start of panic. "I've always told everyone what I've seen, I make no secret of it! A hippogryph bringing the war to an end! A fire priestess guiding the hippogryph to that victory! How much clearer could a vision be, even with Galaxy's claims of another fire priestess in Heraldale?"

Bifrost stopped her pacing, the storm of emotions within her settling into cold disappointment. She fell down beside her sister, every breath a struggle to keep calm and orderly. "Carina . . . ever since that day in the valley, you've been . . . like this. A smug, full-of-herself, blindly trusting fool. And I've tried to tolerate it, because you're my sister, and I love you, and you've never seemed to actually HURT anyone with your prophecies and proclamations. So maybe this is all my fault. But God above damn it all, Carina, where do your visions even come from!? Think about it for just a moment, I beg of you!"

"I don't need to," said Carina without hesitation. Her breathing had calmed, her voice losing its tremor. "I know the source of my life, my power. The Burning King. I know that while you FLED in TERROR, my King gave me a destiny. A grand destiny. So, so YOU get the honorable post as Lady Quetzal's knight and messenger? So, you go out and see the world, and battle, and glory!? So, YOU get the hippogryph's love and favor!? None of it matters because it's MY destiny to save the world, MINE! My King chose ME!"

"Your king chose you for a fool and a tool!" Bifrost screamed.

Silence descended over the palace garden. Guards, drawn to the sounds of arguing, stood watching unheeded. Bifrost's attention remained wholly for Carina below her, gaze hidden beneath bandages but meeting Bifrost's all the same. "No. You don't dare," said the seer.

"The battles were all lost," said Owain, stepping away and off Carina's wing. His voice grew choked, each word a monumental struggle. "King Vigdis is dead. Gwen is dead. Galaxy is . . . is missing."

"You don't dare," Carina repeated. She rolled over onto her belly, stood again on all fours. "You . . . you don't dare."

Bifrost could see now the despair and fear settling over Carina. It was little comfort to know her sister was not a traitor, only a fool. "Empress Nova, through experiments I don't dare imagine, has given herself a hippogryph body. She could Harmonize all of us now.

Lord Beauty is her fire priestess. So, what your Burning King showed you was true, but only by the cruelest measure."

The seconds passed and Carina said nothing, and Bifrost did not reach out a wing to comfort her, Bifrost's own pain still too great. Talons trembling, Carina reached up and tore away her blindfold. Owain whinnied and backed away. "What horror is this!?"

Carina gave no response. The small balls of white flame serving as her eyes stared straight ahead, past the pair of them, past the guards, past the trees of the garden and the city of Gateway, to places Bifrost could not begin to guess. With a flap of her wings, the seer of the Burning King rose above the confines of the garden, turned to the south, and flew, soon gone from all sight. And Bifrost, watching her go, somehow knew with a sinking heart she would never see her sister again.

***

The hours passed and Carina flew. Away from the palace and its mourners. Away from Gateway. Away from Bifrost, who in the end had well and fully proven herself the better of the two, no matter how Carina's pride rebelled.

The hours passed and Carina flew. Over the deep waters of Gateway's surrounding seas, their rare fishing craft and common soldier patrols. Then she reached the land and flew over the black marshes full of snakes and the dead. And past them came the long miles of ash-smothered hills and cliffs, short at first and then growing taller and taller, rising almost into mountains in their own right as they transitioned into the Dragonbacks.

Carina flew and the Dragonback Mountains burned beneath her. All but the most remote patches of ice and snow had melted, and in their place the smoke and ash poured forth to poison the sky. Caves had burst and chasms split wide, drooling rivers of burning lava across the width and breadth of the volcanic mountain range. Carina had to fight the heat of the lava, lest it force her flight upward enough to smother her in the toxic clouds.

The stone was hot beneath her as she landed upon the lip to the crater lake where the Prime Dragon, Kur, had once held domain. The waters of the lake had been steamed away by the volcano waking beneath them, and from the pit wide cracks ran, and from the cracks poured forth a new lake of lava, hissing, spitting, burning the air over it. Fires burned upon the lava surface, flames of strange shades grasping ever for more than rock to engulf.

"What is this," Carina asked, begged the waiting fires. Then, as she felt the magic come to her, she bellowed it louder, demanding. "WHAT IS THISSS!?

"What is this?
To discover my life is a lie
In destiny I found my bliss
Now all about me dies!

"Was I blinded ever by my jealousy
Told I could be truly important
Sowing unthinking my own misery
And to unicorn plans bent!?"

The fires below roared. A great plume of lava spat forth and fell with a terrible crash, singing Carina's feathers even from the distance she stood.

"I swear I was a good gryphon
I only wanted to end the war
I saw a path that seemed so true
I never meant to be a traitor.

"No,

"I served my loves all well and true
As we drifted apart year by year
My king, he promised us safety
My every word to allay fear.

"No . . .

"Do I still stand believing those lies
Or were they ever lies at all?
How can I ever find the truth
When I stand here, ready to fall."

Carina looked away from the fires, scanning the high cliffs around her with a mounting desperation. Her heart felt in total opposition to the fiery chaos of her surroundings as she stood poorly balanced on her rear legs, a cold, black pit spreading through her. She wanted to cry, to sob and wail as she reached her talons out and tore the feathers from her wings, but her eyes of fire allowed no tears to form.

> "There is nothing for me now
> No answer as I yearn
> And I have cast myself aside
> Nowhere to run, nowhere to hide
> All hope now scattered ash
> Before the Empire's furnace blast
> There is nothing for me now
> SO NOW I MUST BURN!"

And even as the last word echoed from her beak, Carina allowed her balance to fail, pitching her forward. Off the crater's edge, down through the rising smoke, down into that last, hungering fire. Never to be seen again by waking eyes.

CHAPTER TWENTY-THREE

Exhausted, scared, in pain deep through her muscles and bones, Bifrost flew south. A flight of hours, leaving Gateway not long after her sister had, the fear and desperation at last getting to her.

"Bifrost, wait!" Owain galloped after her across the palace roof. "Where are you going!?"

Bifrost didn't slow. She didn't dare slow, didn't dare look back, afraid if she did her resolve would leave her. "I'm going to get the last help I can think of!"

Hours of flying passed without a word spoken. Over Gateway, over the surrounding seas, over the marshlands and hills, following the course of the vast river system leading from Gateway's seas to the southern oceans. She flew, who for long years had been courier and scout, messenger, knight for the Lady of the Floating Mountain. But no flight before had ever been so important, nor so terrifying.

She passed to the east of the towering Dragonback Mountains. The light dimmed, dying beyond the heavy clouds and ever-falling ash. Bifrost put on a pair of goggles stashed among the folds of her blue scarf to protect her eyes, then adjusted the scarf to cover her beak. Ahead, all around, the world disappeared into a grim grey haze, no sounds but the flapping of Bifrost's wings, nothing but her innate gryphon senses to keep her sure her flight remained southward.

Out of the ash haze ahead loomed a slim tower of metal and glass. The guard tower marking the halfway point between Gateway and the Floating Mountain. Bifrost angled for it, calling out for the soldiers stationed there to not be surprised by her arrival. No answering call came, and fear fell over her heavy as the blankets of ash. She landed on the main platform, her wings near-dead with exhaustion. Bifrost turned warily. All was silent. The guard tower stood like a post for the dead, the glass domes stained with ash, the landing platforms piled high with drifts of the grey foulness, more drifts spreading through the doorways and windows, driven there by wind.

"Hello!" Bifrost cried out, her voice doubly muffled, once by her scarf, twice by the thick, oppressive air hanging like a guillotine upon the whole scene.

"Hello?" she called again, trudging forward. She found the bodies of the tower guard in the central dome, gathered at a table for a game of cards which now would never be finished. They lay sprawled across the floor or against the table, their faces the faces of gryphons who had died suddenly, yet not so suddenly enough to escape from the agony of the end, choking on a sudden flood of cinders or poisonous volcanic gasses, their tongues lolling out of their beaks, their throats torn from where talons had grasped desperately at them, eyes wide but now beginning to sink in, blind and unblinking.

Bifrost stood among the dead for a long moment, unthinking and unfeeling. Then the terrible thought came to her, the horrid certainty that any moment the dead eyes all around were going to fill again with life and LOOK AT HER. She nearly screamed as she turned to flee this sudden horror. As she tripped and fell onto one of the surrounding bodies, her beak clacking the corpse's in a horrid mockery of a kiss through her scarf, she did scream. The scream echoed all through the tower, chasing after Bifrost long after she regained her feet and took flight once more.

Southward, on and on until the weariness became a refuge. She focused on the agony of her wings, the shortness of her breath, the stinging in her eyes even despite her protective goggles. When she didn't, she began to think again about the bodies in the guard tower. About the vats of misshapen horrors in Hiraeth

Arian, monstrosities against nature, all dead—and if they had not stayed dead in their preservative fluids, Bifrost would surely have lost her mind—all far behind her. She began to think there were figures in the falling ash around her, following her. Half-glimpsed shadows, like the impression of a shark swimming swiftly below the surface of the water, nothing but darkness until the fin broke the surface.

"If I hear a voice," she thought to herself, wings beating faster, trying to eat away the distance between her and the safety of the Floating Mountain, *"If I feel someone—something—touch me out here, I am going to scream. Oh God, I am going to scream and I won't be able to stop. Oh God, it's behind me. It's behind me! No, no, no—"*

Bifrost spun to look behind her. But she saw nothing but the falling ash, darker behind her, lighter ahead. The winds of Lady Quetzal had turned against it.

The rain of ash was lightening up, but it had not ceased completely by the time Bifrost reached the outermost isles of the Floating Mountain. She collapsed upon the rock, unable to stop herself, her wings simply refusing to work anymore after the half-day spent in near-endless flight. Bifrost lay where she had fallen, letting her eyes close for a moment, only a moment . . .

A few scattered stars could be seen peeking through the shattered sky when Bifrost woke. She groaned and stood, body protesting. She weathered the aches enough to shake herself free of the worst of the volcanic filth clinging to her, then took flight again for Lady Quetzal's palace at the heart of the Floating Mountain. It felt like an unbearably slow journey, after the race to reach Vogelstadt. She passed few gryphons along the way, the gryphons gawking at her, shying away from the ashen ghost come suddenly among them.

Then there were soldiers, a dozen of them flying from the palace to meet her, to block her way. Bifrost slowed to a stop and they did likewise, keeping a careful distance from her as they eyed her in horror and wonder. "Bifrost?" asked the nightingale-gryphon at the head of the group, her spear half-raised and uncertain. "Is that you?"

"Get out of my way, Anna," said Bifrost, still weary despite her unwanted sleep, knowing terribly how little she had time for this.

"It is you," said the nightingale-gryphon, voice growing hard. "It is. I can't believe it. When you left with the unicorn and the hippogryph, we were all sure you'd never come back. You never should have come back. Lady Quetzal was outraged, is still outraged. She'll want to throw you in the dungeons the moment she sees you—"

"Look behind me," snapped Bifrost, her patience dead in the water as she drew closer to the gaggle of soldiers. "Look at the steaming, smoking, belching Dragonbacks, at all their ash and dribbling lava. On the other side of them are a hundred, a thousand worse things all heading straight for Gateway, horrors you wouldn't believe, birthing tragedies you could never imagine. I have seen it all, and right now you are hovering between me and the last hope I can think of to stopping all of it, and if you think your spears mean a damn to me, then you can stay right there and see!"

Silence reigned for a moment after Bifrost's tirade. The soldiers remained hovering in place, uncertainty running roughshod through their ranks, every moment teetering on the brink of violence. But then Anna lowered her spear, stared frightened at Bifrost. "Lady Toqeph tells us everything is fine out there. That everything's under control. But she lies, doesn't she?"

Bifrost gave no answer as she flew past the soldiers. She flew faster now, across the palace courtyard and through the thrown-open doors into the meeting hall, down a corridor, past elegant paintings and further doorways to ivy-wrapped verandas. The memory of long,

long ago led her on, the memory of childhood before Bifrost had found herself.

Down pillared halls he led the Royal School group, commenting on this mural or that statue as they ventured deeper into the palace. Bifrost kept his head on a swivel to see everything. Memorialized around them were the great heroes of gryphon history. Elsa, slayer of the hydra hordes. Sigurd, first king of Schwarz Angebot to the far north. Brunhild, who alone held the Featheren Valley pass for three days against a platoon of sphinx raiders. Judith, the first robin-gryphon to earn the title of knight alongside her faithful kitsune companion. Those two were Bifrost's favorites.

Bifrost turned a gilt-edged corner, then stopped, landing. She stood and stared down the hall, filled with sudden foreboding.

Holes filled the walls, Bifrost imagining arrows or crossbow bolts shooting from them at intruders. Above, the hooked heads of spears could just be seen glinting in the shadowed reaches of the high ceiling ready to drop. At the far end of the hall, 30 yards or so, stood a pair of onyx double-doors. Silver and gold flowed like air currents over its surface. Where the doors met at the center stood four peafowl-gryphons in armor as dazzling as their plumage, shields and spears at the ready.

Aside from the eagle-gryphons now guarding the door to Quetzal's Vault, the sight before Bifrost remained the same as in her memory. The gryphons on the far end of the hall watched her warily, their weapons—crossbows now instead of spears and shields—half-lowered, half-aimed her way.

Bifrost swallowed, removed her goggles and lowered her scarf from over her beak, and started forward. She walked, resting her wings. Her steps rang along the hall, the only appreciable sound in the otherwise-overwhelming silence. Bifrost kept her gaze straight, refusing to look to either side. She did not want to risk seeing the glint of arrows and bolts in the holes perforating the walls to either side of her. She did not want to catch a glimpse of the cruelly hooked spears hanging overhead, waiting for the wrong move on her part to be dropped. She did not even want to see the guards at their posts, their crossbows lowering to aim at her as she approached. She kept her gaze on the swirls of silver and gold covering the Vault door as she walked and waited.

Halfway there, one of the guards called out "Halt!"

Bifrost kept walking, a silent prayer in her heart.

"Halt!" the guard repeated. "State your business at once, or we will be forced to stop you!"

"I am Sir Bifrost," she called out, not stopping, not slowing. "Sworn knight of Princess Galaxy. I come on behalf of her whom I love, on behalf of Gateway, on behalf of Heraldale, to demand you let me into that vault! You must stand aside!"

"They will follow no commands but my own, oh sworn knight."

Her steps as she approached from behind had been as silent as snowfall, yet now that she had announced herself, a soothing warmth seemed to filter through Bifrost and the others, like a long-awaited embrace from a most cherished person. A soft glow emanated from behind them, dancing across the marble floor and walls in a kaleidoscope of colors. The sense of foreboding enveloping the area vanished.

Bifrost stopped, turned, stared up at Lady Quetzal, unmoved. The Prime Gryphon stared back at her, relaxed and smug, full of a staggering self-assurance. "So," Quetzal spoke, stepping easily over Bifrost, sitting between her and the Vault. "You came back. Things didn't go well with the hippogryph, hm? King Vigdis all bark and no bite, perhaps? I am, of course, magnificently forgiving when one of my gryphons learns the error of their ways, and since this was your first offense, I'm more than happy to put this whole Grand Harmonium nonsense behind us—"

"It's real," said Bifrost, staring unflinching.

Lady Quetzal stilled. Her blind eyes narrowed. "I will tell you once. Don't say that again."

"It's real," repeated Bifrost, barely keeping herself from screaming. She, Galaxy, and King Vigdis had sent copies of all their memories to the Floating Mountain for Quetzal to review, had sent reports of all which had been happening and all their plans leading up to the attack on the Grand Harmonium, and yet the Prime Gryphon still insisted on burying her head in the sand.

"It's real," Bifrost said again, stepping closer. "And it's built like an Imperial warship. It FLIES. Nowhere in Heraldale or beyond is safe. We need the weapons of your treasure vault, my lady. We need them now, before it's too late. I am begging you."

Lady Quetzal scoffed and rolled her eyes. "Lies. Insanity. We are safe here, young gryphon. My people are safe here. My lands are safe. The rest of the world can simply . . . get by—"

"No, you don't get it!" screamed Bifrost. She could not stop them anymore, neither the screaming nor the tears. "Haven't you looked outside? Haven't you tasted the air? Haven't you felt how the world trembles, on the verge of ending? Your people need you!"

"My people are right here," said Quetzal, gesturing with a wing as if to take in all of Vogelstadt. "My people are sweet and safe. I have always kept them safe. War has never touched our sacred soil, and it never will. Let those who followed other leaders live with their choices."

"Is that all this is?" asked Bifrost, struck nearly dumb as she realized the full scope of pettiness before her. "Your jealousy at gryphons serving and following people other than you? Well, good news! The best news! Because you're the only one left! Don't you get it? Princess Galaxy is missing. King Vigdis and Queen Gwendolyn are dead. You're it, you are the only one left! Do something, damn it!"

And for a moment, a blessed moment, fear and genuine concern graced the Prime Gryphon's features, and Bifrost felt a moment's hope. But Quetzal schooled herself, all warmth lost beneath the cold, blind steel of her gaze. "If the people of Heraldale can't save themselves, I don't see why I should bother. Vogelstadt stands safe and alone, and will remain so. My Vault will remain closed. My people will stay."

And standing there in the same corridor where she had decided the course of her life so many years before, Bifrost saw the Prime Gryphon would not, could not, be swayed, not if all the world begged her in one voice. Beaten, she turned to leave, her thoughts only on the return to Gateway and on whatever final bloody end she and her friends would find there—

Grinding stone and the squeal of metal long unaccustomed to movement reached Bifrost from behind. She looked, eyes wide, saw the guards with their talons on the doors. Their expressions were strained, wings beating laboriously, lit by the glowing metal runes across the doors' surfaces as they slowly swung open to a room of utter darkness.

"What is this!?" Quetzal snarled, a fist striking a wall and shattering the stone to pieces in her rage. "What is this!? Treachery and filth, sworn oaths discarded like loathsome—"

"This is a stand, my lady," said one of the golden eagle-gryphon guards, turning from the work of drawing the doors open with an outpouring of his inner magic to look at Bifrost. "Some of us can't help but look out the window at the apocalypse. Go, hurry."

Bifrost nodded and flew, barely dodging as Lady Quetzal grabbed for her with a blind swing of her talons. She sped past the guards and through the half-open doors, felt the tingle of magic at her entrance into the darkened vault. By magic, flames leapt into life in braziers across the vault, in sconces along the walls, in crude, dust-draped chandeliers to shine upon a towering mural—

Bifrost landed, nearly ramming a trinket-laden table in her shock. She clung to it for support, body weak and heaving, eyes wide as she looked around her in mounting confusion and horror. She might have vomited in her horror, had she any food in her stomach to lose. She knew the room she now found herself in. She had spent many hours of the last few days helping Galaxy and friends to clean it. The vault's door had been another portal, taking her back to Gateway.

"No . . ." She half-staggered, half-dragged herself to the end of the table, heedless of the mixed ash and dust she left in her wake. She spied the antique globe the Twins had teased Carina with, and seeing it she did loose a spatter of stomach acids onto the floor, enough to set her throat burning. "No! It can't be, please!"

Behind her, she felt the giant form of Quetzal settle down. Bifrost wiped her beak and turned to look up at her, shaking and grabbing for anything solid and true to cling to. "Where's the vault? Where are the treasures, the weapons!?"

"There . . . is no vault," said the Prime Gryphon after a long pause, long enough for some of the guards of the hall to come in after their lady. "There are no treasures. There are no weapons. It was all a lie."

Bifrost stood before her first vow, broken by these words. She dragged her talons through the feathers of her head and down her face, eyes stinging with tears, watching the disturbed ash rain to the floor. She wanted—

"Perhaps there are such noble souls within this group? I perceive much potential before me. Who among you think you could stand proudly one day in these vaunted halls as a warrior of the Floating Mountain?"

"I do!" said Bifrost, ignoring Carina's flinch. As Lady Quetzal turned her full gaze on him once more Bifrost only stood taller, near-shivering with excitement. Brave, he hoped, for a child of 9. Hopefully not merely stupid. "I will be a great warrior! The greatest warrior to ever guard the Vault!"

"That means you'll have to be better than me," snarled Carina in a whisper. "That'll never happen."

"But why?" asked Bifrost. She stared down at the floor, unable to bring herself to look up at such a monumental betrayer of her faith. "Why the lie?"

"To hide the secret of Morgana le Fay's connecting portals between Gateway and the Floating Mountain," said Quetzal, in a tone like this should have been answer enough. "To prevent exploitation of the portal or others like it. To present an image of strength and stability to Vogelstadt and all our enemies, to tell them we were powerful and should not be challenged. To preserve even a little of the old, golden order in this . . . dreadful world of change."

"If . . . if the weapons and stuff in there are really so powerful . . . why don't the guards use them against the enemy? We could use Gungnir to stop the horrible unicorns, just like you did with the dragons!"

"And . . . the Oath Spear?" asked Bifrost, looking up at last. "Where do you keep that, then?"

Quetzal's blind gaze met Bifrost's, the grey against the rainbow, both unblinking. "I gave that long ago to someone I trust even more than myself. And if she kept her vow, it is far beyond the reach of any in this terrible war."

CHAPTER TWENTY-FOUR

The first wave of the Imperial assault crashed upon the Gateway defenses, hundred-thick swarms of crystal drones and undead wyverns against a blistering hail of spell bolts from defensive positions across the northern shoreline and nearest buildings. The waters there become littered with the bodies of the now twice-dead beasts, the streets and the docks glittering with the shards of shattered and smoking crystal.

A long stretch of minutes passed, then came a fresh swarm of undead wyverns and gryphons. With them came air-yachts and troop carriers in the dozens, speeding low across the churning waves of the sea in a mad rush for the coastline. Most were destroyed by fire bombs dropped from high above. The half-dozen to make it to the city docks were met by gryphon and Elk defenders and cut down after brief but fierce fighting.

The orange skies deepened to an evil, bloody red, the whole world, or at least Gateway and its seas, turning red beneath it, the shadows long, the air thick and putrid. Far, far to the south, the Dragonback Mountains vomited their lava and black, ashen vapors.

The Imperial assault continued. More crystal drones, more of Lord Beauty's undead, more air-yachts and troop carriers, led now by Wolf-Lords riding armored wyverns, their lances ablaze with spellfire. The shore and northern streets became choked with the debris, and still the sides fought. Owain galloped through the ranks of the defenders, his efforts focused on healing and casting spell filters to protect the fighters from the worst of the breath-stealing foulness in the air. Sascha and Siegfried went about with him. When his reserves of magic ran low, they offered theirs for him to draw from.

Across the north waters, the looming shadow of the Grand Harmonium and its escort could be seen. Ahead of it, two of its four warships sped forward to clear the resistance. At last, High General Shan called for a retreat.

"Fall back! Fall back to the palace! High flyers! High flyers, go!"

They fell back, fighting as they went, Owain and Hywel bringing up the rear of the ground-bound soldiers. High overhead, high enough to be beyond sight from the ground, flights of geese-gryphons joining their ranks from Vogelstadt dropped 200-pound steel rods.

15 found their mark, weight and momentum punching through spell shields to obliterate one of the warships in a sudden eruption of twisted, screeching metal. Five missed their mark, reducing a square mile of the city to rubble.

The other warship continued on, firing its anti-dragon cannons upon the city as wyverns swarmed above it to ward off any potential second bombing run. But none came. The fighting continued.

Owain, exhausted, his own and Sascha and Siegfried's magic reserves brought perilously low, found his way to the palace roof to watch. Pillars of smoke now rose throughout the burning city to join the falling ash and cinders. The sky turned darker, like old and dried blood. From all around, Owain heard the distant lamentations of the gryphons of Gateway. Where the fighting had not yet reached, those who had not fled through the portal to the Floating Mountain before Quetzal destroyed it lay scattered and prostrate upon the streets and roofs, giving in to their despair at the loss of King Vigdis and the war tearing through their homeland. Others had fled Gateway entirely, going east to the guarded and wary borders of the United Zakarian Confederacy, or south, trying for the river passages along the eastern edge of the Dragonbacks to reach the hoped-for safety of Lady Quetzal. A few gryphons, and even Elk, had cast themselves into the storm-driven seas.

The air stirred around Owain. He looked up, the smallest measure of relief striking him as Bifrost landed to his left. It was a rough landing, the raven-gryphon's rainbow eyes wet and bloodshot, promising no good news. But even so, to get to see even one friend again before the end . . .

"My God," said Bifrost, looking out over the destruction. "Not since the defeat of the Wolf-Lords has there been fighting in the very streets of Gateway."

"Maybe this is our punishment for that crime," said Owain. He lashed his tail and tapped at the ground with his hooves, kicking off the accumulating ash. "Nobody's winning out there. Even Nova is only going to rule over a land of the dumb and the dead. Maybe we deserve this."

A bone-jarring BOOM shook the city as General Odin strategically detonated one of the taller towers to slam its burning hulk against the side of another Imperial warship. The warship began to list, smoke rising and fiery debris falling from its damaged side, but still, it advanced.

"No," said Bifrost. "We don't deserve this. Nobody deserves this. It's just the work of evil people and those who couldn't stop them."

"Those who couldn't stop them," said Owain, voice trailing away. He thought about his friends and loved ones. Brynjar, Galaxy, even Bevin. He thought about his father, dead before him, a weak unicorn who had tried to do the right thing in the end, even knowing he would fail and die. Owain thought about the numberless people, gryphon and unicorn and Elk and dragon, who had tried and failed to stop the nightmare unfolding all around them. Failure heaped upon failure, the indifference of others the mortar binding it all together.

"But still," said Owain at a whisper, "we have to try."

"What's that?" asked Bifrost.

"We have to try," Owain repeated. He turned and galloped as fast as his exhausted body could to the section of the palace roof dedicated to air-yacht landing and maintenance. One such craft remained, the troop carrier he, Owain, and Hywel had escaped Avalon in. Damaged as it was, it had been mostly stripped down for parts to repair and maintain the more usable airships in Gateway's meager collection, but to Owain's relief, the communication spell array remained untouched.

"Communicating with who?" asked Bifrost.

"Everyone," answered Owain. He tore away the paneling from the floor of the troop carrier directly beside the pilot's station and pulled free a metal cable

as thick as his horn. "Take this to the rear of the craft—
"

"Directly into the primary spell batteries to overcharge the array." Bifrost spoke as she worked, Owain barely noticing out of the corner of his eye as he adjusted the half-dozen newly-exposed crystal spars to—hopefully—hit a broader band of receivers. "You want a general broadcast rather than a one-to-one transmission."

Owain nodded, then looked up. Through the troop carrier's forward window, he saw the fighting across the city, the spreading wave heralding the Grand Harmonium. It had grown closer in the spare minutes of their work. "Done?"

"Done."

Owain nodded again, breathed deep, shut out the fear from his mind with warm thoughts of Galaxy and Brynjar. He pushed his magic directly into the troop carrier's communication array, seeing at the edge of his vision as the ship's systems activated, felt the hum in the back of his head as connections were made to every other array in range, more connections than he could count. There came the faint flurry of confusion as others noticed the connection, the sounds fading as Owain cleared his voice and sent his own presence over the line. It was probable nobody would listen. It was probable Empress Nova would terminate the transmission before it could do any good. But he had to try, all the same.

"Attention, soldiers of Avalon. I am Sir Owain. You may know me as the traitor, the deserter. I am a unicorn. I am a son of Avalon like so many of you, and you hear me now because I am here to tell you the truth, whether you want it or not."

Owain paused a moment, thought. "It's all a lie. Avalon greatness. It is a lie told to us by our masters to make us their eager tools of destruction. I have been among the people of the world, not as a soldier but as a traveler, a student, and I learned that the people of the world fear and loathe us! We are not the valiant heroes wading out into the darkness of barbarity, spreading the light of our grand civilization. We are the fiery destruction of civilization! Everywhere I have gone, the world has been scarred by us and our domination. Look around you! Look up from your work and see how the world is falling apart all around us! That is us! That is our work! Does this look like we're making a better world? Does anything around you look better for how we have gone about our blissful and ignorant lives!?

"Maybe you all already know this. Maybe you know perfectly well what you're doing and you're happy to do it for greed or hatred. I'm sure you're out there. But I also have to believe there are some of you out there who know what you're doing is wrong, who know that Empress Nova is evil, who dream of a new, better way of things, who dream of peace instead of war. And I beg those unicorns to stand up and say no just like I did. Even if you're alone, even if it might mean death at the hooves of those around you. The world needs you. I—"

And then a new voice came over the communication crystal, the harsh and terrible voice of Empress Nova, deafening and full of fury and hate, magnified a million times across a million crystals throughout Gateway and beyond.

"BE QUIET! I WILL KILL YOUR SOUL! I WILL TEAR YOUR MIND APART! THERE WILL BE NO NEW ORDER! THE OLD SHALL STAND FOREVER! THIS IS MY WORLD, THIS IS MY HOUR, AND NONE ARE LEFT TO OPPOSE ME!"

CHAPTER TWENTY-FIVE

Though she knew now the dream vision to be a cruel, needless taunt Galaxy was helpless to stop its coming, sweeping over her mind like the tide dragging her to the darkest depths.

Forests of the richest green covered the world below Galaxy. The sky swelled with blue immensity, puffs of clouds like breaking waves. The sun was a gentle warmth upon her back and wings. Unable to stop, Galaxy sang a wordless song into the bracing wind. She saw unicorns among the shadows of the trees, unicorns and Elk, laughing and whole and free.

A break in the forest revealed a winding river. Unicorns and gryphons lounged together along the banks. Owain and Brynjar. Bevin, proud Bevin. Bifrost, whom Galaxy loved, and Carina, whom Galaxy hated.

Something was wrong. Carina only stood there and watched Galaxy fly past, insubstantial, the grassy hillside visible behind her. A ghost.

Unsettled, Galaxy left the river behind and flew on over the forest. She dreaded what came next—

"Galaxy."

Galaxy looked left. A yard away flew Ida. Past her the swan-gryphon twins Sascha and Siegfried, Galaxy's other brother and sister. The three smiled at Galaxy, but the sight brought only pain. Ida was dead, had been dead a long time, and as she flew there beside Galaxy, she as was insubstantial as Carina in the clearing behind.

"Failing us all, Gal. Failing us all."

Before Galaxy's eyes, the three gryphons broke apart into flame and ash, laughing as they crumbled. Galaxy cried out in pain as the flames leapt over and consumed her left front leg from talons to shoulder, a battering gust of wind scattering the limb and her family to the void.

Chains shot up from the forest, countless chains, wrapping around Galaxy's limbs, her torso, her throat, squeezing the breath from her. She kicked and fought as they dragged her down, past the trees and into a shallow, black-rocked gully dotted with muddy pools. The chains drew tight to the ground, holding Galaxy flat. Sharp rocks drew pinpricks of blood from her belly.

Hooves clacking on stone drew Galaxy's gaze forward. Before her stood Lord Beauty, her snowy coat blinding in the gully's gloom, her storm-grey mane and tail lashing with lightning. Her silver horn shone with might. Her star sapphire gaze struck Galaxy with the most horrible, amused contempt.

"Why?" Galaxy begged. She strained, pushing herself up onto her quivering legs. "I know everything know. I know! Why torment me with this again!?"

"Blind!" The unicorn's muzzle split open into an impossible smile. The skin pulled back, back, back, tearing down the length of Lord Beauty's neck, her chest and torso, dropping away, revealing a blood-smeared white coat beneath. Before Galaxy's eyes now stood a Wolf-Lord, white-furred and grey-haired like Lord Beauty, cackling.

"Blind!"

Even as she spoke, Lord Beauty shuddered. Cracks appeared in the white-furred Wolf-Lord's body, glowing red, spreading. Flames licked the edges of the cracks, the skin and flesh crumbling away, leaving behind a scorched stench and blackened bones wreathed in fire.

The laughter returned now as screams, echoing all around Galaxy. She turned a circle and beheld the whole world consumed by flame and smoke, the burning ash falling heavy into the gully, rendering all in black and white and grey. Galaxy saw burning unicorns and gryphons stumble out of the forest to fall headfirst into the gully, friends and family, people she knew from Gateway. They stared at Galaxy all the way down. Each CRACK of their bodies hitting the gully floor and shattering into cinders threatened to break her. Shield spells kept the ash from burning her eyes and stealing her breath as she struggled for certain footing.

Suddenly, vast flames hid all else from Galaxy. Before her HE stood, a unicorn stallion 40, 50, 60 feet tall, nothing but black bones and white fire scorching Galaxy where she lay. The skull's eye sockets stared down at her, fire dancing within them. He spoke, voice like the grave.

"BLIND!"

But Galaxy was not blind, not anymore. She had traveled through oppression and war, had felt suffering and healed it, had loved and lost in equal measure. And Carina, whatever her true intentions, had taught Galaxy to see magic and see with her magic. No, Galaxy was not blind anymore.

And right then, Galaxy could see again the bright, cool light of magic, shining like the brightest star beyond the Burning King, THROUGH the Burning King. Recognizing the light, Galaxy summoned forth and reached out with the Waters of Life within her, like magic toward like magic. She reached, and the vision around her shuddered as if its foundations had been broken, and Lord Beauty's voice echoed from all corners. "Stop that! Give in and die!"

"Never!" snarled Galaxy. Before her, the image of the Burning King had been reduced to smoke and shadow, scattering even as she watched, her Waters of Life piercing through for whatever magics lay beyond. "It's like Carina warned me. Visions can be dangerous for all parties involved!"

Galaxy grasped the distant magic in her own and pulled. In a blink and with a terrible wrenching sensation, the black void all around was replaced, to Galaxy's surprise, by another familiar sight. She stood now on a cold, grey beach, a storm-lashed ocean half-covered in breaking, grinding ice spreading beyond sight before her. The vision of the Burning King was gone, but Galaxy was not alone.

"Nnngh . . . you . . ." Paces away down the beach, Lord Beauty struggled to regain her hooves upon the ice-slick stone. "You . . . Who do you think you are?"

"I am Princess Galaxy," she said in answer, halving the distance between them with her head high and her wings spread. "Defeater of Spell Virus and Lord Mordred. Bearer of the Waters of Life. Heir of Schwarz Angebot. Daughter of Queen Vigdis and Sir Lancelot . . . and Sir Ida. Who do you think YOU are?"

"You already know," said the creature before Galaxy, tail and mane lashed about by a harsh, frigid wind. Her struggle for footing ceased, gemstone eyes glowing with inner power even as a darkness stole over the land, spreading from the ice-wracked ocean. "Once, this cursed form was a punishment, but it proved so useful for manipulating bloodthirsty egotists like Nova and reckless dreamers like you. Stupid, stupid hippogryph."

The creature reared back onto her rear legs. As she did, the unicorn melted away, revealing again the bone-thin, white-furred Wolf-Lord within. The darkness swirled in around them, wrapping the grey-haired wolf within a cloak of shadow. The silver horn melted away, reformed and grew into a face-concealing antlered helm, dripping down into pauldrons and cuirass. Galaxy, wary, watched this all with grim fascination.

"Stupid, stupid hippogryph," the Wolf-Lord repeated. "I have been with you every step of the journey, watching you in your dreams, teaching you in your scrolls. I am the Heart of Magic. I am the first daughter of Toqeph, the Prime Unicorn! I am Queen of Dark Realm! I am Morgana le Fay, and you will BOW!"

The vision exploded. It was the best Galaxy could do to describe it. Against the roar and rush of Morgana's magic blast, the beach, the ocean, the sky all caved and shattered like the thin frost upon a window, throwing both into a realm of utter darkness. Galaxy reeled head over heels from the blow, every bone in her body feeling bruised.

Morgana thrust her magic forth with a roar again and Galaxy cried out as a titanic force battered her. She tumbled through the black nothing and Morgana followed after, smashing against her with magic again and again, laughing when she was not roaring.

"DIE! DIE, DIE, DIE!"

Galaxy flared her wings to still herself, turning hurriedly to face Morgana hurtling toward her, a white and silver dart in the all-encompassing darkness of the broken dream. Galaxy screeched and loosed a burst of the blue magic of the Waters of Life from her horn. Morgana sped under the blast, one clawed hand thrusting out. The Wolf-Lord's silver magic streamed from the grasping claws and wrapped tight around Galaxy's neck.

At once, Galaxy's attack faltered. She fell through the darkness, gasping for breath which wouldn't come, talons burning as they grasped vainly at the magic squeezing her throat tighter, tighter. The panicked thought came that Morgana wasn't merely going to strangle her to death, but break her neck—

Then, a burst of light, white fire bursting into existence beside Morgana le Fay, engulfing the whole of her right arm and much of her right leg. The grip of magic around Galaxy's neck broke as the Wolf-Lord shrieked in pain and terror. The fire flared brighter, spreading, trying to consume Morgana—

But then the Wolf-Lord was gone. Galaxy fell for a moment more through the deep darkness, and then she found herself back on the grey, ice-wrapped beach, the air cold and filled with the crushing rush of the ocean.

The white fire, too, was gone. In its place stood Carina a few paces down the beach, insubstantial and wavering where she stood with her rear to Galaxy.

"You . . ." Galaxy winced and sat, rubbed at her sore throat. "You saved me. How, why . . ." Her words failed her as Carina turned to face her, blindfold gone and beak turned in a sad smile. The white fire had faded in her eyes.

"You're dead," said Galaxy.

"Many of us are dead," said Carina. Her voice seemed weak and distant, as if it echoed up from some deep, deep well. "And many more, before this is all over."

"I'm sorry," said Galaxy. She didn't know what else to say.

"It's alright," said Carina, continuing to smile. Even as she spoke, the raven-gryphon grew ever more insubstantial, fading away in voice and body. "I'm sorry too. Just keep an eye on Bifrost for me, please. Tell my sister I loved her, however else things turned out between us."

"I will," promised Galaxy. A moment passed with the rush of the waves and the creaking groan of the ice. Galaxy looked around, took in the desolate beauty, felt she could have lived there in another life. It felt like a reprieve, a gift. One she had needed more than she'd known. "It seems Lord Beauty, or Morgana le Fay, really played us out there."

"Aye."

"I don't know what to do next. I don't know what I'm going to be waking up to. There's not much hope left out there in the waking world, is there?"

"There's enough." Carina's voice was barely a whisper on the wind, the image of her now barely a glimmer in Galaxy's eyes. "Enough to fight on with horn and claw. But you'll need to find the right help. Someone to counter Morgana."

"Who?" asked Galaxy. "Who is left in all of Heraldale who can help, or even wants to?"

"To answer that, you're going to need to wake up."

CHAPTER TWENTY-SIX

Galaxy woke up from the vision and found herself sprawled on her side in front of a merrily crackling fire inside an old but well-tended cabin, the floor warm and the air cozy all around, and she the focus of extreme interest from a wide-eyed unicorn filly. The young unicorn was a pinto, and her blue eyes were startlingly familiar to Galaxy.

"Are you dead?" asked the filly.

"Not . . . yet?" said Galaxy, sounding more like she was asking than she'd intended as she slowly pushed herself up into a sitting position. A quick glance down told her what she already knew, that the Waters of Life had healed Morgana le Fay's stab into her side as she'd been unconscious.

"Are you sure?" asked the filly, sounding suspicious.

Galaxy blinked and looked at her again, wishing she didn't recognize those blue eyes so well. "Y . . . yes?"

The unicorn filly nodded solemnly, backed away until her rear bumped into a table, and then looked to a nearby doorway. "MOMMA! SHE'S NOT DEAD!"

Galaxy startled at the lungs the young unicorn possessed, then startled again as an answering shout echoed from some other room. "DID YOU WAKE HER UP, BRAT!?"

"NO! SHE WOKE UP ON HER OWN!"

Galaxy's mind boggled at this apparent family of screamers, wondering how she had ever been unconscious enough for her dream-vision against Morgana le Fay at all if this was the norm.

An orange-furred kitsune appeared in the doorway, paused a moment as she eyed Galaxy, slowly padded in to rest a hand on the filly's head. Behind her, Galaxy noticed four black-tipped tails curled, poised warily in the presence of the unknown. "Hello," the kitsune said. "I assume you must be the Princess Galaxy of Heraldale I have been hearing so much about recently?"

"That's right." Galaxy glanced around again, deciding after a few brief seconds that she was safe, wherever she was. There were toys in a corner and books stacked haphazardly on almost every available surface. There were scarves draped across the backs of a beaten-up old couch, and on the walls were numerous drawings of fish, or flowers, or most common of all, the three people before Galaxy in various combinations. It reminded Galaxy, with heartbreaking intensity, of her old home in Featheren Valley, long lost now to Lord Mordred's cruelties.

"I'm Shun," said the Wolf-Lord, refocusing Galaxy's attention back to them. "This is my daughter, Nessa. You caused quite the scare in our little town when you appeared out of nowhere like that, looking half-dead. Eishaven is mostly immigrants and refugees from Heraldale, so seeing a hippogryph in such a state . . ."

"I'm sorry," said Galaxy, genuinely so. "I was barely conscious when I felt a familiar magic and reached out for it. I guess I had thought it was my sister, Bevin . . ."

The filly, Nessa, shuffled nervously on her hooves. Shun grimaced and stroked her hand down the filly's neck. "Yes, that would make sense. Nessa, why don't you go see if there's any crystal candy left in Laura's alchemy lab from her last visit here?"

"It tastes like rocks!"

"That it does, kid, that it does."

Galaxy smiled softly at the touch of regular family shenanigans, watching after the filly until she disappeared from sight, followed seconds later by the sound of a door slamming shut. Then Galaxy looked back to the kitsune, her smile dropping. "I feel a little out of the loop on a lot of things, like who you are and where I am, and I know I don't really know my half-sister all that well yet, but please, oh please, do not be about to tell me I'm an aunt, because today has been a really long day—"

"The war's going badly," said Shun. It was not a question.

Galaxy hesitated to answer, slowly nodding her head. "I don't know all the magic or science behind it, but using material from my lost leg, Empress Nova made herself a new hippogryph body. Well, Morgana le Fay made it for her, I guess, but that distinction really doesn't matter. She'll be able to Harmonize unicorns AND gryphons now, I can only assume."

Shun's shoulders slumped with the news. "Bevin told us about the Grand Harmonium. It still stands?"

"It teleports and flies," said Galaxy.

At the news, the kitsune looked quickly in the direction Nessa had gone, fear coming over her features like a mourning veil. "Then nowhere in all the world is beyond range of Harmonization."

Galaxy watched her host in quiet thought. It was easy to put the pieces together. Years before, Bevin had gone east to retrieve a stolen child; her own. This kitsune, Shun, and perhaps others had protected the child long enough for bonds to form. Bevin, stern and unrelenting at first—Galaxy did remember the misery of being pursued by the unicorn—still saw these bonds and accepted them. Yes, it sounded about right to Galaxy. "You love the child?"

"More than anyone still living in this world," said Shun, tails batting the back of her legs.

"Even with all the horrors her kind inflicted upon your kind?" Galaxy knew it was not a light question. Her visions into the past with Carina had shown her clear the nightmares of the war to drive the Wolf-Lords and their kin from Heraldale. Lord Mordred had made clear the sort of monsters birthed by the war, how long the hurts could linger and fester into fresh evils.

At the question though, the kitsune looked back at Galaxy, an eyebrow raised. "You're rather suspicious of the power of love for a hippogryph, aren't you?"

Galaxy bowed her head in acknowledgment of the point. "Alright. How long was I out?" she eventually thought to ask.

"Most of a day."

Most of a day. Galaxy stared. Most of a day since Hiraeth Arian, since the lab of monstrosities, since the hippogryph Nova. Since Morgana le Fay. Anything could have happened.

With a deep breath, Galaxy closed her eyes. For a minute, and then another, she allowed herself to remember all those she knew or feared had died to lead her to that moment, that place. The last she remembered before the desperate teleport spell, Vigdis had been fighting Empress Nova and Morgana le Fay. Fighting and losing. He was, more likely than not, dead. Her efforts to save him in Markhaven and the miracle of the Waters of Life doing no more in the end than buying the brave, loyal gryphon time.

Gwendolyn was also most likely dead, the thought of which drove a stake of grief through Galaxy's heart, wrenching a breathless whisper of a sob from her. Gwen had been her friend. So had Vigdis. She felt their loss more powerfully, more totally, than she had felt the loss of her left arm. And all the brave soldiers who had followed them into battle, gryphons and Elk, betting everything on a final act of bravery overcoming the dauntless odds.

Past her grief, Galaxy found calm. She sat in silence and let the seconds tick on, until in the silence she found a noise, low and steady and seeming from both near and far to the north. She opened her eyes with a shot of excitement and stood, looking around for a moment before looking past Shun to what looked to be the cabin's rear door. "What is that? I haven't heard it so strongly since the days of Port Oil."

"What's what?" asked the kitsune, blinking and following after Galaxy as she moved for the door. "If you're hearing anything that's putting you in mind of ports, I reckon it's the ocean. Eishaven is right on the coast of the Glacial Sea."

"The Glacial . . ." Galaxy muttered to herself, thoughts trailing off. She pushed the door open with a shove of magic and hobbled outside. At first, she could only stand there, nearly blinded. The sun blazed overhead. The sky was blue, blue, blue. Hills and drifts of snow covered the land, as bright as the sun overhead, broken sparingly by more cabins, by trees of holly and fir gathering into forest to the east. Outside, the rush of the tide was louder, stronger, nearer. With it, Galaxy heard another sound, sharper, erratic, the breaking and grinding of ice against itself.

Galaxy took wing and flew northward until she came to the black stone beach, no more than a quarter of a mile away. She landed, burdened by an overwhelming sense of déjà vu.

In her mind she saw the magic as a frosting ocean, battering at the shores to be loosed. She grabbed for it, felt it slip from her like water from talons, the rising panic whipping the ocean of magic into a deeper frenzy.

"No, please, I need you!" She grabbed again, holding tighter this time and pulling. A shock of ice spread over a stretch of the ocean, bulging up to her, only to burst the

moment she thought she had it. "No! Someone's going to die! I need you, power!"

The magic swelled into a wave. When it fell, it did so with a BOOM shaking deep into Galaxy's bones . . . Ice spread through it again, glaciers forming and shattering, water plumes shrieking like banshees.

Galaxy sat, scooped some of the smooth black stones of the beach up in her talons, watched them trickle away with a light clatter before looking up again. The ocean spread away to the unseen horizon, grey and frothing, choked white with drifts of ice. It was all familiar to her, not only from her own mind, but from elsewhere, as if from a previous life . . .

Holly le Fay stood on the black-rock shore, the sky a sullen grey. Her crow-feather cloak pulled tight around her as she watched the tumultuous northern sea. Waves tossed and churned white by storm winds crashed against the black shore, filled the air with frost and the tang of salt. Holly beheld it all, barely felt the cold, lost in her thoughts and memories.

Galaxy stood again and turned away from the ocean, walked up the short slope to the snowfields spreading between the dark forest and the refugee town. Shun waited for her there, watching with wary curiosity. There were others as well, crow-gryphons whispering excitedly among each other, minotaurs, Wolf-Lords. Nessa was there, the filly unicorn looking like she was seeing a ghost. Galaxy hobbled among them, past them, her attention caught by the statue of Holly le Fay.

"There's enough." Carina's voice was barely a whisper on the wind, the image of her now barely a glimmer in Galaxy's eyes. "Enough to fight on with horn and claw. But you'll need to find the right help. Someone to counter Morgana."

Galaxy circled the statue, gently dragging the talons of her right arm across the stone surface. On steadying wings, she looked up at a stone face full of love and grief and resignation which reached to her through the years, through the lifetimes. She had felt the very same more than once for Brynjar, for Owain, for the twins, for Bevin. "This is no ordinary statue. She—"

"She lived, once." Shun stood beside the statue, looked at it with love enough to ignite the moons. And grief enough to swallow it. "Holly was my wife. She gave her life to save me and our daughter and this whole, wretched town, and this is all that's left of her. Her final act. It's enough to make you wish the love itself had never been there."

"I know the feeling," said Galaxy. She looked at the statue which had once been a person, living and breathing, and wondered. She remembered Port Oil, and one of the first proper spells she learned, after the shield spell. Remembering, she closed her eyes and touched the tip of her horn to the statue's chest. Breathed out and focused, first summoning up her own hot, red personal magic, then pushing it out, out and into the cold marble-like stone.

"What is she—" Nessa began to ask, Shun swiftly shushing the young unicorn.

For several seconds, nothing seemed to happen. Galaxy kept up the flow of her magic, mixing in as little of the Waters of Life as possible, some instinct born of experience telling her it would not be needed here. After half a minute, she felt it, a warmth greeting her as her magic ignited the Wolf-Lord's core enough to begin generating its own magic again.

"Oh my God," whispered Shun, the kitsune's voice fallen to almost nothing.

Galaxy gave a last, hearty burst of personal magic into the stone, then opened her eyes and drifted away with a stroke of her wings. Before her and the gathering crowd, the statue shone, red and white light pouring from the scant cracks across its surface. The flowers and wreaths of holly decorating the statue caught fire and burned away. The mixed magics thickened, swept over the stone, and suddenly there was no stone, only flesh and fur.

"Oh my God!" cried Shun, nearly lost beneath the gasps of the onlooking crowd. "Holly!"

Holly le Fay breathed for the first time in more than two years, chest heaving with inexperience. The tall Wolf-Lord, powerfully built, staggered forward a step and caught herself, much of her shock hidden behind drapes of red hair. A shudder struck the Wolf-Lord, then from her back grew broad wings, the feathers as red as Galaxy's own.

"Oh, oh wow, that hurt," said the Wolf-Lord, her voice startling Galaxy with its familiarity. "Oh, but now it hurts so good. I don't need to sit down, but I kind of want to."

"Welcome back to the land of the living, Holly le Fay," said Galaxy, trying and mostly failing to keep her fascination in check. She could not help but look at the Wolf-Lord in front of her and think this was what she'd look like if she was born a Wolf-Lord instead of a hippogryph.

Holly le Fay slowly stood back up to her full height, yellow eyes meeting Galaxy's blue. The pair stared at each other, the Wolf-Lord as fascinated by the scenario as Galaxy was. They circled each other, the wolf's wings twitching half-spread, a hand distractedly brushing the red locks from her eyes. "You look so much like your mother, it is uncanny."

Galaxy blinked. She couldn't imagine how the Wolf-Lord before her could possibly know what the late Queen Grimhilt looked like.

Finally, Holly turned away from Galaxy, eyes sweeping the growing crowd. As she did, the gryphons, the minotaurs, the Wolf-Lords; all but the dragons in the crowd bowed or knelt before her as they would have for a queen. But Holly ignored them, her attention wholly for Shun and Nessa close at hand. A bright smile lit up Holly's face and she stepped forward the same moment the kitsune stepped forward. The pair embraced.

***

It took time, and more grandstanding before the awed, jubilant crowd than Galaxy preferred, but she and the reunited family managed to return to the cabin. Inside, as Holly sat on a stool before the hearth and idly brushed a hand down the mane and neck of the unicorn filly so desperately pressed against her side, Galaxy told her everything she knew and most of what she only guessed at. From where she stood behind her wife, cutting her hair, Shun chimed in to fill in the gaps where needed, simultaneously telling Galaxy where Bevin, Brynjar, and Blackbird where and why.

"Dragons come to the Wolf-Lords," Holly said after a while, more to herself than to the room. "Nations falling, the Dragonbacks awake, my mother working alongside Empress Nova, who is a hippogryph. Gryphons and unicorns alike in danger of Harmonization."

"It's a lot to take in," said Galaxy. "I know. It's been a . . . very, very stressful half a year for me."

Holly laughed. Shun lowered her scissors and stepped back. The Wolf-Lord gave a final pat to Nessa's head before standing, combing a hand through her shortened locks. When she turned to Galaxy, none of the laughter was in her face, a look in her eyes reminding Galaxy for a startling moment of Lord Mordred.

"But of course," Galaxy thought to herself, amazed and horrified by the realization. *"She's Mordred's cousin."*

"I am glad Commander Bevin has made a better mare of herself," began Holly. "But we should—"

There came a knock from the front door. A look passed between the three adults, Shun frowning as she was the first to speak. "It's a bad time for visitors when we're discussing the fate of the world."

"It would be rude to just ignore them," said Holly, and Galaxy could not tell how serious the remark was meant to be. "I would not like the first day of my resurrection marred by rudeness."

The knock came again. Shun sighed, dropped her scissors onto a nearby cough, and went to answer it. After she had left the den, Holly turned and leaned toward Galaxy with an unexpectedly conspiratorial air. "You said you are acquaintances with a pair of raven-gryphons of Vogelstadt named Bifrost and Carina?"

Galaxy thought back to the night of comfort spent with Bifrost on the even of battle and felt her cheeks flush. "I would say . . . more than acquaintances with Bifrost, but yes."

Holly grinned. "More than friends?"

The flush grew, hot but blessedly invisible beneath her feathers. She wondered what this was all about. "I . . . yes? Yes. More than friends."

The Wolf-Lord nodded, still smiling as she straightened back up. "Good. I am glad they are doing well. A previous life of mine knew them as newborns, but then she died. As people do, eventually."

Galaxy blinked, unsure of how to unpack all of this. Before she had to, Shun returned to the cabin's family den, bringing with her the oldest-looking unicorn Galaxy had ever seen, a veritably decrepit mare with a thin grey coat and a ragged mane. An awkwardly long package lay strapped to her back, half again as long as Galaxy stood, wrapped tight in old brown leathers.

At the sight of the unicorn, Holly grew happy, but solemn. "Lady Nimue! It is good to see you again. I thought you would be dead by now."

"Thankfully not," said the mare. She moved with an aching-joint stiffness to stand close to the fire in the hearth, then looked at Galaxy with wide, wondering eyes. "You did survive free, after all. That's good."

"Do I know you?" asked Galaxy. It was beginning to feel like everyone knew someone or two.

"No," answered Nimue, "but your parents did. I was the priestess of the Knights le Fay responsible for the guardianship and use of the Waters of Life. When Queen Grimhilt and Sir Lancelot wanted to have you, they came to me."

Some inner part of Galaxy relaxed. She even managed to feel an old excitement well up in her, the childhood excitement of finding a chance to learn something new, to ask all the questions she could think of and get answers which only sparked more questions.

But Galaxy was not that eager child anymore, had not been her for a long time. She reined in the urge, said only "It's an honor to meet you, Lady Nimue. Thank you for helping me exist."

Nimue coughed and tossed her mane dismissively. As she used her flickering magic to remove the long package from her back, she said "It was the least I could do after . . . after many things it is not right to speak of in the presence of children."

Nessa, almost forgotten, pressed tighter against Holly's leg, whinnying softly. Holly smiled down at her, pat her head, looked back at the former knight. "I assume this is not a social call. What is the package?"

Nimue set it on the floor at the center of the small circle of folks, magic unwrapping it with the greatest of care—and, Galaxy recognized, with disgust. "It is something I've guarded for many years now," said Nimue. "Guarded very carefully. It's one of Heraldale's great sins, and with the dragons among the Wolf-Lords, parleying for land and home, it is a sin I hope our hippogryph can at last set right."

The last of the leathers was removed. Galaxy stared, nonplussed. A long spear lay revealed on the rug, the whole weapon a single, solid piece of glimmering, silver-like metal. The blade at one end was a narrow tear drop as long as Galaxy's arm, and into its flat side were inscribed runes she could not begin to decipher, so small and tightly-packed they were. And the more she looked, the more she saw, the runes spiraling down from the blade and over the shaft of the spear down to the knobbed bottom. "Are those Wolf-Lord runes?" she asked.

"No," said Holly, voice hushed. She squatted beside the weapon, eyes wide as she reverently ran a hand down the shaft. "No, these are Prime runes. The ancient, private language of the Prime Unicorn, the Prime Dragon, and the Prime Gryphon. Known only by them . . . and the first Wolf-Lords, Queen Morgause and Morgana le Fay."

She looked up at Nimue, suddenly frowning. "This is Gungnir the Oath Spear, isn't it?"

The unicorn nodded. Galaxy, startled, squawked. "But that's supposed to be inside Lady Quetzal's treasure vault, at the heart of the Floating Mountain!"

"Not for nearly 20 years," said Nimue, looking at Galaxy. "Not since I learned your Lady Quetzal planned to use it on Avalon the same as she had used it on the dragons. Then I stole it."

Holly stood, the spear in her hand. As tall as she was, the blade rose over her head, and with the weapon in hand, a new viciousness seemed to slink into the look of her, reminding Galaxy again of Mordred. "We need to take this to Cairn Romulus at once. To the representatives assembled there."

Galaxy nodded, her thoughts traveling the same lines once she learned the full weight of the weapon in their hands. "Agreed."

"Whoa, hold on!" Shun hurried forward, a hand moving to rest on Holly's arm. "Just, wait. I know everything is . . . just the worst right now, but please promise me you aren't thinking of USING that cursed . . . THING on—"

The Wolf-Lord looked down at her wife, scandalized. "Never! We will do as Lady Nimue said. Fix one of Heraldale's great sins."

The kitsune still looked lost. Galaxy, thinking of the crimes of Lady Quetzal and Queen Grimhilt, and of getting to see Brynjar and Bevin again, said "We're going to destroy the spear."

CHAPTER TWENTY-SEVEN

They plucked his primary feathers so he could not fly. They bound his wings tight against his body in thick steel chains. More chains connected arm to arm and leg to leg. They threw him into his quarters which had once been an animal's pen, taking for themselves every bag, every scrap, every weapon found there for themselves.

Brynjar put up no fight against any of this. He avoided every accusing look as he was dragged to his prison by Wolf-Lord guards, hung his head as he felt the burning gazes of Ashe and Kanti. The cries for murder and justice from Mammon echoed after him.

Abandoned in his cell, Brynjar closed his eyes and let time pass unmarked. He dwelled in his thoughts of Galaxy, Owain, the twins, Bifrost, all the others left behind back west. If all had gone well, the war might already be over. Galaxy would be getting nervous, urgent for any word from them. The twins would make a pithy remark to calm her, and Bifrost would flirt with her, and Owain would already be readying an air-yacht to come find him and Bevin.

"Since when do things ever go well," Brynjar whispered to himself, and slept.

When not sleeping, he thought of how close he thought they had come to bringing the duke over to their side. He thought of Kanti, if she was still trying to win favor, if she had been lumped in with him and Bevin and held prisoner somewhere else in the castle. He wondered if Bevin had really attacked the strange but helpful guru, and if so, why. He could only think of one reason, but at that late hour of woe, he could barely care.

No visitors came, but after many missed meals and fights for sleep, the guards returned. Once more, Brynjar gave no resistance as they slipped a thick iron collar around his neck and lead him by a chain out of his confining quarters. A cold wind blew from the west, but overhead the sky was clear of all clouds and the sun shone strong in the glory of its azure throne room.

Brynjar stopped and closed his eyes for a moment, basking in the ghost of warmth in the air. Somehow, it had never felt clearer in all his life that winter was on the retreat, at least in that part of the world, and soon it would be spring again.

The guards dragged him on, back through the castle. There were more soldiers filling the place than he remembered, more Wolf-Lords and kitsune bearing arms and armor, all watching him more warily than the dragons beginning to swarm the skies and surrounding mountaintops.

Duke Managarm, the Nameless Monk, and Lady Gauri waited for him in their seats, Guru Veda's remaining empty. A dozen wolf guards roamed the outer walls of the old hall, as Mammon and Ashe loomed large behind the delegates.

As Brynjar was brought to a stop before the thrones, Managarm leaned forward, head turning aside. Brynjar followed their gaze and saw Kanti leaning against a stone pillar half in the gloom, her arms crossed and eyes refusing to meet Brynjar's. A curiously curved sword was strapped to her back, and from her hip hung a short-handled mace with an impressively large head. It didn't seem a good sign to him.

"Sir Brynjar of Heraldale," spoke the Nameless Monk, voice dragging Brynjar's attention back to the assembly like a barbed spear. The kitsune gazed down at him with a perfect sneer. "Do you know why you stand so before us?"

Brynjar said nothing. He looked from the Monk to Ashe behind the row of seats, but though she met his eyes, he gained nothing from her.

"The esteemed Guru Veda's life still hangs in the balance," continued the Monk when he received no answer. "Neither she nor your . . . compatriot, have awakened. The dragons, in their time here, grew fond of Guru Veda. She has ever been their greatest champion in establishing their home and rights here. And your compatriot attacked her. The dragons demand justice for this and many other things. For once, we are in accord."

Lady Gauri leaned forward in their seat neat, their gaze alone pleading, not hardened by anger or hate. "Don't you have anything to say for yourself?"

Brynjar stood as tall as his chains would allow and looked to his judges. To him, despair came in the furious boom of Lord Mordred, the heartless whispers of Lord Beauty, the hateful contempt of Lord Thoth; even the prideful tones of General Madara in the dark of his dungeon cell, tempting toward the worst of ends. Brynjar shut the despair out, thought of family and friends still surely fighting, gave himself hope when none seemed ready to come from elsewhere. "Veda seemed our ally here, but I know Bevin, and I can't believe Bevin would attack her without good cause. I don't know that good cause. Self-defense, perhaps. Perhaps Veda isn't who we think she is."

These last words, Brynjar spoke not to the judges, but to Ashe behind them, meeting her gaze with his own, willing her silently to understand his meaning. The dragon's eyes widened the barest twitch, perceptible only to his keen gryphon sight. Her nostrils flared as she took a slow, probing sniff of the hall.

"Guru Veda's honor is unimpeachable," snarled the Monk. "The same cannot be said of unicorns or gryphons. As our first act as a united people, we condemn you—"

"WAIT!"

The shouted rang through the hall, silencing every voice and stilling every step. Kanti moved to stand between Brynjar and the assembly, shoulders squared and head high. "I call for the old ways of wolf and dragon to settle this! Trial by combat!"

Murmurs of rustles of bodies turning to look at the from her to the delegates rang through the grand ruin. Looks were exchanged among them, and behind them Mammon loosed a deep-throated snort which had short plumes of flame billowing from the blue dragon's nostrils.

Among them all, the Nameless Monk looked exultant. "Why?"

Kanti's fists clenched as her attention seemed to focus entirely on the magical fox. "You. You bear a grudge against Veda for her old association with the late Holly le Fay. And earlier, we refused your offer of assistance in the war for a price we could not pay. I accuse that you attacked Veda and framed Bevin.

"And more . . . I just don't like you."

The Monk's shoulders bunched, a low chortle slipping from him as he rose from his chair. Tails lashed the air, trailing cool orange fires and smoke. Brynjar looked from him to the Wolf-Lord closer at talon and felt a sudden doom in the air. "Blackbird . . . why? You're sticking your neck out for . . ."

"I have to believe it's what she'd do," said the Wolf-Lord, Brynjar unsure of what she meant. At last, she looked away from the Monk, to him. "And I'm sure I told you, it's Kanti among my friends."

From across the hall, Mammon's voice came in a towering snarl. "Bring me the right head, fox, and the alliance between our peoples will last until the stars themselves fall."

"Elder, please," begged Ashe, small and pink as she struggled in vain to get the larger dragon's ear. "Please!"

"Guards!" shouted the Monk. "Drag that gryphon back and bring me my sword."

His chains grew taut, Brynjar grimacing as he was dragged backward by them. All guards, all servants, all dragons, all delegates backed away to the crumbling walls of the ruin, leaving only Kanti and the Monk alone at the center, among the clear pools and growing moss, the thin sunbeams falling over them heavy with motes of dust. To the kitsune a plain-dressed Wolf-Lord of brown fur came, knelt, presented in their open palms a long katana and scabbard. The Monk drew the sword, the blade gleaming thin and bright, and the servant retreated.

To Kanti came Duke Managarm, movements stiff as they adorned her in a hip-length armor coat of leather and gilded scale mail, vambraces, a helmet offered and rejected. The duke made no effort to lower their voice. "This is suicide. That is an eight-tailed kitsune standing opposite you. You have to understand that no mere Wolf-Lord can win this fight."

Kanti rested a hand on the handle of the heavy-headed mace secured at her side. "If I've learned anything from working alongside gryphons all these years, some impossible fights are worth the odds. Besides, I have a trick or two up my sleeve."

Managarm looked unconvinced, but backed away to stand beside Gauri. Brynjar took the chance. "Kanti . . . good luck."

The black-furred Wolf-Lord's head turned, only enough for Brynjar to see the sad smile she wore in answer. Then her focus returned wholly to her approaching foe.

"You should have listened to the duke," said the Monk, letting his katana hang loose at his side as he stalked slowly toward Kanti so the tip of the blade dragged along the pebbled and uneven ground. "Do not let my age convince you that this will at all be a fair fight!"

"You're talking to a pirate and smuggler," answered Kanti, drawing the talwar from her back. "I wouldn't know a fair fight if I saw one."

As if to put proof to her words, even as she spoke she dropped to one knee, free hand reaching to rest the thick scabbard of her sword on her shoulder. A click of a hidden button in what Brynjar had first thought to be only gold ornamentation, and a trio of small black bolts flew from within the hidden weapon.

The Monk stopped his stride and whip-cracked his tails. Shields of flame sprang to life before him, catching two of the bolts and reducing them to ash. The third slipped through and buried into the Monk's gut—

The Monk burst into smoke. Kanti swore brought her sword up in a spin. Steel clashed and the illusion hiding the true Monk faded, katana bare inches from a beheading.

Brynjar watched from the sidelines as the pair separated, clashed again, drew back to circle each other with raised swords and hard gazes. A feint, a poor guard, a cut shocking in its reach, and Kanti retreated, a thin cut along her muzzle. A mocking wound, something which could've been a killing blow if the Monk cared even a little. Deep nausea roiled in Brynjar's guts, a voice of doom he tried to squash as Kanti growled and plunged back into a blistering exchange of blows. Half were blocked or turned aside. Almost half were wasted on illusion copies. One slipped through, a shallow stab which somehow found its way to the Monk's right thigh.

A burst of yellow-hot fire in all directions paid Kanti back for the trouble, threw her clear across the makeshift arena to land with a splash among the pools.

"Stay down," demanded the Monk.

Kanti climbed back to her feet, panting hard, the front of her armor blackened by the fire. For a moment, Brynjar saw her hand stray to the mace at her side, letting go just as swiftly. "No—"

A thick stream of orange fire arced over the pools, trailed by billows of steam. Kanti's scream of pain as the flames washed over her half-raised right arm filled the hall, accompanied by the eye-watering stench of burnt metal and cooked meat. Gasps rose from many of the onlookers. Gauri, tears shining in their eyes, looked away. Brynjar, bellowing, lunged forward to intervene, dragging the four Wolf-Lords holding his chains a yard before they managed to rein him back him. His heart lurched as those screams went on.

The fires died away and Kanti fell back to her knees. Her sword arm hung slack, scorched black and smoking, fingers barely keeping their grip on her sword. Shivers of pain wracked her whole body. It didn't sound like she could get enough air. Brynjar wondered in horror at how she even remained conscious, well aware that fire was one of the few things Wolf-Lords could not heal from.

The Monk lowered his smoking fists and remained in place, glowering across the yards separating them. "Stay down. You're not fooling anyone here who knows anything."

With what looked to be a titanic effort, Kanti lifted her head to glare at the kitsune. Fangs were bared as she gritted her teeth against the pain, tears shining in her eyes as she hissed out "Shut . . . up!"

"Every Wolf-Lord and kitsune worth their salt knows the story," continued the Monk, flames wreathing their hands as they halved the distance between them. "You fell in love with the wicked spawn of wicked Morgana le Fay, but when she needed you, when the forces working toward her death at last her, you did nothing. You fled back to your icy hovel and let her die. So now, whether it's redemption you seek or death, do what I know you do best and STAY DOWN."

For several long seconds, silence was king of the ruined hall. Dragons rustled their wings and Wolf-Lords curled their tails, and Brynjar watched with bated breath and thundering heart as Kanti struggled, got one foot under her, rose wobbling into an unsteady stance. The tears streamed down her cheeks, but though the sword fell at last from her burnt hand to splash forgotten into the pool, her unharmed hand at last drew the mace free from her side. "There's no fire you can burn me with . . . that hurts more than the wound her death left in my life. There's no taunt you can sling worse than what I tell myself in the spare hours of my life, when the years of her absence peel away and the loss is as fresh as that first terrible hour. You . . . are helpless before me."

Brynjar swallowed, throat aching and gathering tears a surprise. All of a sudden, he wanted to hear his mother's voice again and knew he never would.

The next stream of fire burned white-hot and was a pain to even behold. Brynjar raised an arm and turned his head to shield his sight, heart stopping in awful anticipation. But the expected screams never came, and the blinding light shining through his clenched-shut eyelids swiftly dimmed. Brynjar opened his eyes and blinked away the lingering spots, watching first in shock, then horror the sight before him.

The fires of the Monk's attack drained away before the eyes of all in the hall. After the fire came visible streamers of his magic, sparkling and ghostly as it flew through the air toward Kanti. The Wolf-Lord stood panting, looking barely able to hold her mace aloft with head aimed toward the kitsune. But the head had changed. Thin slots had opened in the metal all along its circumference, revealing a glowing blue crystal. Seeing it, Brynjar remembered Port Oil, remembered Spell Virus, remembered the first charged crystal battery Galaxy had thrown into the waters in thoughtless fear. "Oh, God. Kanti, no!"

Kanti gave no answer, gave no sign she heard Brynjar at all. Muzzle set in a growl, she staggered her way forward as the Monk fell to his knees, showing more and more the years of his life as his magic was eaten away. "Your rotten order took her from me! You and the old ruling family! You killed her. Holly was good, Holly was kind, Holly was the most loving Wolf-Lord in all the world and you killed her for her blood! For the sins of parents she had nothing to do with! Death is the best you deserve!"

Gauri and Managarm were shouting for her to stop, for the trial by combat to be over, but Kanti seemed as happy to ignore them as she'd been to ignore Brynjar. Before them all, the Monk continued to wither and die, fur greying and skin thinning, clothes seeming increasingly oversized on his crumbling frame. His muzzle worked and sounds were barely to be heard, a breathless wheeze of ". . . can find . . ."

Kanti, standing before the fallen kitsune, lowered their perilous weapon so that the magical drain lessened. "What was that!? Where can I find them? Caelestis, Maurus, where!?"

The Monk's voice fell further silent, eyes rolling in their bruised sockets and katana fallen from his hand. Kanti growled and with a press of a switch in the handle of the mace the slots closed, securing the shard of Spell Virus once more. "Where are—"

But even as Kanti shouted, the Monk's expression hardened. Brynjar watched, too far and too secured to do anything, as the illusion of the katana faded from the floor, the true weapon still in the Monk's hand, gleaming as it swung up and under Kanti's armor, through her gut and out her back.

"NO!" Brynjar charged forward, scrabbling across the cracked stone, one of the dragon onlookers needing to add its might to those holding him back by chains.

The thud of Kanti's mace hitting the floor rang through the hall. Blood bright and thick burst from her muzzle in a gasp, a shudder passing through her body before she fell away and to the floor, the bloody blade drawing from her with a horrible, wet noise. She lay there, amongst the crowd but alone, gasping and shaking, dying with a slowness which made Brynjar want to vomit.

The Monk towered over her, still ancient and withered but undeniably victorious. He raised his sword for a killing blow—

"STOP!"

Billowing flames accompanied the roar as Ashe crashed through one of the larger openings in the roof, Wolf-Lords cowering from the heat and the Monk gracelessly tumbling aside as the pink dragon landed between him and Kanti. Brynjar had a moment of relief to wonder if this is the miracle he had hoped for, before Ashe slung the limp body of Guru Veda from her back onto the floor and roared again "This is your true enemy!"

Tumult filled the ruin, Wolf-Lords howling, baying, shouting their outrage at the audacity. Swords were drawn. Spears were raised. Duke Managarm screamed for blood and death with flanged mace held high. But Mammon outshone them all, the mountainous blue dragon rearing back with wings spread, a pillar of flame scorching the stone of the roof black.

All fell silent. Mammon fell to all fours. Gazes fell back to Ashe as he growled "Explain yourself, whelp! You slander one wolf who has argued and bled for us!"

"I beg your mercy, elder, but I reveal a deceiver who has made puppets of all of us!" proclaimed Ashe. She stood tall and unwavering beneath the collective glare of the room, such that Brynjar at once wanted to go to her side so she did not have to stand so alone, with only gasping, dying Kanti beside her. He could hardly believe she was the same dragon his small band of friends and family had once found cowering in a cave, lost and alone.

"I spent decades captured by Empire," continued Ashe, one clawed hand left to rest on Veda's still form. "Decades. Learned heart-deep the smell of master torturer, Lord Beauty. Would know smell anywhere. Smelled it here, all time with the delegates. Brynjar and Bevin tell us that Lord Beauty was Morgana le Fay, great evil. Today, I stood among those three and realized I DID NOT smell Lord Beauty, Morgana le Fay." The dragon snarled, the hand moving to grip the body by a shoulder and lift it up for all to see. "I DO NOW! THIS IS MORGANA!"

One second passed. Enough time for sharp intakes of breath throughout the hall. Enough time for Gauri to catch Brynjar's eye. Enough time for Kanti on the floor to cry out in rage and pain. Enough time for Duke Managarm to march forward a single step, flanged mace in hand and raised.

Veda's eyes opened, revealing star sapphire orbs burning with magic. Her twisted around on her neck to glare up at Ashe holding her, the sound of breaking bone clear and sickening. She screamed, in the clear voice of Lady Beauty, of Morgana le Fay, "YOU STUPID, WORTHLESS DRAGON! I WAS ENJOYING WATCHING THEM TEAR THEMSELVES APART, AND YOU HAD TO OPEN YOUR BIG, STUPID, WORTHLESS MOUTH!"

Ashe dropped the body with a yowl of pain and staggered back with wings flapping in a panic, eyes wide and watching the scales from her hand crumble and fall away with a sudden black rot.

Morgana stayed in place as if still held. Rotated to float upright, hair and cloak billowing in the unseen breezes of her magic. An annoyed flick of her hand and Ashe flew backward, faster than those bystanders between her and the wall could get out of the way.

CRACK.

THUMP.

Screams rang throughout the ruin, dragons and some Wolf-Lords fleeing, others falling to hands and knees in terror or worship. Morgana cackled and cast crackling bolts of magic into the backs of those who tried to flee, sending them to the ground in writhing agony.

Amidst the chaos, Brynjar felt the hold on his chains slacken and tore himself free, at once diving forward to grab Kanti and carry her away from the horror suddenly walking amongst them, talons clamping over her stab wound to staunch the blood loss as best he could. The Wolf-Lord groaned for all his efforts, barely clinging to consciousness. "The . . . the mace . . ."

"Not in the cards right now, buddy," said Brynjar, staring at the weapon in question where it lay at Morgana's feet. "Just try to hold on there until help arrives."

It was clear no help would be coming from those within the ruin. Mammon moved to stand protectively between Morgana and Ashe's dazed form, the blue dragon roaring and spreading his wings to their full width as he unleashed a blinding torrent of flame at the floating Wolf-Lord.

Morgana looked his way, and the fire turned to soap bubbles floating harmlessly toward the roof. She tilted her head, tone bored even as the dragon charged forward to swipe at her with his claws. "You should be careful, getting into fights with your scales made of such brittle glass."

A new, peculiar sheen appeared over Mammon's body wherever there were scales, followed immediately by the sound of shattering glass at every joint. Roars of fury turned into screams of pain and the blue dragon fell, Brynjar turning his gaze at the sounds of more glass breaking, the glimpse of blue staining red in the dragon's death throes.

"Oh, God, Veda, stop this," mumbled the Nameless Monk, katana half-raised and trembling. "I don't . . . I don't understand . . ."

Morgana looked down at him, muzzle turned in a mocking smile. "You never understood much of anything, really. Your hatreds and prejudices made you so easy to twist to my needs without you ever being the wiser." Her smile turned brighter, meaner. "Or maybe it's because your skull's made of lead!"

A moment for terror to fill the Monk's eyes, an unspeakable sound from his muzzle, and then his neck bent from the sudden weight with a SNAP. He fell with a clang of his head against the floor, eight tails at last stilled.

"Oh, God," moaned Managarm. They knelt in the shadow of one of the pillars lining the walls, one arm wrapped protectively around a shaking, sobbing Gauri. "Oh, God, please. We're sorry, we're sorry, please, stop! Don't hurt us!"

Morgana looked to them, smile dying though the amusement remained. "Hurt you? Nonsense. Why would I bother hurting you? Little duke, you can't hurt me. You can't hurt anyone. You're nothing."

Gauri sat sprawled in the shadow of the pillar, sobbing and alone.

At last, Morgana turned her crystal gaze toward Brynjar. He stiffened at the attention, swallowed moved to stand protectively over Kanti. He knew there was little he could expect to do even compared to the other victims of the wolf witch's wrath, bound and chained as he still was, but even so . . .

"And so, we meet again," whispered Morgana as she floated toward him, silvery magic dancing between her clawed fingers. The flickers of magic grew, sparked into a ball of blue-hot flames. "I did tell Lord Bevin I would destroy all her family, but I had hoped to wake her up and let her WATCH. Oh well, we can't have everything . . ."

The flames came, thick and blinding. Brynjar took a last breath, thought of Owain—

The flames crashed against an overlapping pair of shield spells, one white, the other a familiar red. Immediately, Brynjar relaxed, shook Kanti back to full consciousness as his every hope came true. The sensation of déjà vu was unreal.

The flames stopped. Morgana backed off, eyes wide as the shields fell away and Galaxy flew up before her. "Enough!"

CHAPTER TWENTY-EIGHT

"That is enough!" Galaxy repeated, staring the dark Wolf-Lord down. She let her magic snap and crackle over her horn, mixing eddies of red and blue magic. With barely a flicker of thought, wary of the foe before her, she let the Waters of Life reach out from her to fill the ruined hall with the weight of her power. Not so much to crush and debase as Empress Nova did, but enough to heal body and harden will against the horrors she could see had been inflicted.

"Princess Galaxy," whispered Morgana, edging away with hands raised warily. "So far away from Heraldale. You have such work to do in Gateway, what brings you here . . . ruining my fun?"

"I can answer that." With a rush of wings and swirl of her sleeveless black robe, Holly le Fay landed to Galaxy's left. Gasps and murmurs ran through the throne room. A disbelieving whimper of "Holly?" from a black-furred Wolf-Lord as Brynjar helped her back to her feet. But more satisfying still to war-weary Galaxy was the breakneck shock writ large across Morgana's features. "Mother."

"Holly," the other Wolf-Lord whispered. No more than this, for the next moment Ashe rose on broad wings and roared a heavy stream of fire at Morgana from behind, followed a spare second later by Mammon. Together, the dragons completely engulfed the dark Wolf-Lord in their fire. All shadows were banished before the overwhelming light of the assault. Wolf-Lord onlookers scrambled away or sought shelter behind their dragon fellows, while Galaxy's heart skipped a beat.

"Enough!" Below, Brynjar seemed to wilt against the heat. "Enough! Hold your fire!"

Mammon let up. Ashe did not. Not until Galaxy flew forward and gripped the young dragon's shoulder. "Ashe, please. That's enough. You got her already or you can't get her at all."

With a low snort, the dragon slowly let the stream of fire peter out to nothing. She stumbled back, suddenly exhausted from the ferocity of the attack, Brynjar and Galaxy catching her with a splayed wing each to keep her from falling. For nearly a minute, the gathered host watched the flames burn where Morgana had fallen, the floor around her melted to slag, nothing seen beneath the flames but a black, ashen mass.

"You killed her," said Managarm, looking from the dying fire to Ashe. Their hands trembled as they clutched to the albino Wolf-Lord beside them for dear life, eyes wide and unseeing within their helm. "You killed her, right? I was . . . I was nothing, and then there was this cold magic, like water, and then I was something again, and there she was, and—"

A clawed skeletal arm reached up from the last dregs of flame and Managarm shrieked. The rest of the withered, fire-blackened Wolf-Lord skeleton pushed itself up from the floor, nothing left to the creature before them but the swaying bones, a fleshy and pulsing mass within the chest cavity, and the glowing star sapphire orbs in the eye sockets. Even as they watched, the mass in the chest began to burn away, the pulsing— a heartbeat, Galaxy decided—slowing, losing its rhythm.

"Ignore the Heraldans," spoke an old, commanding voice from the skeletal figure. Brynjar and Bevin recognized it as the voice of Lord Beauty. Holly and Kanti recognized it as the voice of Morgana le Fay. "Turn from them. Repulse them from your lands. Leave them to their fates at the talons of Empress Nova of Heraldale. This is my command. Obey it and be spared my wrath. Hear the Heraldans, welcome them, help them, and you will be destroyed. That is my promise!"

The black mass burst into scattering cinders and the bones crumbled to ash. The star sapphire eyes remained in place, floating there and staring at them before flying for the door.

"Not so fast!" cried out Holly, lunging and grabbing one of the crystal eyes as it sped past her. Immediately she reeled, a pained and twitching look coming over her. "Oh God, that is loud. There is a voice. There is her voice. It is screaming for me to let her go. Muscles in . . . my arm, they . . . they do not feel like . . . my own . . ."

"Powerful necromancy," muttered the Nameless Monk. "Mind casting into corpses, the gems the receivers . . ."

"Let go of it," said Kanti, moving to Holly's side. "Let go now!"

"I'm . . . trying . . ." Holly trembled where she stood. Blood trickled from both her nostrils and tears welled in her eyes. She screwed them shut and grit her teeth, and with clear, tremendous effort to those near her, forced her fingers apart. The gem eye flew away at once to catch up with the other.

Holly sagged, Kanti caught her before she could fall and cradled her close, peppering kisses across her fellow Wolf-Lord's muzzle and cheeks. For a moment, it was like they were the only two in the room. "Oh God, you're alive again. I'm sorry. I'm so sorry. I tried, I tried so hard."

"I know," said Holly, returning the kisses once before clambering back up to her full height. The brief weakness was behind her. "I know. You were wonderful."

Galaxy kept her peace as she watched the reunion for a moment, then looked to Brynjar beside her. "Where's Bevin?"

Ashe answered. "Unconscious. Left so by . . . Morgana. Nobody has been able to wake her, some sort of spell. Physically, there doesn't seem to be anything wrong with her."

Galaxy closed her eyes at this news and weighed the moment. Her heart yearned to go to her sister, to wake her if this was something the Waters of Life could fix. But she didn't know the first thing about sleeping spells and if they counted as injuries to be healed, and time was already growing terribly, drastically short for Heraldale, and she knew Bevin would want her to make the most pragmatic choice. And so, she opened her eyes and looked to the remaining representatives of the Wolf-Lord nations and of the dragons. They looked put through a warzone, the cavalcade of sudden returns and shocking reveals. She sympathized, but there was simply no more time. "We need to talk."

"Gal," said Brynjar. "What happened at the Grand Harmonium?"

"A lot," answered Galaxy. "The Grand Harmonium can fly and perform mass teleports like any of the Imperial warships. I don't think anywhere is beyond Avalon's reach, now. And it gets worse. Morgana le Fay used my lost limb to create Empress Nova a new body. A hippogryph body. She can Harmonize unicorns and gryphons now."

Brynjar's eyes widened. "The others in the attack with you. Owain, Hywel—"

"I don't know," said Galaxy, her own thoughts going to Bifrost. "But whoever remains, we need to get back and help them. Together." She looked again to those surrounding them and spoke loud and with authority, summoning forth what she knew Brynjar and Owain called her "Princess" voice. "Empress Nova will not stop with Heraldale. Especially not with Morgana le Fay at her side. If we don't stop her together, we will all fall to her in our own time. I came for alliance."

Voice still tinged with the hysteria of the last half hour, Duke Managarm scoffed. "You came out of madness. Even if we could stand against Morgana le Fay and your empress, you ask for Wolf-Lords to stand beside gryphons and unicorns as if centuries of bad blood do not stand between us. It is impossible."

"Not impossible," said Holly. "I have lived and fought beside gryphons, even against Morgana. I will do it again."

"But even so," began the duke.

"You don't speak for us!" said Gauri, stepping to the forefront at last, a tremor in their step but a young resolve in their yellow eyes Galaxy found admirable. When the duke turned to glare down at them, teeth bared, they bared theirs back. "You don't speak for us," they repeated, more firmly. "Right now, nobody apparently speaks for Akela, unless Lady Kanti there wants to step up. Nobody speaks for the kitsune. But I speak for the country of Tabaqui for as long as we're here, and I will make my own decisions. And one question I have to ask that I know you are too prideful to," and here they turned to Galaxy, "is what's in it for us?"

Galaxy stared. Gauri went on. "Perhaps our people feel the same, that it is time to put old grudges aside for the greater good. But my teachers tell me no alliance can stand where resentment stands also. And so, amends. You are hippogryph. You come from both unicorns and gryphons, who savaged us Wolf-Lords and kitsune to the brink of genocide. You stole our lands from us. How will you make amends to us?"

Galaxy swallowed, took a moment before answering, having thought this question over already. She knew many of those at her side would hate her answer. "I, Princess Galaxy, daughter of the late Queen Grimhilt, heir to the throne of Schwarz Angebot, hippogryph . . . relinquish my claim to the throne and offer it to the Wolf-Lords."

Silence for one stunned moment. Then, Brynjar, horrified, "Gal!"

"I know what I'm doing," said Galaxy, wishing the claim did not feel like such a lie in her beak. She kept her gaze to the representatives. "The lands will remain open to gryphons. Any gryphons displaced by the war with Avalon will be free to return to their homes, their communities, and they will be able to live in the same peace and security they could anywhere else. But the governing of the lands will be in Wolf-Lord hands. And I will help however I can in restoring whatever old Wolf-Lord cities are within the bounds of the realm, if such is your wish. I swear this."

"Then I swear myself and the soldiers here with me to your cause." Gauri turned and glared up at Managarm. "Satisfied yet? Or will you wait until the horror of Morgana we saw here today invades our own lands?"

The grey Wolf-Lord's fists clenched. Their gaze swept the scorched and shattered hall around them, the wolves standing there frightened and uncertain. When it returned to Galaxy, it was filled with new resolve. "Aye, then. One last war for this old wolf."

"And what to the dragons?" added Mammon, towering to his full gargantuan height as the moment passed. "What amends for your mother's crimes? For Lady Quetzal's?"

Here at last, Galaxy was able to smile. "Holly?"

At her name, Holly held a hand out. All felt the charge of magic in the air. And then a quick flash, and there in the white Wolf-Lord's hand was the spear Gungnir.

"By the Blessed Magic," said Gauri, looking at the weapon with unabashed reverence.

Mammon reared back, eyes wide and gouts of flame bursting from the edges of his snout. "That accursed weapon!"

"Gal . . ." said Ashe, sounding worried.

"It's alright, I promise," said Galaxy, taking the spear from Holly and holding it aloft in the red shine of her magic. "Yes, this is Gungnir. The Oath Spear. Centuries ago, Lady Quetzal used it to force the dragons into pacifism, to make you unable to ever fight with concerted effort. It is the only reason Avalon was able to hunt the northern dragons to extinction in the first place. They couldn't properly defend themselves.

"I have brought it here to destroy it by Wolf-Lord hands."

The sudden hope, the sudden desperation not only in Ashe's eyes, but in Mammon's, hurt Galaxy straight to the heart. Heedless of it, Duke Managarm scoffed once more. "Noble, but impossible. That was forged by ancient Queen Morgause, who gryphons knew as General Nero. It is one of seven Perfect Tools she made. It is indestructible except by her own blood."

Holly wasted no time with talking, throwing her left hand forward to seize the spear in her own magic. A pulse like a harsh wind spread outward, sending those nearest the scene staggering or sliding back. All but Holly, the Wolf-Lord's knees bent and body leaned forward, fighting the push. To Galaxy, reorienting herself, she looked more like she was hanging on to the spear rather than standing.

"Everyone who is afraid of being caught in the epicenter of a giant magical explosion, leave!" shouted Holly. The rush of the numerous guards to obey this command went unremarked upon. Holly forced herself a step close to the spear, then reached forward with her right hand, encased in a sheathe of her white magic as she waved intricate signs through the air. Before long, the scrolling runes across the surface of the spear began to glow a matching white.

"She's removing the enchantments!" shouted Kanti over the rushing winds as she forced her way back up beside Galaxy. "I've only seen that done once before!"

"Did it work?" Galaxy called back. She had never seen it done before.

"It leveled half the castle!"

Galaxy looked around at her precious people. "You should go! All of you!"

"It's like you've never met us," grunted Brynjar, pushing himself up to Galaxy's other side and shooting her a gryphon's smirk.

"Hold on!" shouted Holly. Her right hand clenched into a fist and drew back again. Before her, the glowing runes quivered, then drew up and away from the metal surface. A sound like the whine of overstressed steel began to fill the air, piercing through ears and making Galaxy feel like her bones were readying to break.

"Look!"

Glowing chains of raw magic had appeared wrapped around Ashe and Mammon. Seeing them, Galaxy imagined similar chains appearing on dragons all across the Wolf-Lord nations, all chained by the Oath Spear.

"Princess Galaxy, shields now!" shouted Holly. "A foot wide around the spear, leave top open. Pink dragon, fire! Now! Hot as you can make it!"

Galaxy began casting her spells before the Wolf-Lord even finished speaking, erecting two, three, four layers of shield spells around the spear, cutting off the worst of the battering winds. The last was barely up before Ashe flew in, head flung back, then forward. A sound like the roar of a mammoth waterfall filled the room, a head-bursting, heart-stopping sound, as Ashe loosed a torrent of blue fire down onto the spear. Even through the multiple shield spells, the light was blinding, the heat toasting the feathers of Galaxy's face. The horrible stench of melting stone and metal struck. Galaxy cast a fifth layer of shield spells, and then a sixth, and it seemed to do nothing.

"Almost . . . almost . . . GRAGH!" With a scream of effort and burst of magical might, Holly whipped both arms out wide. A shriek of twisting metal sounded, then the air itself seemed to crack. Galaxy had a moment to see the chains disappear again from around the dragons in the room. Fire and magic erupted through her shield spells, shattering the pillars, a blinding flash and crush of magic like the end of the world—

CHAPTER TWENTY-NINE

Down in the palace dungeons, the fighting could barely even be heard. Sascha would have laughed at this, any other time. Right then, she didn't feel like laughing. Not one chuckle.

She and Siegfried were two among dozens of noncombatants taken down to hide in the dungeons of the palace while the battle went on, their uses spent. Endless hours of waiting down in the cold and wet dark. Hiding and waiting for the end.

Somewhere in the dark, a baby cried and a mother tried fruitlessly to calm it down, her own voice near to hysterics. Somewhere in the dark, an Elk soldier lay probably dead. He had been brought down bereft a leg and sobbing for his mother, his father, his queen. Somewhere in the dark, Sascha lost track of the last time she'd heard a noise from him.

Something, an explosion, struck the palace. The ceiling cracked, dust and chips raining down on the huddled crowds, who all gasped and screamed.

Sascha closed her eyes and found Siegfried's talons with her own. They held each other as their refuge crumbled in inches and seconds.

***

The hideous red of the volcanic sky died further into utter blackness, an unnatural night in defiance of the very idea of day.

The city had fallen, the defenders driven back to the palace. The crystal drones rained down and the undead scaled the sides of the ziggurat, fires raging, the air choking and foul.

Bifrost flew through the maelstrom of the war, the tattered remnants of her scarf caught on her armor as she fought and fought and fought, her spear in motion from inertia alone. Spell bolts struck glancing blows across her as Imperial air-yachts roared past. Wyverns tore at her as she danced back, their claws more and more leaving their bloody, searing marks.

A crystal drone slammed into her, its forward spike punching into her cuirass. Bifrost fell screaming to the palace roof, body trembling as the drone fired its spell bolts point-blank. She landed on her back, threw the drone off her, buried her spear into its center before it could take off again.

Pain, utter pain, each breath the greatest struggle. Bifrost coughed and spat, then slowly worked herself back up onto all fours, and then onto her rear legs in the Gateway custom, using her spear to support herself. Her talons found a gryphon spellcasting rod on the roof and she began to fire it upon unicorn soldiers charging at her, her voice bloody and roaring.

An eldritch light caught her in the eyes and split the night asunder. Bifrost winced from the harshness of the light, dropped her rod to rub at her strained eyes. Ahead, a thin seam had appeared in the center of the black obelisk at the center of the palace roof, a seam in the stone Bifrost had never seen before. The seam grew, the colorless light reaching from the top of the black obelisk to the bottom. Once it had done so, the new sound of stone grinding over stone reached Bifrost, as before her eyes and the eyes of the whole battle, from the fighters on the roof to the unicorns watching from their warships, the black obelisk split in half. It became not a pillar, but a gate. And beyond the gate, shining forth from it, Bifrost beheld a field of the strange colorless magic stretching out into Dark Realm beyond time and space.

This was it, Bifrost realized, falling trembling to the roof as she was overcome at last by terror and her blasted-apart chest. The power source for the Grand Harmonium's world spell. The last and most legendary creation from Toqeph the Prime Unicorn. The tool which had brought them all to Heraldale in ancient past—

Bifrost's thoughts scattered as she was overcome with a last, wracking bout of coughing, the taste of blood and ash in her mouth and down her throat . . .

***

"The Reality Gate," Owain whispered, fallen exhausted to his knees in the midst of the final battlefield. He swallowed and tore his gaze away, looking back to the slowly approaching Grand Harmonium. "Gal, Brynjar, Bevin . . ."

"OWAIN!"

At the sound of his name, Owain looked to the ruins of the palace roof. Out of the fire-lit fog of war staggered Lord Thoth, the sphinx heaving for breath, mad-eyed as he leveled a heavy sword toward Owain with his telekinesis. He looked as if he had waded through the whole scorched and blasted city, through all the battles and smoking wrecks between the palace and the northern docks. He looked like he had been marching forth for Owain ever since the rainy day Owain, Brynjar, and Hywel gave him and Avalon the final slip. For all Owain knew, perhaps he had.

"I've got you now," the burnt sphinx growled. "Your head . . . your head for Nova . . ."

Owain snorted. He forced himself back to his hooves, his body's protests roundly ignored. He took up his fallen sword in his magic and staggered forward to meet the sphinx. Every hour, every minute of the torture endured in Lord Thoth's grasp in the days of his capture replayed through his mind, every ounce of pain and dreg of fear, all kindling to the anger growing in his heart.

Their swords clashed. Parted. They circled each other, side-stepping the debris and fallen bodies, glares burning. Owain stabbed for the sphinx's throat. Thoth slashed for the unicorn's front leg. Each backpedaled away, wove forward again, swords crashing together.

Thoth roared and pushed. Owain stumbled back, hooves losing purchase. He grabbed a jumble of shattered stone from the palace roof in his magic and flung it at Thoth's face. The sphinx psychically scattered the attack, then flung a burning plank of wood from a wrecked air-yacht.

"Augh!" Owain cried, magic grip on his sword failing as scorching, grating pain scoured across his snout and cheek, dancing over his right eye.

"Ah! Now you can be Queen Gwendolyn's twin!"

Another telekinetic shove and Owain fell, breath lost, back aching as it bent awkwardly over another fallen body. General Odin, an axe buried to the haft into his chest.

Somewhere, fire roared. Lightning flashed and thunder rumbled through the sky.

One of Thoth's front paws slammed down onto Owain's throat, bruising, cutting off air. Owain gagged, gasped, legs feebly kicking as the sphinx leered down at him, dragging his sword along Owain's side. "Where's your Elk friend to hide you? Where's your gryphon lover to protect you? Where's your daddy to die for you? Looks to me like you're all alone, 'Sir Owain'! All alone like you would always be after turning against your empire, against the future!"

"No, not alone!"

Lord Thoth's eyes widened. He lifted away from Owain and turned, into the swing of a great axe. His head flew and his body fell, and Lord Thoth was dead at the talons of Sir Brynjar of Featheren Valley.

Owain could breathe again. He reclaimed his wobbly hooves, helped by a supportive wing from Brynjar. The war around them fell away into utter silence.

Owain moved forward, pressing close against the golden eagle-gryphon, his tears falling freely as he felt a heavy wing drape over his back. More thunder sounded across the sky.

"Not alone," Brynjar said again, looking upward. Owain followed his gaze and gasped. White fire had burst to life in the skies high over Gateway, bright as a star fallen near enough to touch, scattering the ash and storm all around it. Down out of the fire came an army the likes of which had not been seen since before the driving away of the Wolf-Lords many centuries past. Dragons formed the vanguard, dozens of dragons of every size and sort. Wolf-Lords and kitsune came following after them, hundreds in the diverse arms and armor of each of their nations, some grown wings for the battle, some riding upon armored wyverns or brass-toned troop carriers. There were gryphons, minotaurs, sphinxes, even unicorns, hundreds volunteering from their scattered refugee villages.

And at the forefront, vanguard to the dragons' vanguard, the bright crimson light of Princess Galaxy.

***

Bifrost could feel again. She could hear and think and even smell again, beyond the jumbled mess of unconsciousness. But most of all she could feel, not the cold numbness of nearing death, not the thought-breaking pain of all her injuries, but a gentle warmth all around her, filling her and healing her. She knew the sensation of powerful healing spells at once.

"Gal?" she asked, opening her eyes. Instead of her hippogryph lover, she found herself staring up at a white-furred Wolf-Lord dressed all in black, hands enveloped in burning white magic as they waved intricate patterns over Bifrost's sprawled body. So observed, the Wolf-Lord smiled and stood, dropping the healing spell. "Oh good, you are awake again. I am glad for that. Got close there. Someone is going to have to do something to take care of all those undead. I have an idea for that."

"Who—" began Bifrost.

"If you are still weak or disoriented, there is no shame in leaving the fight to others," continued the Wolf-Lord, an offered hand helping Bifrost back onto her feet. She looked around and Bifrost did the same, her confusion growing with every moment. The battle still raged, but new combatants had joined the field on the apparent side of Gateway, Wolf-Lords and dragons wading through the streets and scorching the skies. The Imperial forces wavered, their strength breaking against the refreshed defense. Yet, onward the Grand Harmonium still came, guarded still by two Imperial warships.

"I never introduced myself. I am Holly le Fay," said the Wolf-Lord, snapping Bifrost's attention back to her. In the brief moment of battle-stunned distraction, Holly had grown wings, broad red wings the same plumage as Galaxy. With an easy flap of them, the Wolf-Lord rose into the air, smile flattening into a look of calm certainty. "I am glad you grew up so brave and so strong.

I am going to take care of those undead now. Everything will be okay."

With a flash of white magic, the Wolf-Lord disappeared in a teleport. Bifrost stared at where she had been for a moment, body working on its own to pick her spear back up from where it had fallen. Finally, she found the words to say "What?"

***

A crack of the teleport spell, and Holly landed with a light patter of paws on stone. She turned a slow circle in place, taking in the gold and platinum swirls decorating the marble pillars and floors, taking in the countless statues of every species sitting dimly, half-seen in shadow. All were turned to face the open center of the pyramidal structure, like audiences to a drama. Holly had read of the Great Temple of the Knights le Fay, once their home and headquarters, and before them the home and lair of Morgana le Fay. She had read and she had heard, but to actually stand there in the Statue Hall . . .

The war raging beyond the thick stone and metal walls of the temple could only barely be heard. The smoke from the war was more noticeable, drifting in from somewhere to turn the upper levels hazy, the stench of it sweet and foul. Holly shivered and threw off her black feather cloak. Her magic rose in her, a thick and flowing white fire. The battle needed to be ended, and soon.

"Secrets of le Fay. Power of le Fay. Spells of le Fay! Seize the stone, awake the stone, march to battle, defend the home!" She dropped, slammed both palms against the floor. The spell flared and her magic poured out, through the veins of crystal and copper, spreading through the vast statue hall in a crackling flash of white.

For a moment, silence. Holly remained kneeling, catching her breath from the titanic exertion. She looked up to the sound of grinding stone. Around her, statues of Wolf-Lords, of gryphons, of unicorns, of dragons, of minotaurs and sphinxes, stood and began to march—or in the case of the gryphon and dragon statues, fly—to the temple exits. Kings and queens of Heraldale's past, great knights and beloved saints, heroes and villains, and all manner in-between. Some carried weapons, spears and axes of the same marble as them, others went with only their talons and their horns. All went fast, faster than mere flesh could have gone, hurrying to the battle so near, yet so distantly heard.

"Go!" commanded Holly, though she knew by the workings of the old spell how no more command was needed. "The old order has had its day, but refuses to give way! Take the undead out of the equation!"

A quick look with her spell sight to see all the magics in the boundaries of the city told Holly this work had already begun. The statue army spread out from the temple thousands strong, catching the Imperial forces from behind as Nova's unicorns and Morgana le Fay's Wolf-Lords pressed forward for the Reality Gate. The sight brought a smile to her muzzle. The smile lasted only as long as it took her to notice the singular Wolf-Lord approaching her through the now-emptied statue hall. "Mother."

"You know," spoke Morgana le Fay's voice, "It's really a miracle how you can make me so proud of you even while opposing me at literally every turn. A very terrible daughter, but a truly incredible Wolf-Lord."

Holly turned. The corpse of Lord Mordred came to a stop a few yards opposite her, the family resemblance made all the more obvious by the black robes and antlered helm. From beneath the dark helm shone the star sapphire eyes of Morgana le Fay, who the people of Heraldale had known only as Lord Beauty. "Mother . . . you desecrate the fallen."

"Who, this?" Morgana smiled, arms wide as she made the body twirl. "Oh, please. You met your cousin once. I knew them on and off for centuries! And besides, I got the body for a bargain only a few days ago and just couldn't resist trying it on. What do you think?"

"I think it is sad," answered Holly, and it was the truth. The sight before her was depressing. She had heard the horror stories about Lord Mordred from her gryphon and minotaur friends, heard of the vile, evil, monstrous acts Mordred had inflicted against the world in the name of the Avalon Empire. And she knew, too, the different paths which might have been walked if not for greed, war, and hate. She mourned for her blood and the Mordred who might have been. "I think it is very sad."

"Of course you do," spat Morgana. All the affection fell away, a black staff tipped with a cloudy white orb materializing in her hand. "You bleeding-heart fool!" A fireball rocketed from the head of the staff.

Holly stomped a paw and a slab of stone rose from the floor, blocking the incendiary spell. "You are an old wolf and a monster."

Morgana snarled and cast two more fireballs, each blocked the same as the first. A lightning bolt crashed through the wash of flames and exploded the stone slab, forcing Holly to back away. Morgana advanced. "Gateway was our city! Gateway was the crown jewel atop my sister's head! They stole it from us! They stole EVERYTHING from us!"

An icicle as long and thick as one of Holly's arms skewered her through the chest. The next moment, she scattered into a swarm of red and white butterflies, allowing the icicle to clatter harmlessly to the floor. Holly flew up, reforming in a crouch a floor above Morgana. "I know! I know."

"No, you don't!" Morgana rose level with Holly, and then higher, jabbing her staff forward. No fireball this time, but a raging, serpentine dragon of fire raced down toward Holly, who thrust both hands forward. A thick wave of water materialized from the air and rushed upward to meet the fire dragon, engulfed it, rushed on toward Morgana. The dark Wolf-Lord spun her staff and the water was gone, falling as harmless snow around her.

For a long moment, the two Wolf-Lords stood at an impasse, watching the other, neither willing to make the next move in their sorcerer's duel.

"This temple is a headstone," said Morgana at last. "And all of Heraldale is the graveyard. Our cities are tombs. They left our bones where we died and walk among them like they're incredible relics of a forgotten age! No dignity, only the slow rotting to dust. And then they go and start doing the same to each other. They deserve Empress Nova! She is all they deserve, every last one of them!"

Holly answered with a whip of fire lashing the other Wolf-Lord's face. Morgana reared back with a snarl, muzzle burned and helm scorched. "Gah! Damn you!"

"You damn yourself!" shouted Holly. She spread wings and rose to face her mother as equals, the air crackling around them. "I was not blind in that stone you left me in. I saw through my other incarnations. I saw through the eyes of the hippogryph. I have seen the courage, the nobility, the heroism of those you call our enemies. I have seen them struggle, fail, and triumph. I have seen them form their bonds, I have seen them love. I have seen them hope for a future after war, and I choose to grab for that future with both hands."

"You choose nonsense!"

Fireballs flew, breaking harmlessly against Holly's shield spells.

"You choose nothing! You think there is even a chance that whatever alliance you have made between Wolf-Lords and unicorns and gryphons will last!?"

Lightning struck the ceiling high above, sending rubble falling toward Holly. She flexed her magic and the rubble turned into dozens of iron swords, swerving to fly at Morgana instead. She turned into smoke to let them pass harmlessly through her.

Returning to flesh and fur, Morgana dropped to the nearest floor, landing in a crouch. She drew a dagger from a sleeve and plunged an arm into the floor as if it was water rather than stone.

The next moment, sterling pain erupted from the back of Holly's right leg. She fell to her knees with a cry of pain, gaze turned to see Morgana's arm thrusting from the floor behind her, dagger buried into Holly's leg, halfway up to the heel. Even as she watched, the blade pulled free and the limb disappeared back into the stone, safe from reprisal.

Holly turned forward again, watched as Morgana drew a half-dozen disks of blackness into empty air and scattered all but one of them around Holly. The dark wolf's crystal eyes blazed with power, the head of her staff crackling with bolts of spell lightning. "You've put up a better fight than I expected. Another few centuries of experience and you might've beaten me. But I am Morgana le Fay! The first Wolf-Lord alongside my sister! I alone now carry the burden of our revenge against our foes, and my plans will not be undone by one cocksure whelp!"

Morgana cast the lightning through her remaining disk and it shot from the five surrounding Holly. She barely cast a shield spell in time to catch the multi-angled attack, the force of it driving the young wolf back to her knees. For a mere heartbeat her defenses wavered, and then she poured more of herself into the spells until they held strong. Trembling with the effort, Holly rose back to her feet, and beneath the cover of the blistering, blinding light of the spells, she cast her mind out and away, far away to where her help was needed.

***

In the dream Bevin floated in an endless black sky. The world around her was the cold of the wind before a terrible storm, heavy and charged with the greater power she held within herself.

The Lightning Elemental came to her in a form she knew and wished she didn't. A black unicorn wreathed in lightning, with black mane and black tail, with glowing yellow eyes and a curved horn as white as clean bone.

"Why are you here?" demanded Bevin. "I don't want you here! I don't want anything to do with you anymore! Go away!"

The phantom of Lord Mordred said nothing.

"You were a monster! Do you even understand that? Lord Mordred was a monster! They raised me to be a monster! It's good that they're dead!"

"I raised you to be a survivor," spoke the phantom in kind. "I made you who you are today."

Bevin would have stomped her hooves against the ground, if there'd been any. "You don't get to act like that means I owe you anything. I remember my birth parents now, I have Galaxy, I have Brynjar. That should be enough!"

The phantom of Mordred drew closer. "You don't get to act like I never happened. Not if you want this power. You don't get to just throw me away."

"YOU THREW ME AWAY FIRST!" The world echoed with Bevin's scream. The skies flashed with lightning and trembled with thunder, the palest hint of the storm tearing her heart apart. It had been easy, before. Easier when Mordred had been alive, had been a threat to deal with. Easy to forget the love, the pain. In death, the only thing to do was think and remember. "In Port Oil, when you were ready to blow up the whole city! I . . . I was your daughter! Your soldier! Saved by you, raised by you, trained by you! I loved you! Why!?"

The question passed unanswered into the surrounding void. But from the storm came a new voice. "It's okay to miss people who weren't good for you, commander."

Bevin startled, then turned. A distance behind her stood Holly le Fay, the smile on the white Wolf-Lord's muzzle sad and understanding. "It's . . . you. You took care of my, of, of our Nessa. You gave up everything for her."

"I did. She was worth it." Holly drew closer. "And believe me when I tell you, it is okay to mourn the loss of people who were good or important to you once. To mourn the loss of what once was, however much you have grown or changed in the time since the parting. Especially if you never had the chance to say goodbye. Grief does not know morality, it simply is. Remembering and mourning are not forgiving. That is not something you owe to anyone but yourself."

Bevin knew Holly told the truth. But even so, she fought against it, swung her legs and tossed her mane, whinnied and snorted and SCREAMED. But however she fought, the tears still came. They streaked down her cheeks and away into the void, sparkling like Diamond stars in the dark. Pain like a rupture in her chest, a full-body sob from her hooves to her horn. She remembered the years of bone-breaking training sessions, the blood, the betrayal on the night of Spell Virus. She remembered the guardian demon of her childhood, shielding her from all the abuses other soldiers wanted to inflict, avenging when it could not protect. She remembered lessons in how to protect herself, the gift of the Stone Elemental, the pride shining in yellow wolf eyes.

At last, Bevin could look at the phantom of Mordred again. They seemed diminished to her now, lesser to her. Her heart ached, but held firm. "You were a part of my life. You did make me part of who I am. But I've outgrown you, and it's time I go protect my own family. Goodbye."

***

As Galaxy landed, the Grand Harmonium's throne room was much the same as last she had seen it. The wrecked outer walls from the earlier confrontation were the same, and the glowing control orb at the room's center, and Empress Nova seething with anger and self-righteous hate upon her dais throne. The container for Nova's hippogryph body was gone, replaced by a gathering of chained and beaten gryphons, though they rose unbowed at the sight of her and of the unimagined succor, the light of hope returning to their eyes.

"What have you done?" snarled Empress Nova, rising from the dais with a flap of her wings. Her horn lit up with her blinding white magic, and with a rush of air the full weight of her magic settled over the throne room. "What have YOU DONE!?"

As before, Galaxy stood unbowed with the aid of her own magic as counterbalance to Nova's. Though this time, as she spread the magic thinner to keep the captive gryphons from being crushed, Galaxy's remaining three legs trembled from the effort.

"What have you done!?" Nova spat again, ignoring all else as she advanced toward Galaxy. "Beneath my supreme authority, Heraldale would have risen once more to greatness, instead of splintered by the whims and failures of the weak and degenerate! I promised greatness, and you have brought our enemies right to OUR VERY SHORES!"

"YOU brought these people here, oh Empress," said Galaxy. "You have wrought nothing but war and suffering upon the world, upon these people, and now at last, these people unite and push back! And you are going to lose!"

Nova shrieked and slashed out with her talons. Galaxy beat her wings and rose enough the talons scratched harmlessly across her armor rather than tear off her cheek. Then she flipped back and kicked both her rear legs into Nova's belly.

"OOF!"

The white hippogryph floundered backward. The weight of her magic over the throne room dispersed, the gryphon captives staggering. Galaxy flew, pinning Nova against her dais while she was still down, talons tight around her throat. "Yield!"

"Nev . . . never!" Nova twisted and squirmed beneath Galaxy, unable to get a good angle to bite at Galaxy with her beak, unable to put any effective strength into her clawing talons. Her horn lit up for a spell and Galaxy tightened the grip of her talons on her throat, Nova gasping for breath.

"Yield!" Galaxy screamed again.

Suddenly, Nova loosed a breathless laugh. Before Galaxy could question it, a Harmonized swallow-gryphon tackled her from the side and off of Nova. Galaxy shoved him away with a shield spell, hurriedly swinging the spell around to block a barrage of spell bolts from her fellow hippogryph.

Through their exchanged volleys of spells, neither gave much ground. As she always had, Galaxy held firm to her shield spells, blocking whatever came her way which could not be easily ducked or sidestepped. Nova, meanwhile, remained devoted solely to the offensive, ever aloft on her wings to dodge Galaxy's spells as the Empress slung her fire spells, her cutting spells, her blasting spells. Again and again their magics clashed, pressed, dove, lighting the world in red and white, neither at first able to gain the advantage—

Then, a Harmonized gryphon dove down and into the path of one of Galaxy's blasting spells, forcing her to dispel it before it struck. A second later another Harmonized gryphon charged in, tackling Galaxy and wrapping around her tight in a hug. Galaxy struggled within the tight hold for a moment before shoving the gryphon off with her magic, but already more Harmonized gryphons and unicorns were charging into the fight, some moving to guard Empress Nova from attacks, others moving to tackle Galaxy once more.

"No!" Galaxy cried, conjuring shield spells to push the horde away, unwilling to risk hurting them. "No, please, stop this! Nova, stop this!"

"Never!" came the white hippogryph's answering scream. Then, Nova loosed a blast of raw magic from her horn, bashing through her own assembled defenders, bashing through Galaxy's shield spells, bashing Galaxy across the throne room and into the floor.

When Galaxy came to, the battle had begun to fall silent. For a moment, Galaxy could not picture why. Then she saw Empress Nova standing before the central control orb, talons gripping the crystal tightly as she looked at Galaxy in triumph. The control orb glowed the same eldritch light as the swirling energies of the Reality Gate.

Mind washing clean, Galaxy beheld in her mind's eye a vision of the scene. All around, the battle faltering as the Grand Harmonium at last reached the Gateway palace and the Reality Gate at its center. A deep, bone-rattling hum rose in the air as the Grand Harmonium activated, the Cosmic Magic beyond the Gate drawing up in a reverse-waterfall into the Grand Harmonium, powering it up beyond imagining, charging it toward—

"My time is now," Nova sang, magic crackling over her talons. "The time is right. Now all shall bow, before my might!"

As Nova sang, the magic built up in the orb, built, built, Galaxy able to feel it even without drawing on her magic sight. At the last word the dam broke, the magic of Nova's Harmonization spell bursting forth in a flood. It spread out from Nova at the Grand Harmonium's center, all-encompassing and growing stronger as it went. To her horror, Galaxy could feel as the magic struck indiscriminately. Unicorns and gryphons throughout the city fell screaming into Harmonization. Others, dragons and Wolf-Lords, were struck by the overwhelming magic and paralyzed as their bodily systems were overpowered, falling helpless toward the ground.

> "Feel my magic over you
> As every free thought slips away
> My every word is now true
> You can never disobey!"

Galaxy stood, untouched by the Harmonization spell. The Waters of Life within protected her. Knowing this, she began to hobble toward Nova and the control orb, wings raised against the pressing magic trying to force her back. A last, desperate idea had come to her.

> *"Worship me, adore me,*
> *Keep Heraldale MINE!*
> *Devote your every thought to me*

As my glory—"

Lunging forward with her wavering strength, Galaxy placed her talons upon the control orb, forcing the Waters of Life into it. Nova's song faltered, the Harmonization spell pausing its advance across the countryside beyond Gateway's borders. Nova snarled at Galaxy from across the orb, but Galaxy forced herself to stand, to sing, even as she felt the full focus of the white hippogryph's magic bearing down on her.

"Who will now stand with me
In this hour of destiny?"

She could feel them, both the spell and the magic draining from the Gate, responding to her call, but it was not enough. Nova's hold on it was too great, too complete, and as they stood there opposed, Nova sent the magic forth to burn away at Galaxy. The pain rocked her, Galaxy's rear legs giving out beneath her, leaving her barely clinging to the orb, desperately pushing on, hopeless.

"Who will now stand with me
In this hour of destiny?
With our enemy at our throats
And in our final act—"

A bolt of lightning the likes of which neither combatant had ever seen, as blinding as the Sun, as fiery as the Dragonbacks, crackled with a roar and BOOM through the broken roof and struck Nova across her back and shoulders. She shrieked her pain and fell, connection to the Grand Harmonium broken. Galaxy staggered from the sudden lack of resistance, her own connection fluttering in her surprise and relief, and as more bolts of lightning cascaded through the iron cage of the ruined throne room, her heart soared with hope rekindled. "BEVIN!"

The unicorn strode into view from off to Galaxy's left, shining with the power of her Lightning Elemental, stride and gaze steady toward the suddenly-uncertain Empress Nova recovering across the room. Teeth bared in a battlecry.

***

No matter how the aura of Nova's magic rose and ebbed around them, the struggle for the soul of the Wolf-Lords raged nearly untouched. Another moment and Holly took a knee, strength flagging. Morgana's magic rose triumphant at this, distracted from all else.

"It won't last! Nothing will last, nothing will have the chance to! If the Dragonbacks don't wipe Nova's Harmonized Empire off the map, if your precious hippogryph somehow prevails over MY hippogryph, I will bring the Burning King himself through the Reality Gate and—"

Shun's invisibility spell dropped. Kanti lunged forward, closing the scant yard between them and

Morgana in a moment to press her magic-eating mace into the witch's gut.

"Much love from Port Oil," the smuggler growled, backing away the next moment from the collapsing strands of lightning.

Morgana stared aghast, spell and staff dropped, her hands having gone to clutch the mace on instinct. Stone spread through her body as her magic drained away, eaten away by the trapped and ever-ravenous scrap of Spell Virus. She had a moment to look to Holly dropping her shield spells, and then it was over.

Slowly, Holly staggered over to stand beside her kitsune and Wolf-Lord wives, eyes never leaving the new statue before them, even as they each took one of her hands into their own. The moment was more bitter than Holly had expected.

***

Forward, ever forward, with every stomp of hoof another lightning bolt to send Nova staggering back, away from the control orb. Bevin's voice rose on the wind, a desperate scream of command. "GALAXY! NOW!"

Without a moment of hesitation, Galaxy seized control of the Grand Harmonium pouring her all into it. The Waters of Life at last burst forth from the Grand Harmonium as Nova's Harmonization spell had moments before, an expanding wave of rainbow light as cool and refreshing as a tree-shaded stream in the spring. And at the Waters' passing, the Harmonization spell was utterly washed away, every fire from the battle was quenched, and every hurt and injury was healed. The magic swept across the vastness of Heraldale, even to Avalon, and there, minds were freed and bodies mended as Galaxy wished. Overhead, the frothing storms and choking ash were driven back over the inland seas, and for one sweet moment at least, winter was over and spring had come.

As the spell finished and the work was done, Galaxy felt the magic taper away. The Reality Gate far below closed with a thunderous bang, not to open again until another equinox in another far distant year. Galaxy hoped it would not come again in her lifetime.

Across the control orb from her, Empress Nova lay collapsed on the floor of the throne room, still but for a ragged breathing. As Galaxy watched, the white hippogryph stirred, raised her head, opened eyes no longer Nova's violent red, but the same bright blue as Galaxy's own, as Bevin's. At the sight of the sisters, the eyes widened. The hippogryph lurched to all fours in mortal terror, then turned and took wing out of the nearest broken wall.

Bevin growled and made to chase after. Galaxy hurried forward and spread a wing to stop her. "No! No. Morgana le Fay created that new hippogryph, that new living thing, and then Nova took her over. Now Nova is gone. Leave the hippogryph be. She didn't ask for any of this." Not to imply, Galaxy thought to herself, that ANY of them had asked for any of this.

Bevin looked down at her for a moment, looking as tired as Galaxy felt, slowly nodded. Before either could say more, there came a heavy fluttering of wings as Bifrost landed among the ruins of the throne room, rainbow eyes wide as she took in the scene. "Is it over? Is it really done?"

Galaxy didn't know, not yet. Her body tired and aching despite the palpable charge of magic within it, she hobbled her way to the northwest edge of the throne room and looked out over Gateway. She watched, relief flooding through her, as the remaining Imperial warship turned its battered hulk away from the Grand Harmonium, the last scattered crystal drones and air-yachts retreating back into it.

No cheers rose on the wind at the retreat. No roars or songs of celebration, the war won and the day saved. The smoke still rose across Gateway, the land still grey and air still bitter with ash. The volcanic clouds crept once more from the south. Those on the palace roof below milled about, wary of each other as they began to take stock of things.

Galaxy watched all of this, her vision blurring with tears as an indescribable emotion swelled inside, joy and sorrow and so much simple exhaustion.

Behind her, she felt as Bevin and Bifrost parted, going to check on the now-freed gryphons Nova had been using as living shields. In their place came another pair of unicorn and gryphon. The first pair. Galaxy felt them beside her and, still crying, she spread her wings. Brynjar and Owain lay down and leaned in against her, the unicorn tucking his head beneath Galaxy's to hold her high, the gryphon draping one of his great wings across to hold the both of them close. Galaxy, welcoming their closeness, would have had no others there with her, there at the end.

And it was an end, she knew. An end, of a sort.

EPILOGUE

"The Winter War, as it has come to be known, did not end that day with Empress Nova's defeat and the foiling of Morgana le Fay's plans. The Imperial war machine, as exhausted as it had become by the decades, was too ingrained for any mere declaration of surrender. The last victory came two months later, as the hippogryph Galaxy rent asunder the very foundations of the late Nova's palace, aided by a civil war spurred on by Sir Owain's desperate plea for the people of Avalon to rise up and do the right thing. Some listened. Not many, not enough, but some.

"The Grand Harmonium was destroyed, fully and utterly, flown until over the boiling heights of the Dragonback Mountains and there cast down into the molten depths. Calls for its secrets to be learned, its unparalleled fusion of magic and technology broken down and reused in other matters, were ignored in their entirety. Nobody was willing to push the matter too far with Galaxy, who took for herself the final word on this and many other matters in the months and years to come.

"In the months that followed, Galaxy was thorough in her dismantling of the Imperial government. In its place she forced upon the unicorns a parliamentary system in the same model of the United Zakarian Confederacy. For months more she traveled the Avalon Isles, using the Waters of Life to free all the unicorns she could find of Harmonization. This has softened the war's end for them, at least a little. Galaxy killed those most vocally calling for unicorn pride, for violence and reprisal. Monstrous or not, the peace has held in that quarter of the world.

"The same cannot be said for the rest of Heraldale. With the death of Queen Gwendolyn, the Elk retreated back into their secluded isolationism within the depths of the Elderpine Forest. Those lands have been closed to travelers and none have heard word from there in many years. For all any of us know, the Elk have all died, lost in the diseases and famine which have dominated Heraldale these many years following the eruptions of the Dragonback Mountains.

"More troubles. The gryphons of the lands of Schwarz Angebot, freed of unicorn lordship but with Galaxy abdicating her claim to the throne, utterly refused a Wolf-Lord ruler in their place. Despite every promise from Galaxy, every wolf emissary has been killed or driven away. Mere distance alone has kept the Wolf-Lord nations from a military response. Few on either side of the growing divide expect this to last forever.

"Yet more troubles. With the death of King Vigdis, the last of the royal families for Gateway and Gryphonbough were fully wiped out. Anarchy threatened to turn the months of mourning bloody, with General Madara once more attempting to seize power for himself, this time garnering far wider support among the Gateway gryphons with his calls for isolationism and strength from within.

"A week before the one-year anniversary of the Winter War's end, General Madara died. I am not sure who did it, Galaxy or Brynjar or Bifrost, but it was Galaxy who returned the throne of Gateway to its original holders. Queen Holly's rule has been tumultuous these past few years, and it has received little love from the common folk of Gateway, even less love from Lady Quetzal in secluded Vogelstadt or from Quetzal's puppet king in Gryphonbough, but the peace holds. For now.

"I pause here in my recollections to give assurance that the years following the Winter War and the Second Dragonback Eruption have not all been politics and drama. There's been time for love. There remains, always, time for love."

***

"Are you nervous?"

"What?"

"Nervous, are you nervous?"

"Gal, we went through war together. We fought cockatrices in this very clearing together. I laughed in the face of Empress Nova herself. You're asking if I'm nervous on my own wedding day?"

Galaxy's raised eyebrow and flat, unamused expression were all the answer Brynjar needed. He coughed and looked away from his sister, finding no help in Siegfried and Sascha a few paces away, giggling like fools at the overheard conversation. Brynjar sighed. "I . . . yeah."

"Well, if it helps," said Galaxy as she looked away from Brynjar to the opposite edge of the Rotwald clearing, "I've never officiated a wedding before, so just imagine how nervous I am."

Brynjar chuckled. The thought did help.

Three years to the day since he and Owain had first met, beneath the red-hued trees of the Rotwald, they and their closest friends and family gathered beneath the scarlet canopy once more, this time for a unicorn-style wedding. Galaxy stood at the head of the group,

Brynjar to her right and the twins to his right, and Bifrost to their right, the raven-gryphon repeatedly glancing with longing of her own to Galaxy. On the hippogryph's other side stood Holly le Fay, Shun the kitsune, and Ashe the dragon, who kept looking around in full amazement. The spells Galaxy had set up to protect the surrounding mile from the ever-falling ash and breath-fogging cold had returned a rare sliver of summer to the Rotwald, the trees rich and vibrant in color, a gentle breeze sending leaves dancing in slow and graceful drifts. Though all the hives were long dead and the colonies driven farther north, the sweet scent of fire-bee honey still lingered in the air.

From somewhere a light bell tolled once. Immediately, Brynjar stood straighter and followed Galaxy's gaze to the opposite edge of the clearing. He felt his breath leave him and his heart skip a beat as Owain, his Owain, stepped out of from the thick-set woods, Sir Bevin beside him as honor guard. The unicorn stallion had never looked more regal, adorned now in a deep brown caparison to match Brynjar's wings, a blue rose embroidered onto each side of his collar and a gold ring set over his horn.

"Breathe, brother," said Galaxy, her voice light with laughter. "Remember to breathe."

Brynjar breathed, smiling with a mounting giddiness as Bevin led Owain across the clearing to the gathered group, waiting until he stood opposite Brynjar a horn's length away before bowing to each in turn and taking her place at Galaxy's side.

"Sir Owain," began Galaxy, speaking from memory in the unicorn tradition, "Sir Brynjar. You have each trod life's roads a fair distance. You have tasted life's sweet waters and felt life's harsh sting. By miracle or chance, your roads have crossed, and you choose now to continue together on the road, for however long you may. In love. In honor. In deepest friendship. If any now feel cause to object to this bond . . ."

Brynjar didn't know if any in the small gathering made a show of objecting, the twins pulling one last prank. He barely heard Galaxy speaking. He looked down into Owain's soft, warm eyes, and Owain smiled up into Brynjar's, and all seemed right with the world.

"The silence speaks," said Galaxy. "I dub you wed. May your love see you through to days everlasting."

Then, per gryphon custom, Galaxy began to sing. It was an old song in an old language, from the old days before Heraldale, and though Brynjar did not know the words, as he took the wedding scarf Sascha offered him and wound one end of it around Owain's neck with careful talons, and Owain used his magic to wind the scarf's other end around Brynjar's neck, he felt his heart lifted all the same, and every worry faded. And the magic of the song lasted long after the ceremony, long after the feast and dances, long into the cold ash and long nights of the years to come.

***

"To the surprise of few, Brynjar and Owain chose to remain in Featheren Valley. There, over the course of many years, they and the twins Sascha and Siegfried rebuilt their old valley home, and it became a refuge for gryphons who felt lost anywhere else. The mines were sealed tight and the river unclogged of debris, so that it flowed once more from the mountains down to the red expanse of the Rotwald.

"There is a school, now, too, as Galaxy and the twins wished. It is built from the former governor's mansion, a proud place of humble learning. In the days that followed, people from all walks came to the school to learn under the tutelage of the twins, and myself, and many others. If it will live up to Galaxy's hopes of making a better world remains to be seen, but it is still young, yet. There is time.

"Galaxy did not remain to see her school finished. A few months after her brother's wedding, she took wing and left, flying away to parts unknown alongside Ashe and many other dragons, who did not, despite the wishes of many, return to Heraldale at war's end. We were all devastated, but few of us were surprised. The war broke us all to various degrees, but her more than most, and the disappointments of trying to rebuild and keep the peace afterward . . . some people cannot heal the way we might want them to. Some people become strangers even to themselves, and the shadows of the familiar all around them become a torture.

"Sir Bifrost searched for her. Bifrost still searches for her, even after these many years. Even though other duties draw the raven-gryphon back to Heraldale for a month or two at a time, Bifrost continues to search for our lost Galaxy. I don't think anything will stop her except actually finding the hippogryph.

"I don't know where Galaxy has gone. I only hope that wherever she is and whatever she's doing, my sister is happy."

***

Far to the west of the nameless forest, the sun was setting. Far to the east, the moons and stars were rising. It promised to be a sweet fall night, and the celebrations for the latest harvest would run long and wild.

Galaxy walked beneath the boughs of the forest without aim or guide, listening first to the jubilant dragon-song behind her, and then, as it grew distant, to the silence of the woods. The shadows were cold and dark, deep, pierced blindly by colder shafts of silver moonlight. Galaxy basked in this, the darkness and the silence. They cooled her heart and calmed her thoughts, and turned her memories sweet. A younger her might have sung, but as she was, the silence felt too good to spoil.

But then, there was a sound. Galaxy paused in her walk, frowning, head tilted to listen. From somewhere nearby there came the sound of splashing water. New thoughts stirred in Galaxy. Curious, she took to the trees in flight and followed the sound northward, soon finding a wide, starlit clearing.

Galaxy perched atop a high, thick branch and looked down into the clearing. A pond took up most of it, sitting there in the dark like a fallen piece of night sky. At the pond's edge, to Galaxy's surprise, sat a raven-gryphon, no older than Brynjar, drinking from the star pool. A long blue scarf trailed from her neck.

Her heart struck dumb, Galaxy dropped from the tree branch to the floor of the clearing. "Bifrost."

The raven-gryphon raised her head and turned to look for Galaxy's voice, rainbow eyes finding her and latching on. Her breath hitched and soon those rainbow eyes grew wet. "Galaxy."

Galaxy stepped deeper into the clearing, the stars heavy overhead, filling the scene with their light. It had been years since she'd seen the gryphon. Years since she had seen anyone from her old life except Ashe and the fleeting encounter with the clone hippogryph. All Galaxy could think to say was "Why did you come for me?"

"Because I made a promise." Bifrost came to her, kneeling before Galaxy, a wingtip brushing away the tears she hadn't realized were falling. "You are my queen. Now, and always."

***

"I do not know now, where our paths will go from here. It has been eight years, to the day, since the end of the Winter War. The days are returning to normal, the worst of the Dragonback Catastrophe behind us. This peace, as tenuous as it is, as doomed to eventual failure as it surely is, we earned together through fellowship and struggle. Even now, for many those days of war and the feats accomplished therein pass into mere legends of Heraldale, to be told and retold. But for those of us who lived them, the pains and the joys will last forever, or at least for however long these days of peace will last. It really is a fragile peace, and takes much work from all of us, but it's worth it, all the same."

Bevin set down her fountain pen and looked over the last few words she had written. Satisfied they were her own, she stood and turned from her desk, leaving the book open so that the ink could better dry without staining. She gathered up some relevant books with her magic and, sliding them into a side-slung satchel, she checked the grandfather clock ticking away softly in the corner of her university quarters before moving for the door. The first bell would ring soon, and it would be poor form for her to be late on the first day of the spring semester.

The sun shone beautifully down over Featheren University for Bevin's walk. In the courtyard, a trio of gryphons were singing a bawdry tavern song, slowly so that their minotaur companion could sing along. Farther on, a pair of unicorns with a free period laughed as they played discus, catching it on their horns and flinging it back to the other, a lounging sphinx keeping score. Nearby, a one-tailed kitsune sat perched on the edge of a sparkling fountain, brow creased as he wrote out his own translation of a book of traditional gryphon lays.

Bevin left the castle proper, walking the short, heavily-flowered path to the cliff where she favored giving her lessons in practical magical theory. Distracted as she was by thoughts of lesson plans and proper schedules, she did not notice she was not alone on the path until a low, timid voice said "Mother?"

Bevin stopped, her breath catching in her throat as she looked up. A young unicorn mare stood a few yards along the path, her satchels stuffed nearly to bursting with books and scrolls. Her coat was the same brown and white of her father, but her eyes were the startling blue eyes of Sir Lancelot, of Galaxy, and of Bevin herself.

"Nessa," managed Bevin, her next few words escaping her.

The young unicorn, Nessa, dared a step forward, hoof clacking on the stone of the path, a careful, wary smile appearing on her muzzle. Bevin swallowed and dared a step of her own, wondering if this was a dream. The sun shone warm, and the breeze carried honey and wildflowers to them, and mother and daughter, reunited, watched each other with hope.

www.ingramcontent.com/pod-product-compliance
Lightning Source LLC
Chambersburg PA
CBHW021839010726
47493CB00005B/1470